s Defiant
Mistress

HERINE GEORGE
OLE MORTIMER
ANDRA FIELD

MILLS
BOON

First published in Great Britain 2013
by Mills & Boon, an imprint of Harlequin (UK) Limited,
Eton House, 18-24 Paradise Road, Richmond, Surrey TW9 1SR

HIS DEFIANT MISTRESS © by Harlequin Enterprises II B.V./S.à.r.l 2013

The Millionaire's Rebellious Mistress, The Venetian's Midnight Mistress and *The Billionaire's Virgin Mistress* were published in Great Britain by Harlequin (UK) Limited.

The Millionaire's Rebellious Mistress © Catherine George 2008
The Venetian's Midnight Mistress © Carole Mortimer 2008
The Billionaire's Virgin Mistress © Sandra Field 2008

ISBN: 978 0 263 90546 5
ebook ISBN: 978 1 472 00119 1

05-0313

Printed and bound in Spain
by Blackprint CPI, Barcelona

THE MILLIONAIRE'S REBELLIOUS MISTRESS

BY
CATHERINE GEORGE

Catherine George was born on the border between Wales and England in a village blessed with both a public and a lending library. Catherine was fervently encouraged to read by a like-minded mother and developed an addiction to reading.

At eighteen Catherine met the husband who eventually took her off to Brazil. He worked as chief engineer of a large gold-mining operation in Minas Gerais, which provided a popular background for several of Catherine's early novels.

After nine happy years the education of their small son took them back to Britain and soon afterwards a daughter was born. But Catherine always found time to read, if only in the bath! When her husband's job took him abroad again she enrolled in a creative writing course, then read countless novels by Mills & Boon® authors before trying a hand at one herself. Her first effort was not only accepted, but voted best of its genre for that year.

Catherine has written more than sixty novels since and has won another award along the way. But now she has come full circle. After living in Brazil and in England's the Wirral, Warwick and the Forest of Dean, Catherine now resides in the beautiful Welsh Marches—with access to a county library, several bookshops and a busy market hall with a treasure trove of secondhand paperbacks!

PROLOGUE

ALEXANDER MERRICK achieved the vice-chairmanship of the
Merrick Group before he was thirty, but no one who worked
for him was in the slightest doubt that his appointment was due
to ability rather than nepotism. They soon found he ran as tight
a ship as his father and his grandfather before him, but with a
more humanist approach. He had made it clear from day one
that the door of his top floor corner office would always be open
to any member of staff with a problem, and this particular
morning he sat back, ready to listen, when his assistant came
in looking gloomy.

'What's up, Greg? Girlfriend stand you up last night?'

'No, Alex.' Not long out of college, Greg Harris still got a buzz
from being on first-name terms with his dynamic young boss. 'I
just had a phone call. Bad news. Our bid was unsuccessful.'

'*What?*' Alex Merrick shot upright. 'So who the hell got them?'

'I don't know that yet.' Greg cleared his throat. 'I asked
my—my friend to let me know the result of the sealed bid right
away, as a personal favour, which is why I'm ahead of the
game, but no other details yet.'

Alex swore volubly. 'It must be some local builder with
friends in high places. He'll probably demolish the Medlar Farm
cottages and build God knows what in their place—' He broke
off, eyeing his assistant speculatively. 'Is your friend a girl?'

Greg nodded, flushing.

Alex gave him the crooked smile that few people could resist. 'Excellent. Take her out to dinner; charm her into finding out who got the bid. I'll pay.'

CHAPTER ONE

THE VIEW of the sunset over sweeping lawns and tree-fringed lake was so perfect the dining room could have been part of a film set.

Sarah's escort smiled at her in satisfaction. 'You obviously approve of my choice, darling?'

'Of course. Who wouldn't?' But she was surprised by it. Oliver normally wined and dined her in more conservative restaurants, where the *cuisine* was less *haute* than Easthope Court. 'Is this a special occasion?'

His eyes slid away. 'Let's leave explanations until later. Our meal is on its way.'

The waiter set Sarah's entrée in front of her, and with a hint of flourish removed the cover from an offering of such culinary art she looked at the plate in awe, not sure whether she should eat it or frame it. But instead of sharing that with someone who took his food as seriously as Oliver, she asked about his latest triumph in court.

Sarah listened attentively as she ate, made appropriate comments at intervals, but at last laid down her knife and fork, defeated. Artistic creation or not, the meal was so substantial she couldn't finish it.

'You didn't care for the lobster?' asked Oliver anxiously.

'It was lovely, but I ate too much of that gorgeous bread before it arrived.'

He beckoned a waiter over. 'Choose a pudding, then, while I excuse myself for a moment. Cheese as usual for me, Sarah.'

She gave the order and sat back, eyeing her surroundings with interest. The other women present—some young, others not—were dressed with varying success in red-carpet-type couture, but their male escorts were largely on the mature side. Though a younger man at table nearby caught her eye, if only because his head of thick, glossy hair stood out like a bronze helmet among his balding male companions. He raised his glass in smiling toast, and Sarah looked away, flushing, as Oliver rejoined her.

'So what are we celebrating?' she demanded, as he began on a wedge of Stilton.

'Now, you must always remember, Sarah,' he began, 'that I have your best interests at heart.'

Her heart sank. 'Go on.'

Oliver reached out a hand to touch hers. 'Sweetheart, there's a vacancy coming up in my chambers next month. Make me happy; give up this obsession of yours and take the job. With your logical brain I'm sure you'd enjoy legal work.'

Sarah's colour, already high, rose a notch. 'You mean you brought me here just to pitch the same old story? Oliver, I love you very much,' she said with complete truth, 'and I know you care about me, but you really must let me live my life my own way.'

'But I just can't believe it's the right way!' Oliver sat back, defeated. 'I hate to think of you messing about with plaster and paint all day in that slum you bought.'

'Oliver,' she said patiently, 'it's what I do. It's what I know how to do. And I love doing it. I'd be useless—and miserable—as a legal secretary, even in illustrious chambers like yours.'

'But you're obviously not taking care of yourself or eating properly—'

'If you just wanted to feed me before I go back to starving in my garret you needn't have wasted money on a place like this,' she informed him.

'I chose somewhere special because it's my birthday tomorrow,' he said with dignity. 'I hoped you'd enjoy helping me celebrate it.'

'Oh Oliver!' Sarah felt a sharp pang of remorse. 'If you're trying to make me feel guilty you're succeeding. I'm sorry. But I can't take the job. Not even to celebrate your birthday.'

He nodded, resigned. 'Ah, well, it was worth a try. We won't let it spoil our evening. Thank you for the witty birthday card, by the way, but you shouldn't have bought a present.'

'Didn't you like the cravat?'

'Of course I liked it. But it was much too expensive—'

'Nothing too good for my one and only godfather!'

Oliver smiled fondly. 'That's so sweet of you, darling, and of course I'll wear it with pride. But you need to watch your pennies.' He leaned nearer and touched her hand. 'You do know, Sarah, that if you're in need of any kind you only have to ask.'

'Thank you, Oliver, of course I do.' But she'd have to be in dire straits before she would.

As they got up to leave, the man Sarah had noticed earlier hurried to intercept them.

Oliver beamed as he shook the outstretched hand. 'Why, hello there, young man. I didn't know you were here.'

'You were too absorbed in your beautiful companion to notice me, Mr Moore.' He turned to Sarah with a crooked smile. 'Hello. I'm Alex Merrick.'

Quick resentment quenched her unexpected pang of disappointment. And as if his name wasn't enough, something in his smile made it plain he thought Oliver was her elderly—and wealthy—sugar daddy.

'Sarah Carver,' she returned, surprised to see comprehension flare in the piercingly light eyes in an angular face that was striking rather than good-looking.

'Sarah is helping me celebrate my birthday,' Oliver informed him.

'Congratulations! It must be an important one to bring you down from London for the occasion.'

'Not really—unless you count each day as an achievement at my age. I'll be sixty-four come midnight,' said Oliver with a sigh, and made a visible effort to suck in his stomach.

'That's just your prime, sir,' Alex assured him. 'Are you from London, too, Miss Carver?'

'She is originally.' Oliver answered for her. 'But Sarah moved to this part of the world last year. I've been trying to persuade her to return to civilisation, but with no success. She's in property development,' he added proudly.

'Snap. That's partly my bag, too,' Alex told her.

Oliver laughed comfortably. 'Not exactly on the same scale,' he informed Sarah. 'Alex is the third generation of his family to run the Merrick Group.'

'How interesting,' she said coolly, and smiled up at Oliver. 'Darling, it's past my bedtime.'

'Right,' he said promptly, and put his arm round her to lead her away. 'Nice seeing you again, young man. My regards to your father.'

Alex Merrick's eyes travelled from Oliver's arm to Sarah's face with a look that brought her resentment to boiling point. 'I hope we meet again.'

'You weren't very friendly,' commented Oliver in the car park. 'You might do well to cultivate young Alex, darling. The Merrick name carries clout in these parts.'

'Not with me,' Sarah said fiercely.

The journey home was tiring. Oliver returned to his proposition, and argued all the way, but when he paused to draw breath Sarah told him it would turn her life upside down again to move back to London.

'I did all that in reverse not so long ago, Oliver. I don't fancy doing it again for a while, if at all. I like living in the wilds, as you call it—'

'But what do you do with yourself in the evenings, for God's sake?'

Glossing over the weariness which more often than not sent her early to bed with a book, Sarah said something vague about cinema trips and concerts, hoping Oliver wouldn't ask for details.

'A lot different from London,' he commented, as they reached Medlar House.

'Which is entirely the point, Oliver. Would you like some coffee?'

'No, thank you, darling. I'll head straight back to Hereford. I'm meeting with a local solicitor first thing in the morning.'

She leaned across and kissed him. 'Thank you for the wonderful dinner, *and* for the job offer. But do stop worrying about me. I'll be fine.'

'I hope so,' he said with a sigh. 'You know where I am if you need me.'

'I do.' She patted his cheek. 'Happy birthday for tomorrow, Oliver.'

Sarah waved him off, and with a yawn made for her ground-floor retreat in a building which had once housed an elite school for girls. Advertised as a studio flat, when the school had been converted into apartments, she'd agreed to take a look at it without much hope. It had been the last on the list of remotely possible flats shown her by the estate agent, who had rattled through his patter at such speed he'd been unaware that the moment she'd walked through the door Sarah fell in love.

The agent had given her the hard sell, emphasising that it was the last available in her price range in the building, and offered interesting individual touches.

'If you mean a ceiling four metres high and one wall composed entirely of windows,' Sarah remarked. 'Heat loss must be a problem.'

Crestfallen, the young man had informed her that it had

once been a music room, which explained the lofty dimensions, and then he'd pointed out its view of the delightful gardens and repeated his spiel about the building's security. Sarah had heard him out politely, and when he'd eventually run out of steam, he saw her back to her car, promising to ring her in the morning with other possibilities.

She'd forced herself to wait until he rang, praying that no one had beaten her to it overnight with the flat. When his call finally came he'd given her details of a riverside apartment. Way out of her price range, she'd told him, and then as an apparent afterthought mentioned that since there was nothing else suitable on his current list she might as well take another look at the Medlar House bedsit. He'd uttered shocked protests at the term for such a picturesque studio flat, but once they were back in the lofty, sunlit room again Sarah had listed its disadvantages as her opening shot, then begun haggling. At last the agent had taken out his phone to consult a higher authority, and agreement had been reached on a price well below the maximum Sarah had been prepared to pay to live in Medlar House—which, quite apart from its other attractions, was only a short drive from the row of farm cottages she was about to transform into desirable dwellings.

All that seemed a lifetime ago. Feeling restless after her unaccustomed evening out, Sarah loosened her hair, then sat at the narrow trestle table that served as desk, drawing board, and any other function required of it. She booted up her laptop, did a search, and gave a snort of laughter. To say that Sarah Carver and Alexander Merrick were both in property was such a stretch it was ludicrous. These days the Merrick Group also had extensive manufacturing interests, at home and abroad—and the biggest buzzword of all—it was into recycling on a global scale. She closed the laptop in sudden annoyance. It was irrational to feel so hostile still. But the look the man had given her had annoyed her intensely. Oliver was sixty-three—she glanced at her watch—sixty-four now. She was almost forty years his junior. So of course Merrick Mark Three had jumped to the wrong conclusion about Oliver's role in her life. Her eyes kindled. As if she cared.

She went through her night-time routine in her minuscule bathroom, then climbed up to her sleeping balcony and hung up the little black dress she hadn't worn for ages. She got into bed and stretched out to gaze down through the balustrade at the moonlight streaming through the shutters, hoping the lobster wouldn't give her nightmares. She had to be up early next morning, as usual. The first of the cottages was coming along nicely, and once furnished it would function as a show house to tempt buyers for the others in the row. Harry Sollers, the local builder who worked with her, would be there before her, in case, as sometimes happened, he knocked off half an hour early to do a job for a friend.

When the row of cottages had gone up for sale by sealed auction Harry's circle of cronies at his local pub had fully expected some big company to demolish them and pack as many new houses as possible on the site. When the news had broken that a developer from London had snaffled the property there had been much morose shaking of heads in the Green Man—until the landlord had surprised his clients by reporting that the property developer was a young woman, and she was looking for someone local to work on the cottages. At which point Harry Sollers—semi-retired master builder, committed bachelor and misogynist—had amazed everyone in the bar by saying he might be interested.

Sarah never ceased to be grateful that, due to Harry Sollers' strong views on the demolition of perfectly good living accommodation, he'd agreed to abandon semi-retirement to help her turn the one-time farm labourers' cottages into attractive, affordable homes. Gradually Harry had helped her sort out damp courses, retile the roofs, and deal with various basic faults shown up by the building survey. He had been openly sceptical about her own skills until he'd seen proof of them, but openly impressed when he first saw her plastering a wall, and completely won over the day she took a lump hammer to the boards covering up the original fireplaces.

But from the start Harry had drawn very definite lines about his own capabilities, and told Sarah she would need to employ local craftsmen for specialised jobs. He'd enlisted his nephew's experienced help with the cottage roofs, recommended a reliable electrician to do the rewiring, and for the plumbing contacted his friend Fred Carter, who soon proved he was top-of-the-tree at his craft. The houses had begun to look like real homes once the quality fittings were in place, but to his surprise Sarah had informed Fred that she would do the tiling herself, as well as fit the cupboards in both bathrooms and kitchens.

'I'm good at that kind of thing,' she'd assured him, without conceit.

This news had caused a stir in the Green Man.

'You might have to put up with a few sightseers now and again, boss, just to prove Fred wasn't having them on,' Harry had warned her.

He was right. Harry's cronies had come to look. But once they'd seen her at work they'd agreed that the city girl knew what she was doing.

But much as she enjoyed her work there were days when Sarah felt low-key, and the next day was one of them—which was probably due to Oliver and his coaxing about the vacancy in his chambers. It was certainly nothing to do with the lobster, which had not, after all, given her nightmares. Nor, she assured herself irritably, was it anything to do with meeting Alex Merrick. She'd slept well and risen early, as usual. Nevertheless her mood today was dark. She would just have to work through it. Fortunately Harry was never a ray of sunshine first thing in the morning either, and wouldn't notice. But for once she was wrong.

'You're early—and you don't look so clever today,' Harry commented.

'I was out socialising last night,' she informed him, and went on with the cupboard door she was hanging.

His eyebrows shot up. 'Who was the lucky lad, then?'

Sarah sometimes joined Harry for a ploughman's in the Green Man at lunchtime, where the clientele was mainly male. Some of the regulars were retired, and came out for an hour's chat over a pint, but the younger set were mainly tradesmen of varying kinds on their lunch-breaks. Harry had put up with a lot of teasing from the old hands about his pretty young boss, but some of the new ones tried to chat Sarah up. The more enterprising among them had even asked her out, and it had taken all the tact she possessed to refuse in a way that made no dent in local egos, so she could hardly blame Harry for being curious about her night out.

'Much as he'd love to hear himself referred to as a lad,' she said, with her first smile of the day, 'we were celebrating my escort's sixty-fourth birthday. He's in Hereford on business for a couple of days so he drove over to take me to dinner at Easthope Court last night.'

He whistled, impressed. 'I hear it's pretty fancy there since it was done over—pricey too.'

'Astronomically! I could have fed myself for a week on what Oliver paid for my meal last night. He comes down to check up on me now and then, convinced I'm starving myself to death, but usually all he asks of a restaurant is a good steak and a glass of drinkable claret.' Sarah sighed, feeling a sudden need to confide in someone. 'He's a barrister by profession, Harry. He wants me to work in his chambers.'

'Does it need building work, then?'

'No.' Sarah explained about the office job.

'He thought you'd like that?' Harry said, scratching his head. 'Can you do typing and all the computer stuff?'

She nodded. 'After I left college I ran the office at my father's building firm.'

'You did a whole lot more than that, I reckon. Your dad taught you his craft pretty good.'

'Thank you!' Coming from Harry, this was high praise

indeed. 'By the way,' she added casually, 'I met someone called Merrick last night. Do you know him?'

Harry grunted. 'Everybody knows the Merricks. Old Edgar started off in scrap metal. A right old villain he was; so slick at making money you'd think he'd found a way to turn scrap into gold. His son George made an even bigger packet when he took over and started expanding. The family's got a bit gentrified since Edgar's day, with college education and all that. Easthope Court was one of their jobs. Lot of publicity at the time. Was it George you met?'

'No. This one's name was Alex.'

'George's son. Don't know the lad myself, but word has it he's a right ball of fire now he runs the show up here. I hear George is at the London branch these days.' Harry's lined blue eyes gave her a very straight look. 'I hear a lot of things in the pub, boss, but I just listen. Nothing you say to me will go further.'

'No need to tell me that, Harry!'

He nodded, satisfied. 'I'll get on with the window frames in number four, then. You're doing a good job there,' he added gruffly, eyeing the cupboards.

'Thank you!' Sarah smiled at him so radiantly he blinked. 'How about a snack at the Green Man at lunchtime? My treat?'

'You're on! Betty Mason bakes pasties on Wednesdays.'

Sarah felt a lot better as she went on with her cupboard doors. She worked steadily throughout the morning, with only a short break for coffee, and got to her feet at last, back aching. She went to the door, put two fingers in her mouth and gave a piercing whistle.

'Ready, Harry? I'm starving.'

Harry chuckled as she scrambled into his pick-up.

'What's up?' she demanded.

'You don't look much like a city girl these days, boss.'

Sarah grinned as she tucked a stray curl behind her ear. 'The great advantage of the Green Man is not having to prettify myself to eat there. But if you're ashamed to be seen with me in my working clothes, Mr Sollers, I can always eat my pasty in the pick-up.'

He guffawed. 'Get away with you.'

The knot of regulars in the bar greeted Sarah with their usual friendly acceptance, which put paid to the last traces of her blue mood.

'Your boss let you out, then, Harry?' called some comedian.

'Reminded her it was Betty's day for pasties, so I hope you lot left some for us.' Harry hoisted Sarah up on a stool at the bar, and gave their order. Fred came to join them, to ask about their progress, and Sarah willingly obliged as she tucked into flaky pastry wrapped round a savoury mixture of meat and vegetables. When it struck her that she was enjoying it far more than the elegant meal of the night before she sighed in such remorse that Fred peered under the peak of her cap.

'Something wrong with your pasty, my dear?'

'Nothing at all—it's delicious.' She explained about the meal with Oliver.

'The man must have deep pockets if he took you to eat at Easthope Court,' put in another man.

'It was to celebrate his birthday, Mr Baker,' said Sarah, and looked at him speculatively. 'Actually, I'm glad you're here today—'

'He's here every day,' someone shouted.

'But I'm not, so I must grab him while I can,' she called back, grinning. 'I hear you're a very keen gardener, Mr Baker.'

'I do a bit,' he admitted warily.

'When you can spare the time, would you come along to the cottages and give me some advice on planting?'

'Any time you like,' he assured her. 'Let me get you another half.'

'No, thanks—too much to do this afternoon,' she said regretfully.

There was immediate interest in exactly what, and the conversation was general for a moment, until a voice with the accents of expensive education rose above the hubbub to make itself heard to the landlord.

'I'm looking for a Miss Carver, Eddy. Has she been in here today?'

Sarah winced, wishing vainly she could make herself invisible. Resigned, she let Fred help her down from the stool and turned to face Alex Merrick. 'You were asking for me?'

His formal dark suit looked out of place in the homely environs of the Green Man's public bar, but it was his look of blank astonishment that amused Sarah. Last night, because Oliver adored being seen with a 'pretty young thing', as he put it, she'd been tricked out in her best babe outfit, clinging black dress, killer heels, full warpaint and hair swept up in a knot of curls. Today the hair was rammed under a baseball cap, her face was as nature had made it, her overalls and trainers were covered in streaks of paint and glue and without her heels she was four inches shorter. She couldn't blame the man for mistaking her for a boy apprentice, and felt grateful when Harry and Fred ranged themselves alongside her in protective, burly support.

Alex glanced round the watchful faces in the bar, lips twitching. 'Good afternoon, Miss Carver. I didn't recognise you for a moment. My apologies for interrupting your lunch.'

She shrugged. 'Not at all. I was about to get back to work. What can I do for you?'

'I'd like a word—in private. Today, if possible.'

Sarah eyed him speculatively. 'I generally finish about six. I can see you then, if you want.'

'Thank you. Where?'

'At the site. I'm sure you know where it is.'

'I do. Until six, then. Good afternoon, gentlemen.' He gave a comprehensive nod all round and walked out, leaving a brief lull in the conversation behind him before everyone started talking again.

'You want to watch that one,' said Harry.

'Why?' she asked, downing the last of her cider.

'He's a Merrick, for a start.'

No need to remind her of that!

'Besides, you've only got to look at him,' said Fred. 'Fancies his chance with the ladies.'

'Not one dressed like this,' she said, laughing.

'Don't you be too sure of that,' said Fred darkly.

Harry grinned, and drained his glass. 'No need to worry. One swing of her lump hammer and he'll be done for.'

They left the pub to a burst of laughter, but Harry looked thoughtful as he drove back to the site. 'Just the same, boss, I think I'd better stay behind out of sight in one of the cottages tonight. Just in case.'

Sarah stared at him, surprised, 'The man wants to talk to me, that's all.'

'Yes, but what about?' said Harry grimly. 'Word is that the Merricks were none too pleased when you got those cottages.'

'Because they're on land adjoining theirs?'

He nodded. 'So be warned. I reckon young Merrick's going to make you an offer.'

'So he can knock them down?' Sarah's mouth tightened in a way her father would have recognised only too well. 'Not a chance.'

It took work, but she finally persuaded Harry that she would be perfectly all right alone when he left.

'Just the same,' he said, as he got in his pick-up, 'you be careful.'

'I shall keep my trusty hammer close to hand,' she assured him, only half joking.

Once he'd gone, Sarah almost wished she'd asked Harry to stay after all. Which was ridiculous. It was broad daylight on a summer evening. What could happen? She thought about tidying herself up but couldn't be bothered. Mr Alex Merrick would have to take her as she was. She leaned back against her car, arms folded and ankles crossed, blocking out the site's building gear as she studied the cottages objectively. Harry had replaced the gingerbread trim over each front door, and soon he'd begin painting the exterior walls creamy white. The front gardens were just bare patches of earth as yet, but she would plant them up after some advice from Mr Baker. She'd lay some cobbles on the paths, get the waist-high dividing walls repointed, and once the lawns had been sown with seed...

She turned her head as a Cherokee Jeep cruised down the lane.

Alex Merrick sprang down from it, but instead of jumping to attention Sarah stayed leaning against her car.

'Hello,' he said, smiling. 'I'm a few minutes late. Thank you for waiting. I got held up.'

'I didn't notice the time,' Sarah said with complete truth.

'Because you were lost in rapt contemplation of your work. Understandable,' he said, looking along the row. 'The houses look good.'

'Thank you. So why do you need to speak to me, Mr Merrick?' she asked, cutting straight to the chase.

The smile vanished. 'I could have done this officially, requested a meeting at my office, but it's probably better to talk here on site. What are your plans when the houses are finished?'

'Why do you ask?'

'Professional interest,' he said briefly.

She eyed him warily. 'I shall put them up for sale to first-time buyers, or city dwellers with a fancy for a bolthole in the country.'

'I can save you the trouble.' He took in the cottages with a sweep of his hand. 'On behalf of the Merrick Group I'll buy all six from you—if the price is right.'

She stood erect at last, eyeing him with suspicion. 'What for, exactly?'

Alex Merrick frowned, as though he couldn't believe she wasn't overwhelmed with delight. 'The usual reasons, Miss Carver.'

'I'd like to know exactly what they are, just the same. Because the land they stand on borders yours you might have demolition in mind—in which case nothing doing.'

His eyebrows snapped together. 'I assure you that provided they meet with Merrick standards I want them as they are. May I take a look?'

'Of course. Follow me.'

Sarah felt rather like a new mother showing off her baby as Alex followed her inside the first house. She'd done nothing about her own appearance, but she'd gone on a whirlwind tour of all the houses with broom and cleaning rags, determined to present them at their best in the evening sunlight pouring through the windows.

She found she was holding her breath as Alex inspected the kitchen in the first cottage, but in the sitting room she relaxed a little as he nodded in approval at the horseshoe fire-grate gleaming like ebony under its creamy marble mantle. 'Original feature, Miss Carver?'

'Yes, but not the genuine Victorian article, of course. It's a copy, dating from the twenties, like the houses. The fireplaces were boarded up before I rescued them,' Sarah told him. 'The sitting rooms were a bit dark, so we replaced the original windows with French doors to give access to the back courtyards. Some of the flagstones out there were already *in situ,* and I found more in a reclamation yard. After a check with building regulations I removed the dividing walls between the kitchens and dining rooms. Fortunately they were neither party walls nor load bearing, so I achieved more space and light, and at the same time catered to the current preference for combined cooking/eating areas.'

'Good move.' He followed her upstairs to inspect the small bathroom Sarah had created by stealing a sliver of space from the main bedroom.

'There were no bathrooms in the houses originally, of course, just the downstairs lavatory I replaced with a small cloakroom,' she told him, finding his silence oppressive.

'You've utilised all the space very cleverly,' he said at last, 'and installed high-end fittings. Very wise. Which firm did your plumbing?'

'When I embarked on the project I made a conscious

decision to use local craftsmen, and I had the most enormous stroke of luck when master builder Harry Sollers agreed to work with me. He knows all the local tradesmen. He recommended an electrician for the wiring, and introduced me to his friend, Fred Carter, a semi-retired plumber who installed the fittings. But I did all the tiling, and I installed the cupboards in the kitchens and bathrooms myself.'

He shot her a startled look as they returned to the kitchen. 'This is your work throughout?'

She nodded. 'I stripped and sealed the wood floors, and plastered all the inside walls, too, but I asked Harry to paint them because his finish is so superb.'

'But you did the plastering?' he repeated blankly.

'Yes. Next I'm going to tackle the gardens.'

'You found someone local to help you with those, too?'

Sarah nodded. 'But only to do the digging once all the building site gear is cleared away. I need advice on what to plant and where, but I'll do the rest myself.'

When they were outside in the lane Sarah could tell that Alex Merrick looked back at the row of cottages with new eyes.

'So what do you think?' she couldn't help asking.

'I'm impressed. Congratulations on your achievement.' His manner suddenly changed. 'So, Miss Carver, I repeat my offer. If your terms are realistic I'll buy the lot, but I want the houses ready to inhabit on the day of completion, also cleared parking space at either end of the row. So name your figure.'

Sarah shook her head. 'Impossible right away. I can't say to the day when the cottages will be completely ready, and costs may increase before I can get them valued.' And, much more important than that, no way would she sell to a Merrick.

'If you hang about too long, Miss Carver, the offer may no longer be on the table.' His eyes, which had opalescent grey irises with dark rims, which gave them an unsettling intensity, held hers. 'Have a chat about it with Oliver Moore. I assume he's your financial backer?'

Her jaw clenched. 'No, he's not, Mr Merrick. His sole involvement in my project is on legal matters.'

He raised an eyebrow. 'A bit minor league for a Queen's Counsel!'

'But not for the local solicitor Oliver found for me.' She turned away. 'Now, I'd like to get home, Mr Merrick. I'm tired and dirty—'

'And hungry? In that case let's discuss the deal in more detail later over dinner,' he said promptly.

'No, thank you.'

'Another time, maybe? Contact me when the houses are finished.' He reached for his wallet and took out a card. 'Here's my office address and my various phone numbers.'

Sarah tucked it into a pocket without looking at it. 'I'm surprised you came yourself, Mr Merrick. Surely you pay people to do this kind of thing for you?'

'True. But after meeting you last night it seemed best to sort it myself.' He smiled crookedly. 'Though I confess I didn't recognise you in the pub today.'

'I could tell.' She walked round the car and got in.

His eyebrows rose as he glanced down at the passenger seat. 'Do you always carry a lump hammer round with you?'

'Only when I'm meeting strange men.'

'Nothing strange about me,' he assured her. 'Where do you live?'

'Medlar House,' she said, and started the car. 'Goodbye.'

Sarah drove up the lane and out on to the main road, grinding her teeth in frustration when a look in the mirror confirmed that Alex Merrick was following her home. When he'd parked the Cherokee on the forecourt beside her car he jumped out, holding up his hands in mock surrender.

'I come in peace! But seriously, Miss Carver,' he added, 'forget the deal for a minute. I would very much like to take you out to dinner. Unless Oliver Moore would object?' he added, then cursed his mistake as her eyes flashed under the peak of her cap.

'Nothing doing,' Sarah said flatly.

He frowned. 'Why not?'

'Last night, Mr Merrick, your thought processes were insultingly obvious, just because I was dining in an expensive restaurant with a man old enough to be my father.' Her chin lifted. 'But in the unlikely event that I did socialise with you Oliver would actually approve, because he knows you—or knows your family. I'm not Oliver Moore's bit of fluff, Mr Merrick. He's my godfather.'

CHAPTER TWO

ALEX cursed under his breath as he watched the small figure march into the building. He'd noticed her the moment she entered the restaurant last night. Big dark eyes, and a full-lipped mouth just a shade too wide for her face had attracted his attention early on. And not only because her companion was a barrister his father knew. The age gap between the pair had convinced the cynic in Alex that she was Oliver Moore's trophy girlfriend, whereas in actual fact Sarah Carver was something of a surprise package. How she'd managed to pull a fast one with the sealed bid was still a mystery.

Greg Harris's useful girlfriend had soon learned who'd acquired the Medlar Cottages site, and passed on the information that the unknown Miss Carver intended renovating and restoring the cottages instead of demolishing them to build on the land. At which point Alex had instructed a manager in one of the group's subsidiary firms to make an offer for the site and cottages as they were. When it was turned down flat Alex had decided to sit back and let Miss Carver do exactly what he'd intended for the houses in the first place. Regular checks would be made on their progress, and then, when they were nearing completion, he would simply step in and make his bid for the lot. Decision made, the small, relatively unimportant venture had been relegated to a back burner—until he'd run into Sarah with Oliver Moore at last night. At which point it had shot straight to the top of his priority list.

At Easthope Court Sarah Carver had appealed to him strongly in that sexy black dress, yet today, minus make-up and plus a layer of dust, she'd somehow managed to look equally appealing in her working clothes. She'd made no attempt to tidy up to meet him tonight, not even to wash her dirty face. His mouth tightened. He was accustomed to women who polished themselves to a high gloss for him, while Sarah Carver obviously didn't care a damn what he thought of her. Suddenly he felt an urge to strip those grubby overalls from her curvy little body and— His mind stopped dead as his hormones prodded him. Watch it, Merrick. Stick to the rules. Never mix business with pleasure.

Alex strolled over to the imposing front door of the school he'd known quite well when he was a teenager. He'd come here for dances in the old days, and had fond memories of some hot and heavy necking in concealed corners when the chaperones weren't looking. And, because the Merrick Group had converted the building into pricey flats, he was in a position to know that Miss Sarah Carver could hardly be penniless if she owned one of them. Unless Oliver Moore had bought it for her. Alex found her name on the row of doorbells, considered pushing it, then shrugged and went back to the Cherokee. To hell with it. He'd ring Sarah's bell some other night. One way or another.

Sarah cursed herself and Alex Merrick in the same breath once she was safe in her flat. In her rush to escape him she'd forgotten to shop on the way home. Even more annoying, she'd half expected him to ring the bell the moment she was inside, and felt an irritating sense of anti-climax when it didn't happen. She shrugged angrily. Forget him and think supper. It was a long time since her pasty with Harry. But first on the agenda, as always, she needed a shower.

After that she rang Oliver to wish him happy birthday, thanked him again for the meal at Easthope Court, and finally made for her narrow, high-ceilinged kitchen. She concocted a rarebit from an elderly piece of cheese and the last of her bread, and carried the tray over to the window seat she'd built with her own hands to curve round the bay which formed half the windows. The materials had come from the building supply merchant who'd put her in touch with Harry Sollers; a stroke of luck she gave thanks for daily.

Sarah looked out on the gardens as she ate—something she did every evening when the sun shone, and most times when it didn't. A double row of white-painted shutters controlled the flood of natural light, and even just watching the rain pour down on lawns and trees was relaxing. Her mother had done the gardening in their North London house, but after Louise Carver died her grieving husband had been too involved in comforting his inconsolable daughter while trying to keep his failing business afloat to maintain the garden to his wife's standard. Sam Carver had been adamant about fulfilling his wife's wish to send their daughter to college, even when Sarah had fought tooth and nail against the idea and pleaded to work for her father straight from school. In the end she'd given in, but had taken a Business Studies course instead of her original intention to study art and design. And after classes and at weekends she'd worked with the construction crew and pulled her weight.

To please her father she'd socialised with girls from college occasionally, but had felt happier in the company of the bricklayers and carpenters, electricians and plumbers she'd known all her life. The old hands had treated her like one of the boys, but when nature had finally added curves to her shape, some of the newer, younger ones had begun treating her very much as a girl. It was a new phase which had added considerably to her father's worries, as Sarah had gone out several nights a week with one young man or another.

'It's all right, Dad, safety in numbers,' she'd assured him when he had commented on it. 'I'm having fun, nothing heavy. They're just friends.'

'They're also men,' he'd warned her. 'So watch your step.'

But once she'd left college to manage the firm's offices, it had been Sarah's turn to worry when Sam Carver had grown older and greyer before her eyes, losing contracts to bigger outfits. She had put her social life on hold to stay home to cook proper meals every evening, and to share them with her father to make sure he ate them. Eventually, it had been during one of those meals that Sam had faced Sarah across the table and told her he'd had an offer from Barclay Homes for the firm.

'*No!* You're selling it?' she said, appalled.

'Yes, I am, Sarah,' he said heavily. 'At least this way we'll salvage something out of it.'

Horrified, Sarah argued that they should carry on, *must* carry on, but Sam was unshakeable.

'I've made up my mind, pet. I had a chat with the Barclay Homes manager, and there's a job for you in their local branch if you want it. Though if you don't you should find a job anywhere now, with your experience in the building trade. But I'm jacking it in.'

She swallowed her tears and clutched him tightly. 'But, Dad, what will you do?'

'Retire,' he said, patting her. 'I've been running on empty for a while now, my darling, I need a rest.'

'But I don't want to work for someone else,' she cried, then, shamed by her whining, managed a smile. 'But of course I will. And a job with Barclay Homes means I can live at home with my dad.' And look after him.

Within days the contract was signed and Sarah was given an interview with the manager of Barclay Homes. The night before her start in the new job she made a special dinner to share with her father, and tried not to worry when he ate so little. Afterwards she drank coffee with him in the garden in the warm twilight, relieved to see him looking relaxed for the first time in months as he stretched out in a deckchair.

'I'll be able to get your mother's garden in proper shape

now,' he said later, yawning. 'You should have an early night, pet, to make sure you're on top form in the morning. I think I'll stay out here in the cool for a while.'

Knowing it was where he felt closest to her mother, Sarah bent and kissed him, told him not to be too late, then went up to bed. When she woke in the night and found his bed hadn't been slept in Sarah ran downstairs, panicking, and raced barefoot into the garden to find Sam Carver still in his deck-chair, fast asleep. Scolding, she hurried to shake him awake, then let out a cry of raw anguish when she realised he would never wake again.

The following period remained a blur in Sarah's mind. The only thing constant had been the solid presence of her mother's cousin, Oliver Moore. Like a rock in her sea of grief, he had seen to all the arrangements, and supported her through the well-attended funeral. Sam Carver had been a popular employer, and it had seemed to Sarah that anyone who had ever worked for her father had turned up to pay their respects. Financially Sarah was well provided for. Her mother had left a sum of money in trust for her, and this security, together with the proceeds from the sale of the business and the sum expected for the large, well-maintained house in a sought-after North London location, had given Sarah breathing space to consider her future.

But constantly keeping the house up to inspection standards had been tiring on top of a day's work, and living alone in it had been hard. Keeping strictly to office work in her new job had been even harder. She'd missed the camaraderie of the building site. The final blow had come when the family home had finally been sold and she'd had to find somewhere else to live. When two office colleagues had offered her a room in their flat she'd jumped at the chance, glad of their friendly company, but her Sundays had usually been spent with Oliver. He liked to drive her into the country and feed her substantial meals at some inn he'd seen reviewed in the

Sunday papers, and during one of their trips they'd come across the Medlar Farm cottages. At first glance she'd thought they were part of a Merrick Group hotel site, but when she'd found they were up for sale by auction Sarah had known at once how she wanted to spend her inheritance. Oliver had objected strongly at first, but eventually bowed to the inevitable by paying a building surveyor to value the houses and confirm that they were worth buying. When Oliver had been informed that the cottages were sound and the auction was to be sealed bid, he'd advised Sarah that if she were really determined she should bid slightly more than the properties were considered worth.

Sarah had taken his advice, confident that her father would have approved. Her euphoria when her bid was successful had gone a long way to reassuring Oliver, but he'd had serious qualms when she'd immediately resigned from her job. His reaction to the one-room 'studio' flat had been equally gloomy, but Sarah had been adamant that it was a good investment. The former school building had charm, and she'd assured him that she was more than capable of making the flat so inviting she would make a tidy profit on it when she came to sell.

But now she'd knocked it into shape she didn't want to sell it. Sarah frowned as she looked round her lofty, uncluttered space. After working on the flat practically every evening since she'd moved in, she was at a loose end now it was finished. But the cure for that was easy enough. She'd spend the long, light evenings working in the cottage gardens instead, and at night pore over gardening magazines instead of the building manuals and style publications she'd studied while doing up the cottages. And maybe, just maybe, she'd say yes some time if one of the likely lads at the Green Man asked her out.

Having fully expected Alex Merrick to hound her over the purchase of Medlar Cottages, Sarah was surprised—and rather nettled—to be proved wrong. She heard nothing more from him, and assumed that the offer from the Merrick Group, just as he'd warned, was no longer on the table. Not that it mattered.

'That's a ferocious frown, lass,' said Harry, as he climbed down a ladder. 'Something wrong?'

'I haven't put the cottages up for sale yet, but I can't help wondering how well—and how soon—they'll sell when I do.'

'Don't you worry. You'll have no trouble selling this lot,' he said with certainty. 'They're attracting a lot of attention locally. Mind, it doesn't hurt that the developer's a pretty young female—'

'Harry, are you by any chance being sexist?' she accused.

'If I was you'd sack me,' he said, chuckling, then shook his head as a van came cruising up the lane. 'More visitors,' he grumbled. 'I reckon we should start selling tickets.'

Sarah's eyes lit up. 'It's Mr Baker.'

Charlie Baker heaved himself out of the van and came to look at the houses in approval. 'Morning, Miss Carver, Harry. I've brought the plants you wanted, my dear, and a few bags of compost to get you started.'

Sarah rushed to inspect the plants, and helped the men carry everything to the parking space cleared at the end of the row. 'Lavender for fragrance and buddleia for butterflies,' she said, delighted. 'My mother's favourites.'

'I brought you some viburnums and a couple of hollies, too,' he told her. 'No point in putting in bedding plants, otherwise you'd be down here every night watering.'

'I'm not really clued up about gardening. I wish now I'd helped my mother more in our garden at home,' said Sarah with regret. 'I was always making a nuisance of myself on one of Dad's building sites instead.'

'It paid off,' Harry reminded her. 'Now, we'd better get back to the real work. I want to finish painting number six today.'

'Thank you so much, Mr Baker,' said Sarah as she paid him.

He handed her a receipted bill in exchange. 'Come down the pub some time and I'll buy you that drink.'

'Done,' she said, as they walked back to his van, 'By the way, I was wondering about some trees.'

Harry grinned as he waved at the tree-lined lane. 'Plenty of those here already, boss.'

She made a face at him. 'I meant a smallish flowering tree in the courtyard, and maybe another in the front. What do you think, Mr Baker?'

'I'll bring some catalogues to the pub and you can have a look,' he promised.

Later, when Harry had finished for the day, Sarah waited until his pick-up was out of sight, then, feeling ridiculously furtive, took her mother's garden tools from the boot of her car. It wouldn't take long to plant some of the shrubs in front of what would be the show house. Now that the machinery and skips of rubbish had been hauled away and the parking spaces at either end of the row were clear, the site was beginning to shape up as a very attractive proposition. It was also a mere half a mile to the bus stop on the main road, and only another five to Hereford; a selling point Sarah intended to stress when the houses were advertised.

When her doorbell rang later that evening Sarah's eyes widened as she heard Alex Merrick's voice on the intercom.

'It's very late, Mr Merrick,' she said coldly.

'I wouldn't disturb you if it wasn't important,' he assured her. 'I need a word.'

Thankful she'd bothered to get dressed after her shower for once, Sarah pressed the release button for the main door, then opened her own as he strode across the hall, hand outstretched.

'Thank you for seeing me.'

Sarah touched the hand briefly, but, startled by the contact, dropped it like a hot coal. 'You'd better come inside,' she said—with reluctance, he acknowledged with a twitch of his lips.

Looking disturbingly tougher and more formidable in jeans, and a sweatshirt which showed off impressive shoulders, Alex walked into the room and stood stock still, his eyes wide instead of showing their usual narrow gleam. 'I don't remember anything like this!'

'You mean when your company did the makeover?'

He gave her the crooked smile Sarah felt sure he practised in the mirror.

'I was thinking more of the old days, Miss Carver. My school socialised with the Medlar House girls. I used to come here to dances.'

Of course he had. 'I believe this was a music room.'

'Is that why you have a balcony?'

'No. It's a sleeping platform I built myself. The flight of steps as well. Once I'd sanded and sealed the floor I built the windowseat, too, and installed the shutters,' Sarah couldn't help adding. 'The room was originally just an empty shell with huge windows—plus a tiny kitchen and bathroom, of course, or I wouldn't have bought it.'

Alex looked round slowly, taking in the art nouveau chandelier, the trio of antique mirrors on the wall and the framed family photographs hung between them. 'It's a uniquely attractive room,' he said, with gratifying respect. 'I congratulate you.'

'Thank you. Perhaps you'd like to sit down and tell me why you want to see me?' She returned to her perch on the windowseat.

Alex sat on the edge of the small sofa, his expression grave enough to worry her. 'I took a detour past the cottages tonight on my way home.'

Sarah stared at him in surprise. 'Do you often do that?'

'I do sometimes, to get away from traffic. But tonight I had a different reason. As you know, we're building a spa-type hotel on the site of the old Medlar Farm, a couple of miles from your project. Don't worry,' he added, 'it's not high-rise. It's designed to look organic, blend into the environment. It won't affect your property—particularly if you agree to sell me your cottages.'

'I see. So is there a problem?'

He nodded. 'Security. Late this evening someone got into

our night watchman's cabin at the hotel site while he was on his rounds. He heard a car drive off, and got back to find the Portakabin vandalised.'

'Did they get away with anything?'

'One small television—the solitary thing worth taking. The place was probably trashed in frustration, or just for the sake of it.' Alex looked grim. 'From now on two men with dogs will be on permanent night duty at the site. I drove back via Medlar Cottages, to see if you'd arranged any security there.'

'No,' she said unhappily, 'I haven't.' She brightened. 'But the problem's easy enough to solve. The first house is ready to live in, so I'll move in there until the others are finished.'

Alex gave her a patronising look. 'And what if someone decided to break in one fine night?'

'I'll spread the word in the pub that it's inhabited,' she said promptly. 'Then with the security lights and burglar alarms functioning I'll be fine.'

He shook his head. 'Your decision. But I don't like it.'

'You don't have to like it,' she pointed out.

'I know,' he said morosely, and stood up. 'Give me your mobile phone.'

'Why?'

He held out an imperative hand.

Sarah took the phone from her holdall and handed it to him. 'It's charged and working,' she assured him.

He keyed in some numbers. 'Ring me anytime if you need me, or just feel worried,' he ordered, handing it back. 'Make sure you lock up behind me. Goodnight.'

Sarah glared, incensed, at the door he closed behind him. What earthly right did the man have to come ordering her about? Being fast-tracked to group vice-chairman so young had obviously gone to his head. Damn him for disrupting her life. The last thing she wanted was to move into one of the cottages. Until Alex Merrick had shown up tonight she'd been quite pleased with herself. The cottages were well on schedule, and she was likely to make a sizeable profit on the sale. But now she would have trouble sleeping tonight.

Next morning Sarah was waiting in the lane when Harry arrived. 'Good morning. Could you do me a big favour?'

'Depends, boss,' he said, with a smile which would have surprised his cronies at the pub. 'What do you want?'

She told him about Alex's visit, and the reason for it. 'I haven't given much thought to security,' she said, depressed. 'So I'll just have to move into number one for the time being. Will you cart my sofabed down here in the pick-up, please?'

'No,' said Harry, so flatly Sarah eyed him in dismay.

'But, Harry, I'll never sleep at the flat for thinking someone might be breaking in down here and wrecking the place.'

'And you'll sleep better here on your own? What good would a little thing like you do if someone did break in?' he growled.

Sarah pushed her cap back on her head. 'I'll be straight with you, Harry, I can't afford a security firm.'

He gave it some thought. 'I'd offer to move in myself,' he said at last, 'but better I get Ian to sleep here, bring his dog.'

Her eyes lit up at the thought of the young giant who'd helped with the roofing. 'Would Ian do it?'

'Slip him a few quid and he'll jump at it. He shares a bedroom with his kid brother at home, so he'll be glad of some space for a bit. And he's nearer to his current job here. You've got a kettle, and the fridge is working, so with his portable telly and Nero for company he'll be in clover.'

'We need to fetch my sofabed just the same, then.'

Harry laughed. 'Ian's six foot five in his socks, boss. He'd have your sofa in bits. He can bring his camping gear.' He looked at his watch. 'I'll give him a ring when he's on his break.'

'And while you're at it could you ask Peter Cox to spare us a minute some time today, to make sure the security lights and alarms are all working?' said Sarah.

'Stop worrying, boss. I'll see to it all.'

Ian Sollers was only too happy to do a bit of easy moonlighting, as long as Miss Carver didn't mind Josie coming round of an evening to watch telly with him.

'The girlfriend,' said Harry, reporting. 'Nice kid, Josie.' His lips twitched. 'And if the youngsters get a bit wrapped up in themselves there's always Nero to keep watch for intruders. He's a German Shepherd, and a big lad—like his master.'

Once the security lights and alarms had been checked and confirmed in perfect working order Sarah finally relaxed enough to laugh when Harry teased her about her clandestine gardening.

'You must have started before I was down the lane.'

'I was dying to see how the plants would look.'

'They look good.' He shook his head. 'But it doesn't seem right, a lass like you with nothing better to do with her evenings than grub about in the garden.'

'It makes a change from the carpentry and painting I did every evening until I got my flat sorted—' She broke off as her phone rang.

'I'll make some tea while you answer that,' said Harry, getting up.

'Miss Carver?'

'Yes.'

'Greg Harris here, personal assistant to Alex Merrick. He asked me to let you know that one of our security men will take a drive out to the Medlar Farm Cottages at regular intervals tonight, so there's no need for you to sleep there.'

Sarah rolled her eyes. No use losing her cool with the monkey, she'd wait until she met the organ-grinder again. 'Thank Mr Merrick for me, but I've made my own arrangements. Please pass the message on to his security people.'

'Are you sure about this, Miss Carver?'

'I beg your pardon?' she said icily.

'I mean, after what happened last night I hope you're not going to sleep there yourself after all—'

'I repeat, Mr Harris,' she snapped, 'I've made my own arrangements. Goodbye.'

Mindful of Harry's words about young people getting wrapped up in themselves, Sarah took time to hang curtains at the windows of the show house to give them some privacy. Her plan for decorating a cottage of this era was to keep it simple, with quality curtain material and a rug in muted colours on the gleaming wood floor in the sitting room. When the house was ready for the public she would transfer some of the furniture she'd put in storage, hang a picture or two, and the cottage would look so good she would hate to part with it.

Sarah stood in the doorway of the sitting room, which looked different already with just the addition of curtains and a few things she'd brought from the flat. Much as she resented his high-handedness, Alex Merrick's warnings had given her a wake-up call. It was only common sense from a security point of view to make the house at least appear inhabited.

She heard Harry coming down a ladder and went out to beckon him inside.

'What do you think?'

He whistled. 'Very cosy!'

'Will it con a would-be intruder?'

'No matter. Nero will start barking long before anyone gets near enough to take a closer look.'

Sarah drove back to the flat that evening in high spirits. Ian had turned up in his van with his handsome dog before she left. After a few rapturous minutes spent in making Nero's acquaintance, Sarah had talked money with Ian, and assured the young giant that his Josie was welcome to join him any time.

'Thanks, I appreciate that Miss Carver. But she's at her kick-boxing class tonight so I just brought my telly for company.' Ian had looked round with deep approval. 'Josie will love it here. I wish we could afford one of these.'

When Sarah's doorbell rang very late she pulled on her dressing gown and climbed down from her platform, stiffening when she heard the angry, clipped tones of Alex Merrick over the intercom. She buzzed him in, and smothered a snort of laughter as he came storming across the hall in his shirt-sleeves, hair on end, and a great tear flapping in one expensive trouser leg.

'I'm glad you think this is funny! Why the hell didn't you tell me?' he demanded, advancing on her with such menace Sarah had to force herself to stand her ground.

'Good evening, Mr Merrick. Come inside before you wake my neighbours. What should I have told you?'

'That you'd sold one of the cottages,' he snapped.

'I haven't. Harry Sollers' nephew Ian is doing me a favour by sleeping there, that's all. I made it perfectly clear to your Mr Harris that I had my security arrangements in hand,' she added frostily.

Alex controlled himself with obvious difficulty. 'He relayed the message, but it obviously lost something in translation. I took it for granted you were sticking to your plan of sleeping there yourself. I was at a charity dinner earlier, and went home by way of Medlar Cottages to check on you. I got savaged by a bloody great monster of a dog for my pains.'

'That was just Nero, doing his job. Did he bite you?' she asked solicitously.

'No. I fought him off.' Alex glared at the ragged tear. 'I was fond of this suit.'

'If you'll tell me how much it cost I'll reimburse you,' she said promptly, and won a look of such blazing antagonism she backed away a little.

'I didn't come here for money,' he snapped.

'What, then?'

The angular, good-looking face hardened. 'I should think that's obvious,' he snapped, and started towards her.

CHAPTER THREE

SARAH BACKED away in such knee-jerk rejection Alex glared at her, incensed.

'For God's sake, I'm not in the habit of hitting women!' He controlled himself with obvious effort. 'My sole aim was to make sure you came to no harm, alone in one of those cottages. If you'd had the courtesy to let me know what you'd arranged all this nonsense could have been avoided.'

She took in a deep breath. 'I suppose you feel I made a fool of you?'

'Not at all. I made a fool of myself,' he said bitterly, and turned to go.

'Have some coffee first,' she offered, surprising herself as much as Alex. 'You look a bit shaken.'

'Is it any wonder?' he demanded morosely. 'I've never thought of myself as a coward—dammit, I love dogs. But that one scared the hell out of me.'

She felt an unexpected pang of remorse. 'Please have some coffee. Sit there for a minute and relax while I make it.'

When she got back with a couple of mugs Alex was looking round the room, frowning.

'It seems emptier in here tonight.'

'I took a few things down to the cottage for Ian. He provided his own bedroll, plus a couple of garden chairs and a television.' She smiled demurely as she sat on the windowseat with her mug. 'On future evenings his girlfriend Josie will be keeping him company, but tonight she was at her kickboxing class.'

'Kickboxing?' Alex stared at her in horror. 'Then thank God I missed *her*, if she's as big as the boyfriend.'

'I don't know. I hope not.'

'Frightening thought,' he agreed, and drank deeply. 'This is wonderful coffee. Thank you.'

'The least I could do. Though a shot of caffeine is probably the last thing you need right now.'

'It hits the spot just the same.' He yawned suddenly. 'Sorry. I don't suppose I could have a refill?'

Sarah eyed him doubtfully. 'Is that wise?'

'Probably not.' He heaved himself up, but she waved him back and took his mug.

When she returned with the coffee Alex gave her a speculative look. 'This is a very attractive flat, but it's obviously the home of a single woman.' His eyes followed her as she crossed to her windowseat. 'That must surely be from choice?'

Her chin lifted. 'It is.'

'And you obviously think it's none of my business! Though I already know you don't lack for male admirers, Miss Carver,' he added wryly. 'The day I came looking for you it was like trying to detach Snow White from the Seven Dwarfs—only you're the small one. Those pals of yours may be getting on a bit, but they're a hefty bunch.'

Sarah unbent a little. 'I'm a constant source of entertainment to them. In the beginning they were thunderstruck, because I was doing some of the work myself. They kept popping round to check up on the city girl.'

Alex laughed, his eyes dancing in a way which put her on her guard. This man was dangerous.

'I suppose they think it's an unsuitable job for a woman?' Alex commented. 'How did you get into it?'

'My father was a building contractor. I was brought up on

building sites, so I'm doing what I like best and hopefully making a living out of it.'

'With no distractions allowed.' He smiled wryly. 'Once you put me right about your relationship with Oliver Moore, I wondered if you'd shut yourself away in your ivory tower here to mend a broken heart.'

Sarah gave him a scornful look. 'Even if I had it would be none of your business, Mr Merrick.'

But damned interesting, thought Alex, wondering just what there was about this girl that got under his skin. Right now her narrow face was scrubbed and shiny, her hair—the colour of bitter chocolate instead of the blonde he normally preferred— was a tangle of unruly curls. And her pink dressing gown was elderly and faded, and a shade too small, even for someone of her size, which probably meant she'd had it for years but couldn't bear to part with it.

Sarah decided to give him a hint by relieving him of his coffee cup, and he promptly stood up.

'Time I was leaving.'

'I'm sorry about your near-death experience with Nero,' said Sarah, on her way to the door. Though she wasn't in the slightest.

He paused, giving her the crooked smile she was surprised to find she was beginning to find attractive, whether he practised it or not. 'You may laugh, but it wasn't at all funny at the time.'

'No, indeed. And you ruined your suit—or Nero did.'

'No point in sending him a bill, either. Nor,' he added quickly, 'will I send one to you, Miss Carver. I shall write tonight off to experience. Thanks for the coffee.'

'The least I could do after you'd risked life and limb to make sure I was safe,' she assured him, and eyed him curiously. 'But why did you feel you had to?'

'Because I want the cottages. I had to make sure they wouldn't be vandalised,' he lied.

'I see. By the way, did Nero actually hurt you?'

Alex shook his head and raised a muscular leg to show her

an unmarked shin through the rip. 'I had a fight to detach him from my bespoke suiting, but he stopped short of actually savaging me.'

'So no worry about rabies, then?'

He blenched. 'Good God! I hadn't thought of that.'

She eyed him with derision. 'You're in no danger from an aristocrat like Nero.'

'Just the same,' he said with feeling, ' I'll give your property a wide berth from now on—at night, at least.'

'Very wise.' She opened the door, but Alex seemed in no hurry to leave.

'How about changing your mind?' he asked casually.

'About what, exactly?'

'Having dinner with me one evening. We could just talk business, if that would make the idea more attractive.' He listened to himself in disbelief. This kind of persuasion wasn't his style. Probably because he'd never had to use any.

'No—thank you,' she said distantly.

His jaw clenched. 'Why not? Do you find me repulsive?'

'No.'

'Then have you sworn off men as some kind of vow?'

Instead of saying *Just you, Alex Merrick,* as she yearned to, Sarah shook her head. 'I'm just not socialising with anyone right now.'

'Except Oliver Moore,' he reminded her.

'That's right.' She smiled sweetly. 'After all, he is my godfather.'

'So you said.' Alex moved closer, struck by sudden compassion. 'Are you still in mourning for your father? Surely he would want you to get on with your life?'

Sarah's smile vanished. 'As I keep pointing out, my life is my concern, and no one else's, Mr Merrick.'

'Message received,' he said stiffly. 'Goodnight, Miss Carver.'

Sarah felt very thoughtful as she climbed back up to bed later. If she were honest, and she tried hard to be most of the time, she knew she should have told Greg Harris that she'd arranged a night watchman for the cottages. But Alex's high-handed message had really ticked her off. Though he'd certainly paid for it. Sarah grinned at the thought of the vice-chairman of the Merrick Group fighting off a large German Shepherd.

But what had actually sent Alex storming round here after-wards? He'd been so blazingly angry when she'd opened the door to him Sarah had felt a thrill of apprehension, afraid for a split second that he'd throw her on the floor and take his revenge in the time-honoured way. He'd certainly been hot to vent his rage in some way on the person responsible for his clash with Nero. But she hadn't known he'd check up on her himself—had she? Sarah thought about it, and reluctantly admitted that she'd been aware of the possibility. Visiting the cottages to make sure she was safe had been a chivalrous gesture, and maybe—just maybe—she'd hoped that he would do it. But she would have expected Nero just to bark, not launch himself at Alex in attack mode. She would have a word with Ian on the subject. Injury to innocent visitors was something to be avoided. But, chivalrous or not, she reminded herself tartly, Alex's name was still Merrick. And her reaction to it was still the same as the first time she'd heard it.

On her very first day at Barclay Homes she'd found that the firm was actually a subsidiary of the Merrick Group, which had swallowed up other building firms in the area. A small outfit like her father's had never stood a chance. Sarah knew with the logical part of her that the Merrick Group had not caused his death. But the illogical, emotional side of her still held them accountable.

CHAPTER FOUR

SARAH SAW no more of Alex Merrick after their midnight encounter. But to her surprise—and disgust—she kept wondering if he'd ring, or call in again. To counteract this she worked like a demon on the last touches to the cottages while Harry painted the exteriors, and Ian moved into number two at night, rather than spoil any of Sarah's work on the show house. When she ran out of indoor jobs she repointed the waist-high walls dividing the front gardens, and when she'd finished those Charlie Baker drove her to a local nursery to choose a flowering cherry for the back courtyard of the show house, and a Japanese maple for the front. It was only sensible to go the extra mile to make the properties as attractive as possible to prospective buyers.

'Is something worrying you?' asked Harry, as he helped her plant the trees one evening.

'Yes. I'm wondering what on earth I'm going to do with myself when this lot goes up for sale.'

'What are you doing this weekend?' he asked, surprising her.

'Nothing much. Why?'

'How do you feel about barns?'

Sarah straightened, eyes gleaming. 'Are we talking barn conversion?'

He smiled as he trampled the earth in round the cherry tree. 'Could be.'

'Tell me more—' Her face fell. 'But if they're up for sale I can't do a thing about it until I sell this lot.'

'These barns are not for sale. Leastways, not yet.'

She wagged a dirty finger at him. 'Stop teasing, Harry!'

He chuckled. 'My sister's married to a farmer. When I was there for dinner last Sunday Bob told me he's had to cut back a bit, so he's got three smallish barns he doesn't use any more. He's got planning permission to do them up, but not enough cash to do it with. If you offered to buy them for development I reckon he'd jump at the chance.' He nodded in approval as Sarah's eyes sparkled. 'That's better. You've been a bit down in the mouth lately.'

'Have I? Sorry. Anyway, when could I have a look at the property?'

'I'll talk to Mavis when I get home and let you know.' He looked up as a van came up the lane. 'Here comes the nightshift.'

Sarah bent to hug Nero as he came bounding to greet her. 'Hello, my lovely boy. How are you today? Hello, you two,' she added, as the others came up the path.

'Hi, there,' said Josie, eyeing the newly planted Acer. 'Gosh, it looks better and better here every time I come. Don't you dare go lifting your leg on that tree, Nero.'

'Don't worry, Miss Carver, I'll tell him not to, and he doesn't need telling twice,' said Ian proudly.

'Of course you don't, you clever lad,' said Sarah, giving the dog a last stroke. 'Right, then, time I went home and got cleaned up. See you tomorrow, Harry.'

'I'll give you a ring later, boss.'

Sarah felt weary as she drove back, conscious of a sense of anticlimax now the cottages were ready to sell. Tomorrow three estate agents were coming at different times to view.

When the phone rang while she was eating her supper Sarah seized it eagerly. 'Harry—'

'Afraid not. It's Alex. Alex Merrick,' he added, in case she was in any doubt.

The unexpected pleasure of her reaction struck her dumb for a moment. 'Oh, hello,' she said at last.

'How are you?'

'I'm very well.'

'Glad to hear it. Are the cottages finished?'

'Just about.'

'Then let's meet to discuss the sale. Friday would be good for me.'

He still wanted them, then. 'Sorry. I can't make Friday.'

'When then?'

Never, for a Merrick, if she followed her instincts. But it would be interesting to see how high Alex would go with his offer.

'Are you still there?' he demanded.

'Yes. I could do Saturday morning.'

'Right. I'll see you at the cottages at ten.'

When the phone rang again shortly afterwards it actually was Harry, with an invitation to Sunday dinner at the farm so she could have a look round.

'How lovely! Please thank your sister for me, Harry.'

The houses passed the building inspector's final examination with flying colours, and the visits by the estate agents went equally well. They forecast figures much higher than Sarah had dared hope—the highest from one of the more exclusive agents, who assured her he'd have no trouble in shifting all six houses if she put her business in his company's hands.

But if she did Sarah knew only too well she'd lose a hefty percentage of her profit to them. But that was far preferable to selling them to a Merrick. Though she might as well meet Alex Merrick and know what figure he had in mind, if only for the pleasure of turning him down. The vice-chairman of the Merrick Group would probably beat her down mercilessly. Just let him try, she thought fiercely.

Instead of spending the evening glued to columns of figures on her laptop Sarah went early to bed that night, feeling more relaxed now the die was cast. She achieved a good night's sleep for once, and turned up at the cottages next morning full of energy for the last minute touches. She swept and dusted throughout, then buffed up the latest thing in stainless steel door furniture on each of the cottages while Harry cleaned the windows.

'But don't let on about me doing women's work,' he warned, when they went down to the Green Man at lunchtime.

Sarah zipped a finger across her lips. 'Not a word. Though you've done it miles better than this woman would have done.'

'You mean there's something you can't do, then, boss?' he teased.

'Lots of things—and cleaning windows as well as you do is way up there on the list.'

'Have you decided which agent's going to handle the sale?'

'Not yet. I'll have a chat with Oliver over the weekend and let them know on Monday.'

Close as she'd grown to Harry, Sarah felt it best to keep her meeting with Alex Merrick to herself.

She spent some time next morning over her choice of clothes for her Saturday rendezvous. Her aim was somewhere below the full-on babe outfit of an evening with Oliver but well above the scruffy look of her working day. And, most important of all, Sarah was determined to obliterate Alex's last impression of her in striped pyjamas and the dressing gown her mother had given her for her fifteenth birthday. She felt a little uneasy about seeing him again after the disaster of his encounter with Nero. But this was different; it was a business meeting, she reminded herself, though not the occasion for one of the suits she'd worn in the office. She settled for a pair of black linen trousers and a plain white shirt, and because the forecast was showery armed herself with the short black trench coat she wore for trips into Hereford. She'd treated her unruly curls to a blow-drying session for once, and tied them back with a silk scarf, then surprised her face by applying some make-up for a change, instead of just the usual smear of moisturiser—though this last came in handy when she found she'd run out of polish for her flat black shoes.

Sarah drove down to the cottages at nine to relieve her house-sitters, who had tidied all their gear away and left milk for her coffee. She thanked them warmly, and after a romp with Nero waved them off to enjoy their weekend. Sarah went on a tour of all six houses, then sat down in the show house to read the paper she'd bought on the way. She skimmed through the news items, and even did half a crossword, but at last felt too restless to stay indoors and went outside.

After a week of sunshine and showers, the gardens in all the cottages were looking surprisingly well established. Sarah had time to make a thorough check on all of them before the familiar Cherokee nosed down the lane. When Alex got out, holding a briefcase but otherwise looking casual in jeans and sweater, she strolled up the lane towards him.

'Good morning.' He met her halfway, smiling that smile of his, and shook her hand. 'Congratulations. You've done a great job here.'

'Thank you. Take yourself on a tour, if you like.'

'Come with me—please?'

'Certainly.'

This time Alex was in no hurry. He put his briefcase down on the kitchen table, then made a thorough exploration of every house, taking such minute notice of every feature that Sarah was more glad than ever that she'd bought top-quality fittings—especially when he commented on the Belfast sinks installed in the curving, custom-built counter tops in all the kitchens.

'You've achieved a very clever balance between traditional and modern,' he said, when they eventually returned to the show house.

'Thank you. My aim was a country cottage with local appeal, but which would also tempt a town buyer looking for a weekend retreat.'

'Where did you get the vintage furniture?'

'I put the contents of my family home into storage when the house was sold. I sent for some of them last week, so I could make the show house look like a real home. At which point,' she added, 'Ian Sollers promptly moved into number two at night, to avoid any possibility of his damaging anything.'

'Not to mention any Nero might cause,' said Alex with feeling.

'Nero doesn't do damage. He's a very well-behaved dog,' said Sarah firmly. 'He was just doing his job that night.'

'You obviously love dogs!'

'I do.' Sarah shrugged. 'But even if I had room for one dogs aren't allowed at Medlar House.'

'So sell your ivory tower and move to a place where you *can* keep a pet. In your kind of job you can take a dog with you on site.'

'True,' said Sarah. 'But I don't want to move right now. I've only just got my flat into shape. Talking of property,' she added, suddenly brisk, 'would you care for some coffee while we get down to business?'

'Thank you.' Alex promptly sat at the head of kitchen table, as though chairman of the board was his rightful place.

Sarah made coffee in china cups with saucers, and carried a tray to the table. 'Only instant, I'm afraid.'

'Fine,' he said, waiting for her to sit down. 'Now, then, Miss Carver. How much do you want for the entire property?'

Sarah multiplied the highest price by six and gave him the answer.

Alex stared at her in disbelief. 'That's totally unrealistic.'

'It's the price I was advised to ask,' she assured him.

'But any other buyer would want only one cottage,' he reminded her sharply. 'If I buy the entire row you'll have to come down, Miss Carver. A long way down,' he added.

Sarah had done her homework in so much depth and so repeatedly she knew exactly how low she could go and still make the profit necessary to make her venture a success. 'I suppose I could come down a trifle.'

Alex snorted. 'You'll have to do a lot better than that!'

'Look,' she said reasonably, 'if you don't want them I'm assured I'll have no problem finding other buyers.'

He stared at her in exasperation. 'I do want them, but only at a reasonable figure.'

'You mean what the Merrick Group considers a reasonable figure!'

'Exactly. Nothing personal. It's just business.'

'I know all about the business done by the Merrick Group,' she retorted, before she could stop herself.

His eyes narrowed. 'And what, exactly, do you mean by that?' he asked, his voice dangerously quiet.

Her chin lifted. 'Merely that your group is big enough to submit tenders which put smaller companies out of business.'

Comprehension dawned in his eyes. 'You said your father was a builder—'

'He was taken over by Barclay Homes, which as you well know is a subsidiary of the Merrick Group.' Sarah wished now she'd kept her mouth shut. 'Shall we return to the matter in hand?'

'By all means,' he said curtly, and made her an offer only a little higher than the lowest possible she could accept to make a profit.

'Now *you're* being unrealistic,' she said scathingly.

The coffee cooled in the cups while they haggled, Sarah coolly resolute and Alex growing more and more exasperated as he fought a battle he'd expected to win with barely a shot fired. In the end he slapped a hand down on the table, making the cups rattle, and named a figure which was, he said very emphatically, his top offer, and Miss Carver could take it or leave it.

'Do you want your answer now?' she asked.

Alex fought for control. For God's sake, he thought furiously. He faced tougher customers than Sarah Carver every day of his working life. 'Yes,' he snapped.

She shook her head. 'I need time to think about your offer,

Mr Merrick. I quite understand,' she added, sweetly reasonable, 'if you want to back out.'

To hell with it, thought Alex. Only the prospect of unsuitable tenants on land adjoining his luxury hotel kept him from doing just that. He got to his feet and snapped his briefcase shut. 'Ring my office at nine sharp on Monday morning with your answer, or kiss the sale goodbye, Miss Carver.'

Sarah nodded briskly. She got to her feet to see him out, and followed him down the path.

'Thank you for coming. Goodbye.'

'Goodbye, Miss Carver,' he said formally, and made no further reference to the deal before driving away.

Sarah watched him go, frowning. Now she had to get through the rest of the day with nothing to do. From a practical, purely financial point of view she knew very well that she should have said yes to Alex's offer there and then. But because his name was Merrick she was not only going to turn him down, but make him wait all weekend before she did.

Sarah decided to stay on site all day, until Ian and Josie turned up in the evening. Perhaps she could persuade her young caretakers to spend the entire day here on Sunday while she was out with Harry. The weather forecast was good, and they would probably enjoy a day spent in the sun in the courtyard of number one. She'd offer to stand them a takeaway lunch as inducement. Until the cottages were sold—whoever bought them—she would need the services of her young security guards. Sarah locked up with care and drove back to the local Post Office stores to buy food, added a paperback novel to her haul, and then returned to Medlar Farm cottages for the day.

She passed some of the time with more gardening in the sunshine, though by now there was very little left to do. The shrubs looked healthy, the lawns were greening up satisfactorily, and the property as a whole was very different from the barely habitable row of houses she'd first seen with Oliver.

Sarah rang him later, to tell him about the offer she'd had from Alex Merrick.

'Splendid, darling. I'm very proud of you. Is it all signed and sealed?'

'Of course not. I haven't *accepted* the offer, Oliver.'

'You mean you didn't jump at it?' demanded Oliver in astonishment. 'My dear child, what were you thinking of?' He paused. 'I suppose if he were a rose by any other name you would have said yes to Alex right away.'

'Exactly, Oliver. How percipient of you.'

'Far be it from me to try to run your life,' he said, an edge to his voice, 'but if you're going to succeed in your line of business sentiment's a luxury you can't afford, Sarah.'

'I know, I know,' she sighed. 'Don't worry. The agents who valued the houses assure me they'll have no trouble in selling them.'

'Or in creaming off some of your profit,' Oliver reminded her.

'True. But it would be worth it,' said Sarah. 'I can't bear the thought of Merrick hotel guests living in my cottages.'

'Ah, but that's not the plan. I had a little chat with George Merrick the other night and put out some discreet feelers on the subject. Apparently young Alex intends to use the houses as retirement homes for long service employees of the Merrick Group.'

'*What?*' Sarah's eyebrows shot to her hair. 'Are you sure about that?'

'I'm merely passing on what his father told me. In confidence, by the way,' warned Oliver.

Sarah shook her head in wonder. 'I was sure Alex Merrick meant to put them to work to make money, as an annexe for his hotel.'

'I hinted as much to George. But he said that Alex, much to old Edgar's disgust, is hell-bent on philanthropy. And he makes it very plain who's in charge these days. So instead of making them pay for themselves, the cottages will house deserving ex-employees who will live in rural, rent-free bliss in your first venture into property development, Sarah. Should you sell to him, of course.'

'Well, that's a turn-up for the books,' she said, deflated, and stayed silent for a while, thinking it over.

'Are you still there, Sarah?' demanded Oliver.

'Yes. I was thinking. Much as it grieves me to say so, if what you say is true I suppose it would be a pity not to let Alex Merrick have them.'

'At the money he's offering it would be downright stupidity to turn it down, my girl. Forget about his name for once and accept his offer. As your practical father,' he added with emphasis, 'would have urged you to. And take my advice— which to anyone else is inordinately expensive—in future trans- actions use your head, not your heart, Sarah. And ring me on Monday to let me know what happened.'

Harry collected Sarah from Medlar House at twelve next day, in cords and a tweed jacket, and sporting a new haircut.

'You look very smart, Harry,' she told him, and dumped her rubber boots in the back of the pick-up.

'So do you,' he said, eyeing her crisp striped shirt and newly laundered jeans. 'A mighty big improvement on those overalls of yours.'

'Practically anything would be. I hope it's not putting your sister out to have an extra guest for lunch,' added Sarah.

'If you can put Mavis and Bob in the way of making a bit of money she'll be glad to do it every Sunday,' he assured her. 'They never had sons, which means paying for labour now the girls are married and can't help out any more, so things are a bit tight on the farm these days. Mind,' he added awkwardly, 'I didn't say that to influence you.'

'I know that, Harry! But it struck me yesterday that I'm going to be like a lost soul with no work to do. I do so hope the barns are a feasible proposition.'

To Sarah's intense relief they were. After introducing her to his sister and her husband, Harry kept in the background while Mavis, a smaller, jollier version of her brother, insisted on serving coffee before she let her large, amiable husband take Sarah on a tour of the barns. The meal giving out savoury aromas in the big farm kitchen would be ready in one hour exactly, Mavis informed them.

'So you'd best go too, Harry,' she said, 'and make sure Bob brings Miss Carver back here on time.'

Sarah was jubilant later, on the way home. The barns were small enough to be viable for conversion, though not to the holiday lets the Grovers had intended. Permanent dwellings were essential for Sarah to gain her necessary profit. A lane separated the barns from the main farm, and gave good access for the equipment Sarah would hire—also for the tenants who would eventually occupy the finished houses.

'What do you think, Harry?' she asked. 'If I make an offer to your brother-in-law are you game to go on working with me?'

'Wouldn't have mentioned the barns else,' he assured her. 'So you see them as a workable proposition?'

'I certainly do.' She gave him a sparkling look. 'Mr Grover told me he owns fishing rights on a short stretch of the river, too, which could appeal to male buyers. And for women who don't fish it's not far to Hereford for retail therapy.'

Harry laughed. 'You had all this worked out in your head before Mavis dished up the rhubarb crumble.'

Sarah grinned. 'I certainly did.' She sobered. 'But I can't make a firm offer until I sell the cottages. With luck I should be able to some time next week.'

'You've got someone interested in one of the cottages?'

Sarah nodded. 'I've got a possible buyer for the lot, but I haven't clinched the deal yet.'

'All six houses?' Harry took his eyes off the road for a second to look at her. 'You don't look all that pleased about it.'

Sarah smiled ruefully. 'We've been working on those cottages for quite a while now, Harry. It's a wrench to part with them.' Especially to a Merrick. 'But if the sale goes through I can start planning the new look for the barns right away. Do you think Ian and Fred will fancy helping again?'

'Try stopping them,' said Harry dryly as he drove into Medlar House. 'Now, get a good night's rest. I'll check up on the youngsters myself on the way back.'

Sarah did her best to take Harry's advice, but after a phone call from Oliver to confirm that she still intended to sell to Alex she was too wound up to sleep much—partly from excitement over the barns, but mainly because she couldn't rid herself of the idea that now, when she'd finally, reluctantly, made up her mind, Alex Merrick would say his offer had been withdrawn when she rang him to accept it.

When the sun began streaming through the shutters next morning Sarah gave up all pretence of even trying to sleep and got dressed. She let herself out of the flat, and later enjoyed her morning coffee all the more for the mile long round trip to buy a paper. She ate some toast while she caught up on the day's news, then just sat with her phone in her hand, gazing out at the sunlit garden as she waited for the appointed hour. Exactly on the stroke of nine she rang Alex Merrick's office number, and in response to Greg Harris's familiar accents told him Miss Carver wished to speak to Mr Merrick.

'I'll see if he's free,' said the young man stiffly, obviously still smarting from their previous exchange. 'Will you hold?'

'Certainly.'

'I'm putting you through,' he said a moment later, and her stomach clenched as the familiar, confident voice came on the line.

'Good morning, Miss Carver.'

'Good morning, Mr Merrick.'

'I take it you have an answer for me?'

'Yes. I accept your offer for the Medlar Farm Cottages.'

Alex was silent for so long Sarah's stomach did a nosedive. Had she been right to worry? Had he changed his mind?

'Good,' he said at last.

Her eyes kindled. Swine! He'd done that on purpose.

'I suggest,' he went on, 'that we meet here at my office at eleven tomorrow to make the exchange. Is that convenient for you?'

'Yes.'

'One of the Merrick Group lawyers will be present, and you will naturally wish to bring your own legal support.'

'Naturally,' she said crisply, praying that the solicitor Oliver had found for her would be free to accompany her into the lion's den.

'In the meantime, I'll send our chief surveyor round to the cottages today at ten to make our own official inspection—if that's convenient?' Alex said, hoping Sarah couldn't tell he was grinning from ear to ear.

'Of course,' she said coolly, and disconnected to call her solicitor and make her request.

Charles Selby, it appeared, was only too glad to accompany her, and promised to pick her up at Medlar House well before the appointed hour. Probably because she was the goddaughter of Oliver Moore QC, thought Sarah the cynic, then rang Oliver's chambers, as ordered, to give him the glad news.

'Splendid, darling,' he said, delighted. 'Congratulations. I wondered if you might change your mind at the last minute.'

'So did I,' she admitted ruefully. 'By the way, I've asked Mr Selby to go with me tomorrow, Oliver.'

'Good girl. He can brief me later. Louise and Sam would be so proud of you, Sarah. I'll drink a toast to all three of you tonight.'

Once Sarah had swallowed the lump in her throat, she rang Harry to put him in the picture.

'Well done, boss,' he said gruffly. 'But if it's not signed and sealed until tomorrow you'll need Ian again tonight.'

'I will, indeed. Then tomorrow the Merrick Group can take over. I'm driving down to the site right now to wait for their building inspector, Harry. How about celebrating with a ploughman's at the Green Man later?'

'I'm here at the cottages now,' he told her. 'Ian had to go off early this morning, so he asked me to come over.'

'Thank you, Harry, you're a star!'

'Get away with you. I'll put the kettle on.'

Sarah spent a tense morning with Harry, praying that the Merrick surveyor would find nothing wrong when he arrived to inspect the houses.

'Stop worrying,' Harry told her. 'The official building inspectors were satisfied with it, so I doubt this fellow will find anything wrong.'

'I just hope you're right,' she said fervently.

The inspector had finished by lunchtime, but to Sarah's disappointment he made no comment on the properties other than to tell her he would pass on his findings to Mr Merrick.

'I wish I knew what his findings were,' said Sarah, frustrated.

'You will, soon enough. The surveyor Bob Grover hired for his barns was just as thorough,' Harry told her.

'I'll take Mr Grover's outlay into consideration when I make my offer,' Sarah assured him. 'Though I'll need a second survey on the barns. The original intention was holiday lets, so it's vital I make sure I have the necessary permits for permanent dwellings.'

Lunch at the Green Man cheered Sarah up considerably, though Harry advised her in advance against giving the regulars her news. 'Time enough for that when the deal's gone through,' he warned.

'Don't worry, Harry. I won't breathe a word to anyone until the money's safe in my bank account.'

When they went into the bar to a chorus of greetings Sarah had to put up with some good-natured teasing about being dressed up today, instead of in her working clothes.

'You clean up pretty good, I must say,' said Fred, handing her a half of cider. 'I don't think you've met Eddy's son,' he added, indicating the man who'd just come through into the bar. 'Daniel, this is Miss Sarah Carver—the prettiest property developer in the business.'

Daniel Mason put up the flap to come round the bar and shake Sarah's hand. Unlike his stocky father, he was tall and slim, with smooth fair hair and confident blue eyes. 'I'm delighted to meet you,' he said fervently.

Sarah smiled. 'I haven't seen you in here before.'

'I'm London-based, but I'm down for a few days' break from the city grind.'

'He works in a bank,' said Harry, his tone pejorative.

Daniel laughed. 'But don't hold that against me, Miss Carver.'

'Sarah's from London,' Fred informed him. 'But she's not like any city girl you know. Brought up on a building site, weren't you, my dear?'

'Mostly,' she admitted, and smiled. 'Though I did go to school now and then.'

'Maybe you could see what's happened to our meals, Daniel,' interrupted Harry.

'Certainly,' said the son of the house, unfazed. 'Back in a minute.'

'You watch that one,' said Harry in an undertone. 'He's too clever by half.'

Since this was more or less the same comment he'd made about Alex Merrick, Sarah smiled, amused. It was obviously Harry's general attitude towards the young and successful male.

When Daniel came back with their lunches he leaned on the other side of the bar while Sarah and Harry ate, asking about the project Sarah had just finished.

'I didn't do it on my own,' she assued him. 'I had Harry's invaluable input all along, plus some from Mr Carter here, and from several other people Harry roped in along the way.'

Daniel raised an eyebrow. 'I thought you were semi-retired, Mr Sollers?'

'Miss Carver needed my help,' said Harry flatly, and turned away to talk to Fred.

'He doesn't approve of soft city-types like me,' said Daniel in an undertone, then grinned. 'Though he's best known for his disapproval of the female of the species, so how did you get him work to work for *you*?'

'Harry works *with* me,' Sarah said with emphasis. 'Lucky for me he approved of my aim to restore the cottages rather than demolish them.'

'Ah, I see! I'd like to see the result of your labours,' he added. 'May I come and marvel some time?'

'By all means.'

'Let me get you another drink.'

She shook her head, smiling. 'I must get back.'

Harry turned back to her. 'I'll drop you off, boss, then I'm going to the vicarage to measure up the window Mrs Allenby wants replaced. I'll get back to you after that and wait for Ian.'

'No need, Harry. Just run me back now and I can do the waiting. I've got nothing planned for this afternoon. I'll potter around in the gardens, then read until the night shift comes on.'

'In that case maybe I'll do a bit in my own garden.' He lifted her down from the bar stool, and Sarah said a general goodbye to everyone, including Daniel, who smiled back with a warmth so marked that Harry teased her about it as they drove back.

Sarah felt restless as she wandered through the cottages later. It would be wonderful to sell the lot, even if it were to the Merrick Group. But work on them had taken up almost her entire life until recently, and she felt a sharp pang of regret at the thought of parting with them. Idiot! As Oliver so rightly said, if she were to make any kind of success there was no room for sentiment as a property developer, even for a fledgling one like herself. Though if money had been her only aim she could have sold the cottages to a buyer who'd offered for them before she'd even left London. But the offer had been so unrealistic she'd turned it down without a second thought.

Right now she just had to get through the rest of the day, hope the building inspection had gone well, and meet with Alex in the morning. Then, once the money was in her account, she could concentrate on getting the Westhope barn development off the ground. With this cheering thought in mind, Sarah curled up with her book and settled down to wait until her young security staff arrived.

A knock on the door brought Sarah to her feet, surprised. She'd been enjoying the book, but not so much that she wouldn't have heard an approaching car. She opened the front door to find Daniel Mason smiling down at her.

'Hello, Miss Sarah Carver. I fancied a stroll, so I took you at your word.'

CHAPTER FIVE

SARAH RETURNED the smile, not sorry for company on an afternoon which was already beginning to drag. 'So you did, Daniel Mason. Come in. I'll give you the tour.'

'Thank you. Only I prefer Dan. May I call you Sarah?'

'Of course.'

'After you left,' said Dan, as she took him round, 'I was told all sorts of tall tales; how you do your own plastering and tiling and God knows what besides. That can't possibly be true?'

'Yes, all of it,' she assured him. 'But Harry saw to the basic, essential things required by the building survey. And he put in new windows and did all the finishing after I'd done my bit.'

'And no one does it better than Harry Sollers. But he's well known for preferring to work solo. So how come he agreed to work for—I mean *with*—you?'

'I asked him and he said yes.'

Dan gave her a head-to-toe scrutiny rather too personal for comfort, and grinned. 'Of course he did.'

Sarah turned to lead the way downstairs. 'This is the only one I've furnished, but otherwise the houses are all the same.'

'You've done an amazing job,' he told her. 'If they were in London they'd sell in a flash—and for a lot more than you'll get down here. I'd like to stay a while, Sarah,' he added. 'Unless you're busy?'

She could hardly say she was, since he'd spotted the open

book. 'For the first time in ages I'm not. I was reading when you came.'

'Fred told me that you've got young Ian Sollers staying here at night. What time does he get here?'

'About six, as a rule.'

'What will you do after he gets here?'

'Go home.'

'And where's home?'

'You ask a lot of questions!'

He smiled. 'It's the quickest way to get answers.'

'You could have asked around in the bar.'

Dan shook his head. 'I was pretty sure you might not like that. Though I was told,' he went on, 'that you don't socialise with the local lads. Why?'

'It seemed best to steer clear of complications in a community like this.'

'Is there a non-local man in your life?'

'Yes. My godfather. They were pretty impressed at your pub because he wined and dined me at Easthope Court recently,' she said lightly.

'Well-heeled godfather, then!'

'He's a QC, and successful, so I suppose he must be. More important from my point of view, he takes his responsibilities as godfather very seriously. He wasn't happy when I insisted on bidding for this lot,' said Sarah wryly. 'He doesn't like my flat, either.'

'At the address you didn't give me,' he reminded her.

'It's no secret. I live in Medlar House.'

'Really?' Dan grinned. 'I used to go to dances there when it was a girls' school.'

Another one! 'They were obviously popular, those dances.'

'I went to an all-male school. You bet they were popular.' His eyes gleamed reminiscently. 'Socialising with the Medlar House girls was one of the great perks of getting to the upper sixth in my place of learning, believe me.'

'Oh, I do,' she assured him.

Dan glanced at his watch. 'Damn. Time I hiked back. I promised to give Dad a hand. But I'm free later, so will you have dinner with me, Sarah? Please?'

She looked at him thoughtfully. The evening promised to be long, with the prospect of tomorrow morning's transaction hanging over her. And Dan Mason, though a lot too confident of his own charms for her taste, was here on a temporary basis, not a permanent fixture.

'I can see you weighing up the pros and cons, so just for the record I'm happily unmarried,' Dan informed her.

'Then, thank you. Dinner it is.' Why not? It would be a good way of passing what would otherwise be an interminable evening.

'Great,' said Dan, his smile a shade too smug for Sarah's taste. 'I'll pick you up at seven-thirty. Any preference for eating places?'

'Not really—as long as it's not Easthope Court.'

When Ian and Josie arrived with Nero, for their last evening as caretakers, Sarah thanked them warmly for their help.

'We'll miss coming here,' said Josie wistfully.

'If you need us somewhere else any time,' added Ian, 'you just have to say.'

'I certainly will,' Sarah promised him, and bent to give Nero a goodbye hug.

She felt quite wistful herself on the way back to the flat, but cheered up at the thought of going out. Not sure where Dan was likely to take her, she wore the tailored black linen trousers with their jacket over a cream silk camisole, and brushed her hair into a mass of loose curls. She was glad she'd taken the trouble when Dan came to collect her wearing a formal lightweight suit, topped by a look of deep approval which was highly gratifying.

'You look wonderful,' he told her.

'Thank you. Where are we going?'

'A London chef recently opened a country inn type restaurant a few miles from here. I thought you might like it.'

'Sounds perfect—' Sarah whistled as she spotted the banana-yellow Ferrari parked in the courtyard.

He patted the bonnet lovingly, then held the passenger door for her. 'This baby is my reward for slaving long hours on a City trading floor. I won't make you blush with my father's comments. Boy's toys and all that. And, as he says repeatedly, it's not even necessary. I walk to the bank from my flat.'

Sarah laughed. 'So when do you drive it?'

'At weekends.' He slanted a grin at her as he turned out into the road. 'To some country hostelry—with a charming companion on board, of course.'

'Of course. In the company I used to keep they were known as bird-pullers,' she informed him.

'Bird-pullers!' he exclaimed, laughing. 'Exactly what kind of company did you keep?'

'The kind you get on building sites.'

As Dan had promised, the inn was picturesque. Baskets of flowers hung outside a rambling low building divided inside into several small dining rooms.

'Choose anything you like from the menu. It's all first class,' Dan assured her.

He was right. But Sarah enjoyed the perfectly cooked sea bass rather more than Dan's company while she ate. Because his conversation centred on his success in his job, and the bonuses which had enabled him to buy his expensive car and his equally expensive flat, she found her attention wandering, and surfaced guiltily to hear him describing a recent holiday in St Tropez. Her brief encounters with Alex Merrick had been stormy, she thought suddenly, but a lot more interesting. Though after tomorrow there would be no more encounters. She was unlikely to see Alex again once the sale had gone through.

'That's a very thoughtful expression in those big dark eyes, Sarah Carver,' remarked Dan.

'It seems odd to think that my first venture into property development is over,' she said, smiling brightly.

'Is a second on the cards?'

'Of course. Once the sale of this one goes through.'

'Something local?'

'Yes.'

'Good.' Dan gave her his irritatingly cocky smile. 'With you around I'll be visiting the old folks more often in future.'

Sarah got up to leave. 'Around doesn't mean available.'

'I put that badly,' said Dan penitently, on their way to the car. 'Have I shot myself in the foot?'

'Not at all.'

'Then let's do this again. I'm here until the weekend. What day would suit you?'

'Sorry. I'll be too busy getting to grips with the new project.'

When they reached Medlar House Dan turned off the engine and undid his seat belt. 'I'd love a look at your flat.'

She shook her head. 'I have to be up early in the morning, so I'll just say thank you for the meal and wish you goodnight, Dan.'

He bent his head to kiss her, but Sarah put a hand on his shoulder and held him off, then released the seat belt and got out of the car. 'Thank you for dinner,' she repeated, as he followed her to the door. 'And for a pleasant evening.'

'Pleasant!' he repeated, an ugly set to his mouth. 'You really know how to cut a guy down to size.'

She smiled as she put her key in the door. 'Something you're not used to, I imagine?'

'No. Women like me as a rule.' He eyed her, baffled. 'I just wanted a kiss, for God's sake.'

'But I didn't,' said Sarah gently. 'Goodnight.'

Odd, she thought later, as she got ready for bed. Dan Mason was good-looking, and obviously clever to have done so well in his career. But he seemed to feel that his possessions were his main attributes. And he was probably right, because for some reason the thought of having him kiss her had made her skin crawl. Tonight had been a mistake. It served her right for breaking her rule about socialising with anyone local. She should have spent the evening with her book. Now she'd have to stay away from the Green Man until he'd gone back to the loft apartment he'd described in such mind-numbing detail.

Sarah woke long before the alarm went off next morning, aware the moment she opened her eyes that this was a memorable day in her life. She had no doubt about what to wear. This occasion really did call for a suit. And not just any old suit she'd worn to the office, but the raspberry-red number she'd bought for the wedding of one of her former flatmate, a couple of months before. The jacket's nipped-in waist and cleverly cut skirt were flattering, and with four-inch heels to give her height she could face up to Alex Merrick and whoever else he had on board.

By ten-thirty her solicitor hadn't arrived, and Sarah was just about to take off without him when her doorbell rang. About time, she thought irritably as she lifted the receiver.

'Sarah,' said a familiar voice. 'Are you ready?'

'*Oliver?*'

'Yes, darling. Charles Selby's here, too, so come along.'

Sarah locked her door, then rushed out into the courtyard to embrace her godfather's substantial person. 'It's so lovely to see you, but what on earth are you doing here?'

'Is that the way to greet someone who rose at the crack of dawn to fly to your side?' he asked, and kissed her cheek fondly, then looked her in the eye. 'I wanted to make sure you hadn't suffered a change of heart.'

She shook her head. 'No. I haven't.'

'Good. In that case my professional support will do no harm. Selby here has no objection.'

'Forgive my bad manners, Mr Selby.' Sarah turned to him in remorse. 'Good morning.'

The solicitor shook her hand, smiling. 'Good morning, Miss Carver. I'll follow you to the Merrick Group offices.'

Oliver ushered her into his Daimler, smiling rather smugly. 'I didn't mention my presence here beforehand, in case something unforeseen cropped up to prevent it. And my usual hotel room is free for me tonight, so I shall drive back first thing in the morning. You look utterly delightful, Sarah.'

'Good to know, because it took work,' she said with feeling, and beamed at Oliver. 'Thank you so much for coming.'

The Merrick Group offices were housed a few miles away, in a purpose-built modern building surrounded by manicured gardens. The woman at a reception desk flanked by banks of greenery smiled in enquiry at their approach.

'Miss Carver for Mr Merrick. These gentlemen are my lawyers,' Sarah said grandly.

The receptionist rang through to report their arrival, then conducted them across a gleaming expanse of parquet to a trio of lifts, and told them where to find Mr Merrick's office on the top floor.

Sarah grinned at Oliver as the lift doors closed on them. 'What cheek, talking about my lawyers! I hope you didn't mind.'

'Since both Selby and I *are* lawyers, not at all,' Oliver assured her.

'A pity you couldn't have worn your wig and gown,' she said with regret. 'Though you look impressive enough just the way you are.'

He was immaculate, as usual, his silver hair expertly styled, his superb three piece suit complete with watch chain. Mr Selby was similarly dressed, but his receding hair and smaller stature were no contest against the magnificence of Oliver Moore QC.

A tall young man in stylish spectacles greeted them as the lift doors opened on the top floor.

'Good morning, Miss Carver. I'm Gregory Harris, Mr Merrick's assistant.'

'Good morning. This is my solicitor, Mr Charles Selby, also Mr Oliver Moore QC.' A statement which impressed, just as she'd intended.

'Good morning, gentlemen. Please follow me.'

Alex got to his feet as the trio followed Greg into his office, his eyes narrowing as he saw two men flanking the vision of elegance approaching his desk. She'd pulled a fast one again, by springing not just her solicitor but a Lincoln's Inn Queen's Counsel on him as well. 'Good morning, Miss Carver—gentlemen. How nice to see you, Mr Moore.'

'You too, my boy,' said Oliver affably. 'I come *in loco parentis* for Sarah. I trust you have no objection to my presence?'

'None at all,' said Alex, equally affable.

'Good morning, Mr Merrick,' said Sarah. 'May I introduce Mr Charles Selby, my solicitor?'

There was a round of hand-shaking, including an introduction to Lewis Francis, the Merrick Group legal representative.

'Coffee?' suggested Alex.

Sarah opened her mouth to refuse, but Oliver nodded genially.

'That would be very pleasant—I had an early start.'

And, instead of getting straight down to business, as she would have preferred, Sarah was forced to make pleasant conversation with Lewis Francis while coffee was consumed, along with croissants and French pastries, which Sarah refused. She was hard put to it to swallow the coffee, let alone try chomping on a pastry. It seemed an age before Greg Harris came in to clear away and they could finally get down to business.

'Carry on then, Lewis,' said Alex at last.

Lewis Francis opened the file in front of him. 'All six houses on the property known as Medlar Farm Cottages met the standards of the building inspection, therefore the price remains as agreed privately by Miss Carver and Mr Merrick. This sum has now been paid into Miss Carver's account, if she would like to check before signing the necessary documents.'

'Ring your bank to confirm, Sarah,' said Oliver casually.

Sarah took out her phone to do so, and felt a surge of pure adrenaline as she heard the new total. 'Yes,' she said quietly. 'It's there.'

Eventually, when the contracts held the necessary signatures, and all was legally finalised even to Oliver's satisfaction, instead of the expected relief Sarah felt an overpowering sense of anticlimax.

'Congratulations, Miss Carver,' Alex said, holding her hand a fraction longer than necessary after shaking it.

'Thank you.'

'May I ask if you have another project in mind?'

'I do, yes.'

'Locally?'

'Yes.'

'How interesting.' He smiled his crooked smile, his eyes holding hers. 'I wish you every success with it.'

'Splendid,' said Oliver, watching the exchange like a hawk. 'I suggest I take everyone to lunch to celebrate.'

Due to other appointments, both solicitors regretfully declined, but Alex thanked Oliver warmly. 'I know the very place.'

'If you mean Easthope Court, Alex, I'd rather something more conventional at lunchtime,' warned Oliver.

'I promise you'll like the place I have in mind, sir,' Alex assured him. 'And, to let us enjoy a celebratory glass of wine with our lunch, one of the company cars will take us there.'

Oliver sat up front with the driver on the journey, leaving Sarah alone in the back of the limousine with Alex.

'You look dauntingly elegant today,' he remarked in an undertone.

Sarah shot him a surprised look. 'If that's a compliment, thank you.'

'You should always wear that colour.'

'Not a good choice for a building site.'

'Though as a matter of interest,' he added casually, as though discussing the weather, 'you look equally appealing in those overalls of yours.'

Sarah swallowed, her eyes fixed on the passing scenery. 'Practical in my line of work.'

'You didn't tell me your godfather was joining us today.'

'I didn't know. He turned up this morning as a surprise.'

He slanted a narrow look at her. 'When I saw we had the benefit of Queen's Counsel at the meeting I assumed you didn't trust me.'

'Not at all,' she returned. 'Mr Selby's presence was quite enough. Having Oliver along was just a bonus. It was good to have the support of a relative.'

'I thought he was just your godfather?'

She shook her head. 'He's also my mother's cousin, and they were as close as brother and sister, so Oliver's been in my life since I was born. He's a very hands-on godfather. Though he disapproves of my way of earning my living. When you first saw us at Easthope Court that night he was doing his best to persuade me to take a secretarial job in his chambers.'

Alex grinned broadly. 'How did you react to that?'

'Predictably.' Sarah sighed. 'I keep telling him he shouldn't worry so much about me.'

'Then I assume you didn't mention your idea of acting as your own security guard?'

Sarah shook her head vigorously, and laid a finger on her lips. 'Don't rat on me. Please!'

Chatting to Alex had been so unexpectedly easy for once that she hadn't noticed where they were heading, until the car turned into the forecourt of the inn Dan Mason had taken her to the night before.

'This looks very inviting,' said Oliver in approval as Alex helped Sarah out. 'I wonder if they do a good steak here.'

'They certainly do,' Alex assured him, then smiled as the chef himself appeared to welcome them. 'Hi, Stephen.'

'Back again, Alex? I must be getting something right.'

'We want something special today, my friend. It's a celebration.'

Stephen Hicks shot an appreciative look at Sarah. 'What kind?'

'Business deal. Let me introduce you…'

They were settled at their table before Sarah finally managed to say her piece. 'Oddly enough,' she said to Oliver, 'I had a meal here last night.'

'Did you, darling?' He looked at Alex, who shook his head regretfully.

'Not with me, alas.'

'Dan Mason from the Green Man brought me,' said Sarah, irritated to feel her colour rise.

Alex's mouth turned down. 'Son of the landlord and our local *wunderkind*. He's quite a lad, our Daniel.'

'With women?' said Oliver sharply.

'Probably,' Alex agreed. 'But actually I meant that he's a prodigy in the brain department. We went to the same school, but my interests were cricket and rugby while Dan sailed through every exam and took a first in Maths at Oxford.'

'But you went to Cambridge. Your father was very proud of that,' observed Oliver.

Alex smiled. 'My academic results weren't that spectacular.'

'But of course they didn't matter,' said Sarah. 'You had a tailor-made career waiting for you.'

His smile faded. 'Yes,' he agreed shortly.

'Now, then,' said Oliver quickly, perusing the menu. 'Let's get down to the serious business of food. What did you have last night, Sarah?'

'Sea bass,' she said, smiling at him. 'It was wonderful.'

'Stephen does an excellent rib-eye steak with oyster sauce, sir,' said Alex, and looked at Sarah. 'I had that last night.'

'You were here?' she said, startled.

'Yes. But, having interrupted your lunch once before at the Green Man, it seemed best not to incur your wrath by intruding on your dinner with Dan.'

'I'm sure Sarah wouldn't have minded in the slightest,' said Oliver, breaking the awkward little silence, and smiled as a waitress appeared to take their order. 'Have you two decided?'

The lunch party was a success, rather to Sarah's surprise, though looking back on it she thought that might have owed something to the champagne Alex ordered. Whether it was the champagne or the sheer relief of having the sale signed and settled, Sarah found herself enjoying the meal far more than the one she'd shared with Dan Mason the night before. After only a few minutes of Dan's achievements and possessions she'd been bored. Whereas every time she was in Alex Merrick's vicinity she might feel tense, as though she were balancing on a tightrope, but never for an instant bored. After toasts had been drunk to the successful business of the morning, she settled down to savour her triumph along with the award-winning food.

'So, Sarah, what do you have in mind for your next venture?' asked Alex as he refilled her glass.

'Barn conversion.'

'In this locality?'

'Yes.'

'I haven't heard of anything,' he said, surprised.

'You wouldn't have done. I heard of it through a friend.'

'Sarah seems to have established herself very successfully in the community,' remarked Oliver with satisfaction, and raised his glass again. 'To my clever goddaughter.'

'To Sarah,' said Alex, following suit.

Sarah smiled wryly. 'Not so long ago, Oliver, you were trying to persuade me to work in your chambers.'

'I concede my mistake,' he said nobly. 'I was worried about you, I freely admit, but I'm more than happy to be proved wrong.'

Alex eyed her challengingly. 'I'd still like to know how you stole a march on me over the cottages, Sarah. Our original offer was supposed to include them when we bought the Medlar Farm site, but they slipped through some red tape keyhole and went up for separate auction. And a sealed bid at that. So how did you do it?'

'I received very good advice,' she said demurely.

'That was your doing, sir?' asked Alex.

Oliver shook his head. 'Nothing to do with me, dear boy. I merely enlisted some professional advice to make sure the houses were worth buying, and then advised Sarah to bid slightly over the odds. It obviously worked.'

'Are you using the same strategy this time, Sarah?' asked Alex.

'Unnecessary. There's no auction involved.'

'More than one barn, darling?' asked Oliver

'Three, in fact.' She smiled at Alex. 'But I'd rather not give details in present company.'

Alex looked at her levelly. 'Relax, Sarah. The Medlar Farm cottages were a one-off deal because they adjoin the hotel development. Normally we don't deal in property on such a small scale.'

'Which certainly puts me in my place,' she said lightly. 'I wonder if they have more of the hazelnut parfait I had last night?'

When they arrived back at the Merrick building Alex told his chauffeur to drive Oliver back in the Daimler.

'I took it for granted you wouldn't care to drive yourself, sir,' he said, smiling.

'No, indeed. Wouldn't do for a man in my line to risk it after that extra brandy. Thank you, my boy,' said Oliver, shaking his hand. 'Very civil of you. We can drop Sarah off at her place on the way.'

Alex shook hands very formally with Sarah, before helping her into Oliver's car. 'Good luck with the new project.'

'Thank you.' She racked her brains to find something appropriate to say to mark the occasion, but in the end, feeling unexpectedly forlorn, merely smiled back at Alex as the car drew away.

CHAPTER SIX

OLIVER ASKED the driver to wait for a few minutes when they arrived at Medlar House, and followed Sarah into her flat. 'So, then, Sarah. How do you feel after your first success in the property world?'

'A bit flat,' she confessed. 'And a bit headachy, too, after two glasses of champagne at this time of day. Not,' she added with a grin, 'that it normally features in my life at *any* time of day.'

'You can well afford the odd bottle now, darling, if you fancy it,' he reminded her, then smiled lovingly. 'Sit down, darling. There's something I want to say.'

Sarah eyed him in trepidation as she went to her window-seat. 'Is something wrong, Oliver?'

'Not wrong, exactly.' He stood looking out at the view. 'I need to put something right. Your father asked me to keep it from you, but I think it's time you knew that he was asked to stay on as manager of SC Construction when the Merrick Group bought it from him.'

Sarah stared at him for a moment, then shook her head vehemently. 'That's not true. He would have told me—'

'Sam didn't tell you because he just didn't want the job. As long as you had security from the sale of the company, plus the value of the house, he was satisfied. He asked me to take care of you. Not that he needed to ask.' Oliver bent to take her hand. 'Sam's heart was giving out on him. Unknown to me, or obviously to you, he'd been taking medication for years, but when he told me he had very little time left, my darling—'

'But why didn't he tell *me*?' Sarah jumped to her feet. 'He shouldn't have kept it from me. If I'd known I would have taken more care of him.'

'You couldn't have taken better care of him than you did, Sarah.' Oliver took her in his arms and held her gently for a moment or two, then let her go and turned her face up to his. 'Sam made me promise not to tell you, but I have no compunction in breaking that promise because I believe you deserve the truth. Don't be sad. Enjoy your triumph, darling.'

Sarah nodded dumbly as she blinked tears away.

'Good girl.' Oliver bent to kiss her cheek. 'Now, I'd better not keep Alex's driver waiting any longer. Keep me in the picture with the barn conversion scheme.'

'Of course.' She hugged him hard. 'Thank you so much for coming today.'

'Least I could do, dear child.' He patted her back. 'And now I shall repair to my hotel room and sleep off the effects of lunch, before attacking the brief I brought with me.'

Sarah released him, looking at him steadily. 'And thank you for telling me the truth, Oliver.'

He smiled ruefully. 'I just hope I haven't ruined your day.'

'No. I'm glad I know. I also know how busy you are. It was wonderful to have your support today. Goodbye, Oliver. I'll ring you.'

Sarah put her suit away, washed her face, then took a long bath, her brain revolving in circles as it tried to come to terms with Oliver's revelation. At least, she thought eventually, it scotched any last remnants of guilt she'd felt about selling out to the Merrick Group. But when she'd flung her accusation at Alex Merrick why hadn't *he* told her the truth? But if he had would she have believed him? Probably not, she decided honestly. Believing anything good of the Merricks would have been difficult after years of looking on them as the villains of her particular piece. Yet in some ways she was relieved, because no matter how much she'd tried not to she liked Alex. And she was pretty sure her father would have liked him just as much as Oliver did.

Later, feeling a lot better with that thought in mind, she decided to pass the rest of the day doing girl things for once. As a start she gave her feet a rare pedicure, painting her toenails candy-pink, and then neatened her sorely tried fingernails with an emery board and painted them to match. Afterwards, with an eye on the sunlight filtering through the blinds, she hunted out a white halter top and a thin rose-print cotton skirt she hardly ever wore. Then, armed with a cup of strong coffee to chase away the last lingering effects of the champagne, she made for her usual perch on the windowseat to ring Harry.

'Hi, it's Sarah. Guess what? I've sold the entire row of cottages to the Merrick Group, so Westhope Farm here we come! Will your brother-in-law be available if we pop over there in the morning?'

Harry gave a hoot of laughter. 'No doubt about that, boss. Congratulations! What time shall I pick you up?'

Sarah smiled as she disconnected. The people who thought of Harry Sollers as a gruff old curmudgeon didn't know him as well as she did. Dedicated bachelor he might be, but he felt paternal where she was concerned. And she was grateful for it. But right now she needed to switch off for a while. Tomorrow, she promised herself, stretching, she would think about permits and building inspections and checks on footings and the usual run-up to a job. But tonight she would just chill for a while, savour her first success while she took a walk in the early evening sun round the Medlar House grounds. Afterwards she would watch something mindless on television, or read her book, or even just sit and do nothing at all for once in her life.

Heartily sick of the entire programme by late evening, Sarah was delighted to hear her phone ring—even when she found her caller was Alex Merrick. Or maybe, she decided honestly, *because* it was Alex Merrick.

'If you're not busy,' he said, after the formalities were over, 'I'd like a word.'

'By all means.' She laughed a little. 'Please don't say you want your money back.'

'Not much chance of that, with your heavy legal guns trained on this morning's proceedings! I'll be with you in a few minutes,' he added, surprising her.

'Oh—right.' Sarah's eyebrows rose as she snapped her phone shut. She'd assumed he meant a word on the phone. Now their business dealings were over the last thing she'd expected was another visit from Alex Merrick.

A quick phone call was exactly what Alex had intended, but at the sound of Sarah's voice he'd felt a sudden urge to see her, talk to her face to face. Now the deal was sorted, there was no reason why they couldn't be friends. He was thoughtful as he took the road for Medlar House. The idea of Sarah Carver as a friend was actually very appealing. His old schoolfriends, and others of both sexes he'd made in his Cambridge days, were either married or working in all four corners of the globe. Except for Stephen Hicks. And none of them had as much in common with him as Sarah from a career point of view.

When he pressed her bell Sarah buzzed him in and stood barefoot at her open door. She smiled as Alex crossed the hall towards her, unaware that she was backlit by the light streaming through her thin skirt, giving him an X-ray view of legs and curving hips that struck him dumb. 'Hi. Do come in.'

'Thank you for seeing me,' he said, clearing his throat. 'I thought you might be out celebrating.'

'Not twice in one day,' she assured him as she closed the door. 'Besides, Oliver wouldn't have risked driving here again.'

'You could have been celebrating with someone other than your godfather.' Like Dan Mason, perish the thought.

'True, but as you see I'm not, so can I offer you a glass of wine?'

Alex eyed her hopefully. 'I don't suppose you'd have a beer?'

'Sorry. The only other thing on offer is coffee.'

'Good as yours is, I'll take the wine on an evening like this.' He badly needed something to lubricate the mouth that had dried at the sight of her in silhouette. 'But only if you'll join me.'

Knowing she could depend on the quality of the wine Oliver sometimes brought her to keep in her fridge, Sarah filled two of her mother's best glasses and handed one to Alex. 'Do sit down,' she invited.

He waited for her to take her usual perch on the window-seat, then sat on the sofa, trying not to stare at her pink toenails. Her untidy curls framed a face bare of even lipstick, he noted with amusement. As usual she'd made no attempt to tidy herself up to meet him. But, polished and perfect though she'd been for their meeting this morning, he liked the barefoot dishevelled look far more. So much more it was taking all his will-power to stay on the sofa instead of snatching her up in his arms to kiss her senseless. Whoa! Where had that come from? He swallowed some wine hastily. The first step, Merrick, is to get her used to the idea of you as a friend.

Sarah waited patiently for Alex to speak. His lean, clever face looked very brown in the light above his open white collar, and for once she considered him solely on the merit of his looks—which, she had to admit, were considerable. She had always been attracted to brains rather than muscles, but Alex had both. He had a degree, so he obviously had brains, and if the muscles came from playing cricket rather than hard, physical work, at least he had some.

'What did you want to discuss?' she asked, after an interval where he seemed inclined just to sit and look at her rather than talk.

With effort, Alex removed his gaze from the hair curling on her bare shoulders. 'Have you forgotten about the furniture, Sarah?'

Not Miss Carver any more, then. She frowned. 'What furniture?'

'The first Medlar Farm cottage in the row is full of your belongings,' he reminded her.

Sarah's eyes widened. 'Good heavens!' She shook her head in disbelief. 'I can't believe I'd forgotten that. No more champagne at lunchtime for me!'

He shook his head. 'You were merely enjoying your first triumph too much to remember.'

'Which is pretty stupid of me, because it's my mother's furniture!'

'You think of it as hers rather than belonging to both your parents?' Alex gave her the benefit of his crooked smile. 'Forgive my curiosity.'

Sarah was pretty sure most people forgave him anything when he smiled like that. But she wasn't most people. 'I was speaking literally. It actually *was* my mother's. She inherited it from her parents, along with the house—but I mustn't bore you with my life history.'

'It wouldn't bore me—quite the opposite. I'd really like to hear it. Unless you find it painful to talk about your parents?' he added quickly.

To her surprise, she found she wanted to talk about them. 'My mother was a landscape gardener. She was working in the grounds of a big property when my father arrived with his crew to do restoration work on the house. One look and that was it— for both of them.' Sarah smiled wryly. 'Dad said her parents were not exactly thrilled when their only child told them she'd fallen in love with a builder brought up in a children's home. But when they met him they liked him. So much so that eventually they suggested he moved into their home with Louise after their marriage, instead of taking her away from it. Dad told me that he was only too happy to be part of a family at last, and from then on he did all the maintenance work on their sizeable North London home as a way of showing his gratitude.'

'As a son-in-law he was a valuable asset, then?'

'In every way,' Sarah agreed. 'He helped Mother care for her parents as they got older and frailer. How about you?' she added. 'I heard that your father's based in London these days?'

Alex nodded soberly, and drank some of his wine. 'Did your source tell you he'd remarried?'

'No. My "source", as you put it, is Harry Sollers. He's not big on gossip. He just gave me the bare bones of the Merrick success story.'

Alex smiled wryly. 'Then he must have mentioned Edgar, my grandfather, scrap baron extraordinaire. The old boy's a bit of a legend in this part of the world.'

'For turning scrap metal into gold?'

'That's not far off the truth. He started from nothing, which is hard to believe when you think of the group's present level of expansion.'

'Is he still alive?'

'God, yes. In his late eighties and still alive and kicking. My aunt—a saint by any standards—lives with him, and does her best to care for the cantankerous old devil.' Alex grinned at the look on Sarah's face. 'Don't look so shocked. I say exactly the same to his face.'

'If your father has remarried, did you lose your mother when you were young, like me?' she asked with sympathy.

He was silent for a moment. 'I suppose you could say that,' he said at last. 'After I graduated she divorced my father and bought a house near her sister in Warwickshire.'

'Alex, I'm so *sorry*. I wouldn't have asked if I'd known,' Sarah said remorsefully.

'At least it shocked you into calling me Alex at last.'

'I could hardly do that while you were still addressing me as Miss Carver.'

'I make it a rule never to mix business with pleasure. But,' he said, holding her eyes, 'we concluded the business part this morning, Sarah.'

'So we did.' She took his empty glass. 'Let me give you a refill. Or I could make you some coffee.'

'Does that mean you'd like me to stay awhile?'

She nodded. 'I was feeling a bit lost until you came. I've been so busy lately it was strange to have time on my hands.'

'You could have contacted Dan Mason to keep you company.'

'No, I couldn't,' she said flatly.

'Why not? You were having a good time with him last night.'

She glared at him. 'You were *watching* me?'

Alex's eyes glittered coldly. 'From where I was sitting I had no option. You didn't notice me when you arrived, but Danny boy did. He deliberately seated you with your back towards me, so he could catch my eye now and again to make sure I noticed what fun you were having together.'

'Why would he do that?' she said, astonished. 'Besides, just between you and me, it wasn't much fun. In fact it was boring. Whereas—' She stopped dead.

'Whereas?' he repeated suavely.

'I never feel bored with you,' she said, and flushed, eyeing him so warily he almost threw the 'good friends' idea to the wind and snatched her up in his arms.

'Then now we've got the business deal out of the way, there's no reason why we can't be friends.' He smiled persuasively. 'We have a lot in common, Sarah. We property developers should stick together. Which is why I offered you the services of our security men. Your crack-brained idea of sleeping at the cottages worried the hell out of me.'

'Did it?' she said, surprised.

He nodded grimly. 'I would have hated the thought of anyone at risk down there on their own, but in your case it was even worse.'

'Why? Because I'm a girl?'

'And a small one, at that.' Alex looked her in the eye. 'One I'd like to have for a friend.'

Sarah looked back very steadily. The idea of Alex as a friend appealed to her more strongly than she wanted him to know. The only friends she had in this part of the world were on the elderly side. Besides, since he was in the same line of business, broadly speaking, a friend like Alex Merrick could be very useful.

Alex eyed her curiously, aware that she was debating with herself. 'While you're thinking it over, enlighten me. Why did you say yes to dinner with Dan Mason when you always refused me? Because I'm one of the local lads you won't socialise with? Dan's local too,' he reminded her.

She shrugged. 'Only temporarily. Besides, if you rule out mixing business with pleasure you shouldn't have been asking me out in the first place.'

'For you I broke my rule. Gladly.' His eyes held hers. 'But where you're concerned, Sarah Carver, I had other cards stacked against me. Not only am I local, my name is Merrick!'

They gazed at each other in silence for a long interval. 'Today,' said Sarah slowly, 'I found out I've been wrong about that. Oliver told me my father was offered a job as manager when his firm was taken over.'

Alex nodded. 'It's group policy in those circumstances.'

'Why didn't you put me right about it?'

'Would you have believed me?'

Sarah flushed, and turned away from the bright, searching eyes. 'Probably not. But I feel pretty terrible about it now.'

'Why did Mr Moore tell you the truth today—of all days?'

Sarah raised her eyes to his. 'He obviously thought it was time I stopped gunning for you. He likes you, Alex.'

'I'm glad.' He smiled. 'But I'd be far happier if I thought *you* liked me too, Sarah.'

'I do,' she said simply.

Alex felt a surge of triumph so intense it took him by surprise. 'Good.'

He held out his hand. 'Shall we shake on it?'

'Shake on what, exactly?'

'Our friendship,' he told her, his smile even more crooked than usual.

Sarah smiled back and took the proffered hand, startled

by the frisson of response to the brief contact. 'Done,' she said lightly.

'Enlighten me, Sarah. The moment I introduced myself at Easthope Court that night you turned to ice. I know the reason now, yet you seemed to notice me earlier on. Why?'

'Your hair.'

Alex stared at her blankly. 'It's nothing out of the ordinary.'

'Ah, but the other men at your table were bald, or getting that way, so your luxuriant locks caught my eye,' she informed him, eyes sparkling. 'You were years younger than most of the men in the place, too.'

'It's an expensive restaurant. So unless they're footballers or hedge fund managers the male clientele tends to be elderly.' His lips twitched. 'Unlike their companions.'

'Which is why you took it for granted I was Oliver's current trophy!'

'A natural mistake.'

'You made your opinion so insultingly clear I wanted to punch you in the nose,' she informed him.

'You can now, if you like,' he offered.

She grinned. 'Not in cold blood.'

The last way he could describe his own. Alex itched to run his tongue over her unpainted lips, just to see if they tasted as good as they looked. He raised his glass instead. 'So shall we drink to an end to hostilities?'

She thought it over and raised her glass, nodding. 'I like the idea of being friends, Alex Merrick—'

'For God's sake just say Alex,' he said irritably.

'If we're going to be friends, Alex *Merrick*,' she snapped, ignoring his groan as she hurled his surname at him like a missile, 'we get things clear from the start. You don't give me orders.'

'God knows why I worried about you,' he said, shaking his head. 'You may be small, but you're damned vicious.' He held out his hand. 'Now, sit down and be nice.'

Sarah smiled unwillingly. 'I'll make some coffee first.'

'An offer I can't refuse. You make great coffee. One of several indelible memories from the night I met Nero!' He got to his feet to follow her to the narrow, high-ceilinged kitchen, but she held up her hand.

'You can hover in the doorway if you like, but there's only room for me in here.'

Alex leaned against the doorjamb, admiring the economy of her movements in the narrow space. 'I wanted you as a friend from the first, incidentally, before you even put me right about your relationship with Oliver.'

'You mean you saw me in my dirty overalls in the pub and wanted me for a chum?' she mocked, her eyes wide when she turned round to see Alex nodding.

'More or less,' he said lightly, accepting the mug she gave him. 'Now, this isn't an order, but a friendly word of advice. Say no to future cosy dinners with Dan Mason.'

'Why? Just because you don't like him?'

Alex shrugged. 'I disapprove of him rather than dislike him, I suppose. We went to the same school, but I belonged to a different set.'

'Because you came from a wealthier family?' Sarah couldn't help asking.

Alex held on to his temper with both hands, and sat down on the sofa, patting the place beside him. 'Do you think that one day you might try to think the best of me rather than the worst? I *meant* that I was good at most kinds of sport, and had to work a bit to pass exams, whereas Dan flew through exams but was a total duffer at any sport at all. So we didn't mix.'

'Sorry,' she said penitently, and sat down. 'But why do you disapprove of him?'

'Because, although Ed and Betty Mason are the salt of the earth, and he's their pride and joy, rumour has it that he rarely drives down from London in his Ferrari to see them. And when he does he never stays long.'

'Do you disapprove of his car, too, then?' she asked, smiling.

He looked down his nose. 'Only the colour.'

Sarah laughed, then looked at him thoughtfully. 'Do you see much of your family?'

Alex shrugged. 'I check on my grandfather most days, just to make sure he's still there. He thinks he's immortal, but in the natural way of things even he can't live for ever.'

'How about your father?'

'I see him when I visit the London office.'

Sarah slanted a glance at him. 'So you're filial and Dan is not. Is that your only objection?'

'No.' He thought it over. 'I just don't like him. I never have. He's the type who measures success by the material possessions it buys him.'

'But he's entitled if he's worked hard for them, surely?'

Alex turned to look at her. 'I've worked hard, too. Damned hard. I still do. Just because I was born a Merrick it doesn't mean I had everything handed to me on a plate. Once I was old enough I slogged on building sites or in warehouses every school holiday and university vacation unless I was on a cricket tour. And I always got landed with the hardest, dirtiest jobs.' He stretched out an arm and flexed it. 'I didn't get these muscles behind a desk, Sarah. And there was no gap year for yours truly, either. I went straight from Cambridge into the firm. Not,' he added emphatically, 'that I minded. It was always what I wanted to do. Still is.'

'I can relate to that. Because I'm doing exactly what I've always wanted to do,' said Sarah. 'And my school holidays were spent on building sites, too. But not because I was made to. Dad couldn't keep me away.'

Alex couldn't help touching her bare arm. 'But your muscles are a lot prettier than mine.' He raised her hand to his lips, and on impulse kissed each finger. 'What's wrong?' he asked, as he felt her tense.

'You say you want to be friends, but you behave more like a lover. Or at least,' she added with scrupulous honesty, 'how

I imagine a lover would behave.' None of the boyfriends she'd had in the past had practised subtlety as foreplay.

'You're a very appealing female, Sarah Carver, and I'm your average male, so I want to touch.' Need to—even crave to, more like it. He batted the thought away and smiled down at her. 'But all I ask for is friendship. Unless you're seized with overpowering lust for my body and sweep me off to bed right now, of course.'

Sarah's gurgle of laughter entranced him. 'How would I drag you up there?'

'And, having got me there, would the platform be up to it if I threw you down on the bed?' he said, grinning.

'Are you criticising my carpentry, Alex?'

He shook his head vigorously. 'I wouldn't dare.'

'Besides, I thought I was the one throwing you on the bed.'

'Let's change the subject,' he said, clapping a hand to his heart, 'before I get out of hand and risk our friendship before we even get it off the ground.'

'OK,' she said cheerfully. 'What shall we talk about?'

Alex took her hand again, instead of putting his arm round her as he badly wanted to. 'Tell me what Miss Property Developer has in mind for her next project. Purely as a friend,' he added piously, 'not as competition.'

'Oh, I know that. You made it clear that my kind of project is just chicken feed in the eyes of the Merrick Group,' she reminded him tartly.

'Only to set your mind at rest,' he assured her. 'So talk to me, Sarah. I'm interested.'

'Curious, you mean!' she said, laughing, secretly only too happy to talk at length about her plans for the barns at Westhope Farm.

Alex listened intently, made constructive comments and suggestions, and even offered Sarah any help she might need.

'For free?'

'Of course,' he assured her. 'What else are friends for?'

It was late before Alex forced himself to his feet. 'It's time we were both in bed.' He eyed the sleeping platform and grinned. 'But for various reasons not, alas, together.' He took her hand and kissed her cheek. 'Now we've agreed to be friends, let's have dinner tomorrow night.'

Sarah had to admire his style. 'Why not? Where?'

'You'll probably laugh,' he said, the crooked smile much in evidence.

'Try me.'

'I'd like to go back to Stephen's place and have you all to myself this time, without Oliver Moore watching me like a hawk, or Dan smirking at me. Just you and me, Sarah. Two friends enjoying a meal together.'

In bed later, Sarah tossed and turned, unable to sleep. Her first business triumph would have been enough to keep her awake, but Alex's visit was adding to her insomnia. His visit had been such a welcome interruption to her evening it was hard, now, to believe she'd ever looked on him as the enemy. It would be good, more than good, to have him as a friend. In fact, given the slightest encouragement, she would look on him as a lot more than just a friend— She shot upright as her phone rang.

'Hi,' said Alex.

Sarah subsided against her pillows. 'Hi.'

'Did I wake you?'

'No.'

'The glow of your first success keeping you awake?'

'That's only part of it.'

'So what else is on your mind?'

'I've realised I've agreed to a truce with the enemy,' she said bluntly.

Alex's laugh sent a tingle down her spine. 'Only I'm not the enemy any more, Sarah, am I?'

'No,' she admitted, after a pause. 'Which is pretty hard to believe.'

'I'll help you work on that tomorrow. Now, I'll tell you why I rang.'

'Not just to say goodnight?'

'That too. But I was on my way to bed before I remembered we still haven't settled about what to do with your furniture, Sarah.'

She groaned. 'Not again! I got so carried away with all my talk about barn conversions the furniture went out of my head. I'll contact my storage people and ask them to fetch it.'

'Why not store it down here? You can use one of our container units for a very reasonable fee—much cheaper than in London.'

'Oliver paid for the storage. My only outlay was getting it transported down here.'

'Where it might as well stay, ready to use in future when the barns are finished.'

'That depends on what you mean by a reasonable fee!'

'We'll discuss it tomorrow over dinner. Goodnight.'

'Goodnight.' Sarah closed her phone, then went straight to sleep with a smile on her face.

CHAPTER SEVEN

SARAH WOKE next morning to a feeling of well being. And this, she admitted, was not just due to her success on the first rung of the property ladder. Her new relationship with Alex was the icing on the cake—*and* the cherry on top. Even if he was a Merrick. He was a clever lad all round, she conceded, as she got ready for her trip with Harry. Alex was obviously brilliant at his job, or he wouldn't be vice-chairman of the Merrick Group at his age. Though apparently being born a Merrick wasn't enough to make it automatic. But it surprised her that he'd worked through most of his vacations. She'd imagined him sunning himself in the Bahamas or skiing in Gstaad, certainly not slogging away on building sites.

When Harry arrived to collect her his eyes were twinkling in his weatherbeaten face. 'Who's a clever girl, then?' he said as she got up beside him.

'I am,' said Sarah, beaming. 'But then, look what wonderful help I had!'

'Get away with you. By the way, Mavis is sorry she can't cook lunch today; she was called away late last night. My niece went into labour about midnight.'

'Oh, wow! Panic stations, then. Didn't Grandpa want to go too?'

Harry guffawed. 'Bob drove Mavis to the hospital, then cleared off back home, glad to keep well out of it.'

Sarah rolled her eyes. 'Don't tell me—women's work!'

'Yes, thank God. Bob can help birth a calf without turning a hair, but he was in a right old state about Rosemary when he rang me this morning.'

'If he's not up to it this morning we can do this another day, Harry.'

Harry shook his head. 'Bob's made up because you're thinking of buying, don't you worry. But I told him not to get his hopes up until we take another good look at the barns. Then afterwards I'll buy you a pasty in the Green Man to celebrate.' He shot her a glance. 'I thought you might like to give Fred the news.'

Sarah hadn't the heart to say no, Dan Mason or not. 'Of course. Everyone else, too,' she assured him.

When they got to Westhope Farm Bob Grover was grinning from ear to ear as he came to meet them. 'Good morning both— great news. My grandson arrived half an hour ago, and Rosemary's fine!'

Sarah and Harry opted for coffee rather than alcohol to wet the baby's head, then went on a tour of inspection with the jubilant grandfather. This time Sarah examined every inch of each building, and climbed up ladders into haylofts and down again with a speed and agility the men watched with respect. A surveyor was necessary for the official inspection, but Sarah took sets of measurements inside and out for her own personal record, including the space between each barn and its neighbour.

'You can get a good garden for each one,' Harry told her, casting a practised eye over the land available. 'It's a plus that they're offset from each other. Gives a bit of privacy.'

'I know the buildings are sound from the inspection I had done,' said Bob, not without pride. 'I'll give you a copy of the report.'

'Thank you, Mr Grover, that's a big help.' Sarah smiled at him in reassurance. 'A second one is purely to make sure of permission for permanent homes.'

Eventually Sarah confirmed that she would make a sound offer once she received a report from the building surveyor.

'This is a bigger job all round,' said Harry as they drove back.

'I know. But my dad did quite a few barn conversions at one time. I know the drill. As long as the main structures are sound on the ones at Westhope I don't see any problem. Are you in for the long haul, Harry?'

'Yes, boss,' he said, and shot her a glance. 'But this time we'll probably need more help, so I hope you got a good price for those cottages.'

Sarah nodded happily. 'It took some pretty fierce bargaining, but I did all right, Harry.'

'I don't doubt it,' he said, chuckling.

Secretly, Sarah would have preferred to go straight home. With the prospect of dinner with Alex later she didn't fancy a pasty for once. She fancied a run in with Dan Mason even less, and felt relieved when there was no sign of him when they got to the Green Man. But after she'd managed to convince Harry a sandwich was all she wanted, it was Dan who brought it through for her.

'You still here, then, Daniel?' said Harry. 'You don't usually stay so long.'

'I had my reasons,' he said, smiling pointedly at Sarah. 'And how are you today?'

'She's on top form,' said Harry, and beckoned Fred to join them. 'She sold all the cottages in one go yesterday.'

Fred beamed, and gave Sarah a smacking kiss on her cheek. 'Congratulations. Did you hear that, Charlie?'

Charlie Baker came to add his congratulations, and for a while Sarah was surrounded by well wishers wanting to buy her drinks she promised to accept next time.

When Harry was temporarily engrossed in conversation with Fred, Dan leaned closer to Sarah.

'Lucky lady,' he said in an undertone.

'Hard work, not luck,' she said dismissively.

'Something I know a lot about,' he reminded her, and smiled conspiratorially. 'So let's celebrate over dinner tonight.'

'Sorry. I can't.'

The smile vanished. 'Can't or won't?' he demanded, in a tone she didn't care for. 'I take it you've got a better offer?'

Sarah began to feel uncomfortable as eyes turned in their direction.

'Pity you didn't have a pasty, Sarah,' interrupted Harry. 'Your mother's excelled herself today, Daniel.'

'I'll have one next week,' she promised, and finished her cider.

'By then you'll be back in London, I expect, Daniel?' said Fred.

Dan nodded coolly. 'That's right, Mr Carter. It's back to the grind for me on Monday.'

Fred smiled blandly as Harry lifted Sarah down from her stool. 'Next time we see you it'll be Christmas, I expect. Unless you're off skiing again.'

Dan showed his teeth in a fleeting smile. 'I haven't planned that far ahead. See you later, Sarah.'

She included him in her general smile to everyone. 'Cheerio, gentlemen.'

Dan turned on his heel, and had gone through into the house before they'd reached the door.

'Was young Daniel bothering you?' said Harry, as they reached the pick-up.

'Not exactly. He just wanted to take me out to dinner again.'

'Again?'

'I had a meal with him on Monday night.'

'And you didn't want a repeat?'

Sarah smiled demurely. 'I'm seeing someone else tonight.'

He laughed. 'Good for you. Time you started going out a bit.'

'Exactly,' she agreed. 'But right now I'm off to contact the building surveyor.'

'I've been thinking, boss,' said Harry, as he drove away. 'Young Ian's not very happy with the firm he's working for now. What do you say to him coming in with us on the barns?'

Sarah's eyes lit up. 'I think it's a great idea, if he agrees. Find out what he's earning there and I'll see if I can pop it up a bit.'

'Right.' He got out to help her down when they reached Medlar House. 'I'll give you a ring later.'

'Thanks, Harry.'

His eyes twinkled. 'And you enjoy yourself tonight.'

Sarah spent some time on the phone for the rest of the afternoon. She contacted the offices of the building inspector, and arranged an appointment for the survey of the barns at Westhope Farm in two days' time. She rang Bob Grover with the news, and he assured her he'd be ready and waiting for the inspector, and promised to convey Sarah's good wishes to the new grandmother.

'What with your offer and the baby, Mavis is over the moon,' he said, chuckling. 'So am I, Miss Carver.'

Sarah typed a letter to confirm the inspection appointment at Westhope, then left a message on Oliver's phone to keep him up to date. Instead of driving she took a brisk walk to the Post Office stores to post her letter, and on the way back decided to forget about work for a while. Alex's visit had taken her by surprise last night, though to be fair she'd had plenty of time to tidy up before he arrived if she'd wanted. But tonight she would pull out all the stops. From the expression on Alex's face at the sight of her in a skirt, he obviously liked the girly look, so she'd keep to it tonight.

When she got back Sarah climbed the steps to her platform and slid back the doors on the wardrobe—which was so compact she'd sent a lot of her clothes to charity shops before moving in. She pushed aside the little black number and brought out the dress bought for her leaving party at the flat before moving from London.

Girly was the word for it, she thought with a grin later, as she zipped up the thin poppy-red voile. Slender straps held up the low-cut top, and the fluted skirt stopped just short of her knees. Sarah gave an excited little laugh as she looked at her reflection. Harry and his cronies wouldn't have recognised her. When the doorbell finally rang she went down the steps, carrying her shoes, feeling like Cinderella ready for the ball.

'I'm here,' said Alex.

Sarah buzzed him in, left her door ajar, then slid her feet into her shoes and stood in the middle of the room, waiting for him. He gave a perfunctory knock and came in, to stand very still just inside the door, looking pretty much perfect to Sarah in a linen jacket and khaki jeans which hugged his muscular thighs. They gazed at each other in silence, then, without taking his eyes away from her, Alex reached behind him to close the door.

'You look good enough to eat,' he said, in a tone which did damage to her pulse-rate.

'Thank you.'

'Would it endanger our embryo friendship if I kissed you?'

'You can if you're careful,' she said, offering her cheek.

'Sorry. Can't do careful,' he said, and kissed her mouth, taking so much time over it Sarah's heart was pounding by the time he raised his head. 'You know, I'm not so sure about this friend thing after all,' he said huskily, his eyes glittering.

She heaved in an unsteady breath, trying to damp down the heat his expert, hungry mouth had sent surging through her entire body. 'You don't want that any more?'

'Yes, of course I do. But I have a problem.'

'What?'

'The way you look tonight, any normal guy would want to be more than just your friend, Sarah. But don't worry,' he said softly. 'I'll stick to the rules.'

'What rules?'

'Yours: friendship with the enemy, but no sleeping with him.'

She eyed him quizzically. 'Is that what you want?'

He smiled wryly. 'Of course I do. I'd be lying if I said otherwise.'

'You're honest!'

'Always the best policy, Sarah. But don't let it worry you. Just good friends will do for now.' He touched a caressing finger to her bottom lip. 'So repair the damage, and let's take off to see what Stephen has to offer.'

Outside in the courtyard Sarah looked round for the Cherokee, her eyes wide as Alex led her to the classic beauty parked near the front gate.

'Wow,' she exclaimed. 'A Jensen Interceptor, no less. I do so hope my neighbours are watching. I got some teasing about the yellow Ferrari the other night, then Oliver collected me in his Daimler, and now you turn up with this baby.'

'My pride and joy, and used solely for special occasions,' said Alex, handing her in.

'I'm honoured. Though I would have been equally happy with the Jeep.'

'I know.' He slanted a smile at her. 'That's part of what makes the occasion special.'

It was Sarah's third meal in as many days at the Pheasant Inn, but eating alone with Alex raised the experience to a new level. His kiss earlier had altered things between them, to the point where just his mention of sleeping with the enemy was enough to revive sexual tension, which simmered below the surface while they studied menus and sipped the champagne he'd insisted on ordering.

'But the celebration was yesterday,' said Sarah, her colour rising as he looked into her eyes.

'This is to celebrate something far more important than mere business,' he said, toasting her. 'To friendship—among other things.'

'What other things?' she asked, raising her glass in response.

'Future pleasures.' He gave her the crooked smile that had once irritated her and now had a totally different effect. 'So, what would you like to eat?'

'I know it's a strange choice with champagne—I didn't dare

ask for it at lunch yesterday or Oliver would have had a stroke—but I fancy fish and chips.'

'You can have whatever you want,' Alex said, as the waitress arrived to take their order. 'I'll have the same.'

The simple, perfectly cooked food tasted wonderful, though Sarah had an idea that eating it in Alex's company had a lot to do with it. The small arrangement of flowers on the table had a single fat candle at its centre, with a flame which gave his eyes a more pronounced gleam than usual as they talked shop with the ease of old friends rather than recent enemies. Sarah's barn conversions were the main topic for a while, then she listened, fascinated, as Alex told her about the Merrick Group's acquisition of a manor house its owner no longer had the money to maintain.

'How sad,' said Sarah with compassion. 'To someone brought up to that kind of world it must be a bitter blow to leave it.'

'This particular owner grew up in a cottage much like the ones you've just developed. Ronnie Higgins, aka Rick Harmon, lead singer and guitarist of the Rampage, bought the house at the height of the group's success, but soon got too immersed in the good life to write new songs. The result was inevitable. Their records plummeted down the charts and the rainy day Rick never saved for arrived all too soon. He was forced to sell the fast cars, put the house up for sale and auction the contents.'

'Poor man. What will you do with it?'

'Convert it—with great sympathy—into luxury apartments. We've sold most of them in advance already.' Alex smiled. 'Would you like to live in something like that, Sarah?'

'No way.' She looked up with a smile as Stephen Hicks arrived to ask how they had enjoyed the meal.

'First class, as usual, Chef,' Alex assured him. 'The lady loves your fish and chips.'

Stephen rolled his eyes. 'Marvellous! I honed my craft in Paris and London, and all people want is my fish and chips.'

'I'll try whatever you recommend next time,' Sarah promised.

'You can tell us what to order when I book,' Alex assured his friend. 'What's for pudding?'

Sarah demurred, but gave in when Alex coaxed her to share a dish of sorbet made from blood oranges and pomegranates. She was actually dipping her spoon into their dish before the full intimacy of the process dawned on her. When his eyes held hers as he licked his spoon she felt a tide of red sweep up her face, and she swallowed another spoonful of icy perfection to tone it down.

'I think,' said Alex with constraint, 'that this was a mistake.'

'You want it all yourself?'

'No. But sharing it with you is giving me impure thoughts. Don't worry. I won't act on them.'

'Good.' Sarah laid her spoon down and sat back.

'You haven't eaten much!'

'I pigged on the fish and chips. I'd like some coffee instead, please.'

His eyes held hers. 'I was hoping for that when I take you home, Sarah.'

'Of course, but I'd like some right now just the same.' She smiled. 'And while we're waiting for it you can tell me more about Stephen. Is he an old schoolfriend?'

Alex shook his head. 'We met at Cambridge.'

'Did you read the same subjects?'

'No. His was Archaeology, mine Engineering. But we happened to meet on our first day, hit it off from the word go, and in our third year at Trinity we shared a double set—i.e. a communal living room with separate study/bedrooms.'

Sarah smiled, able to picture it only too well. 'I bet you had a fantastic time with all those clever girls around. Were there lots of parties?'

'Too many. Towards the end we had to buckle down to more serious stuff. Steve and I both played cricket, but like me he had parents who made sure he worked through vacations unless we were on tour.'

'Stephen couldn't have earned much on archaeological digs!'

'True. His Italian mother sent him off to Piedmont every summer, to work in her family's renowned cooking school.' Alex grinned. 'Steve's talent meant our dinner parties at Trinity were hot tickets.'

'So he never did anything with his archaeology?'

'No. As soon as he graduated he took off to France to cook.'

'And you went back home to the Merrick Group?'

'Exactly.' Alex smiled his thanks up at the waitress, and put a sizeable tip on the tray as she set the coffee pot in front of Sarah.

'Is it just coincidence that he opened a restaurant in this area?' she asked.

'No. After learning his craft in places like the River Café and the Savoy, he decided to open a place of his own. He asked me to keep a look out in this area, so when I heard through the grapevine that the Pheasant was going up for sale I told Steve to hotfoot it down here with Jane and take a look before it went on the open market.'

'You get on well with his wife?'

He nodded. 'Jane was at Trinity with us.'

A sort of private club, thought Sarah wistfully. 'Does she do any cooking?'

Alex laughed. 'None at all. That girl can burn water. She's the number-cruncher and takes care of the finances. She sees to the ordering, bullies the suppliers and does front of house. She's away at the moment, visiting her parents, but you can meet her next time.'

Stephen came out to intercept them as they were leaving. 'Nice to see you again, Sarah. Come again soon.'

'Not for a while,' said Alex with regret. 'I'm off to the London office tomorrow.'

'Which doesn't mean Sarah can't come here alone—or with someone else,' Stephen pointed out, and grinned at the look on his friend's face as he escorted them to the door.

On their way back, Alex shot a look at her. 'Would you do that?' he asked.

Sarah eyed him curiously. 'Would it matter to you if I did?'

'It would if it was Dan Mason.'

'How you do harp on about him. I won't go out with him again for the simple reason that I don't want to. But,' she warned, 'I refuse to boycott the Green Man just to avoid him. I enjoy my lunchtime sessions there.'

Alex touched a hand to hers. 'Dan must have gone back to the city by now.'

'He hasn't yet. He was still there when I went in with Harry today.'

'Was he, now? I wonder what's keeping him here so long this time,' said Alex as he turned into Medlar House.

'Could we stop talking about Dan Mason?' Sarah snapped, and stalked in front of him to open the main door. She unlocked her own door, switched on lamps and closed the shutters, then switched on her blinking answer-machine to hear Harry's familiar gruff tones telling her how much Ian earned. Sarah turned at last to find Alex watching her.

'I'll pass on more coffee.' He took her hand to lead her to the sofa, and slid a document from his pocket. 'I've sorted out storage for your furniture, so would you check the inventory Greg took this afternoon?'

'Oh—right. Thank you.' Sarah ran her eyes down the list, and nodded. 'That's the lot. Will you bill me?'

'No,' he said flatly. 'This is a personal arrangement between you and me, Sarah. So indulge me. Accept the storage rental as a gift from a friend.'

She smiled ruefully. 'I can hardly say no when you put it like that. Thank you, Alex.'

He leaned back, long legs outstretched. 'I could have stored it at my place, but I thought you might not go for that.'

'Harry pointed out the Merrick house to me on our way to Westhope. What I could see of it from the road was impressive. Is that where you live?'

'Not for years. When I was growing up we all lived there,

but my grandfather and Aunt Isabel are the only occupants these days. I've got a place of my own a few miles from here. I moved out of the family home when my mother left.'

'Do you see her often?'

'Yes, of course. She lives near Stratford-upon-Avon. I spend Christmas and New Year with her, and she comes to stay at my place quite a lot.'

Sarah turned her head to look at him curiously. 'Doesn't your father ever want you to spend Christmas with him?'

'Not since he's remarried. He takes his wife to a five-star hotel in a ski resort for New Year as her reward for enduring Christmas Day with my grandfather.'

'But you never stay home to endure it, too?'

'Old Edgar respects my wish to spend it with my mother. He doesn't care for her successor.'

'Do *you* like her?'

'We rub along.' Alex took her hand in his. 'Where do *you* spend Christmas?'

'It's not something I've looked forward to since my mother died. Oliver used to take Dad and me out to Christmas dinner at some hotel, rather than risk my cooking, and he still does the same now it's just the two of us.' Sarah smiled brightly. 'But let's change the subject. I'd much rather hear your views on quick-drying membranes for my barns.'

Alex threw back his head and laughed. 'Not a topic of conversation I've discussed with any other woman!'

'But one very dear to my heart right now. So, are you privy to any trade secrets I might find useful?'

For a while, only too happy to have Sarah hanging on to his every word, Alex obliged her with everything he knew on the subject—which was considerable. 'But now,' he said at last, 'let's talk about the weekend. I'll be back by then, so have lunch with me on Sunday. At my place, not the Pheasant.'

'Can you cook, then?'

'I was Stephen's *sous* chef often enough in the old days to learn a thing or two,' he assured her.

'In that case, thank you. I'd like to.'

'Good.' Alex took a card from his wallet. 'Here's my address. I've drawn a rough map on the back.'

Sarah eyed him narrowly as she took it. 'You were sure I'd come, then?'

'No. I lived in hope.' He got up with a sigh. 'I must go. Early start in the morning.'

'Are you staying with your father?'

He shook his head. 'When I'm in town I put up at the flat over the group offices.'

Sarah walked with him to the door. 'Thank you for this evening.'

'My pleasure—literally. Come about midday on Sunday—or I can drive over to fetch you?'

She shook her head. 'I'll enjoy the drive.' And could leave any time she wanted to.

Alex moved closer, smiling down at her. 'I've been very good. I deserve a goodnight kiss, Sarah.'

'In what way have you been good?' she asked lightly.

He took her in his arms. 'By not doing this again until now.' His lips met hers in a kiss which started off gently and then ignited into something so hot and intense Sarah was breathless by the time he released her. 'A goodnight kiss is allowable between friends,' he informed her, and kissed her again. 'Two, even,' he said not quite steadily. 'Goodnight, Sarah.'

'Goodnight.' She pressed the release for the outer door, and Alex smiled his crooked smile and went out into the hall, closing her door softly behind him.

CHAPTER EIGHT

NEXT DAY Sarah had nothing to do except think far too much about Alex Merrick's kisses. Until she heard from the building inspector there could be no progress at Westhope Farm. But in the meantime she would stop daydreaming and pass the time by dealing with laundry, spring-cleaning her flat, and even, horror of horrors, washing her mammoth windows.

She rang Harry after working on her laptop for a while, and told him she could top up Ian's present wage a little. 'Once I get the official report and make Mr Groves a firm offer, you can sound Ian out. If he's keen tell him to come round here to the flat one evening and we'll sort it.'

'He'll jump at it,' Harry assured her. 'So, what are you doing today, then?'

'Housework I haven't had time for lately,' said Sarah gloomily. 'Including the windows, heaven help me.'

'I'd better do that for you,' said Harry, to her astonishment. 'You'd be up and down a ladder like a monkey on a stick with the size windows you've got. Probably break a leg or something.'

'Harry, I can't ask you to clean my windows!'

'You didn't ask, I offered. I'll see you in half an hour,' he said firmly.

Only too happy to be relieved of the task she disliked most, Sarah loaded her washing machine and then got on with her cleaning, her mind on her evening with Alex. It was strange that dinner at the Pheasant with Dan Mason had merely been a way of killing time, whereas with Alex it had been pure pleasure from start to finish. Something she'd never felt with anyone before. Probably because he was nothing like the spoilt rich kid of her first impression. He'd worked hard to earn his crown. And he was no slouch in the kissing department either.

Sarah stood still in the middle of the room, her heart thumping again at the thought of Alex's kisses, until the doorbell brought her back to earth with a bump and she ran to open the door to Harry, who'd come armed with a telescopic ladder.

'Right then, boss, I'll get started.'

'This is very kind of you, Harry,' she said gratefully.

'I had nothing better to do. But not a word in the pub, mind,' he warned.

Sarah grinned. 'My lips are sealed. How about a cup of coffee before you start?'

'No thanks, I'll wait till I've finished. I'd better clean these shutters first,' he said, eyeing them. 'Might as well do the job properly. Got a bucket and some cloths?'

While Harry worked Sarah carried on with her own chores, and at intervals wrung out cloths for him and supplied fresh water. At last he stood back, eyeing pristine white shutters and gleaming glass with a grunt of satisfaction.

'All right if I go out through the long window?' he asked. 'Might as well do the outside and finish the job.'

'You're such a star, Harry,' Sarah said fervently.

'You'd best close the shutters a bit; I'll see better,' he said, and went out, pulling the window ajar behind him.

Sarah closed the shutters to halfway, then went up the steps to put fresh covers on her bed. She straightened in surprise at a knock on her door instead of the sound of the bell. She ran down, expecting one of her neighbours, and opened her door to find Dan Mason grinning down at her, so irritatingly sure of his welcome Sarah found it hard to summon a smile.

'Someone was delivering a parcel as I arrived so I sneaked in at the same time,' he said. 'Can I come in?'

Sarah nodded reluctantly, wishing she could say no.

Dan walked past her, looking impressed as he took in the proportions of the room. 'God, Sarah, what a place!'

'It was a music room originally, but I made some modifications.' Which was an understatement for a work programme which had started with tearing up lino and treating floorboards, progressed to building the windowseat and sleeping platform, and finished with the installation of her double row of shutters.

'But where do you sleep?'

'Up there,' Sarah said, waving a hand at the platform.

He raised an eyebrow. 'Romantic, but not much room for overnight guests.'

'None at all,' she said shortly. 'Why are you here, Dan?'

He smiled, moving closer. 'To get my request in early for your company at dinner tonight. Not the Pheasant again,' he added quickly. 'The weather's good, so we could drive to a place I know near Ross.'

She shook her head. 'That's very kind of you, Dan, but I've got something on tonight.'

'Two nights running with Alex Merrick?' he demanded, his bonhomie suddenly gone.

'As it happens, no.' Her chin lifted. 'But even if it were it's my business, Dan, no one else's.'

His mouth twisted. 'Oh, I get the message. The Crown Prince of Merrick strikes again. Alex always had the girls running after him. That smell of family money on him attracts them like flies. But he's a slippery customer; never gets hooked.' He caught her hands, sudden malevolence in his eyes. 'Did he score any better with you than I did?'

Sarah glared in disgust and tried to wrench free, but Dan jerked her into his arms and crushed his mouth down on hers. In furious, knee-jerk reaction she sank her teeth into his bottom lip, and he pushed her away with a howl of pain, a hand clapped to his mouth.

'Something wrong, Sarah?' said Harry, stepping through the window with his ladder. 'I thought I heard voices. Oh, it's you, Daniel.'

Dan was too taken aback at the sight of him to reply, his face like thunder as blood dripped down his chin.

Sarah fished a crumpled tissue from the pocket of her jeans. 'You'd better have this. You're bleeding.' She looked Harry in the eye. 'Dan tripped and caught his lip in his teeth.'

'Better get off home, then, Daniel,' advised Harry grimly. 'I'll see you to your car.'

'No need, Harry,' said Sarah. 'I'll do that.' She opened her door and waved Dan through, then marched across the hall to the main door. 'Is that why you came here, Dan? Because you heard I had dinner with Alex Merrick last night?'

He shrugged, his eyes like hard blue pebbles as he dabbed, wincing, at his lip. 'By the law of averages it might have been my turn to get lucky tonight.'

Sarah clenched her fists, itching to hit him. 'Not tonight, not ever, Dan Mason. Just go, please.'

'In my own good time,' he snarled.

'Right now, please, or I'll get Harry to speed you on your way.'

'What the hell's he doing here, anyway? Another of your conquests?'

'Oh, grow up, Dan,' she said wearily, and moved to close the main door, but he held up a hand.

'Be very careful where Alex Merrick's concerned, Sarah. At a stretch you could say you're both in the same line of business. But there's just one of you, while he's got his entire bloody group behind him.' He swore under his breath as Harry came out with his ladder.

'I'll just stow this in the pick-up before I have that coffee, boss.' Harry gave Dan a straight look. 'On your way now, are you, lad?'

Dan shot a venomous look at him as he stalked away to his

car, then with a growl of the powerful engine he drove off, barely stopping to check for traffic as he shot out into the road.

'Ed Mason spared the rod too much with that boy,' said Harry, walking back to Sarah. 'I was ready to haul him off you by the scruff of his neck, but you sorted him yourself. Good girl.'

'I try to be,' she said with a sigh. 'Let's have that coffee. I could even rise to a sandwich or two if you've got time to stay for a bit.'

After Harry left Sarah locked up her gleaming flat and went out. The incident with Dan had left a nasty taste in her mouth which would be best cured, she decided, by a trip into Hereford to buy herself something new to wear on Sunday. While she'd been working on the cottages an hour or two on a Saturday afternoon was the only time off she'd allowed herself, and she felt like a child let out of school as she drove into town on a week day.

After a tour of the chainstores in High Town, and diversions along narrow side streets to pricier shops, Sarah bought some delicacies from a food hall to add to her collection of carrier bags, found a couple of paperbacks after a browse in a bookshop, and finally drove out of the city just as rush hour was getting underway. When she got home she put the food away, and then climbed up the steps to put the rest of her shopping on the bed. It was at this point, she thought with a sigh, that she missed having a girlfriend on hand to give an opinion on the clothes she'd bought, or to try out the new lipstick.

Sarah shook off the mood. She had been the one desperate to work in a man's world, so she had no one to blame but herself. She had quite literally made her bed, so now she just had to lie on it. Alone, unfortunately. Unfortunately? She frowned as she hung up her new clothes. When she was building the platform had she deliberately given herself space for only a single bed, like a nun in a convent? Sarah snorted with laughter and went down to make supper.

Later, after Caesar salad and cherry tart bought earlier, Sarah took a stroll in the gardens before tackling a small mountain of ironing. At last, feeling pleasantly tired, she had just stretched out on the sofa to watch television when Alex rang.

'Hi,' she said, quite shaken by her delight at the sound of his voice. 'How's life in the big city?'

'Noisy. I miss the green and pleasant land of Herefordshire. What have you been doing today?'

'Cleaning, shopping—nothing much. How about you?'

'Meetings and more meetings.' Alex yawned. 'Sorry. Any progress on the barns?'

'The survey is booked for first thing in the morning, and the inspector promised to ring me with the result before sending me a written report.' She sighed. 'I'm an impatient soul. I couldn't bear the thought of a whole weekend without any news.'

Alex chuckled. 'So what will you do the moment you hear? Rush over to Westhope and press a cheque into Bob Grover's hand?'

'I shall conduct the sale in my usual businesslike manner.'

'Of which I have experience. You drove a hard bargain over the cottages.'

'Oh, come on, admit it. You got a really good deal there.'

'Fair, maybe, but I draw the line at really good! Now let's change the subject. Things have gone better today than expected, which means I'll be back on Saturday morning. Can you make it over to my place in time for dinner?'

'Instead of lunch on Sunday?'

'As well as, not instead of. Don't worry,' he added. 'I'll let you go home in between.'

'An offer I can't refuse.'

'I hope so.'

'Then I won't.'

'Won't come?'

'Won't refuse.'

'Seven sharp, then,' he said after a pause. 'Don't be late.'

* * *

Sarah went for a long walk next morning, while the inspection was taking place at Westhope Farm. But the phone in her pocket remained obstinately silent as she strolled through intersecting lanes she'd never had the time—or energy—to explore when she was working on the cottages. Eventually her route brought her back past the Post Office Stores. She bought a newspaper and bread and milk, chatted for a while with the owners, then started back at a leisurely pace. She was at home before her phone finally rang.

'Mark Prentiss here, Miss Carver.'

Her heart leapt. 'Hi, Mr Prentiss. Thank you so much for ringing. Don't keep me in suspense. What's the verdict?'

'Good. I did an inspection for Mr Grover in the first place,' he explained, 'so it was merely a case of checking my own work, with a few extras from your point of view. I'll get an official report sent off to you this afternoon.'

Sarah thanked him profusely, then rang Harry. 'We're on,' she said jubilantly. 'Once I get the written report I'll get my solicitor on board, then apply for the usual permits and it's all systems go. When can we pop over to see Mr Grover?'

'Now, if you like,' said Harry, and chuckled. 'Might as well give Bob and Mavis a happy weekend. I'll give them a ring, then come round to get you.'

After her long walk in the morning, topped by her euphoria over the inspection, and then Mavis Grover's vast high tea washed down with parsnip wine, Sarah fell asleep on the drive back, and came to with a start when Harry turned into the courtyard of Medlar House.

'Sorry, Harry,' she said with contrition.

'Too much excitement,' he said, helping her down. 'Watch your step. Mavis's wine is powerful stuff.'

'Tell me about it!' Sarah swayed on her feet as the cool

evening air hit her. 'Wow. I couldn't refuse it because you were driving, but I hope I don't have a hangover tomorrow.'

'Drink a lot of water and a few cups of tea and you'll be fine,' he told her. 'Best get to bed early.'

Sarah nodded, then clutched her head, wishing she hadn't. 'Thank you, Harry. Talking of tea, can I make you some before you go?'

'No, thanks. I'm off down the pub for a game of cribbage with Fred.'

'You can mention the barns to him on the quiet, if you like. And bring Ian round for a chat about the job as soon as Mr Selby has everything legally sorted. I think your sister was very pleased,' she added, smiling.

'Pleased?' Harry gave a snort of laughter. 'I wouldn't mind betting she's taking a glass or two more of her parsnip wine right now. Bob, sensible chap, sticks to beer.'

'You think they were satisfied with my offer?'

'More than satisfied,' he assured her, and jingled his car keys. 'It was a really nice thought to buy that teddy bear for the baby, boss.'

'I had fun choosing it, Harry. Enjoy your game.'

Her house phone was ringing when Sarah let herself into the flat.

'Hi,' said Alex.

'Oh, it's you,' she said in relief.

'Yes, me. Disappointed?'

'Quite the reverse.' She'd been afraid it was Dan Mason. 'But normally you ring me on my mobile.'

'I tried. No luck.'

'I left my phone behind when I went to Westhope. Wish me luck, Alex. I just climbed on the second rung of the property ladder.'

'Congratulations! We'll celebrate tomorrow night.' He sighed. 'I would have come back tonight and called in on you, but I'm dining—reluctantly—in the bosom of my family. My father was so insistent I gave in for once.'

'Think of the filial glow you'll bask in!'

'I'd rather think of tomorrow evening with my new best friend.'

'I thought Stephen Hicks was your best friend.'

'He is. But you have a big advantage over him.'

'What's that?'

'You're a girl.'

'Tut-tut, you can't say that these days, Mr Merrick. I'm a woman,' Sarah chastised.

'That too. Though it's hard to believe when you're wearing those overalls.'

'How you do harp on about them. Anyway, I bought some new ones yesterday. I went shopping in Hereford.'

'Not just for work clothes, surely. What else did you buy?'

'A teddy bear with a blue bow tie.'

'Original—dinner guests normally bring wine!'

'It's for the Grovers' brand-new grandson,' she said, laughing.

'Pity. I quite fancy the teddy—hell, I just noticed the time. Got to go, Sarah. Be punctual tomorrow.'

'I will be, if your directions are accurate.'

'Of course they are. You can't miss it. Turn left past the church, follow the signs for Glebe Farm, and my place is the first turning on the right.'

'I'll ring if I get lost.'

'Why not just let me come and fetch you?'

'I'd rather come under my own steam.'

'So you've got a getaway car if you need to escape?'

'Of course not,' she lied. 'See you tomorrow.'

'Is this the only one on the farm?'

'The only conversion, anyway. Matt Hargreaves uses the other barns for their original purpose, and sold me this one years ago. His farm is half a mile down the road, so I buy milk and eggs from him, but otherwise I don't get in his way much.'

Sarah leaned against the car, taking in every detail of his home's beautifully maintained exterior. Glass panels had replaced the wood in the original barn doors, and a flight of worn stone steps led up alongside the entrance porch to a window set in the former entrance to the old hayloft.

'It's just wonderful, Alex,' she said with a sigh, and smiled at him. 'Come on, then. Give me the guided tour.'

He opened the porch door into a small entrance hall with a small shower room to one side of it, and mouth-watering dinner smells coming from a kitchen on the other. 'The rest is through here.' He ushered her into a vast, open-plan space with a vaulted ceiling and exposed beams. Light poured through the tall glass doors and from the windows at the rear, highlighting the treads of a spiral stair which wound up in shallow, leisurely curves to a galleried landing. To one side of the staircase on the ground floor a handsome stone fireplace had been built into the end wall. In front of it a Persian rug in glowing colours warmed the stone floor between a pair of sofas with end-tables and lamps, and a carved cupboard against the outer wall. In the other half of the room the wall backed a long credenza table, and solid oak chairs were grouped round a long refectory table already laid for dinner, with an open bottle of wine and a board with a rustic looking loaf and a hunk of cheese already in place.

The first, overwhelming impression was of space and light. Sarah gazed up in rapture at the vaulted ceiling. 'I'm so impressed by the way you've done the beams, Alex.'

'They were too dark as they were, so I had them stripped and treated, then lime-washed to get this bleached effect. The idea was to look almost like a ghost of the original structure. Would you like to see the bedrooms?' added Alex, watching her face.

Sarah nodded eagerly, and started up the stairs. Along with his enjoyment of her trim back view, Alex felt a deep sense of satisfaction as he followed her. Unless he was much mistaken, Sarah Carver lusted after his house. Just as he'd hoped. The next step was to get her to lust after its owner. No, he thought, frowning. Not lust. That was too raw and basic for the feelings he wanted to arouse in her. Not that thinking of arousal of any kind was a good idea right now, when he was about to show her his bedroom.

Sarah stood at the gallery rail, admiration in her eyes as she gazed down at the floor below. 'Did you do all this yourself?'

'I was involved at every stage, certainly,' he said, leaning beside her. 'The interior design is mine, the staircase and so on. And the extra windows. Like you, I'm hooked on light and space.'

Sarah shook her head. 'My room can hardly compare with this.'

'But you worked on it yourself, so it's your baby as much as this place is mine. I used to slog away here every weekend I could, and the occasional evening when the job allowed. Some weekends Kate Hargreaves took pity on me, and sent a hot meal over from the farm.' Alex shrugged. 'My father left to oversee the manufacturing side from the London office soon after I acquired this place, so I didn't have too much time to spare for building work.'

'Did you have a pleasant evening, by the way?'

'Relatively, yes.' Alex took her hand. 'Take a look at the bedrooms, then I'll feed you.'

To offset the dark wood of his plain, masculine bedroom furniture, the bedcovers in all the rooms were white. The master bedroom was large, as Sarah had expected, but the two guest rooms were anything but small, and all three had their own bathrooms, fitted to a standard her practised eye could now price very accurately.

'My father thinks I went overboard with the white look,' said Alex. 'Too stark and monastic for his taste. His place in London leans to opulence and colour.'

'I think yours is exactly right,' said Sarah, and smiled at him. 'Will you object if I take a leaf out of your book and do something similar at Westhope?'

'I'll consider myself flattered.' He went out on to the landing, beckoning her to follow. 'Come on, let's eat. I'll just throw some pasta in a pot and dinner will be ready.'

Sarah smiled as she followed him down the elegant curving stair. In the past the only meal a man had ever made for her had been pasta with sauce from a jar. Apparently the vice-chairman of the Merrick Group was no more inventive in his smart kitchen than the boyfriends who had worried her father so much at one time.

Alex pulled out a chair at the dining table. 'Sit down, madam, and I shall bring in the food in exactly five minutes.'

'What are we having?'

'Nothing fancy.' Alex lit two candles in heavy glass holders and went off to the kitchen. When he came back with two steaming bowls, Sarah received hers with a mental apology to the chef.

'*Gnocchi di patate pomodoro e rucola*,' he announced grandly. 'Potato dumplings with tomato sauce and rocket.' He poured the wine and sat down, smiling at her as he raised his glass. 'Your health, Sarah.'

'Yours too,' she said, toasting him. She eyed her meal with respect. 'This looks—and smells—wonderful.' She drank some wine, grated cheese over the *gnocchi*, and then put the first fluffy, melting forkful in her mouth. 'Mmm,' she said indistinctly, as the flavour of the sauce hit her tastebuds. 'It tastes wonderful, too.'

'Good. I enjoy seeing a woman eat.'

'It's one of my favourite pastimes!'

Alex eyed her curiously. 'What are the others?'

She looked up from her plate. 'Other what?'

'Pastimes.'

Sarah thought about it. 'I enjoy my work so much I suppose you could list that as a pastime. I don't seem to have time for anything else other than reading—at least not in summer. This winter I'm going to make an effort to go to concerts and plays, and visit exhibitions and so on. Last winter I was too busy fitting up my flat to go out much, except for a couple of weekends I spent in London with former flatmates.'

'You've been back only twice?'

'The first weekend was fine, because I hadn't been gone long. But the second weekend was a mistake because by that time I was totally out of the loop.' Sarah shrugged. 'Once you're gone, you're gone.'

'These weren't close friends, obviously?'

'No, but I'll always be grateful to them, because they were kind to me after Dad died. I shared their flat after the family home was sold.' She looked at him expectantly as she went on eating. 'What kind of things do *you* do in your spare time?'

Alex smiled ruefully. 'I used to play village cricket, but these days I can't count on being free for net practice sessions, or even for a match itself, so I've given it up and run a bit instead. I cycle as well, but sometimes life's so hectic that lately I've been glad just to potter in my bit of garden on a Sunday, or watch cricket instead of actually playing.'

'You must have more of a social life than that!'

'Corporate entertaining mostly.' His mouth turned down. 'I get invited to private dinner parties quite a bit, too, but I accept only if I'm sure there's no catch.'

Sarah looked at him for a moment. 'A helping hand for the host's career?'

He shook his head. 'Unwilling partner for the hostess's single best friend.'

'Tricky! That kind of dinner party doesn't feature in my life,' said Sarah thankfully. She eyed the rustic loaf. 'I'd love a chunk of that to wipe out my bowl.'

Alex laughed, and jumped up to cut it for her. 'We'll both have some.'

Sarah mopped up every last drop of sauce with her bread,

then sat back, licking her lips. 'It's a sin to waste any of that sauce.' She smiled sweetly. 'How clever of you to make *gnocchi*. I've heard it's a pretty ticklish process. You must give me your recipe.'

Alex got up to refill her glass, but Sarah shook her head.

'No more; I've got to drive home.'

'Confession time.' His eyes gleamed in the candlelight that burned brighter now it was darkening rapidly outside. 'I made the sauce from scratch, I swear, but Steve gave me the *gnocchi*. I called in on my way home this morning and asked if he had any fresh pasta to spare, but he said his *gnocchi* would impress you more than the usual spaghetti.'

Sarah laughed. 'He was right. It was delicious.'

'Stay where you are,' he added as he collected plates. 'Dinner's not over yet.'

Sarah looked round with envy when he'd disappeared into the kitchen, liking the idea of a next time. She felt so at home here. Probably because on a grander scale the vaulted ceiling and open space gave the same sense of breathing room as her flat.

Alex came in to switch on lamps. 'It's raining hard out there.'

Sarah could hear it drumming on the roof as he went to fetch the next course. It gave her the feeling of security experienced in childhood when she'd been tucked up in bed listening to rain spattering against the windows. She smiled at Alex as he came back. 'I love that sound.'

'So do I.' He put a tray on the table, with coffee and a luscious looking dessert. 'I cadged this from Steve, too. Chocolate and almond tart. You'll like it.'

Sarah did like it. So much that she gave in to temptation and accepted another slice. 'But just a sliver, or I won't get into these jeans again.'

'Which would be a pity,' he said blandly, 'when they're such a perfect fit.'

She grinned. 'I suppose you noticed when you were following me up the stairs?'

'A man can't help noticing such things,' said Alex, unrepentant. 'Will you pour?'

They lingered over coffee until the pot was dry, while Sarah listened avidly to Alex's account of his work on the house. But at last he apologised for getting carried away and stacked their cups on the tray. 'Now, you take a sofa over there while I clear away.'

'I'll help,' she said firmly, and started gathering up dessert plates.

While they tidied up, in his compact, well-designed kitchen, Alex demanded a detailed account of her movements since he'd last seen her, and Sarah told him about the meal at Westhope Farm, and Mavis Grover's powerful parsnip wine. But they were sitting on one of the sofas together before she mentioned Dan Mason's visit.

'He came round to your place?' Alex's eyes narrowed. 'And what was that about?'

'He wanted me to have dinner with him again, at some place near Ross.'

'And what did you say?' he asked silkily.

'I said no. And not just because you warned me against him, so don't look so smug.' Sarah shivered. 'I didn't want to go out with him, to Ross or anywhere else.'

'Good,' said Alex with satisfaction, and put an arm round her.

'Dan was so objectionable when I said no—Harry was all for seeing him off,' she added, chuckling. 'He'd been cleaning my windows. You should have seen Dan's face when Harry appeared.'

'Good for Harry!'

'Anyway, Dan went off in a huff, but his parting shot was a warning about you.'

Alex stiffened. 'Oh?'

'He said I should watch my step, because I'm in the same line of business as you, and while I'm just small fry you've got the might of the Merrick Group behind you.'

'That's nonsense,' he said flatly. 'The man's an idiot.'

'He also told me,' Sarah informed him, 'that droves of

women are attracted to your Merrick money, but you refuse to get hooked.'

Alex's mouth curled in distaste. 'I think *droves* may be exaggerating slightly. Besides, I did get hooked. Once.'

'Do you still have feelings for the lady? Sorry,' she added hastily. 'You don't have to answer that.'

'My pride took a beating at the time. But it recovered, and so did I. Completely.' He smiled crookedly 'Unlike those mythical droves of women, mere money doesn't work for you, Sarah, does it? Least of all when it comes attached to the name of Merrick.' He leaned nearer. 'But you wouldn't be here tonight if you didn't like me for myself a little.'

'True. I do like you. And not just a little. I like you a lot.' On impulse she kissed his cheek.

Alex promptly seized her in his arms and kissed her mouth, and when she made no protest went on kissing her with a savouring pleasure she shared to the full. 'I can stop if you like,' he whispered, after an interval.

Sarah shook her head. 'Not just yet. Kiss me some more.'

'Yes, ma'am!' He ran the tip of his tongue round her parted lips, then slid it between them in a caress which she responded to with such fervour he lifted her onto his lap as he kissed her. He felt a surge of triumph as her breath quickened in time with his. He smoothed a hand over the glittering fabric covering her breasts, and felt himself harden as her breath caught. He raised his head, his eyes questioning. 'You don't like that?'

She nodded wordlessly, her breathing ragged as his mouth returned to hers, coaxing and tasting with a new hunger as his caressing fingers slid beneath the tunic to trace the shape of breasts which were suddenly so taut and sensitive she felt fire streak south to parts of her unused to such ravishing sensation. Then suddenly she was back in her place on the sofa, and Alex was on his feet, raking a hand through his hair.

'Look, Sarah, let's get something straight. Just because I

asked you to come to my place doesn't mean I expect you to sing for your supper.'

'That's a relief,' she said breathlessly, 'because I can't carry a tune in a bucket.'

He let out a crack of laughter and sat down again. 'No singing, then. I'm not trying to rush you to bed, either.'

Sarah took in a deep, calming breath. 'If you had something like that in mind you'd do better to stick to a sofa down here. It must be a bit tricky to rush someone up that stairway of yours.'

Alex moved closer and took her hand. 'I've never tried, but you're probably right.'

She gave him a thoughtful look. 'Funny, really. Neither of us owns easily accessible bedrooms. And in my case, even when you get up to the platform, the bed is too narrow to take more than one person.'

'And one small person at that,' he said, smoothing a finger over the back of her hand. 'For my part, I suppose I took it for granted that if ever I did invite a lady to sleep here she'd climb the stair willingly. And of course the lady who does sleep here on a regular basis does exactly that. My mother,' he added.

Sarah smiled, hoping he hadn't noticed her fleeting pang before the penny dropped. 'She must be very proud of what you've done here.'

He nodded, his eyes softening. 'She saw it at various stages on her visits—which, by the way, are not solely to catch up with me. She spends time with my aunt and grandfather as well. The old reprobate positively dotes on her. Which explains his attitude to my charming stepmother.'

'It's an awkward situation,' agreed Sarah. 'Have they ever met? Your mother and stepmother, I mean?'

'Oh, yes, they've met—' Alex's grip tightened as lightning lit up the room, followed by an earth-shattering crack of thunder. He smiled at her. 'That was close.'

She nodded, heart thumping.

'Are you afraid of storms?'

'Not afraid, exactly,' she lied, 'as long as I'm under cover. I don't like being out in them.' She winced as another flash lit the room, followed by another crack of thunder.

'You certainly won't be going out in this one. I have two spare bedrooms, Sarah.'

She gasped as lightning and thunder did their double act again, and Alex put his arms round her. 'Thank you,' she said against his chest. 'I'll take you up on that. I don't fancy driving home in this.'

He held her closer as the storm grew in intensity, and chuckled as the next clap of thunder sent her burrowing against him. 'From a purely personal point of view, I'm grateful to the weather.'

Sudden torrential rain blotted out conversation, and Alex raised Sarah's face to his and kissed her. She wreathed her arms round his neck and kissed him back with a fervour he returned with such intensity that Sarah forgot about the storm. Then lightning lit up the room, followed by a crash louder than anything that had gone before, and the lights went out.

Sarah let out a deep, unsteady breath as Alex released her.

'At least we've got the candles on the table to see by, but sit still and don't move,' he told her. 'I'll see if it's just the trip-switch, in which case I can trip it back on. If not we'll need torches and more candles.' He gave her a swift kiss and got up.

'Don't be long,' said Sarah involuntarily.

'I'll be back in a flash,' he promised, then laughed as lightning lit the room again. 'Right on cue, but the thunder's not so close this time.'

Sarah counted to five before the expected crack reverberated through the room, and she relaxed slightly, chuckling when Alex cursed as he stumbled over something in the kitchen. He came back with a box holding candles and torches.

'Not just the trip-switch, I'm afraid. There must be a line down somewhere—not unusual in these parts.' He set a torch down on the table beside Sarah, put the box on the floor and fetched the candles from the dining table. He put them down at either end of the sofa, then took matches and a selection of saucers out of the box. 'I own just the two candle holders, so otherwise I make do with these.'

'Does this happen regularly, then?'

'Enough to make it sensible to have this kind of thing on hand.' He glanced at his watch. 'It's a bit late to ring my aunt to see if Edgar's all right. But I've told her I'm home, so she'll ring me if he's not.' Alex handed her a candle and saucer and struck a match, and Sarah held the wick in the flame and waited until wax dripped enough for her to secure the candle in the saucer.

When they had four candles alight Alex ranged them along the fireplace, then sat down again. 'Now, where were we?' he said, and pulled her onto his lap, smiling into her eyes. 'I think I was doing this,' he whispered, and kissed her as though the simple, ravishing pleasure of the kiss itself was all he needed or intended.

It was Sarah, to her surprise, who grew impatient first. She wriggled closer on his lap, and Alex groaned and held her still.

'I'm only human,' he whispered against her lips.

'So am I,' she whispered back.

As though her words had triggered some switch inside him, his mouth suddenly devoured hers, their hearts thumping so madly in unison as he crushed her close that Sarah longed to tell Alex to forget any scruples and take her to bed. A shiver ran through her as his hands slid up under the stretchy se-quinned fabric, and she stopped thinking altogether as his fin-gertips played such clever, inciting games with her sensitised nipples that she dug her fingers into his back in demand.

Alex raised his head, his eyes dark 'This,' he said hoarsely, 'is the part where I wish I had an ordinary flight of stairs so I could do the Rhett Butler thing and carry you up to bed to ravish you.' He set her on her feet and stood up, rejoicing as he saw the glittering sequins moving in hurried rhythm with her breath-ing. 'Instead,' he said, holding her eyes, 'I'm going to take you by the hand and lead you up those stairs to my room—and then ravish you.'

'In that case,' said Sarah breathlessly, 'you'd better blow out these candles.'

Alex pulled her close. 'You approve my plan?'

She nodded. 'If you'd said you just wanted to make love to me I might have said no, but ravishing sounds too good to pass up.'

Laughing together, they blew out the candles in the saucers, then took the pair in the glass holders up the winding stair to the master bedroom.

Alex kissed her swiftly. 'Wait there. I'll go down and get the torches.' When he came back with them he put a bottle of wine down alongside the candles, took a glass from each of his pockets and placed them by the wine. 'Since you're not driving anywhere tonight, I thought you might like another glass of this.'

She beamed at him. 'I would. Thank you.'

Alex sat on the edge of the bed and patted the place beside him. 'Come and sit here and I'll pour.'

Sarah kicked off her sandals and perched beside him. He gave her a glass of wine, then took her free hand in his and kissed it fleetingly.

'This is a very good idea,' she told him, as thunder rumbled in the distance.

'I get them sometimes,' he said modestly, and stroked a hand down the sequins. 'I like this sexy chainmail thing you're wearing.'

'It's a dress,' she informed him.

'So why are you wearing jeans with it?'

'It's shorter than my usual stuff.'

Alex grinned, his eyes gleaming wickedly in the candle-light. 'If the dress is short on you, it must be a bit dangerous on taller women.'

Sarah nodded. 'It's meant to be. The woman in the shop said it looked perfect, but then, that's her job.' She sipped more of her wine. 'This is delicious—and hopefully a lot less lethal than Mavis Grover's parsnip wine. When Harry drove me home from Westhope I fell asleep in the pick-up.'

'If at all possible,' said Alex, his hand tightening on hers,

'I'd rather my wine doesn't have the same effect on you. At least not yet.'

Sarah chuckled. 'Before you ravish me, you mean?'

'Exactly!' He slid an arm round her, and pulled her close with a sigh of pleasure. 'This is a very good way to spend Saturday night.'

'Except for the storm.'

'Because of the storm,' he contradicted. 'Otherwise we wouldn't be here on my bed together, and you would probably be driving home by now.'

'True.' Sarah raised her glass in solemn toast. 'To the storm.' She drank the rest of her wine and handed him the glass.

Alex laid it on the side-table with his, then piled his pillows at the head of the bed and pulled her up into his arms as he leaned against them, his breath warm and tingling against her ear. 'To make it even more perfect, would you do something for me?'

Sarah angled her face up to his. 'Sing, or recite from Shakespeare maybe?'

'Later for that. Right now I want to see you in the dress without the jeans.'

She slid off the bed and stood up. Aware in every fibre of his gleaming, intent eyes, she unzipped the jeans and took them off. Deliberately taking her time about it, she folded them and placed them on the chest between the windows, then gave a smothered gasp as he pounced on her and carried her back the bed.

'Is this where I get ravished?' she demanded. 'Because if it is I'll take the dress off too. It was expensive.'

'I'll do it for you.' He took the glittering garment very carefully by the hem and drew it over her head, then laid it over the back of a chair.

Sarah tried to relax against the pillows, but it was difficult when she was breathless, shaking inside, and hot all over even though all she was wearing were some lacy bits of nude satin that had cost more than the dress.

Alex stood very still and tense at the foot of the bed, his eyes so openly eating her up that Sarah held up her arms and he dived across the bed to scoop her up against him. He kissed her hungrily and Sarah kissed him back with equal fervour, one part of her admiring his skill as he removed his clothes without taking his lips from hers, the other part of her hot with anticipation as he drew back to gaze down at her. The possessive look in his eyes was as tactile as the caress of his stroking hands. Then his mouth moved down her throat and she lay with closed eyes, quivering as his lips moved in a slow, erotic trail down her throat, and over her shoulders, her anticipation mounting as he neared the swell of her breasts. Suddenly she pushed him away, her eyes glittering in her flushed face.

'What's wrong?' he whispered.

'Nothing at all. It's my turn. I want to look at you.' Sarah smiled, open relish in her eyes as they moved inch by inch over his broad chest and flat-planed stomach.

She leaned nearer to trail caressing hands down the same path, well aware of the effect they were having on him, and when she laid her open mouth against his chest he pulled her hard against him, his patience gone. With unsteady hands he removed the scraps of satin, and at last they were naked in each other's arms, their kisses frantic as their bodies came into contact. The breath tore through her chest as his lips left hers, his hair brushing her hot skin as he used his mouth on her breasts. She shivered at the touch of his tongue and grazing teeth, then gave a stifled moan as he parted her thighs to cause such unbearable arousal with his caresses her entire body felt bathed in flames.

He leaned away for a moment, then let himself down on her very gently, until every part of his body was touching every part of hers. She gazed up at him, her eyes lambent with invitation, then gasped in delight against his possessive mouth as he slid slowly home inside her. She made a relishing sound deep in her throat, her body taking its lead from his as he made love to her with all the care and skill at his command, until her urgent hips stole the last of his control and he took her at thrusting, break-neck speed towards the goal he reached at last before her. Still erect and throbbing with his own release, he drove deeper and held her impaled until he felt her climax ripple around him, then he collapsed on her, his face buried in her hair.

When Sarah found the energy to move at last she yelped in pain, because her hair was trapped. Alex kissed her in apology as he freed her and brushed the tangled curls back from her face, then slid off the bed to make for the bathroom.

'Well?' he said softly, when he rejoined her. 'Did you enjoy being ravished?'

'I don't think you could describe it that way,' she said, thinking it over.

Alex looked down at her, frowning. 'You mean I fell short of expectations?'

She rolled her eyes. 'Typical man!' She touched a hand to his cheek. 'Of course you didn't. But ravishing implies that the woman is unwilling in some degree. And, as perhaps you noticed, I wasn't. Unwilling, I mean.'

'I noticed,' he said, with deep satisfaction.

Sarah looked at him steadily. 'I didn't know it could be like that, Alex.'

The intense, dark-rimmed gaze held hers. 'How much experience have you had?'

'Not nearly as much as you, I imagine,' she said tartly. A very few episodes in the past, where enthusiasm had featured far more than skill, hardly counted. Whereas at Cambridge alone a man like Alex must have been able to take his pick of the women students. And probably of the damsels at Medlar House before he'd even left school.

'I'm no Casanova,' he assured her, reading her mind, then laughed suddenly into her neck.

'What's so funny?'

'I've just noticed that the storm has gone and the lights are on downstairs, and I think they've been on for some time.'

CHAPTER TEN

SARAH LAUGHED, but stayed his hand as he reached to turn on the bedside lamp. 'Not just yet. Leave me with romantic candlelight for a while.'

Alex slid from the bed to fetch a dressing gown from his wardrobe. 'What would you like? More wine? Or now we have power again I could make coffee.'

'Could you make tea instead?' Sarah said hopefully, controlling an urge to dive under the quilt now Alex was covered and she was not.

'I certainly could. Anything else?'

'My handbag. It's near the sofa somewhere.'

'Right. I won't be long.' Alex bent to plant a swift kiss on her mouth. 'Don't go away.'

Sarah made a beeline for the bathroom, for the swiftest shower on record, then wrapped herself in the towelling robe hanging behind the door. She switched on the bedside lamps and blew out the candles, tidied the bed, and went barefoot downstairs just as Alex came into the main room from the kitchen, carrying a loaded tray.

'What the blazes are you doing down here?' he demanded. 'I was just coming up to you with the tea.'

'I couldn't let you carry it up that staircase when I can drink it just as well down here on the sofa.' She smiled, relieved when his eyes softened.

'I usually take a tray up to bed on a Sunday morning,' he informed her, and raised that eyebrow again. 'At least you're still here. While I was making tea and so on, I wondered if I'd find you dressed and ready to leave when I took it up to you.'

Sarah flushed. 'I can still do that, if you like.'

Alex stalked to the table beside the sofa and put the tray down so hard the cups rattled. 'No. I do not like. I wanted you to stay in my bed so I could rejoin you there. Not necessarily for more sex—though I wouldn't say no—but just to stay there together until we went to sleep.' He cast a look at the robe. 'A trifle large, but it looks good on you.'

'I hope you don't mind,' she said awkwardly. 'I had a very quick shower.'

'I certainly do mind. If I'd known I would have postponed the tea-making and had one with you.'

'I seem to be getting things wrong here,' she said crossly. 'You'll have to forgive me, Mr—'

He held up a hand. 'Don't!'

'I was going to say,' she went on with dignity, 'that I'm not sure of the right procedure on these occasions. My former brushes with—with romance were not sleepovers.'

Alex's eyebrows rose. 'Are you saying you've never slept with a man?'

'Yes,' she said shortly, and picked up her bag.

'You've changed your mind about leaving?' he said sharply.

'No. I just want to slap some moisturiser on my face.' She glared at him. 'If that's all right with you.'

He took in a deep breath. 'Let's start again. Sarah—my darling Sarah—come back to bed with me to drink your tea.'

She thought it over. 'OK.' She glanced at the teapot. 'But I'd better carry that.'

'Off you go, then. I promise not to leer at your back view while I follow.'

'Not much to leer at in this dressing gown!'

Alex smiled. 'Ah, but I know exactly what's under it.' To his delight Sarah flushed hectically, snatched the teapot from the tray and marched over to the stairs.

When Sarah had said yes to dinner at home with Alex, she'd known perfectly well that dinner was probably not the only thing he had in mind. And if bed was involved she had been prepared for that. Welcomed it, looked forward to it, had been so excited by the prospect she'd put new underwear at the top of her shopping list for her trip to Hereford. But her imagination had never gone as far as picturing the fun of a midnight feast in bed with him. It was long past midnight by this time, but the principle was the same. She curled up against his banked pillows, smiling when he offered her thick slices of buttered toast.

'No wonder I had time to shower if you were getting this together,' she commented as he handed her a plate.

'I'm hungry,' he said simply, and smiled. 'Are you still cross with me, or will you eat some of this?'

'I'm not cross.' She grinned at him as she took a couple of slices. 'In fact I'm flattered. *And* I'm hungry. Even though after dinner I was sure I wouldn't eat again for at least a day.' She drank the tea he gave her in one draught.

'You were thirsty,' said Alex, and got up to take her cup as she began to eat.

'I'm amazed you have a teapot,' she commented, watching him pour.

He grinned. 'It was a present from my aunt when I moved in, with instructions to serve tea properly to my mother. In cups, with saucers.'

Sarah relaxed against the pillows as they ate. 'I didn't expect all this when I said yes to dinner,' she told him.

'Expect what, exactly?' He took her cup and plate away and stacked them with his own on the tray, then brushed crumbs from the covers and sat back beside her. 'Making love with me?'

Sarah turned to look at him. 'That did occur to me.'

His eyes held hers. 'Yet you still came?'

'Yes.'

'Is it remotely possible that you wanted it to happen?'

She gave him a smile as crooked as his. 'I thought you might have picked up certain clues about that.'

Alex slid his arm round her and drew her close. 'Let's see. First you actually turned up. Second you fell madly in love with my house. True?'

'Oh, yes,' she sighed, rubbing her cheek against his shoulder.

Alex's arm tightened. 'Then you kissed me of your own accord. On the cheek, admittedly, but a voluntary kiss for all that. I was, to put it mildly, encouraged.' He dropped a kiss on her hair. 'The storm finally clinched it. And here we are, *on* if not *in* my bed, relaxing in the aftermath of what I can only describe—poetic fool that I am—as a trip to heaven and back. How am I doing? Is there anything I missed?'

'The underwear.'

His eyebrow rose. 'I noticed it was pretty mouth-watering before I parted you from it, but is there more to it than that?'

She nodded. 'Normally I wear a chainstore white cotton bra, and the kind of knickers that come three in a pack. I bought the sexy stuff specifically to wear today.'

Alex put a finger under her chin to turn her face up to his. 'To seduce me?' he said incredulously.

'Of course not,' she said impatiently. 'But I thought there was a possibility you might want to seduce *me*.' Her eyes fell. 'And if you did,' she muttered, 'I wanted to look good.'

'*Good?* I wanted to fall on you and gobble you up,' he growled, and kissed her hard. 'I still do,' he said, and threw off his dressing gown and laid a hand on the tie securing hers. 'Do you want me to?'

'Yes,' she tersely, and abandoned any last lingering inhibitions to show him how much.

When Sarah surfaced again it was daylight. She found an arm round her waist, and a long, muscular leg hooked over both of hers, and opened her eyes on Alex's intent gaze.

'Good morning,' he said softly.

'Good morning.' She blinked sleepily. 'What time is it?'

'Just after nine. Want some breakfast?'

She thought it over. 'Could I have another shower first?'

'Certainly.' Alex slid to his feet and scooped her up in his arms. 'But this time I'm sharing.'

The shower involved a great deal more than just getting clean, and led them straight back to bed, and to lovemaking that was different from the night before. Alex in playful mood was irresistible. In the bright light of day his way of making love was a light-hearted process, and great fun—until heat and need took over and rocketed them to orgasm in each other's arms. After that there was another shower, and the morning was half gone before they got dressed to sit down to toast prepared by Alex, and eggs scrambled by Sarah.

'Teamwork,' he said with satisfaction. 'You do good eggs.'

'I'm not bad in the kitchen!'

Alex's eyes gleamed. 'Not bad in the bedroom, either.'

'Is that all you can think about?'

He forked in more eggs before replying. 'You're here, in my house, across the table from me eating breakfast, after a night no mere words can describe, so of course I'm thinking about it. I'll probably be thinking about it all week while I'm in endless meetings.'

Sarah smiled and blew him a kiss. 'I'll probably be thinking about it, too, while I get on with the Westhope barns.'

Alex reached out a hand to touch hers. 'Don't expend all your energy on those barns of yours, Sarah. Leave some for evenings with me.'

Sarah was more than happy to do this for the following fortnight, which was a period of marking time for her until the permits came through to start on the barns. Some clearing work in them was all that was possible, and since Ian was now helping them this took very little energy on her part or Harry's.

For Alex certain social commitments were unavoidable some evenings, but they spent the others together at his house—most of them in bed. But Sarah always drove back to Medlar House, and in spite of Alex's persuasion refused to stay overnight at Glebe Barn.

'I'll be happy—deliriously so—to sleep here at weekends,' she promised. 'But because Harry picks me up every morning I'd rather keep to the usual routine during the week.'

Alex eyed her sardonically. 'You don't want him to know about us?'

'Lord, no,' she said, grinning. 'Can you really picture me telling Harry Sollers that my new friend is the vice-chairman of the Merrick Group?'

There was no answering smile from Alex. 'Is that what I am? Your friend?'

She bit her lip, flushing. 'A very special friend. But I can't tell Harry that, either.'

'Why the hell not?'

'Because it's too private to talk about to anyone,' she said, and kissed him so passionately he stopped arguing and made love instead of war.

They spent the weekends in much the same way as the first one. Sarah was now so much at home at Glebe Barn that it was a huge effort to leave it to go back to her flat on Monday mornings, and one particular Monday was worse than usual, because Alex was going away for a while.

'I'm in London, at a conference on global recycling,' he said morosely.

'Just as well,' said Sarah cheerfully. 'Bob has said we can start on the foundations this week, even though the deal isn't final, and when I'm working flat out on that kind of thing I'm tired by the evening most days. And Westhope is a twenty-mile drive for me, instead of just five minutes away like the cottages.'

He nodded moodily. 'I wish you had a less demanding job, Sarah.'

She busied herself with pouring coffee and buttering toast. 'But I don't, so from now on I'll be much better company if we just see each other at weekends. Why the smile?' she added suspiciously.

'Out of all these droves of women apparently languishing for me—or at least my money—I have to fall for the one who doesn't have enough time to fit me into her schedule,' Alex said sardonically. 'I'd begun to hope our relationship meant something to you.'

'It does,' she said, and eyed him warily. 'I'm just not sure what you expect of it, Alex.'

'A hell of a sight more than you're prepared to give,' he snapped, and jumped up to stalk round the table.

She put out her hands to fend him off. 'So tell me what you want.'

'Wasn't last night—and this morning—explanation enough?' He pulled her to her feet. 'You know damn well what I want.'

'Alex, don't rush me,' she said urgently. 'I've only just got used to the idea of you as a friend.'

'Even as a mere friend I'd expect to see more of you than the odd weekend!'

Sarah gazed at him in appeal. 'Once I get the job off the ground at Westhope things will settle down enough for us to see more of each other than that.'

'How generous of you.' Alex stood back, shaking his head in mock wonder. 'I never learn, do I? I should have remembered from past experience of your sex that priorities for a man are not necessarily the same for a woman. Like a fool, I thought you cared for me, Sarah.'

'I *do*.' Sarah blinked hard. 'Surely after what's happened between us you must know that?' She flushed miserably. 'But to strip this down to basics I'm not used to—to this kind of thing on top of a working day. I get tired.'

'By "this kind of thing" you mean sex?' he asked brutally.

The word struck her like a physical blow. 'It's not the word I would have used, but, yes, I suppose that's what I do mean.'

'For me it was a great deal more than that,' he said harshly.

'It was for me, too.'

'But still not enough to combine it with your busy schedule? Or is there something you're not telling me, Sarah?'

She frowned. 'What do you mean?'

His eyes stabbed hers. 'Perhaps you need time away from me to pursue other interests during the week? That's the way it usually goes when a woman pleads for time to herself.'

She stared at him, incensed. 'If you mean seeing another man, it may be usual with the women you know, but it certainly isn't for me!'

'If you say so.' Alex raised a cynical eyebrow. 'But even if your excuses—'

'Reasons, not excuses,' she said hotly.

'Reasons, excuses—it makes no difference. Do you honestly expect me to hang around waiting for whatever crumbs of your company you can spare from your project?'

Sarah looked at him in disbelief. 'If that's the way you feel, no, I don't,' she said, after a tense pause. 'No hanging around expected.'

'Or required!'

'I didn't say that.'

He shrugged. 'It's how it came across.'

Sarah took in a deep breath. 'Talking hypothetically—'

'By all means let's do that!'

She hung on to her temper with difficulty. 'All right. Would you put your London trip off to spend more time with me?'

His shook his head impatiently. 'That's different.'

'Why? Because you're the vice-chairman of the Merrick Group and I'm just an amateur, one-horse property developer—and a female at that?' she demanded.

'Hell and damnation, Sarah, you know I don't think of you

like that.' The sudden burst of heat vanished from his eyes, leaving ice in its place. 'Besides,' he drawled, 'I was merely requesting some of your leisure time, not your hand in marriage.'

She stared at him in disbelief, feeling the colour drain from her face. 'Right,' she said, when she could speak. 'I think that's my cue to leave. Goodbye, Alex.'

Instead of sweeping her into his arms, as she'd half hoped, he nodded formally and carried her overnight bag out to the car.

'Good luck with the barns,' he said distantly, as she got behind the wheel.

Sarah took a last look at his house, then nodded glacially. 'Thank you.'

'Goodbye, Sarah.' Alex walked down to the gate to open it for her, waited as she drove through into the lane, then added the crowning touch to her day by walking straight into the house instead of watching her out of sight.

During her working days she was able to push it from her mind, but in the evenings Sarah seethed constantly over Alex Merrick's parting shot. And sometimes regretted laying down rules about how often they saw each other. But deep down she knew her problem was his typical male assumption that now she'd begun sharing his bed she would be happy to drop everything, any time, to do it again. Presumably whenever he had a moment to spare from the demands of his far more illustrious job, no matter how involved she was with hers.

She shrugged. It was her own fault for getting entangled with someone who was not only used to women flinging themselves at him, but who had once had a relationship with one of them that gave him a jaundiced view of her entire sex. Sarah ground her teeth as his taunt about marriage came back to haunt her, and wished passionately she'd had a cutting riposte to hurl back at him. Instead she'd just walked out. Which was probably as good a response as any.

* * *

When her doorbell rang as she was clearing up after a belated supper one evening, Sarah's heart jumped hopefully to her throat, then sank like a stone in disappointment when she heard Dan Mason's voice over the intercom.

'Could I see you for a moment, Sarah?'

'What do you want?'

'To apologise.'

With reluctance she pressed the buzzer, then opened her door as Dan crossed the hall, looking far from certain of his reception, she noted with satisfaction. 'You'd better come in,' she said coolly.

'Thank you,' he said, with such humility she eyed him in suspicion as she waved him to the sofa.

'So what's brought you down to these parts again, Dan?' she demanded.

'My mother's birthday. But I'm glad of the chance to apologise to you for my behaviour last time I was here.' He fixed her with persuasive blue eyes. 'I was out of order. I'm sorry.'

She shrugged indifferently. 'Apology accepted.'

'Good.' He looked down at his expensive shoes for a moment. 'Word has it you don't patronise the family hostelry these days.'

'No. The project we're working on is a bit far away to pop back for lunch.'

'How about your evenings?' He looked up. 'I know you've been seeing something of Alex Merrick, according to the Green Man grapevine. Is that still on?'

'I'm too busy to see anyone these days,' she said elliptically. 'The barn conversions we're working on leave me too tired to socialise at the end of a working day.'

'Surely you must want a night out now and then?'

'Not really. I get home fit for nothing more than a shower, supper in front of the television, then early bed.'

'That's not much of a life, Sarah!'

'It suits *me*, Dan,' she assured him.

He leaned forward, his eyes suddenly urgent. 'Now you've accepted my apology let me take you out somewhere tomorrow evening. Or if you're not up to going out I could order something in to eat here—'

'No thanks, Dan,' she interrupted. 'I'm not good company right now.'

His eyes hardened. 'Because Merrick dumped you?'

God grant me patience, thought Sarah. 'My private life is my business, Dan.'

He regrouped hurriedly, and gave her a cajoling smile. 'I just want an hour or two with you, Sarah. We spent a pleasant evening together before. Let's do it again.'

Sarah got up. 'Thanks a lot, Dan, but—'

'But you can't. Or won't,' he said bitterly, and jumped up. 'I suppose you're still hankering after Alex Merrick, like all the others before you? I did warn you about him, remember?'

'So you did,' she said wearily, and walked to the door. 'Goodnight, Dan. Drive carefully.'

He paused in the open doorway. 'If you are carrying a torch for Merrick, Sarah, remember what I said. You're a very small fish in your line of business, and he's a great big shark.'

Thoroughly put out by Dan Mason's parting shot, Sarah blanked it out by immersing herself in the back-breaking work of sorting out the floors in the barns. Not even to herself would she admit she was still nourishing the faint hope of a phone call that never happened.

When her phone finally did ring one evening towards the end of the week, she grabbed it eagerly. 'Oh—hi, Harry. What can I do for you?'

'All right if I come round for a minute?'

'Of course. See you soon.' With a sinking feeling Sarah snapped the phone shut. Harry had sounded grim.

When she let him in a few minutes later he looked even grimmer than he'd sounded. 'Come and sit down and tell me what's wrong.' She took her usual place on the windowseat, and waved Harry to the sofa.

'Bob rang me tonight,' he said heavily, his hands clasped between his knees. 'He said I wasn't to tell you, but I think you should know.'

She eyed him in alarm. 'Is there something wrong with the barns?'

'No, not that. But Bob got another offer for them today. Quite a bit more than you've offered for them.' Harry looked her in the eye. 'That's why he didn't want to tell you—in case you thought he was trying to get more money out of you. Bob said it was a young chap called Harris who called on him to make the offer. Ever heard of him?'

Sarah sat stunned for a moment. 'Oh, yes, I've heard of him,' she said at last. 'He works for Alex Merrick.'

Harry stared. 'Does he, by God? I didn't know that. Bob neither. Tall young fellow with glasses, he said.'

'That's the one.' Her eyes kindled. 'But I seriously doubt that Greg Harris is going into barn conversion on his own.'

Harry grimaced. 'Mavis was blazing. Everything about to be signed and sealed, she reminded Bob, and besides, she'd already spent some of Miss Carver's deposit on the baby. Bob said they had a right old set-to before he could shut her up long enough to say he had no intention of accepting the offer—'

Sarah tried to smile. 'It must be a bit galling for him to know he could have got more money for them, though.'

'Bob's one of the old school,' said Harry, getting up. He'd given his word. As far as he's concerned that's that.' He gave Sarah a searching look. 'Don't worry about it. Have a good sleep and I'll call for you in the morning.'

'Thanks, Harry. But you and Ian take tomorrow off. I'm going to sort this out.' She smiled at him. 'Thanks for coming round.'

'Sorry I brought bad news,' he said gruffly.

She shrugged. 'I had to know.'

Sarah saw Harry off, then booted up her laptop and wrote a short, very explicit letter to Alex Merrick, printed it, and signed it with a flourish. She printed out an envelope, folded the letter into it and put it in her handbag, then lay in a warm bath until she felt calm enough to go to bed.

At ten next morning Sarah parked in front of the Merrick office building and walked into the foyer to confront the receptionist.

'Sarah Carver,' she said crisply. 'I'd like to see Mr Alex Merrick, please. I don't have an appointment.'

The woman smiled politely. 'I'll see if he's available.'

Sarah felt a surge of triumph. At least he was here in the building.

'Mr Merrick is in a meeting, but he'll see you in fifteen minutes, if you care to wait, Miss Carver,' said the receptionist, putting the phone down.

'Thanks.' Sarah took a seat on one of the leather chesterfields, and stared blindly at a magazine until the receptionist came to tell her Mr Merrick was free.

Alex had wound up his meeting sooner than intended, then sprinted to his office to sit behind his desk, all kinds of reasons for Sarah's visit chasing through his brain as he waited for her to appear. It was unlikely she was coming here to his office to mend things between them. Though he hoped to God she had. The knock on the door brought him upright in his seat, but his voice was calm as he bade her come in.

Last time she'd been here, to sign the deal on the cottages, Sarah had been a vision in some kind of dark red, but today she wore a severe black suit. Her hair was dragged back into a ruthless knot and her mood, he saw at a glance, matched the suit.

'Good morning,' he said, rising. 'This is a surprise.'

'Good morning. It's good of you to spare the time to see me.'

'For God's sake, Sarah,' he said wearily. 'Of course I've got time to see you. What's wrong?'

'Why should anything be wrong?' she countered. 'I came to deliver a letter, in case you were away, but since I'm lucky enough to speak to you face to face I won't bother with that.'

'Please sit down, Sarah,' said Alex.

'Thank you, I'd rather stand.'

'Sit down,' he repeated, without raising his voice.

'As you wish,' she said, shrugging, and took the chair facing him.

'Now, tell me why you're here.'

'To tell you I think you're despicable,' she said coldly.

The steady eyes didn't so much as flicker. 'Despicable?' he repeated, and raised an eyebrow. 'Would you care to expand on that? We crossed swords over my desire to see more of you. You didn't want that. What, exactly, is so despicable? Should I have been more persistent?'

'Oh, stop tap-dancing, Alex,' she said wearily. 'You know exactly why I'm here. You topped my offer to Bob Grover for his barns.'

Alex stared at her, no vestige of expression on his face. 'No, Sarah,' he said, after a silence so long she was ready to scream, 'I most certainly did not.'

'Oh, all right, if you must split hairs. It was Greg Harris who made the offer.'

'What the hell would Greg Harris want with the barns?'

'He doesn't want them. You know perfectly well he was acting on your behalf,' she snapped. 'You couldn't take it when I preferred to work on them rather than see more of you. So to massage your damaged ego you put a spoke in my wheel in true Merrick fashion. You won't have any luck, though. Bob Grover won't go back on his word to me.'

Alex subjected her to another fraught silence, then picked up his phone. 'Come in, please.'

Greg Harris greeted Sarah politely, and looked at his employer in enquiry.

'Have you ever been to Westhope Farm?' asked Alex.

The young man thought for a moment. 'No. I don't even know where it is.'

'Are you sure? It's about fifteen miles the other side of Hereford.'

Greg shook his head. 'Sorry, Alex. Do you want some information on it?'

'No. I want you to go there with me, right now. Postpone the rest of my morning appointments, contact Mr Grover at Westhope Farm to make sure he's free, then meet me down in the car park.'

When the young man had gone, Sarah got up. 'I've had enough of this charade. I'm leaving—'

'No, Sarah,' rapped Alex, in a tone so hard it startled her. 'You started this. You're coming to Westhope Farm to see it through.'

'I most certainly am not!'

'Why? Are you afraid you'll be proved wrong?' he asked, with a smile which made her clench her fists. 'I wouldn't have put you down as a coward, Sarah.'

She glared at him, but Alex stood up, his eyes ice-cold as they held hers, and at last, to her mortification, hers were the first to fall. 'Oh, very well,' she said ungraciously. 'I'll follow you in my car.'

'Oh, no! You travel in mine.' Alex held the office door open for her, and Sarah walked out to the lift in stony silence.

To Sarah's chagrin she was shown into the back seat of the Cherokee, and virtually ignored while Alex chatted to Greg in front. The only time he spoke directly to her was to ask directions to the farm when they left the Leominster road.

'I'm sure you know exactly where it is,' she said tartly, though by this time tendrils of doubt were beginning to creep up on her.

'It's years since I've been out this way, so I don't remember precisely,' he said, and told Greg to consult the map. 'Since Miss Carver is uncooperative, we'll blunder on the best we can.'

When they'd passed the turning down to Westhope and driven a mile further on Sarah gave up.

'Go back and take the next left,' she snapped. 'As you well know.'

Greg, she saw with satisfaction, looked hideously uncomfortable, which scotched any doubts she'd been feeling. He was very obviously not looking forward to an encounter with Bob Grover.

When they finally drove past the trio of barns to arrive at the farm, Alex surprised Sarah by staying in the car.

'Greg will go to the door with you,' he said.

'What am I supposed to ask, Alex?' asked his unhappy assistant.

'Just to see Mr Grover. I'm sure Miss Carver will take it from there.'

Greg opened the Jeep door to a chorus of barking, and helped Sarah down. He took out a handkerchief to wipe his glasses and then settled them firmly on his nose, plainly relieved when the stocky figure of Bob Grover appeared, to quiet the dogs.

'Hello there, Sarah,' said Bob, smiling, and looked enquiringly at Greg.

'Good morning. You remember Greg Harris, Mr Grover?' she said. 'Harry told me you've met before. When Mr Harris made you an offer.'

Bob looked at the young man blankly, and shook his head. 'No. This isn't the chap, Sarah.'

'There's obviously been some mistake, Miss Carver,' said Greg stiffly, and turned in relief as Alex came to join them, smiling warmly at the farmer.

'Hello, Mr Grover.'

Bob's weatherbeaten face lit up. 'Alex Merrick? Well, I never. Haven't seen you since you were a nipper. How's old Edgar?'

'In rude health, thanks. Nice to see you again,' said Alex, shaking hands. He cast a cold glance at Sarah. 'Someone's been causing trouble, Mr Grover, by posing as Greg here to make an offer for your barns. I'd like to know who it was.'

'So would I,' said Bob fiercely. 'Come in, the three of you. My wife is out, but I can put the kettle on.'

'That's very kind of you,' said Alex, 'but I'm pushed for time. Could you describe this man for me?'

Bob thought hard. 'He was tall, about your age, and wore a suit and glasses. He drove a fancy foreign car.'

Sarah wanted to dig a hole in the farmyard and bury herself in it as Bob described a yellow Ferrari in detail.

'He'd left it out on a verge, out of sight along the lane,' he explained. 'But it had settled into thickish mud when he went back to it, and he had to ask for help to push it out.'

'Thanks, Mr Grover,' said Alex. 'Mystery solved. An old schoolfriend of mine playing a practical joke. I'll have words with him.'

'I'd like some words with the idiot myself,' growled Bob. 'It upset Mavis good and proper, I can tell you. Not,' he said, smiling at Sarah, 'that it made any difference. Miss Carver knows she can trust me to keep my word.'

'I do indeed, Mr Grover,' she assured him.

'Trust is a very valuable commodity,' said Alex pointedly. 'Good to see you again, Mr Grover.'

'Give your grandfather my regards.' Bob turned to Sarah. 'You'll be here in the morning, then?'

'That's right. Tell your wife I'm sorry I missed her.' Sarah managed a smile for him, then walked to the Cherokee, feeling like Marie Antoinette on the way to the guillotine.

Alex motioned to Greg to get in the car, but barred Sarah's way.

'What the hell was your boyfriend playing at?' he asked in a furious undertone.

'Boyfriend?' Sarah eyed him balefully. 'You know perfectly well that Dan Mason is not, and never has been, my "boyfriend".'

'Then what was he doing at your place the other night?'

'How do you know he was there?' she asked involuntarily.

'I was idiot enough to call to see you,' said Alex with disgust.

'But I saw the Ferrari parked outside Medlar House and thought better of it."

Sarah could have cried. 'Dan came to apologise for his behavious and to ask me out again. I refused the offer. End of story.'

'Do you mean the bastard made that offer to Bob Groves as a form of revenge? It certainly worked—on both of us.' He gave her a look which made her quail. 'Did you really believe I would do something so petty, Sarah? Don't bother to answer,' he added harshly. 'You obviously did. Please get in the car.'

In embarrassed silence Greg Harris helped her into the back, then got in beside Alex, which left her no opportunity to apologise on the endless journey back. By the time they reached the Merrick building Sarah was word-perfect in various speeches, but when Alex parked the Cherokee it was Greg who came to hand her out, and no speeches were necessary.

'I've wasted enough time this morning,' Alex said, looking at his watch. 'See Miss Carver to her car, Greg.' And, without even a look in Sarah's direction, the vice-chairman of the Merrick Group strode inside to rule his kingdom, leaving his assistant to carry out his orders with body language which made his opinion of the morning's fiasco very plain.

Sarah burned with humiliation on the drive home. But gradually it gave way to a cold feeling of loss. One thing was clear. She would have all the time in the world to concentrate on the Westhope job. Alex would never want to set eyes on her again. She'd paid him back well and truly for his jibe about marriage. As she thought of her crack about his ego she shivered, seized by a burning desire to black both of Dan Mason's lying blue eyes.

'Bob told me what happened,' said Harry on the phone later. 'Fancy some lunch at the pub?'

'Oh, yes, please,' said Sarah fervently.

'Right. I'll pick you up in five minutes.'

On the way Sarah gave Harry a detailed account of her morning, and sighed heavily as he drew up outside the Green

Man. 'A good job I'm not in Oliver's line of work. I accused Alex Merrick without a shred of actual proof that he was behind the offer.'

'But why would you think *he* wanted the barns?' said Harry, frowning. 'The Merricks don't do small stuff like that any more. It was different with the cottages. They were next to the hotel site.'

'I've been seeing something of Alex lately—socially, I mean,' said Sarah reluctantly. 'But we had a row.'

Harry's shrewd blue eyes met hers. 'Must have been some row if you thought he'd tried to queer your pitch with Bob.'

'It was.' She smiled brightly. 'But after the insults I hurled at him this morning he'll never want to lay eyes on me again, so my social time is all mine again.'

'Learn to play darts,' advised Harry, as they went into the pub. 'You can play with Fred and me of an evening some time.'

'I used to play a bit,' she assured him. 'In my building site days I wasn't bad.'

'Hear that?' said Harry, as Fred joined them. 'The lady says she's good with the arrows.'

Sarah felt so much better by the time she'd eaten a sandwich and downed some cider that it didn't take much persuasion when Fred fetched some darts and challenged her to a game. She took off her jacket, rolled up the sleeves of her white shirt, projected a mental image of Dan Mason's face on the board, and did so well with her first few throws that a small crowd gathered to watch.

By the time she was well on the way to beating Fred at his own game, Sarah's hair was beginning to unravel from its knot, and she'd kicked off her high heels. She let out a crow of triumph as she beat him with her last throw. When a cheer went up from the onlookers she turned to bow all round, then blushed to the roots of her hair at the sight of Alex at the other end of the bar, talking to Eddy Mason. He nodded coldly, and for the second time that day Sarah wanted to run and hide. She returned the nod, thrust her feet into her shoes, and stood between Fred and Harry, forcing herself to finish her drink before looking in Alex's direction again. And found he'd gone.

CHAPTER ELEVEN

SARAH HAD been so sure Alex had come to the Green Man to look for her she was utterly devastated when he left without a word. Message received, loud and clear, she thought miserably. Even so, she still had to apologise. If she rang him there was every likelihood that he'd refuse to speak to her, so the only option was a letter. But when she'd finished it, the typewritten letter seemed too cold for an apology. With a sigh she copied it in longhand, and then went out to post it before she could change her mind. It had been incredibly difficult to express herself in a way which apologised for her accusations and at the same tried to hint that a reply would be welcome.

When no reply arrived Sarah faced the truth. It was time to forget Alex Merrick, along with fancy underwear and dresses with sequins. Life from now on would consist of overalls, a hard hat, and hard work.

Sarah was grateful to get back to hard labour with Harry and Ian at Westhope next day. In the beginning, because they were too far away for pub lunches at the Green Man, all three of them had taken sandwiches, but Mavis Grover, shocked at the thought of them functioning all day on such meagre fuel, had insisted that she would make lunch for them. Since she was Harry's sister and Ian's aunt, Sarah had had no choice but to accept—but only, she'd said firmly, if Mavis accepted payment. Also, the lunch must be something simple and easy to eat during their break in one of the barns, instead of at Mavis's table. After seeing the state of all three of them halfway through the first day's work Mavis had given in on this, but beaten Sarah down on the sum she considered fair in return for a few snacks.

The arrangement meant that Sarah ate something nourishing at least once a day—which was a good thing, she conceded wearily, when she was too tired to do more than open a tin or make a sandwich after Harry dropped her off each night.

Fred drove to visit them on site a few days later, to tell them Daniel Mason had been mugged outside his London flat. According to his father he'd been lucky to come out of it with nothing worse than a black eye.

'Betty Mason is pretty upset about it,' reported Fred, over a hunk of the steak and ale pie Mavis had insisted he stay to share.

Sarah plumbed a dark side of herself she hadn't known existed as she tried not to rejoice at the news. Her only regret was not blacking Dan's eye herself.

'Serves him right for that trick he tried to play on Sarah and Bob,' said Harry, and gave Ian the details.

'If I'd known about it,' said his large nephew, clenching formidable fists, 'I'd have beaten him up before he ever got back to London.'

'Best you kept out of it, lad,' said Harry.

Sarah broke off a piece of piecrust for Nero. 'Did Dan have much stolen from him?'

Fred shook his head. 'Nothing at all. A crowd of thugs just jumped him for the pleasure of it, seemingly.'

Good for them, thought Sarah fervently.

During one of Oliver's weekend phone calls he suggested coming down to take her out to lunch one Sunday soon. 'I shall put up at the Green Dragon overnight, as usual, and drive back first thing on Monday morning. How about the restaurant we went to with Alex Merrick? What was it called?'

'The Pheasant.'

'That's the one. Good food there; decent wine list, too. You can bring me up to speed on your progress.'

Speed was hardly the word. Securing and relaying the floors was hard, slow work, and Harry admitted he was as grateful as she was for Ian's tireless help. Once that stage was over a footing inspection would be necessary before they could go any further. But by the time Oliver arrived on the appointed weekend, attired in a tweed suit of impeccable pedigree, Sarah reported that once Harry had treated all the wood they would be ready to start on the roofs before they went on to the next step of lining the walls with quick-drying membrane to render them waterproof.

'You look tired, darling,' said Oliver, as he drove her to the Pheasant.

'I've been working hard.'

'You never do anything else.' He shook his head in disapproval. 'It seems entirely wrong for a girl of your age.'

'I enjoy it, Oliver. And this time it's easier because I have Harry's nephew Ian working for me on a permanent basis.' Sarah patted his solid, tweed-clad knee. 'Stop worrying about me. Let's just enjoy our lunch.'

They were welcomed at the door by a smartly dressed redhead Sarah took to be Jane Hicks, Stephen's wife. She showed them into one of the smaller dining rooms, and seated them with a view of the pretty garden at the back of the pub.

'We do Sunday roasts of varying kinds, but you can order from the *à la carte* menu if you prefer.' She handed out menus, gave Oliver the wine list, and with a smile excused herself to see to the next arrivals.

Once a waiter had taken their order for wine, Oliver sat back to peruse the menu with his customary respect for the business of eating.

'Good place, this,' he commented, as he ran his eye down the list of choices. 'I'm torn between the rack of lamb and the roast duck.'

Sarah smiled at him fondly. 'Not your usual steak today?'

'For once, no. I'll keep to Sunday lunch convention.' Oliver was presented with a bottle of wine to inspect. A little was poured into his glass, he tasted, rolled it round his palate, then nodded in approval, and the waiter filled their glasses.

Well used to the ritual, Sarah went on studying the menu, then looked up with interest when a feminine voice said, 'Oliver Moore! How are you?'

Oliver rose to his feet with a delighted smile. 'Helen! How wonderful to see you.'

'Likewise.' The lady was tall, with stylishly cut fair hair and large hazel eyes which smiled at Sarah in enquiry. 'Hello. I'm Helen Alexander.'

'This is my goddaughter, Sarah Carver,' said Oliver, and pulled out a chair. 'Do join us.'

'I'd love to, my dear, but I'm lunching in the next room with my sister-in-law and my son. Our meal will soon be ready, so I must get back. All right, Alex—I'm coming,' she added, as an all too familiar figure joined her. 'Look who's here, darling.'

'Hello, Sarah,' said Alex briefly, and shook hands with Oliver. 'How are you, sir?'

'Very well, my boy,' said Oliver. 'I liked the place so much the day you brought us, I persuaded Sarah to eat here again.'

'Stephen's a fabulous chef, isn't he?' said Helen. 'Do you live nearby, Sarah?'

'Yes.' Sarah found her voice at last. 'I have a flat in Medlar House—the old girls' school.'

'Really? It's such a lovely building. I always wanted to look round it, but I didn't have a daughter as a pretext.' Helen smiled at her son. 'Alex knew it well. He went to parties there when he was young.'

'I've heard about the parties,' said Sarah.

'How is your project coming along?' Alex asked her stiffly.

His mother looked at him in surprise. 'You two know each other professionally?'

'Of course they do,' said Oliver. 'Sarah's in the same line of business.'

'Scrap metal?' said Helen, astonished.

Alex shook his head. 'Sarah's involved in property conversions.'

'Then you really must take her to see your barn, darling.'

'She's already seen it,' her son informed her shortly. 'We'd better get back to our table. Aunt Bel will be wondering where we are.'

Helen Alexander offered a cheek to Oliver to kiss, and smiled warmly at Sarah. 'Come and take another look at Alex's house while I'm staying there. I'll give you tea.'

'Sarah's far too busy to waste time on mere socialising,' said Alex coldly, and won a look of shocked disapproval from his parent.

'Perhaps you'd have tea with me at Medlar House instead, Mrs Alexander?' said Sarah, surprising him. And herself. 'I never work on Sundays.'

'Why, thank you. I'd like that very much indeed. Next week?' said Helen, ignoring her son's stony face. 'I leave for home shortly after that.'

Oliver regarded Sarah with intense interest when they were alone. 'Did I detect a certain *froideur* between you and young Merrick?'

'Yes,' said Sarah baldly, and turned away in relief as a waitress came to take their order.

A past-master at cross-examination, Oliver returned to the subject as soon as they were alone. 'The last time we were here I gained the distinct impression that young Alex was smitten with you.'

'You were wrong,' she said flatly. 'Do you know his mother well?'

'I met her at some party, back in the mists of time. Like a fool I introduced her to George Merrick and lost her to the younger man.' Oliver looked down his formidable nose. 'But now he's lost Helen, which makes *him* the fool.'

The encounter with Alex's attractive mother made Sarah deeply curious to know more. 'Why did she leave him?'

'Usual story—another woman. Stupid idiot,' Oliver added bitterly.

'Cheer up,' said Sarah, as much to herself as to Oliver. 'Here comes our lunch.'

Much as she would have liked to eat and run, to avoid seeing Alex again, Sarah knew from experience that Oliver refused to be rushed when it came to food. And since in this case it was excellent, she did her best to enjoy it while she described her current work on the barns.

'No wonder you're looking thinner,' said Oliver with disapproval. 'Do you cook for yourself when you get home at night?'

'I don't have to. Mrs Grover cooks for the three of us at lunchtime.' Sarah explained the catering arrangement. 'Now, tell me about your latest case. Have you been defending anyone famous?'

While Oliver enjoyed his usual ripe Stilton, Sarah pushed some ice cream round a dish, but put her spoon down when Helen Alexander came back with another woman in tow.

'Miss Merrick,' said Oliver, rising to his feet. 'How good to see you. Let me introduce you to my goddaughter, Sarah Carver.'

Isabel Merrick turned familiar grey eyes on Sarah. 'How do you do, my dear? Helen tells me you're in the same line of business as my family.'

Sarah smiled. 'On a very much smaller scale.'

'What have you done with Edgar today?' asked Oliver.

'Our invaluable housekeeper is giving Father his lunch to let me off for an hour or two,' said Bel Merrick, rolling her eyes. 'But I'd better be back in good time for his afternoon tea.'

'I'll do that today,' said Helen firmly. 'You shouldn't let him ride roughshod over you, Bel.'

'You mustn't bore Miss Carver with our family secrets, Mother,' interrupted Alex as he joined them.

'Old Edgar's tyranny is no secret,' said Oliver wryly.

'Very true,' agreed Helen. 'It keeps him alive. Are you staying the night with Sarah, Oliver?'

'No room at her place, m'dear. I'm in my usual berth at the Green Dragon in Hereford.'

'A favourite haunt of yours, I seem to remember.' She turned to Sarah. 'Next Sunday at about four, then?'

Sarah smiled warmly. 'I'll look forward to it.'

In the general chorus of goodbyes Sarah and Alex pointedly ignored each other—something duly noted by Oliver once they were alone.

'Daggers drawn, obviously,' he said, beckoning to a waitress. 'Have some coffee and tell me why the electricity positively crackles between you and young Alex.'

'We had a disagreement over something trivial,' she said flatly, and changed the subject.

The encounter with Alex gave Sarah such a restless night that Harry eyed her warily when he picked her up next morning.

'Bad head?'

'Bad night.' She tapped her Thermos of coffee. 'A couple more cups of this and I'll be fine.' She explained about Oliver's visit. 'I ate too much lunch yesterday.'

'Not something you do any other day,' he said sharply. 'Don't think I haven't noticed.'

'Your sister always gives me too much,' she protested.

'You give half of it to Nero most times. What are you fretting about, boss? Is it the job?'

'No, Harry. I love the work.' She shrugged. 'But, as you know by now, some days I feel a bit down.'

'When you miss your father?'

'Yes,' she said, which was only half the truth. The other half was Alex Merrick's fault. She'd persuaded herself she was getting over him. But one look at him yesterday had made it clear that wasn't going to happen any time soon. Her mouth set. She'd get there in the end.

Sarah was glad when Friday arrived, and she had two days off to look forward to.

'Will you be wanting me on Saturday this week, boss?' asked Ian as they were packing up.

'No. We're well on schedule,' she said, patting Nero. 'I need tomorrow off for stocking up on food—'

'And eating some of it,' muttered Harry.

'For heaven's sake, stop *nagging* me—' She took in a deep breath. 'Sorry—sorry! I'm a bit tired—which is no excuse for shouting at you, Harry.'

'Let's get you home,' he said gruffly. 'It's been a long day.'

Sarah was glad, not for the first time, that she wasn't driving on the way back. Harry had suggested he took on this job from day one, and after insisting she paid for petrol Sarah had been only too happy to agree.

'You can rip at me again if you like,' he said, once they were underway, 'but you'd do well to stay in bed for a bit in the morning before you do that shopping.'

'I certainly will. I'm looking forward to it,' she agreed, yawning. 'But cleaning comes before shopping. Not the windows,' she added hastily. 'They still look fine.'

Harry's lips twitched. 'I'm not offering to do that lot again in a hurry. Not after the day we've had, that's for sure.'

'That's the trouble with our kind of work,' said Sarah with a sigh. 'It doesn't leave much energy over for going out in the evenings.' Which only proved the point she'd tried to make to Alex. Though if he could see her right now, she thought bitterly, her face grey with fatigue and her hair stuck to her head with sweat, he'd run for his life, offering up thanks for his escape.

By half past three on Sunday afternoon, Sarah was beginning to regret her impulsive invitation to Alex's mother. In part, Sarah knew only too well, it had been a knee-jerk response to his sarcastic crack about her social time. Or lack of it. But there was something about Helen Alexander as a person which called strongly to Sarah, and made her eager to know her better.

So now her flat was shining, she'd arranged flowers at one end of her trestle table, and set a tea tray ready in the kitchen. She'd taken extra care with her hair and face, and wore a pink cotton shirt tucked into the white jeans of her night with Alex. Since it was no use even for an evening with Oliver, the sequinned dress was bundled up in a bag, ready for a charity shop next time she was in Hereford. Her lips twitched as she thought of Oliver's reaction to the dress. Oliver liked to think of himself as broad-minded, but not, she had a fair idea, when it came to his goddaughter.

When Sarah's bell rang promptly at four, she pressed the buzzer for the outer door, then walked across the hall to greet Alex's mother. 'Welcome to my retreat,' she said, smiling as she led the way back to the flat.

Helen Alexander, cool and attractive in a leaf green linen dress, greeted her warmly. But when Sarah ushered her inside the beautiful hazel eyes widened in awe as Helen took in the dimensions of the room. 'My dear girl,' she said, impressed. 'What a wonderful retreat it is. Alex told me it's all your own work, that you actually fitted it up yourself, so show me exactly what you've done.'

In the face of such genuine interest Sarah found herself giving every detail, but at last apologised for going on too long and offered her visitor tea. 'I won't be a moment. My kitchen's a bit small, Mrs Alexander—'

'It's Miss these days,' her visitor corrected, as she followed her to the kitchen doorway. 'I reverted to my maiden name after my divorce. But just Helen will do.'

'Thank you.' Sarah smiled in apology as she poured boiling water on to teabags in her best cups. 'I'm afraid that, unlike Alex, I don't have a teapot. At least not here with me. That kind of thing is still in store in London. But the cups were my mother's.'

Helen eyed her speculatively. 'Sarah, I normally scoff at women who talk about their intuition, but even Bel noticed something in the air between you and Alex. And if you're acquainted with his teapot you must know him quite well.'

Sarah picked up the tray. 'He bought the cottages I restored.'

'He showed them to me. I was deeply impressed.' The hazel eyes were searching. 'But if you've been to his house there's a lot more to it than that. Alex tends to keep his home off limits to visitors.'

'We met occasionally in the run-up to the sale of the cottages, and we've had dinner together a couple of times since,' Sarah said casually, and carried the tray over to the table. 'Would you like some cake? Home made—though by the lady who bakes for the local Post Office stores, not by me.'

'Honest creature! I'd love a piece of cake.' Helen took it, and sat down in the cherrywood rocker. 'So, tell me about yourself, Sarah. I know you're Oliver Moore's goddaughter.'

Sarah explained about the relationship. 'He was always a hands-on godfather, but since Dad died Oliver takes his duties even more seriously.' She smiled wryly. 'My way of earning a living gives him nightmares. Irregular income, plus down-and-dirty physical labour.'

Helen looked thoughtful as she ate some cake. 'Oliver would rather you worked office hours in a pretty dress?'

Sarah grinned. 'Exactly. But that's enough about me. Alex said you live in Stratford? You enjoy that?'

'I do—very much. I bought a flat near my sister, and I've made quite a lot of friends there, not to mention having the Royal Shakespeare Theatre on hand.' Helen smiled wryly. 'It's not too far from London, or to visit Alex—and Bel and old Edgar, of course. After my divorce I wanted to go abroad as far as I could get at first, but I soon got over that. I need to be at least in the same country as my son. Though not near enough,' she added with a smile, 'to be breathing down his neck.'

'From the way Alex talks about you, that's not a problem for him.'

'Does he talk about me?'

'Not in detail. He told me about your visits.' Sarah hesitated. 'He doesn't resemble you at all physically.'

Helen smiled ruefully. 'No. He's his father all over again. When I first met George he looked very much as Alex does now. Perhaps you can understand why I was swept off my feet?'

'Yes, I can,' said Sarah bleakly. 'Alex is a very attractive man.'

'And it's obvious that he thinks the same about you,' said Helen gently. 'So what went wrong?'

Sarah looked into the sympathetic eyes for a moment, then found herself pouring out the entire story—from her initial aversion to the mere name of Merrick, to the hideously embarrassing scene with Bob Grover at Westhope Farm. 'I wrote to Alex to apologise,' she finished forlornly, 'but no reply. And by his attitude the other day at the Pheasant I'm not likely to get one. Not,' she added hastily, 'that I blame him. But I still think he was unreasonable in some ways.'

'And what ways were they?'

'I get pretty tired during the week when I'm working flat-out, so I suggested—no, pleaded with him,' she added bitterly, 'to save our time together for weekends.'

'And of course Alex, typical male that he is—and a Merrick at that—thought he should see you whenever he wanted to,' said Helen, nodding. 'So you took it for granted he was the one who did the stunt at Westhope Farm in petty revenge?'

Sarah flushed hectically. 'I can't believe, now, that I made such a terrible mistake without checking it out.'

'But in spite of all this you still like my son?'

'Much too much for my peace of mind. But don't tell him that,' Sarah added hastily.

'Of course not.' Helen got up. 'How about some more tea while I tell you something which may help you to understand Alex better?' She handed the cake plate over. 'I should put the rest of that in a tin right away, so it doesn't dry.'

When they were back in their former places, holding fresh cups of tea, Helen gave Sarah an odd little smile. 'Tell me if

I'm imagining things, but do you share this rapport I feel between us?'

'I most certainly do,' Sarah assured her. 'It was part of my reason for asking you here.'

Helen chuckled. 'And was the other part due to Alex's rudeness about your lack of social life, by any chance?'

Sarah nodded sheepishly. 'He annoyed me.'

'I could tell! It's obvious that you two have very strong feelings for each other, even if they're not exactly cordial right now. So, be honest with me. Do you love my son?'

Sarah stared at her, startled, her first instinct to deny it vehemently. But the steady hazel eyes were so compelling it was impossible to lie. 'Yes, I do,' she said despondently. 'For all the good it will do me now.'

Helen smiled reassuringly. 'It will, I promise. Because Alex feels the same about you, Sarah. He gives himself away every time I mention your name. So, to understand him you should know that he had a pretty nasty experience at the hands of one young woman. It tends to colour his view of our sex.'

'Which doesn't mean he has to tar me with the same brush, Helen.' Sarah sighed. 'He was totally unreasonable.'

'Of course he was. He's a man! Now, I must go—or Edgar will be giving Bel the third degree about where I've gone. Poor dear, I don't know how she puts up with him. Well, I do, really. She does it because she loves him. So do I, the old tyrant. You should meet him. He'd like you.'

Sarah shook her head as she accompanied her visitor to the door. 'One Merrick was more than enough for me.'

'I have some advice for you,' said Helen. 'You probably won't want to follow it, but I'll give it anyway. Alex will be at home next weekend, because he's doing something to his garden. If you turn up out of the blue I doubt he'll send you away.'

'I can't see myself doing that,' said Sarah ruefully. 'But thanks anyway.'

'By the way,' said Helen, as they walked outside, 'who did cause the mischief with Westhope Farm?'

'A man called Dan Mason. His parents keep the Green Man. Do you know him?'

'I know of him. He was the hugely bright boy who walked away with all the prizes on Speech Day when Alex was in school.' She shook her head in wonder. 'What on earth made him do such a preposterous thing?'

Sarah's mouth turned down. 'It sounds a bit big-headed, but I think it was just to cause trouble because I preferred Alex to him.'

'And are you going to let him get away with it?' said Helen slyly.

Sarah looked into the challenging hazel gaze and came to a decision. 'No. No, I'm not. I'll take your advice and beard the lion in his den next Sunday. Alex can't eat me.'

Helen took two cards from her bag and gave one to Sarah. 'Ring me to tell me how you got on. Ring me any time you want, in fact. Whatever happens with you and Alex, I'd like to keep in touch with you, Sarah. Now, tell me your number and I'll scribble it down. Goodbye, my dear.' Her eyes sparkled. 'Shall I give Alex your love?'

Sarah shook her head. 'I doubt that he'd want it right now.'

'Oh, he would. We mothers know these things,' said Helen, and smiled wickedly as the doorbell rang. 'There he is now, come to drive me home.'

When the bell gave a peremptory second ring, Sarah gave Helen a wild look and picked up the receiver.

'Alex here.' The familiar voice set Sarah's pulse racing. 'Is my mother ready?'

Sarah pressed the button to release the outer door, then opened her own. Helen stood beside her as they watched Alex cross the hall towards them. 'I could have gone outside, but this is so much more interesting,' she whispered.

'Hello, Sarah,' said Alex woodenly as he reached them.

'Hi,' she returned, managing to paste on a smile.

'Thank you for tea, Sarah,' said Helen. 'And for showing me your quite remarkable home. It's amazing, isn't it, Alex?'

'Yes,' he agreed stiffly, then, as if the words were torn from him, 'How are you, Sarah?'

'Absolutely fine,' she lied. 'How are you?'

'I'm absolutely fine, too.' He turned to his mother. 'Are you ready?'

'Yes, dear.' Helen kissed Sarah's cheek. 'Thank you again. I've enjoyed my afternoon. I'm going home tomorrow, so I'll say goodbye. Perhaps you'll give me tea again next time I'm here?'

'I'd be very happy to. Thank you so much for coming.'

Alex gave Sarah a formal nod as he took his mother's arm. Helen turned to wave at the outer door and Sarah waved back, but Alex kept his back turned as he hurried his mother out to the car.

CHAPTER TWELVE

RAIN CAME down in sheets as the Jensen left the courtyard, so instead of a peaceful stroll in the gardens Sarah settled down to the paperwork she'd been too tired to work on during the week. Afterwards she rang Oliver, to report progress and tell him about the visit from Alex's mother.

'Got to go, Oliver,' she said as the doorbell rang. 'Someone's at the door. I'll ring you next week.'

The sound of Alex's voice over the intercom again sent Sarah so haywire her hand shook as she pressed the button to let him in.

He strode across the Sunday quiet of the hall towards her, rain dripping down his shirt from his hair. Without a word he pushed her inside, thrust the door shut behind him, and seized her in his arms, kissing her with a craving she responded to helplessly.

'I can't do this any more,' he said hoarsely, when he raised his head.

'Do—what—?' she gasped.

'I give in. To hell with it. I'll take your terms. Whatever I can get.' His mouth found hers again, and for a hot, breathless interval they kissed with a wildness that left them shaking when she pushed him away far enough to let her look up into his face.

'Let me say I'm sorry, Alex,' she said, in a voice so unsteady it sounded like a stranger's. 'I should have known—'

His kiss smothered the rest of her plea, and for a while it seemed more important to kiss him back than to try and talk.

'No—please,' she panted at last. 'You must let me speak. I should have trusted you. Known you wouldn't do anything so monstrous. I would have apologised as soon as we got back from Westhope, but you didn't give me the chance.'

'Because I was mad as hell,' he said, and kissed her again. 'As soon as I simmered down I went looking for you at Medlar House, but no luck, So I tried the Green Man.' His eyes blazed into hers. 'And there you were, without a care in the world, playing darts, for God's sake.'

'So you stormed off without a word again.' Sarah buried her head against his damp shirtfront. 'It cut me to pieces.'

'It didn't do me much good, either.' He rubbed his cheek over her tangled curls. 'I know the perfect way to put the pieces back together. But there's a snag. We're in the wrong place. My healing process needs a bed.' Alex put a finger under her chin to raise her face to his. 'If I made love to you on your balcony, Juliet, I'd wreck it, the way I feel right now.'

Sarah felt a hot thrill run through her at the mere thought. 'I have a much safer alternative. My windowseat has a secret life. It's really the lid of a storage box.' She ran to raise it and drew out the thick winter duvet stored under it.

Alex's smile lit up the room as he snatched the quilt from her to throw it down on the rug. He held out his arms. 'Then come lie with me, wench, so I can kiss you better.'

'You'd better take that wet shirt off first!'

He smiled his crooked smile. 'I'd rather dispense with yours.'

'You'll have to, if you're going to kiss me better,' she said, her eyes steady on his. 'Because I hurt all over.'

'In that case,' said Alex, eyes glittering, 'you'd better have some cushions, too.' He took some from the windowseat and tossed them down on the quilt, then pulled the blinds closed and drew her down full-length beside him. 'Where shall I start?' he asked, looking down into her eyes.

'The shirt,' she reminded him gruffly.

'Ah, yes.' Alex sat up, undid his shirt and tossed it over his head, then began to undo Sarah's, his lips following his fingers.

'Plain white cotton today,' she said breathlessly, as he flung her shirt to join his. 'I put the fancy stuff away.'

'Why?'

'Not suitable for the kind of work I've been doing.' Sarah bit her lip. 'Besides, I couldn't bear the sight of it any more.'

He frowned. 'You haven't thrown it out?'

'It was too expensive for that.' Her eyes met his. 'But the dress with the sequins is about to go.'

'No way,' he said sternly. 'I have a particular fondness for that dress.' He pulled her close. 'I want you so much, Sarah.'

'Then for heaven's sake do something about it,' she said impatiently, and Alex gave a choked laugh and kissed her as he went on undressing her. 'And now,' he said, when she lay naked in his arms, 'for the rest of you.'

By the time Alex had finished kissing every inch of her better, they were both in such a high state of arousal that their lovemaking was too frantic to last long, and all too soon they lay clutching each other in the healing aftermath of the storm.

'So,' Alex said, when he could breathe again, 'are you better?'

'Not yet.' Sarah fought for breath. 'I shall need more of your medication, Doctor. Much more.'

Alex's eyes gleamed down into hers, the light in them changing to something that turned her heart over. 'I've missed you like hell, Sarah. Can you imagine how I felt when I found Dan Mason's car here when I gave in and came to see you? I wanted to break his jaw.'

'You'll have to stand in line. I'm going to break it first. But let's forget Dan.' She touched a caressing hand to his face. 'I've missed you, too.'

'Even though I'm a Merrick?'

'I told you—I'm over that.'

'Even though you thought I'd tried to queer your pitch at Westhope Farm?'

'I've apologised twice. Once by letter, and once face to face. But,' she added, her eyes kindling, 'I refuse to grovel any more.'

'It wasn't a very warm letter,' he said, smoothing the tumbled curls from her face.

'It took me ages. I was hoping,' she said tartly, 'for a reply.'

'Fond hope! I didn't take kindly to the accusations you flung at me, Sarah.' He scowled down at her. 'It was the final straw when I found you playing darts with your pals at the pub. Though, to be honest, I didn't go there just to look for you. I wanted Dan Mason's London address.'

Sarah propped herself up on an elbow in sudden suspicion. 'Why?'

'To pay him a visit.' Alex piled the cushions up and drew her down against them. 'Dan was notorious for playing nasty little tricks on people in school. Usually on defenceless types who couldn't retaliate. This time he chose the wrong target. Though he knew damn well I wouldn't report him to the police.'

'Why not?'

'No money was actually involved, and he could have passed off the rest as a joke that didn't come off.' Alex's smile turned Sarah's blood cold. 'So I waited for him to come home from work one evening, and pushed him back inside his smart loft the moment he opened the door. When I confronted him about the Westhope farce he started blustering, then suddenly lost it and punched me in the nose,' he added casually.

Sarah whistled. 'I can't see you turning the other cheek, so you must be the one who blacked his eye!'

'Oh, yes,' he said with relish. 'Don't worry. I didn't damage him much. Dan's main worry, the fool, was the blood on his jacket courtesy of my nose.'

She shook her head in wonder. 'I heard about a mugging. In the pub they think Dan was set on by a crowd of thugs.'

'He *would* say that,' said Alex, with scorn. 'The worst part was his stream of invective when I forced him to tell me why he did it. Apparently he hates me because my family's money got me the pick of the girls at Medlar House. Not my personal charm, you note. My other crime was my prowess at cricket and rugby, and winning too many events at Sports Day.' Alex shrugged. 'I pointed out that academically he'd won far more glittering prizes than me, but brains, as he spat at me, are no match for brawn when it comes to attracting women.'

Sarah's lip curled in disgust. 'Dan needs to grow up. It's a long time since you were both in school!'

'You're to blame for reviving his old animosity. He's convinced you were attracted to my family money.' Alex smiled crookedly and drew her close. 'Whereas, unknown to Dan, my name and all it stands for did me no good at all where you're concerned.'

Sarah shifted a little. 'This floor is hard, duvet or not, Alex.'

Alex promptly got up and pulled her to her feet. 'And I must go. Mother's leaving early in the morning.' He held her close as she tried to break away to pick up her clothes. 'Not so fast. We haven't discussed next weekend yet.'

'And we're not going to before I get some clothes on!'

When they were dressed, Alex sat down on the sofa and pulled Sarah on his knee. 'After I see Mother off I'm driving to London to sort out some problems with our restoration work on a riverside warehouse. My father and I have differing ideas on the subject, so I'll have to stay down for a few days to put him right.'

Sarah's lips twitched. 'Or he could put *you* right.'

Alex shook his head. 'He always comes round to my way of thinking in the end.'

'So when will you be back?'

'Friday night. So drive over first thing on Saturday morning. Please?' he added belatedly, and kissed her.

'Saturday afternoon,' she said firmly. 'I do things on Saturday morning.'

'Do them with me.'

'I'm talking about food-shopping and laundry,' she said, laughing.

Alex sighed. 'All right, if you must. Saturday afternoon, then.' He set Sarah on her feet and put his arm round her as they went to the door. 'Goodnight. Don't work too hard tomorrow. I'll ring you after dinner.' He kissed her, held her close for a moment, then gave her the crooked smile she'd missed so much. 'Sweet dreams.'

If Sarah did dream she remembered nothing about it next morning, after the best night's sleep she'd had in ages. And instead of her usual Monday morning reluctance, she approached work with a zest she knew Harry was wary of commenting on in case her mood changed. For once she ate all her portion of cottage pie at lunch, and even accepted a piece of the cake Ian's mother had sent with him for their tea break.

'Ian's reach will come in handy with the membrane on the highest bits,' she told Harry on the way home.

'Reach is one thing you lack, boss,' he said, lips twitching.

'I know. So you two can deal with the membrane. I'll put the cob fixings in to secure it,' she said briskly. 'When the first barn is finished I'll get going with the plastering, while you two put the membrane up in the others.'

'Have you been taking some vitamin pills or something?' asked Harry. 'You're in a very good mood today.'

'Are you suggesting I'm a bit hard to get on with some days?' she demanded.

'Yes,' he said bluntly. 'But so am I. Which is why we work well together, boss.'

Sarah had just finished supper when Alex rang that evening.

'Reporting in,' he said. 'Had a good day?'

'A wonderful day,' she told him. 'Did your mother get away on time this morning?'

'She did. And sent you her love. *Love*, not regards, she emphasised. 'You two really hit it off.'

'We certainly did. I like your mother very much, Alex.'

'Me too. I miss her when she goes back to Stratford. I'll need a lot of loving care from you, Sarah, to console me.'

'I'll see what I can do.'

Alex heaved a sigh. 'It's going to be a long week. Did I mention bringing an overnight bag with you on Saturday?'

'No.' Though Sarah had intended to anyway.

'If I only get you at weekends, Sarah Carver, that means from the moment you get to my place until first thing on Monday morning. Understood?'

'Understood.'

'And the following week I expect the weekend to start on Friday evening,' he informed her. 'I don't care how tired you are. You can doze the evening away on my sofa if you want. No need to drive. I'll fetch you, and drive you back on Monday morning. Do you approve my plan?'

'I just love your plan,' she said, and, since there was silence on the line for a moment, concluded she'd rendered him speechless.

On the way back to Medlar House the following Friday, Sarah was in such high spirits that Harry cast her a sly look

'Got a date tonight?'

'Not tonight. Tomorrow.'

'Good for you. All work and no play's a bad thing at your age.'

'Any age, Harry. So you have a good weekend too.'

Normally Sarah felt so weary on Friday evenings that she was too tired to do anything other than shower, eat and go to bed early with a book. This Friday she felt totally different. Probably because she'd been eating properly all week. And talking to Alex every night. So, instead of wasting part of her Saturday on cleaning and laundry she got on with it straight away, so she could turn up early next day at Glebe Barn as a surprise.

When Alex rang later, she told him he sounded tired.

'I am—whereas you sound full of beans, Sarah.'

'It's been a good week. We've got a lot done. I can now enjoy my weekend with a clear conscience.'

'With me.'

'With you.'

'I can't wait.' He yawned. 'I'm halfway home. I stopped at a service station for coffee to get me through the rest of the journey.'

'For heaven's sake, drive carefully!'

'You sound as though you care.'

'I do.'

'So do I,' he said softly. 'See you tomorrow, darling. Come as early as you can.'

Next morning Sarah did her shopping at the Post Office stores, rather than waste precious time driving miles to a supermarket. When she got back she put the food away, collected her overnight bag, and set off as she was, in jeans and a white cotton shirt, smiling as she pictured Alex's face when she turned up earlier than expected.

But when she arrived at Glebe Barn she found another car there before her, parked alongside Alex's Cherokee. A Porsche, Sarah noted, eyebrows raised. As she got out of the car she heard voices raised at the rear of the house. Helen had told her Alex was doing something in his garden this weekend. Apparently he had help. Female help.

Sarah went round the side of the house, then froze at the sight of a woman in Alex's arms. With a gasp, she turned tail and fled. But her feet crunched on the pebbles, and before she could reach her car Alex caught her.

'Sarah, it's not what you think.' He pulled her close and kissed her very thoroughly. 'You don't know how glad I am to see you,' he said, with feeling.

'Are you?' she said breathlessly.

'Yes. Thank God you came early. Come on.' He led her round to the patio he was building at the back. The woman stood there, tapping an impatient foot. She was tall and slender, with suspiciously voluptuous breasts, and straight blonde hair which framed a stunningly beautiful face.

Alex tightened his arm round Sarah as he introduced her. 'Sarah Carver, meet Maxine Merrick—my father's second wife.'

Help, thought Sarah. And what an odd way for Alex to describe his stepmother. 'How do you do?'

'Hello,' said Maxine curtly, and stabbed a look at Alex. 'Could we speak in private before I go, please? I'm running late.'

'Then take off right now,' said Alex. 'We have nothing more to say.'

Maxine looked at him with such venom that Sarah felt an absurd impulse to stand in front of him, like a bodyguard. 'I'm warning you, Alex, you'll regret this.'

'Oh, for God's sake, don't be such a drama queen, Max,' he said, bored.

Angry colour flared in her face. She slung her expensive bag over her shoulder and, ignoring Sarah, stalked past Alex on her way back to her car, throwing him a look so vicious it turned Sarah cold.

When the Porsche roared into life Alex turned Sarah into his arms, holding her so close she could feel his heart thudding against her. 'As wicked stepmothers go, Maxine takes the prize,' he said, rubbing his cheek against hers. 'Did you hear any of that?'

'No. I didn't wait long enough to hear any conversation.' She gave him a wry look. 'Seeing you with a woman in your arms was a horrible shock.'

'Maxine was trying her famed feminine wiles on me to persuade me into doing what she wanted.' Alex took her hand to lead her inside. 'I need coffee.'

They drank it close together on one of the deep, comfortable sofas. Alex was so obviously in need of the physical contact as much as the caffeine that Sarah kept quiet, leaving it to him to explain the incident. Or not.

'The delightful Maxine,' he said at last, 'came here this

morning to extort money from me. At this point I should tell you that she was once engaged to me—'

'So she's the one?' And Maxine had married his *father*?

Alex eyed her in surprise. 'Did Mother give you any details?'

'Only that someone hurt you badly. Helen thought it would explain you to me.'

'She's right. Maxine made me very wary of getting close to a woman again. Until I met you, Sarah.' He kissed her swiftly. 'Just to make it crystal clear that I'm immune to Maxine's charms these days, I'll tell you the entire sordid story.'

'You don't have to,' said Sarah quickly.

'I do, my darling. And even though it involves my mother, she strongly urged me to put you in the picture.' Alex took in a deep breath. 'There's no easy way of saying this. Mother told me, with great reluctance, that when she turned up unexpectedly at their London flat one day, she found my father enjoying some afternoon delight in their bed. His naked partner in crime was my fiancée, Maxine Rogers.'

Sarah stared at him in utter horror. 'How horrible! What on earth did Helen do?'

'She walked out without a word, and kept on walking—right out of my father's life. The worst part, she said, was explaining to me.'

'I can well believe that!' Sarah shuddered and held him close.

'It hit me for six,' said Alex huskily. 'My world came apart at the seams for a while.' He smiled evilly. 'But, being a true Merrick, I put it back together on my own terms. I can be as ruthless as old Edgar any day. My father ranted and raged in the beginning, but I wouldn't budge. And because he was suffering agonies of guilt he agreed to my terms in the end. So he remains as nominal chairman of the group, and runs the retail end from the London office, but I actually rule over the Merrick Group as a whole.'

'Did that make it easier to cope with the situation?'

'It helped. But I would have coped a lot better if Maxine's

lover had been anyone but my father. That was the pill I found so bloody impossible to swallow.' Alex raked a hand through his hair. 'By then I didn't care about Maxine, but I couldn't understand how my father could do such a thing—to my mother, I mean, not me.'

'I can't either. She's so lovely. And she looks far too young to be your mother,' said Sarah. 'When did all this happen?'

'Six years ago. Mother looked even younger then. As far as I know my father had never looked at another woman until I brought Maxine home,' he said in disgust. 'When I learned the truth my first instinct was to get as far away from my father and the Merrick Group as I could. But once I'd cooled down I realised I'd be a bloody fool to throw my birthright away over a woman I no longer even cared for. My whole life had been geared to taking over one day, so I simply informed my father that the day had come sooner than planned, and there was no room at the top for both of us. When my grandfather weighed in on my side my father caved in and agreed to relocate to London.'

'And married Maxine?'

'After the divorce came through, yes.' Alex's smile turned Sarah's blood cold. 'Maxine thought she'd fallen in the honey pot. My father's a fit, good-looking man, and wealthy. He bought her a penthouse flat in Chelsea, and—best of all to Maxine—she wasn't required to ruin her figure with the children I'd wanted. But things haven't worked out quite as flawlessly for her as she'd hoped. My father is a canny man. He'll give her anything her heart desires, lets her use her credit card as much as she likes, but he checks the bill and pays it for her. Lack of hard cash is her problem, and right now she needs some in a hurry.'

'Has she run up some kind of debt?'

'No.' His mouth twisted in distaste. 'She wants the money for a discreet abortion, plus a holiday with her mother afterwards in some spa-type hotel in the sun to recuperate, without my father being any the wiser. Then she'll return, pampered and massaged and good as new, to the arms of her unsuspecting husband.'

Sarah shook her head in wonder. 'But if your father doesn't want children why doesn't she just ask *him* for the money?'

Alex smiled evilly. 'My mother had such a bad time when I was born he had a vasectomy.'

Sarah winced. 'So Maxine has a lover?'

He shrugged. 'She went to a friend's party while my father was away on a business trip. She says she drank too much champagne, can't remember much about the evening, and now she's pregnant with no idea who's responsible.'

'Do you believe that?'

'Of course not. The man is probably someone else's cheating husband, who either refuses to take the blame or can't put up the money. And whatever Maxine feels—or doesn't feel—for my father, she's too much in love with the luxury he wraps her in to risk her marriage.'

Sarah shivered in distaste, and Alex drew her closer.

'Forget about Maxine. I've been looking forward to this weekend too much to let her spoil it for us.' He kissed her, then eyed her accusingly. 'You were supposed to bring an overnight bag!'

'I did. I left it in the car.'

'Give me your keys and I'll fetch it for you, then I'll get cleaned up and we'll eat.' He smiled and brushed a hand over her hair. 'I wasn't expecting a lunch guest, but I'm sure we can find something.'

Sarah went up to Alex's bedroom with him to unpack her bag, her eyebrows raised when she saw a new plasma television screen mounted on the wall opposite the bed.

'Wow!'

Alex grinned as he dumped her bag down. 'For entertainment on the lonely evenings you won't spend with me.'

'How many evenings have you been home alone this week?' she demanded.

'None. Because I was in London, working. I had this installed when you dumped me.'

'You mean when you dumped *me* because I wouldn't agree to your terms!' She glared at him, and he laughed, holding up his hands in surrender.

'Pax! No fighting before lunch.'

'All right,' she sighed, and melted into his arms. 'I've been looking forward to this all week.'

'So have I.' Alex kissed her hungrily, then with a sigh let her go. 'I need a shower, but I'll only be a minute so don't go away. Unpack your bag while I get clean.'

Sarah felt utterly happy as she unpacked in Alex's bedroom while he sang—quite well, she noticed—in the shower. There was an intimacy about it she liked a lot. And Alex's bedroom had a lot more going for it than her own place when it came to comfort. A thrill of pure delight ran through her at the thought of sharing the bed with Alex.

She smiled at him so radiantly as he emerged from the bathroom that he caught her in his arms.

'What were you thinking just then?'

'Just that I'd be sharing that bed with you tonight.'

He hugged her close, burying his face in her hair. 'If you're very good it's just possible I might let you share it with me this afternoon, too. An afternoon nap would do you good.'

'Would I sleep?'

'No. Do you want to?'

She pressed her lips against his warm, bare skin, exulting at the feel of his heartbeat against her mouth. 'No,' she whispered. 'I want you to make love to me, to make up for all the misery you've caused me.'

'I was miserable too,' he said, his arms tightening. 'Let's start making up for it right now—'

She wriggled away, laughing up at him. 'Not before I've eaten. I'm hungry.'

* * *

The weekend was everything Sarah had looked forward to—right through to the last moment when Alex kissed her goodbye at a brutally early hour on the Monday morning.

'Next week,' he said imperiously, 'you bring your work clothes and drive to Westhope from here.'

'Yes, Alex,' she said meekly, and spoiled the effect by sticking her tongue out at him.

He grinned and bent to kiss her. 'I do so like an obedient woman.'

'Then go find one,' she said, laughing, and kissed him back. 'Are you free on Wednesday evening, by any chance?'

His eyes narrowed to familiar gleam. 'I could be. Why?'

'The weekend is a long way away,' she said, looking up from under her eyelashes.

'Are you by any chance trying to say you'd like to see me before then?'

Sarah nodded eagerly. 'Not to go out. I *do* get tired, Alex. But if you fancy coming to my place for supper, I—I'd like that. Very much.'

Alex held her in such a punishing embrace that she protested against the lips crushing hers. 'Of course I fancy it,' he said roughly when he let her go, and brushed her hair back with a possessive hand. 'I longed to suggest it myself. But, having learned my lesson the hard way, I held my tongue.' He smiled into her eyes. 'Thank you, my darling.'

'Don't mention it,' she said, not quite lightly. 'About eight, then?'

'Don't cook. I'll bring something.'

To Sarah the time seemed to fly by for the next couple of days as she helped the men reline the barns.

'I'll be able to start plastering soon,' she said with satisfaction, as they finished in good time on the Wednesday.

'And how do you reckon you'll reach the top of this lot?' said Harry, indicating the height of the walls.

'Like Michelangelo did for the Sistine Chapel—with ladders and a trestle to stand on. Though I won't need to lie on my back, like him.'

Ian looked at her doubtfully. 'Couldn't you let my uncle do the top bits, boss, and you do the bottom halves?'

Harry shook his head. 'You'd see the difference.' He gave his nephew a fierce glare. 'Don't you ever let on I said this, but she's better at it than I am.'

'Harry actually admitted it,' crowed Sarah to Alex later, as they made inroads on the lasagne he'd coaxed out of Stephen. 'But he's much better at carpentry than I am, so I'm really lucky to have him for the banisters and stairs and so on.'

'And you've got his nephew for the brute strength department. You three make a formidable trio.' Alex helped her to more of the lasagne, then put the rest on his plate. 'Stephen would like you to know that takeout meals are not normally part of the Pheasant's repertoire. In other words, don't tell anyone he's doing us a special favour.'

'Which he does because he's your good friend,' agreed Sarah.

Alex dropped a kiss on her nose. 'And because he approves of you. Highly.'

'That's nice! Did he approve of Maxine?'

'No, because she upset his wife.' Alex grimaced. 'I met Maxine for the first time at Stephen's wedding. She's Jane's cousin, which means that Jane, no matter how much I or my mother try to persuade her otherwise, feels responsible for the mayhem Maxine caused.'

'I can sympathise with her,' said Sarah soberly.

'One more thing, and then let's delete Maxine from the evening. My father flew to New York last weekend, and for once Maxine didn't seize the chance to go with him. Instead she drove to the Pheasant to ask Jane for money.' Alex's eyes hardened. 'Steve turned her down flat. They're still getting established, and just don't have that kind of spare cash. Maxine took off in a temper and came to me—as you saw—then still with no luck, went running to her mother, who never has two pennies to rub together, so I don't suppose she had much luck there, either.'

'So what will she do now?'

He smiled, and rubbed his cheek against hers. 'Frankly, Scarlett, I don't give a damn. So forget Maxine and tell me what you'd like to do next weekend.'

'The same as last weekend,' said Sarah promptly. 'I'll help you finish your patio.'

'No, you won't. You can recline on a deckchair and hand out advice and instructions while *I* finish it. Then you can scrub my back in the bath afterwards. Or any other part of me you think needs attention,' he added with a grin. 'I'll pick you up here at seven. If you're not too tired we'll take a detour to monitor progress on the new hotel, and you can take a look at your cottages at the same time.'

'I won't be too tired for that,' she assured him, and knew she wouldn't be. The weariness of the past few weeks had been due to Alex Merrick's absence from her life. Her energy was fully restored now he was back in it again.

Sarah had just waved goodbye to Harry the following evening when she saw, with sinking heart, a familiar Porsche in the Medlar House car park. Maxine Merrick slid out of it, eyeing Sarah's work clothes with a patronising smile.

'Hello. Have you got a minute? I'd like a word,' said Maxine.

'How did you know where I live?' asked Sarah, making no attempt to hide her hostility.

'Apparently Alex went on *ad nauseam* about this flat of yours to Stephen, so I asked Stephen where it was. Can I come in?'

Sarah's first instinct was to refuse, but after a pause her curiosity got the better of her. She unlocked the outer door and strode across the hall to her flat, then stood aside to let her unwelcome visitor in.

'Heavenly little place,' said Maxine, looking round in surprise.

'Thank you. Why are you here?' Sarah asked bluntly.

'To give you a friendly warning,' said Maxine, her china-blue eyes limpid.

'What exactly are you warning me about, Mrs Merrick?'

'Alex, and how ruthless he can be,' said Maxine, sighing. 'May I sit down?'

Sarah shook her head. 'I've had a long day, and I need a shower. I'd rather you just said what you have to say and go.'

Maxine's mouth tightened. 'All right then, Miss Carver. To get straight to the point, I think it's only right you know that Alex got me pregnant out of revenge, to hurt his father. You probably heard some of that when you walked in on us last Saturday. One look at you gave me the perfect lever I needed. I threatened to tell you everything unless Alex paid up for an abortion. Which he did, finally, but I'm telling you anyway, just to enjoy the feeling.' Her eyes hardened to chips of blue ice. 'No man tells me to get lost and gets away with it. Why are you shaking your head like that?' she added with sudden hostility.

'I feel so sorry for him,' said Sarah.

'Alex?' snapped Maxine.

'No. For his father.' Sarah flung the door wide. 'Goodbye, Mrs Merrick.'

'Hold on, I haven't finished—'

'Yes, you have. Take your lies and leave, or I'll call the caretaker.' Sarah smiled sweetly. 'To quote Alex, Mrs Merrick, get lost.'

Maxine turned a deep, unbecoming crimson, speechless with fury for a moment, but before she could recover Sarah thrust her out into the hall and closed the door, her heart beating like a drum.

Alex arrived fifteen minutes early the following evening. 'Sorry,' he said, kissing Sarah, I couldn't wait any longer. If you're not ready, I'll wait until you are.'

'Harry needed to get away a bit earlier today, so I was home in good time,' she assured him, and pointed to her bags. 'If you'll take those to the car, I'll just lock up.'

'Yes, ma'am!' he said with alacrity, and looked her over with appreciation. 'You look good enough to eat, Sarah.'

She smiled and reached up to kiss him. 'So do you.'

When they called in at the hotel construction site Sarah took a nostalgic look at the row of cottages.

'Note the trees,' said Alex, watching her face. 'I had the rest of the houses planted up to match the first one. You approve?'

'I do. I'm flattered you liked my taste. My cottages look really good. I'll always think of them as mine, you know,' she added, smiling.

'So will I.' Alex kissed her swiftly as he helped her down. 'I'm very glad, now, that you refused my original offer.'

'I should think I would,' she said indignantly. 'It was outrageous.'

'I meant the one I made before you even left London to start work on them,' he said, and sprang back, hands upraised in mock surrender.

Sarah stared at him blankly. 'That was you?'

He nodded, smiling broadly. 'I told the manager of one of our London subsidiaries to put out a feeler for me. When you didn't bite I decided to sit back and let you get on with them.'

She laughed in disbelief. 'You devious devil! Why didn't you tell me this before?'

He laid a hand on his heart. 'Harmony has not been a continuous feature of our relationship, Miss Carver, so I waited until it was on firmer ground before I confessed.'

'Good thinking.' Sarah blew him a kiss. 'Now, show me over this hotel and then take me home. I'm hungry.'

They were in bed together later that night, wrapped in each other's arms in the afterglow of making love, before she dropped her bombshell.

'I had a visitor last night,' she said, as Alex stroked her hair.

'If it was Dan Mason I'll black his other eye!'

'It was Maxine.'

Alex shot upright, his eyes incredulous as he stared down into Sarah's flushed face. 'What the hell did she want?'

'To make trouble for you, Alex.'

'What else is new?' he said grimly. 'What particular brand of trouble did she dish out this time?'

'She said you gave her the money for her abortion.'

Alex took in a deep breath, then caught her in his arms, his eyes looking deep into hers. 'I didn't give her any money, Sarah. I haven't seen her since last Saturday.'

'I know, darling,' she said gently.

He let out the breath, and rubbed his cheek against hers. 'I realise that, now my brain's started functioning again, otherwise you wouldn't be here with me like this—wouldn't have let me through your door tonight.'

'I believed the worst of you without evidence once, Alex,' she said firmly. 'I wasn't going to do it a second time. I did think for a fleeting moment you might have given her the money to spare your father. But her big mistake was saying you'd made her pregnant—'

'*What?*'

'Precisely. After what happened with your mother I knew you wouldn't touch Maxine again with a bargepole.'

'How right you are.' Alex crushed her close again in gratitude. 'You trusted me.'

'Yes, I did.' She smiled up at him. 'I do.'

His own smile was crooked as he returned the smile. 'I like the sound of that.'

'That I trust you?'

'No. The "I do" bit.'

Sarah swallowed, trying to control her somersaulting heart. 'Where do you think she got the money?' she said hastily, in case she was taking too much for granted.

'Don't know, don't care. Maybe her mother came up trumps for once.' Alex paused. 'But Maxine must have got it somewhere if she came round to you to gloat and spit out lies. Though I didn't think even she would be that vindictive.'

'You told her to get lost. She couldn't take that.'

'It's probably never happened to her before.'

'It has twice now.' Sarah smiled victoriously. 'I told her to get lost, too.'

Alex gave a crow of laughter, then grew quiet. 'Thank you, Sarah,' he said at last.

'For telling Maxine to get lost?'

'No, though I wish I'd been there to witness it. My thanks are for trusting me, Merrick though I am.' He held her close in silence for a while, then turned her face up to his. 'Talking of which, I've thought of a foolproof way of getting you used to my name.'

'Oh?'

'If you moved in here with me, and got gradually used to the idea, we could get married—preferably some time soon—and then your name would be Merrick, too. I know,' he added hastily, as her jaw dropped, 'that certain of my relatives leave something to be desired. But you've met my lovely Aunt Bel, and I think you'd even like old Edgar—and to crown it all you'd have the best mother-in-law in the business.'

'Are you serious?' she said, even as a glow of pure happiness spread through her.

'About my mother? Of course I am—'

'I mean about getting married.'

'Sarah,' said Alex patiently, 'you've worked among men all your life. You should know how they tick better than most women. Can you imagine any man saying something like that for a joke?'

'No, thank God!' She threw her arms round his neck in rapture at the thought of marrying Alex Merrick, whatever his name was.

'I wanted you the moment I set eyes on you—even when I thought you were Oliver Moore's trophy girlfriend,' he told her, and curled a lock of hair round his finger. 'Of course I didn't know then what trouble you'd cause me—'

'Trouble?' she said indignantly.

'False accusations for one,' he reminded her. 'You hurt me, my darling.'

'I know,' she said with remorse. 'I'm sorry, Alex.'

'But now you've trusted me rather than Maxine I feel I'm on a winning streak here. So how do you feel about marrying me, Sarah Carver?'

'Ecstatic,' she said, her smile incandescent. 'If I do, will you expect me to give up my work?'

'Hell, no,' he said fervently. 'Maybe you'll get so good at it I can retire early. I've always had a fancy to be a kept man.'

'Have you, now?'

'Well, no,' Alex admitted, kissing her. 'If there's any keeping involved I'd rather do it, because you'd have to have the babies.' He drew back to look her in the eye. 'Do you want children, Sarah?'

She nodded earnestly. 'Of course I do. As long as they're yours, Alex.'

He relaxed and held her closer. 'Then tell me I can keep you, Sarah.'

'Oh, yes,' she said with a blissful sigh. 'For ever, please. Besides, rather than shock Oliver, I'd prefer to marry you before we have these babies of ours.'

He rubbed his cheek against hers. 'I'll take all that as a yes, then.'

'A very enthusiastic one! I think your mother will be pleased.'

Alex laughed, and kissed her nose. 'You're only taking me on so you get my mother as well!'

'Of course. Though I love you madly, too.' She smiled suddenly, her eyes dancing. 'Oliver will be delighted, naturally, but I don't fancy telling Harry Sollers.'

'I'll break it to him myself. In the pub, so that all your pals hear the news at the same time.' Alex gave her his familiar crooked smile. 'And then, light of my life, I'll ask Eddy Mason to pass on the good news to Dan.'

* * * * *

THE VENETIAN'S
MIDNIGHT MISTRESS

BY
CAROLE MORTIMER

Carole Mortimer is one of Mills & Boon's® most popular and prolific authors. Since her first novel was published in 1979, this British writer has shown no signs of slowing her pace. In fact, she has published more than a hundred and forty novels!

Her strong, traditional romances, with their distinct style, brilliantly developed characters and romantic plot twists, have earned her an enthusiastic audience worldwide.

When Carole made her first attempt at writing a novel for Mills & Boon, "The manuscript was far too short and the plotline not up to standard, so I naturally received a rejection slip," she says. "Not taking rejection well, I went off in a sulk for two years before deciding to have another go." Her second manuscript was accepted, beginning a long and fruitful career. She says she has "enjoyed every moment of it!"

Carole lives "in a most beautiful part of Britain" with her husband and children.

"I really do enjoy my writing, and have every intention of continuing to do so for another twenty years!"

Carole now also writes for Mills & Boon® Historical— don't miss any of the fabulous stories in her wonderful Regency series, THE NOTORIOUS ST CLAIRES.

PROLOGUE

'So, I've been having wild, orgasmic sex every day with my tennis coach for over a month now.'

'*What?*' Dani gave a start as she stared across the drawing room at her friend Eleni.

The two women were putting the finishing touches to the décor of the country home Eleni would share with Brad following their Christmas wedding in a week's time. As an interior designer, Dani had spent the last month helping Brad and Eleni choose both the furniture and décor for the spacious house that she knew the two hoped would one day be filled with their children.

'Hang on a minute.' Dani's eyes narrowed with suspicion. 'You don't have a tennis coach, Eleni.'

'True.' Eleni, a beautiful Venetian, laughed at Dani's frowning expression. 'But it caught your attention, didn't it?' She smiled wryly. 'I've been talking to you for the last ten minutes, Dani, and I'm pretty sure you haven't heard a word I've said!'

'Sorry, Eleni,' Dani apologised with a grimace.

She had been doing her best, she really had, but obviously Eleni knew her too well to be fooled for a moment. Well, for any longer than ten minutes, anyway.

The two women had first met when they were both fourteen and Eleni had arrived at Dani's boarding school from her home in Venice, sent there for a year by her brother Niccolo, the head of the D'Alessandro family, in order to improve her English. The two girls' friendship had been so strong by the end of that year that when it had been time for Eleni to return home she had pleaded with Niccolo to let her come back to the English school for four more years and complete her education there. A battle she had lost...

Dani gave a shudder just at the memory of her first meeting with Niccolo D'Alessandro, after Eleni had insisted that Niccolo take both girls out to lunch so that she might introduce him to her English friend. Intimidating didn't even begin to describe the arrogantly assured Venetian.

Head of the D'Alessandro banking family for four of his then twenty-seven years, Niccolo D'Alessandro had been imposingly tall, his shoulders wide beneath his tailored suit, his stomach taut, legs long and muscular. Seeing his overlong black hair that he'd brushed back from his aristocratically handsome face, eyes of deep, brooding brown, high cheekbones, a long arrogant nose, a firm mouth that looked as if it rarely smiled, and a hard square jaw, it hadn't been in the least difficult for Dani to imagine that Niccolo D'Alessandro was descended from pirates as well as princes; she had a little more trouble imagining any D'Alessandro male could ever have been a priest, although she had been assured some of them had.

It had been also obvious what Niccolo had thought of Dani after that single meeting—he had flatly refused to let Eleni remain at school in England, only relenting in his decision when Eleni had reached eighteen and wanted to go to university in London.

'Man trouble?' Eleni prompted knowingly now.

Dani shook her head as she dragged her thoughts back from that first meeting with Niccolo D'Alessandro, almost ten years ago now. 'Not in the way you probably think.'

Eleni, her hair darkly luxurious, her brown eyes warm and glowing, shrugged slender shoulders. 'Let me guess. Either you have a man and he's being uncooperative. Or you don't have a man and you want one.'

'I had a man, remember?' Dani pointed out dryly.

Eleni frowned. 'I'm not sure I would call Philip that.'

'I was married to him!'

'Technically, yes.' Her friend nodded. 'But in reality we both know that the two of you didn't even last through the honeymoon.'

To Dani's everlasting mortification.

Philip had looked like a Greek god, and he had been charming, thoughtful, and funny. Until the honeymoon following their lavish wedding, when the jealousy he had been hiding until that point had suddenly reared its ugly head. He had turned into a monster, accusing her of being too friendly with every man she met, from the elderly porter who had delivered their suitcases to their hotel suite, to the waiter who served them dinner on their first evening in Florence.

The scene that had followed in their hotel suite after that last accusation was something that Dani preferred not to even think about!

The two of them had arrived home from the honeymoon separately. Dani had filed for divorce almost immediately, and since that time she had stayed well away from any sort of romantic involvement, no longer trusting her own judgement when it came to men.

'I don't have a man.'

'Then it's about time you did,' Eleni said, having been happily engaged to Brad for the last year. 'Not all men are like Philip, you know—'

'I have no guarantee of that,' Dani interrupted firmly. 'And until I do, I have no intention of getting involved with anyone again. Well…not by choice,' she muttered, sighing as the heavy weight of her earlier distraction came crowding back.

Damn her grandfather, anyway. What person in his right mind would put a clause like that in his will, for goodness' sake? Her grandfather, apparently. If she hadn't complied with the terms of that particular clause by the time her grandfather died, then her parents were going to lose Wiverley Hall, their home in Gloucestershire, where her father had spent years building up the reputation of his stable for training racehorses.

Eleni raised dark brows. 'That last statement sounded very intriguing…?'

Dani gave herself a mental shake. It was a problem, yes, but not an immediate one when her grandfather was still so fit and well.

'Not really,' she dismissed briskly. 'So, tell me how your plans for the reception are progressing? Have you—?'

'Oh, no, you don't, Daniella Bell,' Eleni cut in. 'I'm not

going to be put off by a change of subject. Tell all,' she demanded, her dark brown gaze avid with curiosity.

Dani couldn't help but smile. It was difficult to believe now that Eleni's English had ever been other than what it was. In fact, apart from the darkness of Eleni's colouring, nowadays her friend was almost more English than Dani.

She should never have given Eleni, of all people, even an inkling that something was troubling her. Eleni was like a dog with a bone when she got her teeth into something, and she wouldn't let this go until Dani had 'told all', as she had so succinctly put it.

But maybe she *should* tell Eleni what was worrying her. Eleni was her best friend, after all, and Dani badly needed to talk to someone about her grandfather's will!

She heaved another heavy sigh. 'Do you remember my grandfather Bell?'

'How could I forget him?' Eleni snorted. 'I met him at your wedding, of course, and once before that, when I came to stay for a weekend at your parents' home years ago. But that was certainly enough! He's even more formidably conservative than Niccolo with his "young ladies should be seen and not heard",' she quoted in a fair imitation of Daniel Bell's harsh tones. 'How your poor mother has put up with him living with them all these years I'll never know! I— Oops.' She gave an apologetic grimace. 'I'm sorry, Dani, that was extremely rude of me.'

Dani shook her head. 'The fact that he's my grandfather doesn't make me blind to his faults. He's always been a tyrant and a control freak,' she confirmed disgustedly. 'But the thing is, Eleni, it's actually my parents who have lived with my grandfather all these years. Not the other way around. He owns Wiverley Hall.'

'So that's why your mother has had to put up with him,' her friend realised.

'Yes,' Dani said. 'And my grandfather has never made any secret of the fact that he's disappointed he only had the one grandchild—'

'How could he possibly be disappointed with you? You're gorgeous!' Eleni looked indignant. 'I've always wanted to be a tiny redhead. Do you remember how I dyed my hair red like yours five years ago?' Her giggle was almost girlish. 'I thought Niccolo was going to shave my head and then send me back home on the next plane!'

Dani remembered only too well Niccolo's visit to England five years ago. And the fury in the accusing look he'd shot in her direction when he'd arrived and seen what Eleni had done to her normally rich brown hair...

'And I've always been envious of your amazing green eyes,' Eleni continued longingly. 'Plus, you've become one of the most successful interior designers in London.'

'Mainly due to you and other mutual friends employing me,' Dani pointed out dryly.

'That's irrelevant,' Eleni said firmly. 'Your grandfather should be proud of you and your achievements!'

Dani couldn't help smiling at her friend's chagrin on her behalf. 'The thing is, my mother couldn't have any more children after me, so that pretty well took care of there ever being a male heir.'

'Your grandfather is only a land-owner, for goodness' sake, not nobility!' Eleni scoffed.

And, being descended from nobility herself, Eleni was in a position to know the difference!

Dani smiled wistfully. 'Same thing as far as Grandfather Bell is concerned. "Land is wealth",' she quoted in almost as good an imitation of her grandfather as Eleni's a few minutes ago. 'Anyway, whatever the reason, he's never made any secret of his disappointment that he only has one grandchild—me. When my marriage to Philip ended in divorce, and childless to boot, I thought he was going to have a heart attack!'

'Doesn't he know *why* it ended in divorce?'

'Can you imagine any of the family even attempting to explain Philip's problem to Grandfather Bell?'

Her grandfather was approaching ninety years of age; trying to explain Philip's pathological jealousy, his violent behaviour after he and Dani were married, would probably only result in her grandfather stating that the demand for equality from woman nowadays—that he so disapproved of!—was obviously to blame.

'But the failure of your marriage wasn't your fault, Dani.' Eleni reached out a hand to grasp one of Dani's. 'You do know that, don't you?' She frowned. 'I only ask because I know there hasn't been a single man in your life since that awful marriage.'

'Nor a married one, either!' Dani retorted cheekily.

Although, in all honesty, it wasn't a subject she found in the least amusing. Not when her sex life, or lack of it, was the basis of her current problem!

'Very funny,' her friend drawled sarcastically as she straightened. 'But I still don't see how any of this affects you, Dani.'

In the normal course of events it shouldn't have; when her grandfather died, Dani's father should quite naturally inherit Wiverley Hall and the stables. Except her grandfather had decided otherwise...

'My father will only inherit Wiverley Hall and the Wiverley Stables if I have produced—or at least shown signs of producing—an heir before my grandfather dies.' Dani winced at just putting into words the terms of the clause that her grandfather had recently told her he had added to his will, let alone actually acting on it! 'Otherwise the whole thing is to be sold and the money given to charity.'

Eleni gasped as she sat back in obvious shock. 'But that's—that's positively Machiavellian!'

'Tell me about it,' Dani agreed, relieved to have talked to someone other than her parents about this at last.

Her parents had obviously been distressed a week ago, when Daniel Bell had called them all together to inform them of the changes he had made to his will, but not as shocked as Dani herself.

As Eleni had already pointed out, Dani had stayed well away from becoming involved in any sort of relationship since her ill-fated marriage to Philip, so how she was supposed to produce this heir any time in the near future she had no idea. Solicit some poor unsuspecting man off the street? Pay someone to get her pregnant? The whole thing was ludicrous!

As she might have known they would, her parents had totally dismissed the clause, advising Dani to ignore it too. They'd stated that when the time came they would move the stables elsewhere.

But Dani knew that was easier said than done when her grandfather controlled the purse strings, too.

Eleni gave a dazed shake of her head. 'So is his idea that you get married again?'

'I have no intention of marrying again. You know that,' Dani said.

'But Dani—'

'I will never put myself in such a vulnerable position ever again, Eleni,' she stated emphatically. 'Even seeing your own happiness with Brad as an example of how good a relationship can be,' she added tactfully. 'Besides, Grandfather hasn't said I have to actually get married again, only produce the Bell heir.'

'Incredible.' Eleni still looked dazed. 'I thought Niccolo was being unreasonable a year ago when he was so against my wanting to marry an Englishman, but your grandfather's behaviour is positively archaic!'

Dani had been present on the day that Eleni told her brother she intended marrying Brad and living in England with him—moral support, Eleni had called it!—and could clearly remember Niccolo D'Alessandro's icy disapproval that his sister should be contemplating marrying anyone who was not a Venetian.

She also remembered the way Niccolo had looked so coldly down his arrogant nose at her that day, as if he suspected *her* of being responsible for Eleni's stubborn refusal to back down. Not true, of course, but Dani had known there was no point in even trying to defend herself against such prejudice.

As Eleni and Brad's wedding was due to take place next weekend it was obvious who had won that particular battle—and that was yet another thing Niccolo D'Alessandro would no doubt blame Dani for!

'I know that, and you know that, but my grandfather has never claimed to be a reasonable man,' Dani said.

'But—'

'Can we please not talk about this anymore today, Eleni?' Dani cut in. 'I've thought of nothing else for the last week, and it just gives me a headache.'

'I'm not surprised.' Eleni frowned. 'You should have talked to me about it before, Dani,' she admonished her friend. 'I can't believe your mother and father would really lose Wiverley Hall and the stables if you haven't—'

'Eleni, please! Can we talk about your wedding next week instead?' Then Dani shuddered as a thought occurred to her. 'Has Niccolo arrived yet?' she asked tentatively.

Eleni, diverted by Dani's obvious aversion to seeing her brother again, shook her head. 'I've never understood why you and Niccolo have never become friends.'

'Probably because we are both of the opinion that the less we see of each other the better,' Dani retorted.

'But you're the two people I love most in the world—apart from Brad, of course—and I can feel the antagonism start to rise the moment the two of you are in the same room together!' Eleni wailed.

Niccolo D'Alessandro was thirty-seven now, to Dani's almost twenty-four, and the crush Dani had once had on the arrogant Venetian had—as Eleni so rightly pointed out—developed into antagonism on both sides. Out of dislike and disapproval on Niccolo's side—especially after Dani's brief marriage and divorce—and out of pure self-defence on hers.

She gave a dismissive shrug. 'We just don't like each other.'

'But why don't you?' Eleni pressed, frustrated. 'I know I'm his sister, but you have to admit that Niccolo is the epitome of "tall, dark, and handsome", and he has such a dangerous sexual aura about him he should come with a public health warning. And you're absolutely gorgeous—'

'So you already said,' Dani teased. 'None of which alters the fact that your brother makes me break out in a rash every time I see him, and that I seem to have the same effect on him.'

'It's a total mystery to me,' Eleni continued. 'Niccolo is usually so stiffly correct, so—so Venetian, that I simply don't understand his behaviour whenever he's around you.'

Dani chuckled softly. 'One of life's mysteries you're just going to have to live with, I'm afraid.' She glanced at her wristwatch. 'Now, I really will have to go; I have another appointment in town later this morning.'

'But I haven't told you about our plans for the honeymoon yet,' Eleni protested.

'And I would really rather you didn't. Besides, I really don't have any more time.'

'Don't forget we have the final fitting for your bridesmaid's dress in the morning,' her friend reminded her.

'As if!' Dani slung her capacious bag over her shoulder. She was wearing her usual work clothes: fitted black trousers and, today, a cashmere sweater the same deep green as her eyes. 'Although I doubt anyone will even notice what I'm wearing once you appear in that delectable froth of white lace.'

'I have every intention of introducing you to all my eligible male cousins next Saturday, you know,' Eleni promised.

Dani shook her head. 'Introduce away, Eleni, but I can assure you I won't fall for any of them.' Especially if they were anything like the arrogantly forceful Niccolo D'Alessandro!

'Maybe not at the wedding next weekend, but how about at my masquerade party here next summer?'

Dani knew that was part of the reason that Eleni had fallen in love with this particular house. Her friend had taken one look at the spacious garden with its numerous trees and shrubs and instantly decided that the following August she would throw a real Venetian masquerade party there. In fact, her friend was almost as excited about the party next summer as she was about her wedding next week!

'Not then, either,' Dani said dryly.

'But *everyone* falls in love during the Venetian Festival,' her friend protested. 'I remember my Aunt Carlotta telling me that she once spent the whole evening at one of the festivals flirting with her own husband—my Uncle Bartolomeo—without even realising it!'

Dani grinned. 'I bet he was surprised!'

'From the becoming blush on my aunt's cheeks when she told me about it afterwards I would say they both were!'

'Eleni!' Dani chided laughingly.

'You'll see at the party next year,' her friend promised. 'The festival is a way for everyone to misbehave without anyone needing to feel guilty about it.'

'Even your brother?' Dani taunted.

'Well…perhaps not Niccolo,' Eleni conceded. 'But the party is months away, Dani, and if you haven't solved the problem with your grandfather's will by then, an evening of anonymity could be the answer.'

'No, Eleni,' Dani said, easily able to guess what her friend was about to suggest, and having no intention of being seduced into the shrubbery by one of Eleni's male cousins in order to become pregnant. 'I know exactly what you're thinking, and the answer is most definitely no,' she repeated firmly.

'But—'

'*No*, Eleni.'

'It was just an idea.' Her friend shrugged ruefully.

'Well, it was a lousy one—oh!' Having intended making her way out of the house to her car in the driveway, Dani instead found herself crashing painfully into something very hard and unyielding.

A man's chest, she realised, once the pain in her jarred chin had abated to a mild throb.

Niccolo D'Alessandro's chest, Dani discovered breathlessly when she raised her gaze reluctantly to look at his handsome face above a black silk sweater.

Brooding dark eyes chillingly returned her startled gaze, and that same coldness was in the derisive twist of Niccolo's sculptured lips as he grasped the tops of her arms with elegantly long hands and put her firmly away from him.

'Daniella,' he acknowledged as he released her. 'I should have guessed.'

Dani's eyes narrowed at his sarcastic tone. 'Should have guessed what, exactly?' she challenged, two bright wings of colour in her cheeks. Colour she knew would not be complementary to the bright red of her straight below-shoulder-length hair.

But at least she had the answer to her earlier question—Niccolo had obviously arrived in England for the wedding next Saturday.

And he was looking even more devastatingly gorgeous than ever, making Dani's pulse race and her breath catch in her throat. The colour burning her cheeks was from physical awareness this time. Complete physical awareness. Of Niccolo D'Alessandro.

Her breasts tingled uncomfortably and a fierce heat gathered between her thighs.

Oh, God!

She had thought she was over this infatuation—had imagined that no man would appeal to her ever again after what Philip had done to her. But she knew she had been wrong as every nerve ending, every part of her, silently screamed her attraction to Niccolo—of all men!

She looked up at him from beneath lowered dark lashes. Maturity had given him lines beside those chocolate-brown eyes and the firmness of his mouth, but instead of detracting from his good looks they merely added another layer to his attraction, giving him that dangerous sexual aura Eleni had alluded to earlier.

Niccolo was dangerous, Dani acknowledged to herself. He exuded power, a complete domination over everything and everyone within his vicinity.

Well, not her. She'd had enough of domineering men—Philip and her grandfather to name but two—to last her a lifetime.

She turned away abruptly. 'Never mind,' she said, in answer to her own question.

'I thought this morning would be the perfect opportunity for Niccolo to come by and look at the house,' Eleni said awkwardly.

Dani knew by the way Eleni refused to meet her gaze that there was a lot more to it than that. By inviting him here at the same time as Dani, Eleni had perhaps been hoping for yet another chance of reconciling her brother with her best friend.

Dani sighed in irritation. 'I really do have to go now, Eleni.'

'Surely you are not leaving on my account, Daniella?' Niccolo taunted softly, his voice moving like husky velvet across Dani's already sensitised flesh.

Dani's chin rose at the challenge she heard in his tone. 'No, I was leaving anyway,' she snapped.

Niccolo watched Daniella Bell from between narrowed lids, noting that she wore her red hair longer than when he had seen her at Eleni's engagement party a year ago. Now styled in layers, it tumbled fierily onto her shoulders and down her spine. Long, dark lashes were lowered over eyes he knew to be an unfathomable green. Her nose was small and pert and dusted with a dozen or so freckles. Her face was thinner than he remembered, her cheeks hollow, giving those softly pouting lips a fuller appearance above her determinedly pointed chin. Her loss of weight was also borne out by the slenderness of her waist and narrow hips, although her breasts were still firmly full.

And unless he was mistaken—and Niccolo felt sure that he wasn't—they were also naked beneath that clinging green sweater!

His mouth tightened. Ten years ago he had not approved of or understood Eleni's affection and friendship for the gawky English girl she had only known for less than a year, and had absolutely refused to allow his sister to complete her education in England so that she could remain in England with her new friend. Eleni had eventually complied with his decision, of course, and instead continued the friendship by telephone and letter.

Then, at the age of eighteen, a much more stubbornly determined Eleni had informed him that she intended attending an English university, and she had instantly met up with Daniella Bell again. If anything, the friendship between the two women had become all the stronger as they had matured.

Admittedly Daniella had grown into a self-assured woman of passable beauty, and Eleni reported she was very successful as an interior designer, but Niccolo still did not approve of her as a friend for his young sister. Even less so after Daniella's brief marriage two years ago, followed by an equally hasty divorce. It just proved how fickle she really was.

'I'll see you later.' Daniella moved to kiss Eleni on the cheek. 'Mr D'Alessandro.' She gave him a curt nod as she straightened.

Daniella didn't exactly approve of him either, Niccolo recognised with wry self-mockery.

'What? You have no parting kiss for me, Daniella?' he asked, a smile curving his lips as she stared at him incredulously.

'We're hardly kissing acquaintances, Mr D'Alessandro,' she finally managed to splutter in disgust.

'Possibly not.' He drawled his amusement. 'Perhaps when we meet again at the wedding…?'

Those green eyes flashed. 'I believe I will forgo that dubious pleasure!' she came back waspishly.

Niccolo's gaze was intent on Daniella as he ignored his sister's snort of laughter at his expense.

Daniella, he knew, had been in awe of him when they'd first met almost ten years ago—an awe that had quickly turned to infatuation. An infatuation he had been aware of, but had chosen to ignore, even to deliberately rebuff; to a man of twenty-seven years of age Daniella Bell's calf-like devotion as she'd watched his every move with those deep green eyes had been a danger as well as a nuisance.

It was an infatuation she'd seemed to have got over completely by the time the two of them had met again years later, when he'd delivered Eleni to England at the start of the university term.

But Daniella had grown up in the last five years, Niccolo recognised, and in her maturity she was certainly no longer in awe of him.

In fact, it was safe to say that over the last five years Daniella had become less in awe of him than any other person of his acquaintance!

As head of the D'Alessandro family, and of D'Alessandro Banking, Niccolo was accustomed to wielding power and authority, to having his every instruction obeyed. His domestic needs at the D'Alessandro palace—his title of prince had fallen into disuse several centuries ago—were supplied quietly and efficiently, usually before he had even made them known. And no one, in any sphere of his life, stood up to him or answered him back in the frank way that Daniella Bell did on the rare occasions they met.

'The prospect of the two of us ever kissing seems just

as unpleasant to me, I do assure you,' he said, deliberately baiting her.

'Then it's so nice to know we're agreed on something!' Daniella snapped, before turning sharply on her heel and leaving.

'Why do you do that, Niccolo?' Eleni asked gently once the two of them were alone.

He turned to look at his sister. 'Do what?'

'Behave like such a—a—an overbearing Venetian!' she accused.

'But Eleni, I *am* an overbearing Venetian,' he returned mockingly.

'Yes, but you don't have to keep proving it!' His sister glared at him.

Niccolo gave a rueful shake of his head. 'Your friend brings out the worst in me, I am afraid.'

'And you bring out the worst in her!' Eleni muttered with a frown.

Niccolo was unconcerned. 'Then it seems we are all agreed it is best if Daniella and I stay well away from each other.'

'I suppose so,' Eleni conceded heavily, disappointed they both so obviously felt that way.

'Cheer up,' Niccolo teased affectionately. 'After the wedding she and I will probably have no further reason ever to meet again.'

'What about my masquerade party in the summer?' his sister protested. 'The two of you are sure to meet again then.'

Not if Niccolo first ensured that he knew exactly which of Eleni's masked guests was Daniella Bell—and then avoided her like the plague!

CHAPTER ONE

Eight months later...

DANI was feeling hot and bothered by the time she arrived very late—it was well after ten o'clock—to Eleni's masquerade party.

A problem with a client had come up at the last moment, delaying her in getting ready. Then, when the taxi had arrived to drive her here, she'd realised she had another problem. It was an extremely warm evening, and her gown was made out of soft gold and very heavy velvet, and the hoops beneath the skirts kept springing up and almost hitting her in the face.

How on earth, Dani wondered wrathfully, had women ever managed to move around in these clothes two hundred and fifty years ago, let alone eat or drink in them?

Dani gave her cloak to Jamieson the butler after being admitted to the house, before moving to the mirror in the hallway to check her appearance. The gold mask she wore covered her face from brow to top lip, and her red hair was covered with the white powder that had been the fashion of those days. The low neckline of the gold gown showed an expanse of breasts pushed up to a creamy swell by a corset, which also held her waist nipped in tightly, and the full skirt billowed out and over the gold slippers that matched the dress.

Yes, she was as ready as she was ever going to be to face all the other guests, who were already outside in the romantically lit garden.

Eleni had telephoned Dani yesterday so that she could tell her all about her plans for the masquerade party. The garden was to be lit only by lamps and strings of coloured lights in the trees and bushes, with a small orchestra hired to add to the romance of the evening. But even so Dani was totally unprepared for the magical appearance of everything and everyone when she stepped outside on her way to the rose garden where Jamieson had told her Brad and Eleni were greeting their guests.

The costumes of the two hundred or so guests were exquisite, and the masks even more so—a lot of them intricately decorated, especially those worn by Eleni's Venetian relatives—giving Dani a feeling of unreality, as if she really had stepped back into another time.

It was easy to see how and why, with so many corners of the spacious garden left in darkness, those flirtations Eleni had spoken of took place!

Dani quickly made her way to the rose garden, keeping a wary eye out for Eleni's obnoxious brother—a man she thankfully hadn't seen in the eight months since Eleni and Brad's wedding, an occasion when they had all but ignored each other.

'Is that you, Dani?' Eleni greeted her warmly as soon as she saw her, her own Georgian-style costume an elegant red, her mask silver and her dark hair unpowdered.

'You aren't supposed to know it's me.' Dani frowned behind her mask.

'We discussed these dresses once—don't you remember?' her friend said as Dani moved to kiss a Duke-of-Wellington-costumed Brad.

As it happened, Dani did remember the time she and Eleni had lain under an oak tree in the school grounds, waxing lyrical about how romantic it must have been to live in the seventeen hundreds, with all those manly heroes from the historical novels they'd devoured. Until they had remembered that there had been no plumbing for instant hot baths in those times, nor the convenience of the telephone!

But like Eleni, Dani hadn't been able to resist wearing a beautiful gown in the style of that century this evening.

'You both look very beautiful,' Brad told them gallantly.

He was nothing like those dark, almost satanic heroes Dani and Eleni had once drooled over, with his hair a golden blond and his eyes blue, but there was no doubting the happiness of Eleni and Brad's marriage, Dani recognised almost wistfully, as Brad turned to give his wife a lingering kiss.

'Just tell me what Niccolo is wearing so that I can once again avoid him!' Dani begged of her friend as she realised she was holding up the receiving line.

'He's a p—'

'Just think of the D'Alessandro ancestry and you'll know him,' Eleni cut smoothly across Brad. 'And you see all those good-looking men gathered by the bar?' She nodded towards five men laughing and talking together as they sipped champagne. 'D'Alessandros every one,' she said with satisfaction. 'You met them all at the wedding last year, and I'm sure that any one of them would be pleased to oblige you, if you know what I mean…?'

'Very funny.' Dani shot her friend a silencing glare before moving off to join the rest of the guests strolling in the garden, knowing exactly what her friend was referring to even if Brad didn't. In the eight months since she had spoken to Eleni about her grandfather's will, Dani hadn't even come close to finding a solution to that particular problem.

But Eleni was right about the D'Alessandro men all being good-looking, Dani acknowledged ruefully as she stood a short distance away from them. All of them were dark-haired, very tall, with athletically fit bodies. In fact any one of them could be Niccolo, she realised in dismay.

One was dressed as a nobleman. Another as a priest. The third as a gondolier. The fourth was a nineteenth-century Italian soldier. The fifth was in Regency-style clothes.

Exactly what had Eleni meant by her cryptic comment about the D'Alessandro ancestry in reference to Niccolo's costume?

'Champagne…?'

She turned to find a rakish-looking pirate standing at her side—another one of Eleni's D'Alessandro cousins? This man's dark hair was pulled back and tied with a black bow at his nape, and a black mask covered his face from brow to top lip. Tight black trousers were tucked into black boots, emphasising the long length of his legs, a black sash was about his waist, and a long black leather tunic was worn over the white billowy shirt that was *de rigueur* for any respectable pirate.

Except pirates weren't respectable by definition, were they?

This one certainly didn't look as if he was. Dark, dark eyes glittered through the slits in the mask as his gaze roamed boldly over Dani, from her toes to her powdered hair and then back to her face behind the gold mask.

'Champagne…?' he prompted again huskily, and he held out one of the two glasses he held in his hands.

Dani swallowed hard, not taking her gaze off the pirate for even a second. It was one thing to fantasise about meeting a man like this when you were an impressionable teenager. Another thing altogether, at the age of twenty-four, to find yourself face to face with a man who looked as if he were every bit as dangerous as the pirate he was dressed as.

Which meant he *definitely* had to be a D'Alessandro cousin!

Still, it was a masquerade party, where no names were exchanged and there would be no expectations after tonight. Eleni was right; it could be fun for Dani to just anonymously enjoy herself for one evening.

Until ten minutes ago Niccolo had been finding the evening tedious. Conversation became louder as bottles of champagne began to disappear, the laughter too shrill, the flirtations more obvious—and the culmination of those flirtations was obvious as couples began to disappear off into the darkness of the garden.

But Niccolo had never particularly enjoyed the Venetian Festival, and he certainly had no intention of being lured into the privacy of the surrounding trees by any of the women who had so far tried to tempt him.

As usual, he had kept a wary eye out for the sharp-tongued Daniella Bell as each of the female guests had arrived, but at ten o'clock he had assumed that she either wasn't here at all or he had missed her in the crowd.

In fact, until he had seen the woman in the gold gown enter the garden, he had been considering taking a bottle of champagne and disappearing into the relative privacy of Eleni's conservatory.

The woman's hair was powdered white, and she had a heart-shaped beauty mark above her top lip. The creamy swell of her breasts was inviting above the low neckline of the gold gown, and her arms were white and slender, a gold fan held in one of her delicately graceful hands.

Her very stillness made her stand out from the rest of the guests as she looked slowly about her with an almost untouchable air of separation from those about her.

It was a feeling Niccolo easily recognised and related to. As head of the D'Alessandro family and banking consortium he had to keep himself apart out of necessity. The fact that he hadn't yet found a woman suitable to become the D'Alessandro bride only added to his aloofness.

But he put on hold his plan to disappear the moment he saw the woman in the gold gown. Instead he collected two glasses of champagne and made his way determinedly towards her before any of the other men present sensed her air of detachment and saw it as the same challenge he did.

She was even more alluring close up, her skin as pale as milk. The colour of her eyes was not discernible behind the mask in the poorly illuminated garden, but somehow Niccolo thought they would be blue. Her perfect bow of a mouth was highly erotic, with that heart-shaped beauty mark above the fuller top lip, and Niccolo believed the hair beneath the powder would probably be a rich burnished gold.

Dani felt slightly flustered by the intensity of that dark gaze—not sure that encouraging this man by accepting a glass of champagne would be a good idea. Although she had no doubt that the more mischievous Eleni wouldn't have hesitated.

'Thank you.' Her voice was husky as she took the glass of champagne the pirate presented to her, not quite managing to avoid touching the man's long, slender fingers as she did so, and feeling something like an electric jolt up her arm as her own fingers briefly made contact with his.

'Our hostess has strictly forbidden us the use of our own names,' he said with a wicked smile. 'So, if you have no objection, I would like to call you Belladonna.'

His voice was very deep and very sexy. Dani suddenly became aware that she was slowly being seduced.

'As in the poison?' she said pertly.

His teeth gleamed very white in the darkness as he grinned at her appreciatively. 'As in beautiful lady,' he corrected softly. 'And you *are* very beautiful.'

Dani's smile widened at the compliment. 'How can you possibly tell?'

'Would you really like me to tell you?'

Slowly being seduced? This man's intent had just gone up a couple of notches!

But it was fun, she realised with dawning wonder. More fun than she'd had in a very long time.

'Yes, please,' she invited.

'You have skin like white satin, a mouth that was surely made for kissing, and breasts—'

'I think perhaps you should stop there!' Had she thought only a couple of notches? Make that a dozen or so! She was starting to feel light-headed from all this flattery, and she had only sipped at the champagne.

'Perhaps for the moment…' He gave in gracefully with an inclination of his head. 'Would you care to dance?'

Would she? The idea certainly had its appeal. But who *was* this man? The dark hair, swarthy skin and slight accent gave no clue other than that he was probably a D'Alessandro relative. What if he should turn out—horror of horrors!—to be Niccolo D'Alessandro himself?

It would be just her luck, when they all removed their masks at midnight, to discover she had spent the evening flirting with Niccolo!

No, she realised with some relief as she glanced briefly across at the other D'Alessandro men. They had just been joined by a sixth man, even taller than they were and dressed very lavishly, and his regal air of arrogance was unmistakably that of Eleni's brother.

Dani relaxed slightly as she turned back to the pirate at her side. 'And what do I call you?'

'What would you like to call me?' he countered.

Dani felt a quiver of excitement down her spine as her body was suffused with a heat that was in no way connected to the warmth of this beautiful summer evening.

This really was a seductive experience, she thought. To be complimented, enticed by a man she didn't know, and who didn't know her, and whose attention seemed to be fixed intensely on her. No wonder the Venetian Festival was so popular!

She moistened her lips with the tip of her tongue, that butterfly fluttering in her stomach increasing as she sensed his dark gaze watching the movement.

'Come, Bella, what is your fantasy? Tonight I will be whoever you wish me to be.'

Dani hadn't even known she had a fantasy until now. 'Morgan,' she breathed. 'I would like to call you Morgan.'

'After the pirate Henry Morgan?' the pirate said with a nod. 'It is appropriate.'

Dani tilted her head. 'Although I somehow think you must be a relative of Eleni's…?'

He laughed. 'No names. No personal details. Those are the rules, are they not? Now, would you care to dance? Or perhaps a walk in the garden would be more to your liking?'

Dani eyed the dozen or so couples moving slowly to the music on the temporary dance floor that had been set up in front of the small orchestra, tempted by the idea of being taken in his arms—more than tempted. But did she really want to be that close to a man who already made her feel like behaving more recklessly than she ever had before?

For the moment, no…

'A walk, I think,' she accepted, careful not to touch him this time as he took the champagne glass from her and placed both of them on the tray of a passing waiter.

Despite her care in not touching him, he immediately took hold of her hand and placed it in the crook of his arm as they strolled through the dimly lit garden. His arm felt like tempered steel beneath her fingertips, the billowy sleeves of his shirt hardly any barrier to the heat of his skin at all.

Niccolo, sensing that his Belladonna was about to remove her hand from his arm, moved to place his other hand over the top of hers, determined not to relinquish this small contact with her.

She was enchanting, tiny perfection, her hand small and delicate beneath his much larger one, and the coloured lanterns and the light of the moon threw the beauty of her breasts and the bareness of her arms into shadowed relief.

He could never remember being this immediately attracted to any woman before. The muted lighting and softly romantic music no doubt added to the seduction of the evening, but nevertheless Niccolo knew it was the intriguing air of mystery that surrounded the woman at his side that gave such enchantment to the meeting and held him captive.

For once he didn't have to be the respected and respectable Niccolo D'Alessandro. His anonymity allowed him to be bolder, less reserved than was his normal custom. And he already knew where he wanted that boldness to take him with this woman... No doubt Eleni would be able to tell him exactly who his Belladonna was if he were to ask her, but Niccolo found that he didn't want to do that, preferring to savour each new discovery about this woman as it emerged.

He turned to her in concern as he felt the slight tremor of her tiny fingers beneath his. 'Are you cold?' he enquired as he looked down at her.

Those softly pouting lips curved into an enigmatic smile. 'Not at all,' she assured him.

Cold? Dani's thoughts echoed shakily. She was so

aware of this man, so sensitised to the almost feline strength of his body as he walked beside her, to the touch of the fingers that curved so possessively about hers, that she wasn't sure she could even think straight, let alone know whether she was hot or cold!

She was hot, she discovered when she concentrated on the question. Hot, hot, *hot*!

Every part of her felt tinglingly alive, and she was totally aware of the man beside her as she breathed shallowly, her breasts feeling full, her nipples hard and oh so sensitive as they pressed against her corset.

Again Niccolo felt the slight quiver of this woman's fingers beneath his. 'You *are* cold,' he insisted.

'Well—perhaps a little,' she allowed breathlessly.

Niccolo's gaze was riveted on the fullness of her slightly parted lips as she looked up at him. Their softness was an invitation he was finding it more and more difficult to resist.

He could no longer resist!

She tasted of champagne and honey, those lips as soft and delicious as Niccolo had imagined they would be. He gathered her close against him and feasted, sipping, tasting, deepening the kiss as he felt the surge of desire course through his body when he moulded her slender curves against him.

Dani was lost from the first moment those firmly sculptured lips claimed hers. And as she felt the leashed power behind her pirate's kiss, the hard throb of his thighs against hers, she knew that he wanted to do much more than just kiss her.

And, dear Lord, she wanted so much more than that too!

Tonight she wanted to forget everything else but this man and the seduction of the evening. Wanted to lose herself in the passion of his kisses and the promised pleasure of the hardness of his body.

She wanted him. Wildly. Frantically. Heatedly.

The realisation shocked her at the same time as she pressed her body longingly against his, her arms moving up about the broadness of his shoulders as her lips parted to deepen the kiss.

Nothing else mattered other than the intensity of the desire, the arousal, that surged through her body. The need to feel. To live only for this moment and to hell with tomorrow.

She moaned low in her throat as his hand moved from her waist to her breast, lingering there, cupping her, those long, warm fingers a caress on the bareness of her skin above the gown before they dipped lower, seeking and finding the hardened nub, and that single touch across the sensitised tip sent rivulets of pleasure throbbing between her thighs.

Her pirate's hands moved to cup her bottom and pull her against his thighs, against the rigid hardness there that told her of his own arousal. At the same time his tongue moved erotically across her bottom lip before surging beyond, capturing, claiming, as he tasted every part of her.

Niccolo wanted this woman now.

Right now!

His earlier aversion to couples disappearing off into the trees was totally forgotten as he held the woman of his dreams in his arms and tasted and caressed her with the same burning need, only the two of them existing as their kisses deepened hungrily.

Then a teasing laugh from somewhere amongst the shelter of the trees permeated the desire that had clouded his brain, and he drew abruptly back to rest his forehead against hers, his breathing ragged.

'I think perhaps we should go somewhere a little more—private. Do you agree?' he murmured ruefully.

She hesitated only fractionally before giving an affirmative nod of her head.

Niccolo moved back slightly, his hand sliding caressingly down her arm before he laced his fingers with her much smaller ones, only lingering long enough to once more kiss her hungrily on the lips before he turned to guide her towards the relative privacy of his sister's home.

Dani felt slightly dazed by the intensity of her arousal, was beyond thought, beyond anything but being the focus of this man's single-minded desire.

She wanted to be naked with him, wanted to touch and caress the broadness of his muscled back, ached to feel all that nakedness against her own. There would be plenty of time tomorrow, all her tomorrows, to be the much more cautious and emotionally bruised Dani Bell.

On paper she was a twenty-four-year-old divorcee. But the reality was different—so totally different.

Her disaster of a marriage to Philip had made her wary of men and physical relationships. As Eleni had once pointed out so succinctly, there had been no one in her life since the end of her marriage to Philip two and a half years ago.

The failure of that marriage had made her doubt her own attractiveness to men. But there was no doubting that her pirate found her attractive, that he wanted her, and part of her so ached to feel wanted, to feel desired, if not loved.

Nevertheless, she kept a wary eye out for Eleni as she and her pirate strolled back towards the house; she would never hear the end of it if her friend should spot Dani disappearing with one of her D'Alessandro cousins!

'I do not intend to do anything you do not want me to do,' Niccolo promised as he sensed the onset of doubt in the woman who walked so gracefully and silently beside him. At least he *hoped* he would have the control not to take things any further than this woman wanted them to go.

The reality was he wanted her so badly that his normally rigid control was in jeopardy of deserting him. Only the earlier interruption of that laugh had stopped him from enticing her into the trees with him and making love to her right then and there.

This immediacy was totally out of character for Niccolo.

There had been many women in his life over the last twenty years, and some of them had become a mistress for several months, but with none of them had he felt this driving need to know, to touch, to make love until they were both weak and satiated. And then start all over again.

Eleni's conservatory was in darkness as Niccolo opened the door and allowed the woman at his side to enter first, before closing and locking the door firmly behind them, shutting out the noise of the other partygoers and all but the muted strains of the small orchestra.

Dani's hand moved to cover his as he would have switched on one of the lamps. 'It's more—in keeping with the evening this way,' she whispered, inwardly knowing that if he switched on a light the magic of this encounter would be broken and she would run away—probably screaming.

Philip's uncontrollable and unwarranted jealousy had made Dani not just wary, but actually fearful of physical relationships, and she was sure that the only thing that was giving her courage now was the mask each of them was wearing and the anonymity the darkness afforded.

In fact, the veritable forest of exotic plants and trees that Eleni nurtured in her conservatory effected such a feeling of privacy, of heightened expectancy, that it seemed to Dani as if the two of them were alone on some lush desert island. Which was very fitting, considering he was dressed as a pirate!

'You've been here before?' he asked, as Dani confidently made her way to where the sofa and chairs were situated.

'Once or twice,' she replied, not wanting to give away even that much of herself.

Behaving with uncharacteristic recklessness was one thing, having this man discover her identity as Eleni's best friend was something else entirely!

She turned to face him, stepping closer to let her hands slide slowly up his silk-covered chest. 'We aren't supposed to be asking personal questions, remember?'

'I remember,' he murmured, as his arms moved about her waist to draw her close against him and his head lowered so that his lips could claim hers.

Heaven.

There was absolutely no other way for Dani to describe the pleasure that surged through her as the kiss deepened, as her lips parted to the silky caress of his tongue before it slowly entered her mouth.

Oh, God!

Dani's legs went weak at this slow, sensuous plundering, her arms tightening on his shoulders as she clung. He moulded her against him from breast to thigh, their legs entwined.

It had been too long, she acknowledged achingly. Far too long. And it had never been like this before. Ever.

Dani's head swam, her body feeling completely, totally alive as the man she knew only as Morgan continued to kiss her. His hands moved restlessly across her back before cupping her bottom and pulling her even tighter against him, allowing her once again to feel the heat of his arousal as her own thighs melted into liquid fire.

That heat intensified, became almost unbearable, as one of his hands caressed the bare tops of her breasts, igniting her so that she longed to have him caress her more fully, and her nipples were hard and aching for his touch as she pressed closer in silent appeal.

But the magic stopped, abruptly ceased, the moment she felt his hand move up to the ties at the back of her mask.

'No!' She broke the kiss to protest, breathing hard as she backed away slightly, cheeks burning, eyes feverish. 'No,' she repeated more calmly, as she sensed him looking at her questioningly. 'It's more—exciting this way, don't you think?'

More exciting? Niccolo mused wryly. If things became any more exciting the two of them were going to go up in flames! But perhaps she was right—perhaps it was the fact that they were both masked, their identities secret, that made this whole experience so uniquely erotic.

She moved her body enticingly against his, the elusive perfume of her skin, the way her breasts swelled above her low-cut gown, once again holding him in thrall.

Niccolo drew in a sharp breath as his body pulsed,

throbbed in answer to all that she was offering. 'I—' He
broke off as she pressed her fingertips against his mouth
and played them lightly over his bottom lip before one
dipped provocatively inside in silent invitation.

An invitation Niccolo was powerless to resist.

He held her against him and his tongue moved moistly
across her finger, licking, enticing, making it hot and wet.
The same way Niccolo wanted *her* as she lay beneath him.
Or on top of him. He didn't care which…

CHAPTER TWO

DANI quivered with excitement, with anticipation, as she turned in silent invitation and allowed him to slide the zip of her gown down the length of her spine, groaning low in her throat as his lips followed the same path before he straightened once again to turn her to face him.

She breathed shallowly as she lowered her arms to allow the gown to fall shimmering to the floor. She slipped her feet out of the gold slippers and dispensed with the cumbersome hoops to stand before him wearing only the tight corset with matching cream silk French knickers.

'No, leave it,' he growled throatily as Dani would have reached up to undo the twenty or so hooks down the front of the corset. His gaze was intent on her masked face as he threw off his waistcoat and the black sash before moving to stand in front of her. 'I have always wondered what it would be like to remove one of these,' he admitted. 'I am going to very much enjoy finding out.' His accent had thickened in his deepening desire.

Dani hoped that it felt as sensually arousing to him as it did to her as he slowly undid the hooks, one by one, as he savoured the moment her breasts were free and he could brush his fingers lightly over their pouting tips. Dani's breath caught in her throat as he lightly caressed the taut and swollen nipples.

She felt her knees go weak as he lowered his head and his lips claimed one temptingly pert bud, his tongue licking slowly, rhythmically, making her skin wet. Her nipple swelled in arousal inside his mouth as his teeth gently rasped against that sensitivity and he continued to taste and suckle.

Her hands moved up instinctively to cradle the back of his head and she held him to her, her back arched, her breathing ragged as pleasure surged hotly between her thighs and dampened her until she was hot and aching.

He moved the attentions of his lips and tongue to her other breast, licking, gently biting, while his hand captured its twin and caressed that hardened nub in the same pleasurable rhythm.

God, she was so excited, so aroused, Dani realised in trembling wonder. She was going to explode into a million pieces right here and now while this man was still fully dressed and she was wearing only her panties!

Her fingers clenched in the dark thickness of his hair as she held him against her. He increased the rhythm of his caressing tongue and his other hand moved from her breast to seek lower, cupping between her thighs. The pad of his palm pressed subtly, rhythmically, against the hardened nub nestling there. Pressing, caressing, until Dani felt an aching pleasure all centred there, before it spread out to every part of her body, hot and fierce, totally encompassing, and she arched against his caressing hand in a climax that seemed never ending.

Her knees buckled slightly and her head dropped forward to rest against the broadness of his shoulder as those spasms of pleasure finally began to lessen, her breathing ragged and sporadic.

'I don't— I've never— That was so—'

'You are beautiful!' Niccolo assured her with husky force even as his arms moved about her and he lifted her up to carry her to the sofa. He laid her down on its length, his gaze once again holding hers captive as he straightened to begin unbuttoning his shirt.

No woman had ever looked more beautiful to him, the glow of the moonlight giving her skin the appearance of alabaster against the cream silk underwear she wore, her eyes dark and satiated behind her mask. The posture of her body—turned slightly sideways on the sofa, with those small graceful hands resting on her thighs and the long silken legs bent slightly at the knees—was sensually enticing.

Niccolo left his shirt unbuttoned, revealing the dark hair of his chest and the flatness of his stomach, as his fingers dealt deftly with the fastening of his trousers.

'Let me.' She held her hand out in invitation. 'It's my turn to undress you,' she whispered, moving over on the sofa to make room for him to lie down beside her.

No part of Niccolo found objection to that invitation— not the surge in his already hardened shaft, the increased beat of his heart, or the clamouring inside him to feel those delicate hands against his naked body.

And God, those hands felt good as she pushed the sides of his shirt aside to lay them flat against his chest, light as butterfly wings as she moved up beside him, expression sultry, her bottom lip caught between tiny, even white teeth as she looked her fill of him and her hands touched and caressed him from shoulder to thigh.

Niccolo breathed in sharply, his stomach tightening, as one hand moved lower, beneath the waistband of his trousers, and she touched him lightly before curling her fingers about his rigid hardness.

He felt like steel encased in silk, Dani discovered as she pushed aside his clothing to slowly caress his arousal from tip to base and then back again. She revelled in the response of his long thickness as he moved slowly, sensuously, against her hand and fingers, in the increased raggedness of his breathing as her thumb caressed the sensitive tip and she felt the slight escape of moisture.

But she wanted more. Wanted it all. To taste him, not just touch and caress him.

She moved up on her knees beside him to slide his trousers and boxers down the long length of his legs and drop them down on the carpet beside them, holding his gaze as she parted his legs to move in between them and cup and hold him.

Then she finally looked down at him. He was long, hard and beautiful, she acknowledged, even as she lowered her head to capture him in her mouth, feeling emboldened, empowered, as she heard his groan of acceptance and surrender.

His hands came up to grasp her shoulders—not to push her away, as she had initially disappointedly thought, but to plead with her not to stop that rasping caress of her tongue or the rhythmic caress of her hands as she cupped and held him.

His groans became deeper, more ragged, with each

caress, and Dani wallowed in his pleasure as surely as if it were her own.

It *was* her own!

She had never known anything like this before, had never felt so uninhibited, so free to express her enjoyment in a man's body. In *this* man's body.

It was a beautiful, perfect male body, muscled and yet silky, his shoulders wide, his stomach flat, his thighs—Oh, God, his thighs…

'No more, little one!' he suddenly rasped fiercely, his fingers tight on her shoulders as he sat up to gently hold her away from him. 'I want to take off the rest of your clothes. Slowly. And then I want to kiss and caress you in the way you have just kissed me,' he explained.

Dani smiled as she knelt back to lift her own breasts to his dark, appreciative gaze before he lowered his head to draw one of those darkened nipples into his mouth as he slid the silk panties down her thighs.

In seconds she knelt completely, unashamedly naked in front of him, knowing by the raggedness of his breathing and the intensity of that dark gaze that he liked what he saw.

It was exhilarating, liberating, to be with a man like this, to just enjoy without doubt or responsibility…

She was perfection in the moonlight, Niccolo acknowledged achingly as she slid the shirt from his shoulders and down his arms. Her breasts full and pert, her waist slender, hips curvaceous, a lush triangle of hair at their apex, and her smile enticing as she lay back against the cushions.

He reached up and removed his mask—it had to be past midnight now—before bending to kiss first one dark-tipped breast and then the other, his hands dark against her much paler flesh as he trailed yet more kisses down her stomach to her navel, dipping his tongue into that sensitive well as he moved to lie between her parted legs.

Her skin was like velvet, and she groaned her pleasure at each stroke of his hand, that groan becoming a soft mewling noise as he moved lower still, seeking and finding the hardened nub between those silken curls to roll his tongue against it slowly, rhythmically, caressingly.

Dani felt boneless as waves of pleasure washed up and through her, turning to rigid tension as she felt another climax rapidly approaching.

It was too much—

She couldn't—

'Please,' she whispered. 'I want— I need—'

'Tell me what you need and want, my beautiful lady,' he encouraged gruffly.

'You,' she gasped, reaching down for him, fingernails digging into those broad shoulders. 'I need you!'

'Then you shall have me,' Niccolo assured her, moving up and over her. 'All of me.'

He gave a primeval groan as he entered her and buried himself inside her heat. He didn't move again for long, pleasurable seconds, just enjoying being inside her, and then he raised his head to watch the play of moonlight across her firm breasts with their deep rose tips.

Perhaps it really was the mystery that surrounded this woman, but he had never felt such incredible excitement, such intense pleasure, as he did here and now. Then he began to move slowly, and he knew that the pleasure that had come before was as nothing compared to what he was feeling now.

The pleasure intensified, grew hotter, stronger, until Niccolo wasn't sure he could bear more without exploding. He began to stroke deep inside her, his body gliding over and in hers as she began to make soft noises of excitement.

Niccolo held off as long as he could, promising himself to take longer next time, to take her to the edge of that peak again and again before taking her over it. But for now the need for release was too urgent, too intense for him to delay. And as he heard the first of her cries of release, felt her tighten and flex hotly about him, he allowed himself to let go too. A release made all the stronger, all the more satisfying, because they had reached it together.

Dani lay entwined with her pirate, their bodies slicked with sweat in the aftermath of their lovemaking. She stroked the loosened, overlong darkness of his hair as his head rested between her breasts. Both of them were too satiated to even attempt to move, and still too afraid of breaking the spell, the magic of the evening, by so much as saying one word.

And it had been magical. Beyond anything Dani had ever experienced before. This man had allowed her the freedom to explore and caress his body in a way she had never dared to do before with anyone else.

This man made her feel beautiful. She was beautiful in his arms. And that he had enjoyed their lovemaking too she was in absolutely no doubt. She could feel his satisfaction in the way he still caressed her body from breast to thigh—not in a sexual way, but out of the sheer pleasure of touching her.

But as she lay there in the silence, as she slowly became

aware of their surroundings, could once again hear the muted strains of the music and the people laughing and talking outside, the full import of what had just happened hit her like a slap in the face.

Dear God—there was recklessness and then there was *insanity*! And this, Dani realised belatedly, was insanity. She had made love with a perfect stranger—probably one of Eleni's *relatives*—in her friend's conservatory. And she continued to lie here naked in his arms when there were over two hundred guests outside in the garden!

Beautiful, ecstatic insanity. But insanity nonetheless.

And now it was over.

It had to be over…

'Have you fallen asleep?' Niccolo asked teasingly at the sudden stillness and silence of the woman who had such a short time ago met and equalled his desire in the most incredible, most erotic lovemaking he had ever known.

Their clothes, he noticed ruefully, were scattered all over the rug beside the sofa, their need for skin on skin having been absolute. He wanted this woman like that again. And again. Not here, in his sister's home, where they could be interrupted at any moment, but somewhere they could be completely themselves, where there would be no need for masks or artifice.

He wanted to know more about this woman—wanted to know everything there was to know about her. Wanted to look at her face, to see her wearing her long hair loose about her shoulders and nothing else.

'Would you like to leave?' he murmured. 'We could book into a hotel somewhere. For a week. A month. Longer!'

At this moment the world of D'Alessandro Banking seemed unimportant. She was the only thing that mattered right now—and for some time to come, he felt sure.

'Belladonna…?' he prompted as he raised his head to look down at her.

Dani gave a muted gasp, and then ceased to breathe at all as she recognised the unmasked beauty of the face above hers in the moonlight.

Her heart seemed to stop beating and the blood froze in her veins.

The world itself seemed to stop spinning on its axis.

The man above her, lying naked beside her, the man she had just made love with so wonderfully, so completely, was *Niccolo D'Alessandro*!

'What is it, *cara mia*?' He frowned down at her with concern. 'Do not tell me that you are suddenly feeling shy?' he teased.

Shy? After the intimacies she had just shared with this man?

Niccolo D'Alessandro…

And she had—

And then he had—

Oh, Lord.

But Niccolo obviously had no more idea of her true identity than she'd had of his. There was no way he would have flirted with Dani Bell in that way. Would have seduced Dani Bell so single-mindedly in the moonlight. Would have made love to Dani Bell with such intensity and passion.

He *couldn't* know it was her!

The D'Alessandro ancestors had been priests, princes— and *pirates*, she belatedly recalled.

And she couldn't bear for this pirate to realise who his lover was. To have the warmth fade from those beautiful dark eyes as they assumed their usual expression of contempt whenever he looked at her. But how could she get out of here without Niccolo discovering the truth?

He had given her the opening himself, she realised with dawning hope.

She moistened her lips before speaking. 'A hotel sounds good. But I don't think we should leave without at least one of us making our excuses to Eleni or Brad.'

Dani's thoughts were racing now. If Niccolo left the conservatory to talk to Eleni or Brad, and if she could get dressed quickly enough, she might—just might—be able to get out of here and away from the house before Niccolo came back.

'The two of us going to a hotel together only sounds "good"?' His expression was amused as he moved to sit beside her on the sofa before turning to trail light fingertips over her body from her throat down to her thighs.

Dani trembled as her body instantly came alive to his touch, her nipples hardening, tightening to aroused pebbles, and the heat returning between her thighs.

This was *Niccolo*, she reminded herself impatiently. The man who made no secret of his utter contempt for her.

'More than good. Wonderful,' she corrected abruptly, just wanting him to leave so that she could get out of here.

'That is better.' Niccolo nodded his satisfaction, his gaze hooded as he stood up. 'I will not be long,' he promised as he moved to pull on his clothes, steeling himself not to lie back down beside her and make love to her all over again.

But there would be plenty of time for that once they

reached the hotel. Plenty of time to learn all there was to know about this beautiful and responsive woman.

Niccolo could never remember feeling such possessiveness before during a relationship—this need to know a woman in every way. Perhaps that was because this wasn't a relationship. Yet. But it was going to be. He didn't intend letting this woman out of his life, his bed, until they had completely slaked their desire for each other.

Which could take some time, he decided, when he only had to look at her for his body to harden with renewed desire!

'The sooner you leave…' Dani encouraged, with a lightness she was far from feeling.

The realisation that she had just made love with Niccolo still made her feel weak at the knees, and she was only just managing to hold down her nausea as she imagined the darkness of his rage if he should learn her identity tonight.

But there was no reason why he should ever find out who she was—if Dani could just manage to get away before he returned…

'Five minutes,' he stated as he strode forcefully towards the door.

Dani's encouraging smile vanished as soon as Niccolo had gone.

She had only minutes in which to dress and leave—to escape like one pursued!

It couldn't be done!

It *had* to be done, Dani decided grimly as she quickly began to throw her clothes back on. Not the corset. She really didn't have time for all those hooks just now—

If she could just make it to the front door undetected she

could make good her escape—would walk all the way back home if she had to.

Once there she didn't ever have to open her door again. Never had to see Niccolo D'Alessandro ever again…

CHAPTER THREE

'DANI! I've been trying to contact you all day; where on earth are you?' Eleni demanded late on Sunday evening, when Dani finally took the call on her mobile.

Dani was well aware of the fact that Eleni had been trying to reach her all day—she had just chosen not answer any of her friend's telephone calls until now.

Mainly because she had no idea what to say to her. Or what Eleni was going to say. Surely that all depended on whether or not Eleni was aware of Dani's...*encounter* with her brother the previous evening?

'I'm at Wiverley Hall.'

'What are you doing there?' Eleni sounded puzzled.

Good question!

Hiding, seemed to pretty well answer it...

Dani had come up with the idea of visiting her parents—of removing herself from London completely—as she'd tried to find a taxi after the masquerade to take her back into the city. She had realised that to stay at her apartment was unthinkable. Niccolo could come storming over at any moment demanding an explanation for her behaviour, once he discovered she had been the woman in the gold gown.

Because it was inevitable that he would find out eventually. After all, Eleni knew exactly which of her female guests had been dressed in the gold gown and mask the previous evening, and Niccolo only had to ask her to find out the unwelcome truth.

Of course there was always the possibility that Niccolo, having returned to the conservatory to find his mystery lady had flown, would be too angry or too proud to actually ask his sister who the woman in the gold gown had been. But as Dani recalled the intensity of the passion they had shared, along with Niccolo's determination to spend the rest of the night with her, she knew it was very likely a remote hope.

'Visiting my parents and grandfather, of course,' she said with false lightness.

'You left last night without saying goodbye,' Eleni reproved.

'I did try, but I couldn't find you in all the crush.'

'Dani?'

'Yes?'

Eleni's sigh could be heard. 'Dani, Niccolo looked for you last night after you left without saying goodbye.'

'For me?' She feigned surprise even as her fingers tightened about her mobile. 'Why on earth would he do that?'

'Dani, please don't,' her friend rebuked her gently. 'I *know* you were the woman with Niccolo last night, and that's why you left the party so suddenly.'

Dani sat down abruptly on the bed in the bedroom that had been hers since childhood. But she didn't see the rosettes she had won as a child at gymkhanas still pinned on the wall. Or the long shelves of books. Or the pretty lace canopy over the bed that had been added when she was a teenager. All Dani could see was Niccolo D'Alessandro's face. His incredibly angry face...

'Does Niccolo know the woman was me?' she breathed tremulously, abandoning all hope of convincing Eleni that she had no idea what she was talking about.

'Not yet,' Eleni said. 'But he's going to,' she warned. 'I feigned complete ignorance last night when he sought me out and pressed me to tell him who the woman in the gold gown had been, but I doubt I'll be able to keep the truth from him for long. Dani, what did you and Niccolo *do* last night?'

What *hadn't* they done? That was probably more the question!

Just thinking about the previous evening, the intimacies she had shared with Niccolo, was enough to make Dani blush—unbecomingly—to the roots of her red hair.

She rushed into speech. 'I didn't know it was him, okay? You've always made such a big thing about your Venetian cousins, how handsome and charming they all are—that I just assumed it was one of them when he began to flirt with me.'

'Niccolo *flirted* with you?' Eleni sounded disbelieving.

He had done a lot more than flirt. They both had.

Dani had never behaved like that in her life before.

And she would never behave like that again either!

Not now she recognised there was no such thing as pleasure without responsibility.

'Yes,' she confirmed huskily. 'I—I didn't know it was Niccolo!'

'You already said that,' Eleni pointed out dryly. 'Didn't you pick up on my hint about the D'Alessandro ancestry?'

'If I had, do you really think I would have spent the evening with your arrogant brother?' she groaned.

'Probably not,' Eleni allowed.

'Eleni, you *can't* think that I wanted to— That I ever intended to spend the evening with Niccolo, of all people?' she gasped incredulously.

'I really don't know what to think, Dani,' her friend replied. 'All I know is that my big brother is behaving completely out of character and insisting on finding the mystery woman he met last night at my masquerade party.'

Niccolo was still looking for her? Dani gulped.

No, he wasn't looking for her, she reassured herself. Niccolo was looking for the woman who had attracted him the previous evening.

The woman who had returned that attraction.

The woman who'd had wild sex with him in his sister's conservatory!

Dani had never experienced anything like it in her life before, and she still felt hot all over just at the thought of it.

'You were the one who told me that was what the masks were for,' she reminded her friend defensively. 'So that people could behave out of character safely hidden behind them.'

'How "out of character" did you behave, Dani?' Eleni asked.

'Very,' she answered tightly.

'How very…?'

'Very, *very*.'

'Oh.'

'Eleni, are you going to tell Niccolo it was me?'

'It isn't a question of my telling or not telling, Dani. Brad knows it was you, too,' Eleni warned. 'So far Niccolo hasn't thought to ask him about the woman in the gold gown, but it's probably only a matter of time…'

'He'll forget about me in a few days, and then—'

'Niccolo doesn't forget *anything*,' Eleni interrupted ruthlessly. 'And whatever the two of you did last night it certainly seems to have made an impact.'

'Eleni, *please*—'

'Dani, tell me that none of this has anything to do with your grandfather's will.'

'My grandfa—?' Dani was stunned. 'What on earth do you mean, Eleni?'

'If you remember, I once joked about you seducing one of my cousins…'

'Eleni, you can't *seriously* think that I— You don't think that I would *deliberately*—' Dani was beyond stunned now—she was speechless.

'Actually, Dani, I don't believe what *I* think is all that important, do you?'

Dani became very still as the full import of the possible consequences of last night struck her.

Eight months ago her grandfather had changed his will to stipulate that Dani had to provide a Bell heir before he died, or her parents would lose their home as well as their living.

And last night Dani had made love with a man she had believed to be a complete stranger, which was completely out of character for her.

All of which Eleni knew.

She had obviously drawn her own conclusions about Dani's motives for her uncharacteristic behaviour the previous evening. Conclusions that Niccolo, if he learnt of that clause in her grandfather's will, would no doubt also draw.

Eleni was right. It didn't matter what she personally thought of Dani's behaviour the previous evening; it was what Niccolo believed that was going to be important…

'Your mother told me I would find you out here.'

Dani almost fell over the bucket of feed she had given her horse while she rubbed him down after her morning ride as she heard the grimness of Niccolo D'Alessandro's voice just behind her.

Niccolo was here—at her parents' home in Gloucestershire?

Dani's movements were measured, carefully precise, as she placed the brush down on the straw before straightening to rub her wet hands nervously down the thighs of her jeans and then slowly turn to face Niccolo. A Niccolo who looked as grim-faced as his tone had implied he was going to be.

There was no mistaking the tension of his body either. In a black tee shirt that stretched tautly over those wide shoulders and fitted jeans, it was as if he were barely repressing his anger.

As if?

If Niccolo was here for the reason Dani thought he was, then there was no doubting he was angry. No—furious, she amended as she found herself unable to break her own gaze away from the intensity of his glacial brown eyes.

'Niccolo.' She forced the muscles in her face to relax as she moved to look at him enquiringly over Jet's back. 'What on earth are you doing here?'

'Do I *really* need to spell it out, Daniella?' Those dark eyes glittered dangerously.

She would rather that he didn't. She had spent the last few days convincing herself that her time in his arms hadn't happened at all! But with Niccolo standing only feet away, and with every nerve ending in her body, every one of her senses, screaming her awareness of him, that was no longer an option.

She knew this man. Had touched and caressed every part of him. And no amount of wishing otherwise was ever going to change that.

Perhaps that saying should be Act in haste, repent at leisure? From the anger she could feel emanating in her direction from Niccolo's rigid body he was going to do more than make her repent.

'The two of us need to go somewhere and talk,' he said icily when she didn't answer him, and that coldness sent a chill of apprehension down Dani's spine.

She wasn't ready for this—would she ever be? She had simply naively hoped as the days, almost a week, had crawled past, with no sign of Niccolo, that he must have returned to Venice without finding out the identity of his mystery woman.

One glance at Niccolo's absolutely livid expression and Dani knew that was no longer true...

'Talk about what, Niccolo?' she stalled lightly, at the same time continuing to keep the black stallion that her father had given her for her twenty-first birthday between them. Jet shifted restlessly in his stall as he obviously sensed her tension.

Niccolo's mouth twisted scathingly. 'Oh, I think you

know, Daniella. Or should I call you *Belladonna*?' he added, his voice now lethally soft.

Dani's stomach felt as if the bottom had just dropped out of it, and she could feel her hands begin to tremble as she fought for breath.

This confrontation was worse, so much worse than she had ever imagined that it would be. In those imaginings she had been able to laugh off the incident as unimportant, as just a bit of fun. Niccolo didn't look as if he found any of this in the least amusing. Or ever would!

But she tried again. 'Belladonna?' She shook her head. 'I have no idea what you're talking about—'

'Do not even *try* to deny it was you that night, Daniella!' Niccolo cut in harshly, not in any sort of mood to play games.

He had spent all his time these last few days discreetly eliminating every woman who had been at Eleni and Brad's party that evening, finally coming down to the one woman no one could account for.

Daniella Bell.

Incredible as that possibility had seemed to him at first, the more Niccolo had thought about it the more it had become a reality. The woman in gold had been the right height and size to be Daniella, and the white powder would have hidden the brightness of her red hair. And she would easily have been able to disguise the normally brisk tone with which she normally addressed him with that huskily seductive, totally unrecognisable voice.

It had been a little more difficult imagining that Daniella could possibly be the sexily uninhibited woman who had made love with him. But having openly confronted Eleni this morning, Niccolo now knew that woman had indeed been Daniella Bell.

Incredible, but nevertheless true.

And his anger hadn't abated in the least during his drive to Gloucestershire in order that he might confront Daniella with the truth face to face. In fact it had settled like a cold, leaden weight in his chest.

Daniella's evasiveness now, as she shot him apprehensive glances from beneath lowered dark lashes, only increased the intensity of that fury.

She was wise to feel apprehensive—at the moment Niccolo was clenching his hands into fists at his sides in an effort to stop himself from reaching out and wringing her slender neck!

'Why did you do it, Daniella?' he growled.

'Why?' she echoed hollowly.

He nodded grimly. 'Explain to me why you made love with me that night and then disappeared before I could discover who you really were.'

Dani drew in a ragged breath. 'Niccolo—'

'Could we get out of here?' he asked impatiently as Jet swung his head dangerously close to him and bared his teeth. 'Your horse obviously does not like me,' he added dryly.

She moved to run a soothing hand down the length of Jet's nose. 'You're making him nervous.'

'And you?' Niccolo spoke softly—dangerously so. 'Am I making you nervous too, Daniella?'

He was frightening the life out of her, if the truth were known!

Niccolo cutting and sarcastic she was used to. Niccolo

totally indifferent to her she could accept too. But this Niccolo, cold and threatening, his anger barely leashed, was terrifying.

But damn it, he had been a willing participant that night—more than willing! And he couldn't deny that he had enjoyed it because he had been the one to suggest they book into a hotel so that they might continue doing more of the same.

Her chin rose as her gaze met his challengingly. 'Why are you making such a fuss, Niccolo?' she asked waspishly. 'We're both over the age of consent, and you can't deny we had a good time that night.' She shrugged slender shoulders. 'So why can't you just leave it at that, hmm?'

Because he couldn't do it. That was why. Much as he had tried, Niccolo hadn't been able to get the memory of the woman in the gold gown out of his head—hadn't been able to forget making love with her.

He had been so determined to find her again that he had delayed his return to Venice by several days in order to continue his search.

He still found it incredible that his search had ultimately led him to this woman.

Had she known it was him that night?

Had she known and found all the more pleasure—amusement, perhaps?—in knowing that Niccolo had no idea with whom he was making love?

He had questions, many of them, and he did not intend leaving until Daniella had answered them all.

His impatience was not improved by the fact that at this moment he was completely aware of Daniella, in the over-large tee shirt she was wearing over fitted jodhpurs and brown riding boots. That he knew exactly what she looked like beneath those clothes and how to caress and kiss that body in order to give her the ultimate in pleasure.

His mouth tightened. 'I have no intention of *just leaving* anything, Daniella,' he rasped. 'I want an explanation for your behaviour last weekend, and I want it *now*!'

She shook her head. 'I'm busy, Niccolo—'

'You will get yourself out of that stall right now, Daniella, or I will come in and get you!' he threatened.

He would too, Dani acknowledged heavily. Even Jet's restless movements, the stamping of his hooves, wouldn't deter Niccolo if he decided to come in and get her.

'Fine—I'll walk you back to your car,' she snapped, giving Jet one last reassuring pat before moving to the stall door. 'But I really don't have anything else to say about last Saturday,' she told him as she let herself out into the yard.

It was busy at this time of the day, all the stable lads and girls having returned from their early-morning canter and now rubbing down and feeding their mounts. Their chatter and laughter was at complete odds with the feeling of rapidly increasing doom that held Dani in its grip.

'Eleni told me these are your father's stables,' Niccolo remarked evenly as the two of them left the busy yard and walked in the direction of the huge manor house.

Dani eyed him warily. 'Yes.'

'I believe he is very well thought of as a trainer?'

'Yes.'

'I suppose you have been riding since before you could walk?'

'More or less.'

'Daniella, can you not at least give me credit for trying to effect some semblance of normality by conversing in this way?' Niccolo glared down the length of his arrogant nose at her.

Normality? How could anything possibly be *normal* between the two of them ever again?

Maybe she should have thought of that last weekend?

Maybe she would have done if she had realised her pirate Morgan was actually Niccolo D'Alessandro!

But she couldn't really say she had been thinking at all that night. She had simply savoured the moment and allowed herself to forget all her troubles, if only for a short time. She had been as devastated that night at discovering Niccolo was her pirate as he probably was now at finding out she was his Belladonna.

She couldn't even look at Niccolo now without remembering the intimacies they had shared—the response of his body to her caresses, the pleasure she had felt as he thrust deep inside her...

This was *not* helping, Dani rebuked herself impatiently.

'Perhaps you would like me to comment on the weather?' she taunted him naughtily. 'I believe that's always good for a few minutes' normal conversation.'

Niccolo turned to give her a narrow-eyed glare, his mouth tightening even further as his frustrated anger deepened dangerously.

If Daniella imagined this was any more comfortable for him than it was for her, that driving to her parents' home in order to confront her with the truth had been easy for him to do, then she was mistaken. She was the last woman Niccolo would have chosen to have this conversation with!

Niccolo turned to look down at her as they reached the black sports car he kept garaged at his house in England. The warm breeze ruffled the fiery length of her hair, revealing the wide brow and high cheekbones that had been hidden by a mask the last time the two of them had talked. Talked? They hadn't really talked at all—they had been too busy kissing and pleasuring each other to talk!

He had to stop thinking about that night, Niccolo told himself sternly. Maybe it *had* been the most sexually enjoyable night of his life, but the reality—knowing it was Daniella Bell he had been making love with—surely made the whole thing ludicrous.

He did not even like her. He had not considered her a good influence on Eleni when the two girls were younger, even less so when Eleni came to London to go to university, and the fact that Daniella's brief marriage had barely survived the honeymoon had only served to confirm that she was no example for Eleni to emulate.

But somewhere in the last ten years, Niccolo acknowledged with grudging awareness, she had matured into a beautiful woman, her body slender and lithe, her movements graceful, her eyes a beautiful translucent green, her mouth—

No! He would not think about that perfect bow of a mouth, nor the way it had pleasured him almost a week ago!

'So?' She looked up at him challengingly. 'What is it you want to know, Niccolo?'

His mouth thinned at her aggression. 'I have already told you,' he bit out. 'I want to know why. I want to hear from your own lips exactly why you did what you did.'

Daniella raised auburn brows. 'Why I did what *I* did?' she retorted heatedly. 'I seem to recall that *you* were the one who talked to me first! Who asked me to walk with him? Who kissed *me*? Who suggested we go somewhere more private? I certainly don't remember hearing you complaining at the time!'

Of course Niccolo hadn't complained—he had been totally sexually enthralled!

As he knew he would be again if he should ever take this woman in his arms....

So long as the lights were out and he couldn't actually see who he was making love with!

'I am well aware of the sequence of events last Saturday evening, Daniella,' he snarled. 'And now I know exactly who they happened with!'

Her expression was scornful as she shook her head. 'If my identity is the only problem you have with what happened, then I suggest you just forget about it and move on.'

'Have *you* forgotten it, Daniella?'

Dani would never forget that night. Not one single moment of it.

It had been magical. Wonderful. Exhilarating. Liberating. And not even the fact that her lover had turned out to be Niccolo D'Alessandro could ever change that.

In fact, Dani had come to realise that knowing her lover was Niccolo only made it more memorable. The infatuation she'd felt for him ten years ago hadn't died or been crushed under the force of his cutting sarcasm, after all, but had deepened into something else. Something she had kept well hidden. Even from herself....

Maybe she hadn't consciously known it was Niccolo she was making love with on Saturday night, but had some inner part of her—some inner sense, the part of her that still found him so devastatingly attractive—actually told her who it was?

The more Dani thought about her impetuous behaviour that night, the more she believed it was more than a possibility.

But she had to protect herself. 'Of course I've forgotten all about it,' she lied.

Niccolo's eyes narrowed to dark slits as he spoke even more icily, if that were possible. 'So you make a habit of making love with men you do not even know and then conveniently forgetting about them?'

He'd meant to be insulting, Dani recognised heavily—and he had succeeded.

But if she defended herself, if she said no she didn't, then Niccolo was going to demand to know why she had made an exception in his case.

And her reasons were too complicated.

Or too simple!

There were those hidden feelings for him, of course, but there was also another explanation. She was tired, worn down by worry over her grandfather's will on her parents' behalf. The attention of her seductive pirate last weekend had lifted her out of all that, had transported her into another world—a world of light-hearted fun that had deepened into intense sexual tension and the indescribable pleasure that followed.

Not an excuse, perhaps, but it was certainly an explanation.

None of which she could possibly confide to Niccolo D'Alessandro!

'I don't make a habit of it, no,' she answered lightly. 'But I very much doubt I'm the first woman to indulge in a little—what was it you called it that night?—fantasy, I believe. *Morgan*,' she added pointedly, and was rewarded by a fierce frown. 'I certainly don't see why you're making such a big thing out of it.'

'You do not?' he grated.

'Not at all. After all—'

'You are the best friend of my sister,' Niccolo cut in furiously. 'Does that fact not make this a "big thing"?' he challenged.

Dani winced. It did make things a little awkward, she had to admit, and it was certainly not something that she and Eleni would ever be able to laugh about. But surely the awkwardness of the situation was for the two women to work out, not Niccolo?

'Hello, there!'

Dani flinched as she easily recognised her grandfather's strident tones, turning slowly to watch him as he strolled down the front steps of Wiverley Hall.

Still tall and erect, his bearing military even though he had retired from the army over twenty years ago, Daniel Bell had a full head of iron-grey hair and a neatly trimmed moustache. His clothes—a checked jacket over a twill shirt worn with brown corduroys—added to his 'country squire' image.

'We've been waiting for you to bring your visitor up to the house, Daniella,' he reproved as he joined them in the driveway.

Introducing Niccolo to any of her family—least of all

her tactlessly outspoken grandfather—was not something Dani wanted to do. But in the circumstances it seemed she had little choice…

'Grandfather, this is Niccolo D'Alessandro,' she said stiffly. 'Niccolo, my grandfather—Major Daniel Bell.'

'Sir.' Niccolo shook the other man's hand.

'D'Alessandro…' Her grandfather repeated slowly. 'Any connection with the D'Alessandro Bank?' He eyed the younger man speculatively.

Niccolo inclined his head. 'It is the family business, yes.'

Dani couldn't help but notice the increased speculation in her grandfather's shrewd expression. Obviously her grandfather was perfectly aware of the prestigious D'Alessandro Bank. And there was one thing that could be said about her grandfather—he was never averse to a little social snobbery!

'Well, I hope you've come here to cheer Daniella up, D'Alessandro,' her grandfather continued briskly. 'Girl's been moping around here for almost a week now—'

'Grandfather!' Dani exclaimed sharply, aware of the amused twist to Niccolo's mouth as he obviously enjoyed her discomfort.

Eyes the same colour green as her own met hers unapologetically. 'Only telling the truth, young lady. I trust my granddaughter has invited you to join us for lunch?' He turned his narrowed gaze on the younger man.

Dani's breath caught and held in her throat as she too turned to look at Niccolo.

She didn't want him to stay to lunch.

And she was pretty sure that Niccolo didn't want to accept the invitation, either.

But that didn't mean he wasn't going to…

CHAPTER FOUR

NICCOLO sensed Daniella's silent plea for him to refuse her grandfather's invitation to join her family for lunch. And a part of him—a large part, he had to admit—wanted to refuse. Now that he had confirmed it had been Daniella last weekend he just wanted to leave—to get as far away from her as he possibly could. But another part of him wanted something quite different….

'Niccolo has to get back to London. Don't you, Niccolo?' Daniella prompted, her gaze forceful as it met his.

He eyed her consideringly. That she wished him to leave—that she wished he had never come here in the first place—had never been in any doubt. The very fact that she obviously wanted that so badly perversely made Niccolo want to stay.

He shrugged. 'I am sure I have time to join you and your family for luncheon before I go.'

Daniella paled. 'I—'

'Well, of course you do.' Daniel Bell nodded his satisfaction with the arrangement. 'I'll take Mr D'Alessandro to the drawing room to meet Beatrice and Jeffrey while you go upstairs to shower and change, Daniella,' he added with a disapproving glance at her clothing.

Dani couldn't believe this was happening!

Niccolo couldn't really have any desire to prolong this torturous meeting, let alone further his acquaintance with any of the Bell family. Her grandfather's motive for the invitation was easy to guess; he just saw Niccolo—as he did any reasonable red-blooded man—as a possible father to the Bell heir. But she was sure that Niccolo's only intent in accepting the invitation was to make her feel uncomfortable.

How could she have been such a fool last Saturday? How could she not have known her fantasy lover was the arrogantly forceful Niccolo D'Alessandro?

Because she hadn't, that was how. Because she hadn't wanted to know. And now Niccolo was making her pay for that mistake.

One glance at Niccolo's face was enough to tell her how much he was enjoying her discomfort. Those dark eyes were glittering with mockery, those sculptured lips quirked into a derisive smile.

It was a self-satisfied smile that she wanted to wipe off those taunting lips!

'Perfect,' she accepted lightly. 'This way I'll be able to join you on your drive back to London, Niccolo, instead of spending hours sitting on an overcrowded train later this evening.'

Her gaze met his in glittering challenge. His expression didn't alter, but those dark, dark eyes took on a glitter as intense as her own. 'It would be my pleasure,' he finally said curtly.

Like hell it would, Dani thought happily. The last thing she wanted was to spend three hours in the confines of a car with Niccolo, but the fact that she knew he didn't want to spend those three hours with her, either, meant she intended doing exactly that.

And she'd thought *he* was being perverse! Feeling as they did about each other, they would probably both end up with indigestion from trying to eat lunch together, followed by three hours of awkward silence on the drive back to London.

But it would be worth it, Dani decided stubbornly, if only to show Niccolo that she had no intention of feeling guilty for what had happened last weekend. That she didn't care about his opinion of her.

Even if she did…

Just seeing Niccolo again, remembering the intimacies they had shared, was enough to show her that leaving London so hastily the previous weekend had achieved nothing. Seeing Niccolo again today only made her ache to repeat the experience.

It was at complete odds with the aversion Dani had felt towards physical relationships after her brief marriage to Philip, but she only had to look at Niccolo, at the broad width of his shoulders, his flat stomach and tapered thighs, to want him all over again.

But maybe she should tell him exactly what he was letting himself in for by accepting her grandfather's invitation to eat with them.

She broke away from the intensity of his gaze. 'Grandfather, would you mind very much if I just have a brief word with Niccolo in private? I promise I will point him in the direction of the sitting room as soon as we've finished talking,' she assured him as she saw her grandfather was about to protest.

'If you really must,' he allowed tightly, but he looked most displeased by this change in his arrangements.

It was a displeasure Dani refused to back down from. 'I really must,' she said firmly.

Her grandfather shot her one last narrow-eyed glare before turning to Niccolo. 'Don't let my granddaughter keep you out here too long,' he advised, before turning to stride stiff-backed into the house.

Dani waited only long enough for him to be safely out of earshot before turning back to Niccolo. 'What do you think you're doing?' she demanded fiercely.

Niccolo had been expecting this—had known from the outset that Daniella did not want him to accept the invitation to lunch; it was the very reason he had accepted!

'Politely accepting an invitation to luncheon with your family, I thought.'

'Why?'

He gave a humourless smile. 'It has obviously not occurred to you that I have driven for almost three hours this morning and would appreciate something to eat and drink before repeating the journey.'

Her eyes narrowed to green slits. 'You don't have to do that here—you could find any number of suitable places to eat on your way back to London.'

Niccolo gave an unconcerned shrug. 'I choose to do so here.'

Daniella shook her head. 'You'll regret it.'

Niccolo became very still as he looked down at her with hooded eyes. 'Are you threatening me, Daniella?'

She gave another shake of her head, her smile as humourless as the one he had given her seconds ago. 'I'm trying to warn you. The Bells, although you haven't yet had the chance to witness it, are your typical twenty-first-century dysfunctional family.'

Niccolo's mouth quirked. 'In what way?'

'In every way,' Dani said impatiently, knowing he wasn't taking this conversation seriously at all. 'My mother runs the house and gardens with grace and style. My father is a very successful trainer of racehorses—'

'And you, Daniella?' Niccolo taunted. 'Eleni tells me that you are a *very successful* interior designer.'

'So they say,' Dani confirmed, choosing to take his words at face value and ignore the sarcasm. 'But the truth of the matter is that my mother and father do not own Wiverley Hall and the stables; my grandfather does. And it is something that he never lets his son and daughter-in-law, or his disappointment of a granddaughter, ever forget.'

Niccolo looked at her searchingly, doubting for a moment that Daniella could be sincere in her warning. Admittedly Niccolo had only met Daniel Bell for a few minutes, and he was sure that Daniella knew her grandfather much better than he did, but the scenario she presented sounded a little extreme.

'In what way is he disappointed with his granddaughter?'

Daniella gave the ghost of a smile. 'I might have known you would pick up on that part of the statement. Probably because you share that disappointment…'

Disappointment was the last emotion Niccolo felt towards Daniella. He wasn't yet sure what emotions he *did* feel for her, but he was pretty sure disappointment was not amongst them.

'Do not change the subject, Daniella,' he advised harshly.

'I've been married and divorced, and all without producing the Bell heir,' she told him flatly. 'An unforgivable omission as far as Grandfather Bell is concerned.'

Dani regretted having even started this conversation; her grandfather's feelings towards her and her parents were none of Niccolo's business.

'Never mind—ten minutes in the company of the Bell family and you'll see exactly what I mean,' she said. 'Come into the house and I'll show you where the drawing room is—let me go, Niccolo!' she gasped as he suddenly reached out and grasped her arm.

He looked at her intently for several long, deliberate seconds before slowing releasing her. 'This conversation is not over, Daniella,' he warned softly.

As far as Dani was concerned it should never have begun!

But she didn't have any more time to argue about it now; she had to get herself quickly showered and changed before returning downstairs. The less time she left Niccolo alone with her parents—and with her obviously matchmaking grandfather—the better. Given the chance, her grandfather, just like her father with one of his horses, was likely to ask Niccolo for his complete pedigree!

'I did try to warn you,' Daniella sighed, as she sat beside Niccolo in the car later that afternoon and he drove them both back to London.

Yes, she had, Niccolo acknowledged ruefully. But even without that warning it would have been all too easy for him to pick up on the undercurrents of emotion running beneath the polite conversation as the five of them ate lunch together. Neither did Niccolo need to ask why Daniella was making further apologies now.

'You did,' he allowed. 'But that warning did not include the fact that your grandfather would be under the misapprehension that I am a prospective suitor for your hand in marriage,' he drawled.

The older man's barrage of questions about Niccolo's family and D'Alessandro business interests had bordered on rudeness. A fact Beatrice and Jeffrey Bell had also been aware of, if the way they had constantly tried to silence the older man was anything to go by.

Daniella turned to him. 'Don't take it personally, Niccolo; my grandfather considers any man under the age of sixty as being "a prospective suitor", as you so eloquently put it.'

Niccolo wasn't sure he altogether liked the image that statement conjured up. He and Daniella might be completely unsuited to each other, but the thought of some other faceless man making love with her in the way that he had was not a pleasant one.

He scowled. 'Why?'

Dani gave Niccolo a hard look, but could read nothing from his—deliberately?—bland expression. 'I told you—Grandfather is very big on continuing the Bell family line,' she dismissed with forced lightness.

Lunch had been as embarrassing as she had imagined it might be, with her grandfather asking Niccolo increasingly personal questions, and her parents doing their best to laugh it off. It hadn't helped that halfway through the meal her grandfather had made a scathing comment about Dani's 'friend Eleni'. And then he'd added insult to injury and remained completely unapologetic when Niccolo had frostily informed him that Eleni was his sister.

Her grandfather really was the most obnoxious man.

What Niccolo had thought of them all Dani had no idea. And she didn't particularly want to know, either!

'Don't look so worried, Niccolo,' she teased. 'I can assure you that I've told my grandfather repeatedly that I have no intention of marrying again.'

Niccolo raised dark brows. 'Was your first experience of marriage so awful, then?'

Awful? Traumatic better described it!

'Oh, yes.' She grimaced.

'Why?'

'I don't believe that's any of your business, Niccolo,' she snapped, too aware of him for comfort in the close confines of the car. Those brief few seconds of triumph she had felt earlier at wrong-footing him had been completely nullified by this self-imposed torture.

In fact, Dani wasn't sure *she* wasn't the one suffering the most discomfort from the arrangement, as Niccolo seemed his normal confidently relaxed self!

The previous mild interest Niccolo had felt towards Daniella's marriage became something much more at her blank refusal to discuss it.

Of course it was a personal matter—very personal—but the marriage had been of very short duration and had taken place two years ago now; surely long enough ago for Daniella to be able to talk about it dispassionately? Unless she still had feelings for her ex-husband....

It was strange, but after years of complete uninterest where Daniella Bell was concerned, Niccolo now found himself wanting to know everything he could about her. Perhaps because the Daniella he had thought he knew— and disapproved of—as Eleni's friend was a complete contradiction to the woman who had made love with him so passionately and unselfishly last weekend.

No matter how he tried, no matter how many times Daniella herself told him it was better for him to do so, Niccolo could not forget the woman in the gold gown. Or that Daniella and the woman in the gold gown were one and the same...

'And If I choose to make it my business?' he challenged her now.

'My advice is, *don't*!' she told him fiercely. 'Go back to Venice, Niccolo, and just forget any of this ever happened.'

That had been precisely his intention before he had spoken to Daniella today. But the more Daniella repeated that advice the less inclined Niccolo was to take it.

He drew in a harsh breath. 'I ask you again, Daniella— will *you* be able to do so?'

Never, came the unequivocal answer, Dani acknowledged heavily.

If her experience with Philip had soured her towards marriage for life, then her night with Niccolo had ruined her chances of ever taking another lover. That time with Niccolo had been so totally perfect that she knew anything else—anyone else—would always be second best.

She sighed. 'Does that really matter, Niccolo, when the two of us intend going back to our normal habit of ensuring that we see as little of each other as possible?'

'You do not think that our night together is reason enough for us to explore this...relationship further?'

She gave a choked laugh. 'The fact that you hesitated in even calling it a relationship should be answer enough!'

'I hesitated simply because I do not know what else to call it!' he growled. 'Damn it, Daniella, we both know that we found pleasure together that night.'

She closed her eyes to block out the image of his fiercely angry face, quickly opening them again as images of that night—being completely naked in Niccolo's arms, the beautiful strength of his perfectly proportioned body—instantly overwhelmed her.

'Have dinner with me this evening.'

'No!' she protested instantly, her hands clenching into such tight fists that her nails dug into her palms. 'No, Niccolo,' she repeated more calmly. 'We made a mistake; let's not compound it by trying to create something out of nothing.'

Niccolo had found her grandfather's interest both in his family and his financial affairs bordering on offensive earlier, but Daniella couldn't have shown him any more clearly that *she* had absolutely no interest in either of those things.

Intriguing.

He knew he was considered extremely eligible, but Niccolo didn't delude himself into believing his person-ality and looks had too much to do with that. Rather it was the D'Alessandro name and millions that gave him his eligible status. Dozens of women had pursued him with those things solely in mind.

But now Daniella was making it more than obvious that neither his name, money, or indeed he himself interested her!

'We will not know whether or not there is a basis on

which to create something until we have…explored the possibilities,' he said slowly.

Her mouth quirked. 'Until we've gone to bed together again, you mean?'

Was that what he had in mind? Possibly, Niccolo allowed grimly. And was that so unreasonable? Did Daniella have no curiosity herself to know whether or not they could recreate that one perfect night together? Did she feel none of the heated desire that churned just below the surface of their every conversation, their every glance? Had she not felt the same jolt of awareness he had just now, when he'd merely touched her arm?

'Are you not the least bit curious to know, Daniella?' he felt compelled to demand huskily.

Of course she was, Dani admitted privately. Only someone who was as blasé about lovemaking as Niccolo had earlier implied that she was could possibly remain immune to that curiosity.

But that curiosity, that daring, had already landed her in this impossible situation; to repeat it, with both of them aware of exactly who the other was, would be the height of stupidity.

'Not in the least, Niccolo,' she lied, with a brightness she was far from feeling, knowing by the angry tightening of Niccolo's mouth that her response had succeeded in alienating him. 'Now, if you don't mind, I think I would like to take a nap before we reach London.' She pointedly closed her eyes on the stony disapproval she could see in his face.

But she was far too aware of his brooding presence beside her for the next two hours to sleep, and her relief was immense when she realised that the increase in traffic and noise meant that they had finally reached their destination.

She opened her eyes to look around her. 'My apartment is—'

'I know where your apartment is, Daniella,' Niccolo gritted, the last two hours of silence having grated unbearably on his already frayed temper.

He desperately wanted to shake Daniella—wanted to physically pick her up and shake her until her teeth rattled.

His only reason for seeking her out today had been to clear the air between them, to somehow come to some sort of understanding that would enable them to meet again in future—as they were sure to do because Eleni was Daniella's best friend—without awkwardness.

But seeing Daniella again, speaking with her, had somehow achieved the opposite effect!

Dani sensed Niccolo was far from happy. Who could possibly have guessed so many complications would arise from what had at the time seemed so uncomplicated? *Come and enjoy the anonymity of a masked Venetian festival,* Eleni had invited her. *Take a lover, if you want one—at a Venetian festival it is allowed.*

Admittedly, Dani doubted that Eleni had intended for her to take Niccolo as that lover, and Dani knew now that any lover would have been a mistake.

Yet Niccolo's reaction to that night was to suggest repeating it—and Dani had spent the last two hours fighting against accepting that invitation!

Her body actually ached from the tension of remaining unmoving in the car beside him. Her jaw ached from the effort it had taken not to speak. And the closer they had got to London, to their parting, the harder it had been for her to remain silent and still.

'Thank you,' she muttered now, as Niccolo parked his car outside her apartment building.

'Daniella—'

'No, Niccolo. Don't say anything else—please!' she exclaimed, before turning to open the car door and scramble outside onto the pavement, immediately breathing in deep lungfuls of the late summer air in an effort to calm her rapidly racing pulse.

Everything looked as it normally did outside her apartment building. People strolling in the early evening sunshine in the park opposite. The ice-cream shop open across the street. One of her neighbours walking his dog.

Only she was different, it seemed.

And perhaps Niccolo a little, too…

Nothing, she realised emotionally, was ever going to be quite the same again…

'Daniella?'

She turned slightly confused eyes to look at Niccolo as he came to stand beside her after placing her overnight bag—all she had taken to Wiverley Hall as she kept some clothes there—on the pavement at her feet.

God, he looked good, she acknowledged achingly. His overlong hair appeared as dark as ebony in the sunlight, and his swarthy features were softened by that light too; deep brown eyes appeared almost golden, high cheekbones less hard, and his mouth—that pleasurably tormenting mouth!—had relaxed into a slightly enquiring smile.

She must not weaken now!

She straightened abruptly, her mouth set, green gaze direct. 'It was kind of you to drive me back to London,' she told him stiffly as she extended her hand.

Niccolo's breath caught in his throat as he looked down at the slenderness of that hand.

Daniella thought to part from him as if he were just any casual acquaintance who had given her a lift to her home? She believed that she could dismiss him, and the intimacy they had shared, so easily?

'Oh, no, Daniella,' he snarled, ignoring that hand to reach out, his hands planted firmly on the slenderness of her waist, and draw her towards him. 'You do not dismiss me so easily!' And with that his head lowered and his mouth took fierce possession of hers.

Niccolo's eyes closed instinctively, shutting out her startled expression as his mouth began to taste, to savour hers.

She tasted like the woman in gold!

She felt the same!

She *was* the same...

Niccolo growled low in his throat as, with a soft groan of surrender, her lips parted to deepen the kiss, and he drew her body close into his to mould her softness against his much harder contours.

His body leapt with remembered, renewed desire, heat rising rapidly between them as he restlessly caressed the curve of her spine, holding her firmly against him so that she could feel his throbbing response.

He wanted her.

Now.

Wanted to feel her naked beneath him as he plunged

deep inside her, as his hardness stroked rhythmically against her arousal. Wanted to once again feel her heat, her passion, as she convulsed around him in ecstasy.

How could Daniella even think of denying them that pleasure—?

Dani wrenched her mouth away from Niccolo's to look up at him with dark, slightly bruised-looking green eyes, her breathing ragged as she pushed against his chest to be released.

'Let me go, Niccolo,' she told him shakily as he still held her tightly against him. 'Let me go *now*!' she repeated fiercely, her eyes glittering angrily.

He blinked once at her vehemence before narrowing his gaze questioningly. His arms slowly fell back to his sides to allow Dani to step back.

She was trembling, shaking—more shaken, more aroused than she could ever allow Niccolo to know.

God knew what would have happened if they hadn't been standing on a public London street! Her jaw tightened and she looked up at him challengingly. 'What was that supposed to prove?'

'I did not set out to prove anything, Daniella. What it did prove is that you are not as immune to me as you claim to be.'

She breathed raggedly. 'You—!'

'It also proved that you will not find it so easy to forget our evening together as you think it will,' he continued ruthlessly.

'Neither will you!' Dani retorted.

'I never claimed I would forget it, Daniella,' he reminded her softly.

No, he hadn't, had he? she thought. In fact, Niccolo had been so affected by their lovemaking last weekend that he had spent the last few days searching for the woman in the gold gown.

Well, now he had found her. Only, as Dani had no intention of becoming Niccolo's latest mistress in a no doubt long line of mistresses, it was up to her to put a stop to this once and for all. Even at the risk of damaging her friendship with Eleni.

She forced a deliberately mocking smile to her lips. 'I really do hate to dent your inflated ego, Niccolo, but our lovemaking really wasn't that memorable, and I can assure you I am going to have absolutely no problem whatsoever in forgetting both it and you!'

To her chagrin, her claim only made Niccolo smile. Widely. Confidently. 'Have you ever heard the saying "the lady doth protest too much"…?'

'Of course I've heard it,' she snapped. 'It just doesn't happen to apply in this case.'

'No?' he pressed.

'No!' Dani scowled fiercely.

'Very well.' He nodded, those sculptured lips still curved into a mocking smile. 'I will be back in London at the end of next month, Daniella. Four weeks from now.'

'Of what interest can that possibly be to me?'

'If your lack of interest is genuine, then it will be of little relevance,' Niccolo allowed. 'But if, as I suspect, your body still burns with the same desire as mine, then it may be of great interest—'

'God, you're unbelievably arrogant!' Dani cut in.

Niccolo knew that his arrogance was a part of his nature,

that it was part and parcel of being the head of the D'Alessandro family and business. But when he talked of the desire that burned between himself and Daniella he knew he was not speaking out of arrogance, but fact. Just now had proved as much. And perhaps the month until he and Daniella could meet again would give her time to realise the truth of that too.

He sincerely hoped that it would!

He gave an elegant shrug. 'I am merely being more truthful, both to myself and you, than you appear to be.'

'You just want to find yourself a convenient mistress for whenever you're in London!'

Niccolo refused to rise to her deliberate attempt at insulting him. 'And what sort of mistress do you think you would make, Daniella?'

'A very unaccommodating one.'

He smiled at the obvious truth of that remark; anyone less like the warm and, yes, accommodating women he had taken as mistresses in the past he had yet to meet!

'I'm glad you find this so funny, Niccolo,' she continued as she saw and obviously misunderstood that smile. The impatience in her tone told him she found it the exact opposite of amusing. 'What do you think Eleni would have to say about all this?'

Niccolo's humour faded, and his mouth tightened at what was an obvious ploy on Daniella's part to halt this conversation by mentioning his sister.

Eleni had had plenty to say to him earlier that morning, before he'd set out for Gloucestershire, leaving Niccolo in no doubt whatsoever that if he intended harming Dani in any way he would have Eleni to answer to.

'What is between us does not concern Eleni,' he stated flatly.

'There is absolutely *nothing* between us, Niccolo!' Dani denied desperately, her unfair use of Eleni as a weapon having failed utterly. 'This—whatever it was—is over.'

'Keep telling yourself that, Daniella,' he drawled as he took the car keys from his trouser pocket before moving around to the driver's side of the car. 'Who knows? By the time I return in four weeks' time you might even have convinced yourself into believing it.' He raised one mocking eyebrow. 'I will then have the pleasure of proving otherwise.'

Dani opened her mouth to tell him exactly what he could do with his *pleasure*, but the words died on her lips as he slid smoothly behind the wheel of the car and closed the door behind him before turning on the ignition.

Arrogant, arrogant man, she muttered to herself in frustration as she watched Niccolo drive away.

It could be four weeks until she saw him again, four years or four decades, and she would not—she *could not*—give in to the desire Niccolo ignited inside her with just a look!

CHAPTER FIVE

'DID you decide that you could not, after all, wait the full four weeks until my return to London this weekend?'

Niccolo's surprise of a few minutes ago, when his secretary had come into his Venetian office and told him of Daniella Bell's presence in the outer room, was completely under control now as he sat behind the width of his imposing leather-topped oak desk and looked at the slenderness of Daniella's back where she stood across the room from him, gazing out of the window at the busy Grand Canal below.

He had stood up when she entered the room, and indicated for her to take a seat across the desk from his. But instead of doing so Daniella had moved to the huge window, her back remaining firmly towards him as she gazed out at the beauty that was Venice in September, with the weak sun bathing the buildings and the water in a soft amber glow.

Niccolo had seen that view dozens of times in his lifetime, both before his father died and then more since he had taken over this office as his own, and he knew exactly how mystical, how beautiful Venice looked as it stretched majestically into the hazy distance.

But Daniella had been in the room for at least five minutes now, and so far had not spoken a word....

'Daniella?' he prompted impatiently, when she did not even respond to the deliberate provocation of his remark.

It was three and a half weeks since he had last seen her. Three and a half weeks during which he had not forgotten a single thing about her or the evening they had made love so beautifully. Three and a half weeks during which he had longed to return to London, but forced himself not to do so to give Daniella time. Time, he had hoped, to discover she wanted him as much as he still wanted her.

When Melina had told him Daniella was here, waiting outside to see him, Niccolo had believed that to be the case and had been filled with expectation. But Daniella's behaviour since entering the room—her silence, the fact that she had barely glanced at him before moving to stand in front of the window with her back towards him—did not fill him with the same confidence.

But by the same token, she could have not have flown to Venice, sought him out at his office, without good reason...

She was dressed more formally than he would have expected. Her black suit was expertly tailored and matched with a cream silk blouse; her slender legs and feet were bare in black court shoes. The formality of her clothing implied this was more of a business appointment than a social call.

'Daniella, your silence is becoming intolerable!' he rasped, his movements restless as he stood up.

Dani was aware of Niccolo behind her in the room, just as she had been aware for several minutes of his rising impatience at her silence.

She hadn't meant for it to be this way. Had intended coming to Venice to see Niccolo, and stating confidently and calmly exactly how she intended things to be between them in future, then returning to her hotel to spend the night there before flying back to England tomorrow.

But one glance at Niccolo when she'd entered the room—just one heart-stopping look at his ruggedly handsome face and lithely muscular body in the lightweight grey suit and pristine white shirt with its neatly knotted grey tie—and Dani had felt her throat close up and her mouth go completely dry, making it impossible for her to force a single word past her lips.

Niccolo was perfectly correct. This silence could not continue!

She straightened her shoulders and forced herself to turn, slightly disconcerted to find he had moved from behind the desk and was now standing only feet away, but determined to stand firm and say what needed to be said.

'Okay,' she breathed huskily. 'This is the way it's going to be. I will continue to live in England, but you may visit whenever you are in London—'

'Stop right there!' he cut in icily. 'Daniella.' His voice softened as he saw her pallor. 'You are discussing a possible relationship between the two of us as if it were a business arrangement,' he chided gently.

Dani blinked, confused for a moment, until she realised exactly what Niccolo was saying. 'You thought I was discussing the two of us having an *affair*?' she said with a frown.

He looked nonplussed. 'What else—?'

'No, Niccolo,' she interrupted. 'You have it all wrong. *I* have it all wrong,' she corrected agitatedly. 'I'm not doing this very well at all.' She groaned, pushing the silky swathe of her fiery-red hair back impatiently. 'I'm a bit flustered, Niccolo. I'm sorry.' She looked at him appealingly.

Niccolo returned that gaze searchingly, having already noted the paleness of Daniella's cheeks, the dark shadows beneath those anguished green eyes, the way her hands were tightly clenched together in front of her until the knuckles showed white.

'Perhaps you should sit down?' he said slowly. 'I will ask Melina to bring us some coffee—'

'No, not coffee!' Daniella grimaced in apology for her sharpness. 'Tea would be nice,' she accepted.

Niccolo didn't bother ringing for his secretary, but instead strode over to open the door and make his request verbally. Much to Melina's surprise, he acknowledged ruefully, before closing the door and turning back to Daniella.

She hadn't moved from in front of the window, and she looked incredibly slender standing there, bathed in the soft September sunlight like a slender reed topped with flame. A slender, vulnerable reed…

'I really do think you should sit down, Daniella,' he pressed gently. 'Before you fall down,' he added more firmly, when she looked up at him slightly dazed.

Dani swallowed hard, knowing Niccolo was right. At this moment her legs *were* feeling more than a little shaky. But she had been so anxious to establish the parameters between them that she had totally missed an explanation as to why those parameters were needed in the first place.

'Thank you,' she accepted, before moving jerkily to sit down on the chair in front of his desk. 'Won't you sit down, too?' she invited, hoping that the formality of their sitting on either side of his imposing oak desk might make this easier for her.

Although she somehow doubted it!

She hadn't given herself time to think once the decision to come to Venice to talk to Niccolo had been made—had simply booked her flight and turned up at his office ten minutes ago, asking to see him.

But being here, face to face with Niccolo like this, it was all too easy to realise the enormity of what she was doing. To realise just how difficult all this was going to be.

It might have helped if she had got her thoughts into some sort of order before coming here, for one thing; at least then she might not have made such a complete muddle of things.

In her haste to get it over and done with, it seemed she had completely misled Niccolo into believing she had come here to work out the terms of an affair with him. When in fact the reason for her visit couldn't be any further from the truth….

Niccolo moved to sit behind his desk and studied Daniella in concern. She didn't look well. In fact, he was sure she had lost weight since he'd last saw her. If just coming here to see him had made Daniella ill, then she was right; no matter what he might have hoped to the contrary, there could never be a relationship between the two of them.

'Don't look so worried, Niccolo,' she murmured ruefully as she saw his look of concern. 'I haven't been feeling too well the last couple of weeks, but I'm not ill. Well—not ill, exactly. Can you really not guess the reason I'm here, Niccolo?'

No, he really couldn't.

And he was feeling too perplexed, too disturbed by this unexpected visit to play guessing games with her!

'Tell me,' he ordered.

Her eyes suddenly looked huge in the pallor of her face, her cheekbones standing out starkly above hollow cheeks. 'The truth is, Niccolo, that I flew over from England this morning to—' She broke off as Melina, after the briefest of knocks, entered carrying a tray of tea things. Daniella looked up to smile her thanks at the older woman as she placed the tray in front of her on the desk.

Niccolo barely held his impatience in check until his secretary had left the room. 'Pour it,' he invited Daniella. 'You look as if you need it,' he added with a frown as she sat forward to pick up the teapot. 'Has something happened to Eleni?'

'No!' Daniella gave him a startled look. 'Oh, no, Niccolo, you mustn't think that.' She handed him one of the cups of tea before putting a liberal amount of sugar in her own cup and taking a grateful sip. She sat back with a sigh, a little of the colour returning to her cheeks. 'No one is ill, Niccolo. I— The fact of the matter is—the truth is that I—I'm pregnant, Niccolo! Over a month pregnant to be exact,' she added shakily.

Niccolo stared at her uncomprehendingly.

Dani's eyes were wide with distress as she looked across at him searchingly, knowing what a shock this must be for him.

What a shock it had been for her, too, yesterday morning, when she had finally plucked up the courage to use the pregnancy testing kit she had purchased from a chemist the day before.

She hadn't even realised she had missed a period until two days ago—had been keeping herself so busy, her thoughts carefully channelled in an effort not to think of Niccolo, that she had completely omitted to notice that her body wasn't functioning as meticulously like clockwork as it usually did.

Even once she had realised she had missed a period she had dismissed the idea that she might be pregnant as ridiculous; surely it was an old wives' tale that it only took the once?

Apparently it wasn't!

Not convinced by the first test she had done, Dani had used the second test in the box. That had shown a positive result too. Still hopeful that she might have got a faulty testing kit, she had made an emergency appointment to see her doctor, at which point he had calmly and kindly explained to her that neither of the tests was faulty, that she was indeed in the early stages of pregnancy.

Which was when complete panic had set in!

No doubt her grandfather would be thrilled by the news, but Dani's first instinct had been to run. Her second and third instinct too! As fast and as far from Niccolo as she could possibly go.

But she had very quickly realised the futility of doing that. She couldn't just disappear, any more than she could carry on running for ever—and certainly not once the baby was born. She had to have some means of supporting the baby, as well as herself, and London was where her business was established. Besides, Eleni was far too astute, and knew Dani far too well, to ever accept her just disappearing like that. By the same token, if Dani remained in London, from the timing alone Eleni would know that Niccolo was the father of Dani's baby. And while Dani didn't doubt her friend's love for her, the love and loyalty Eleni also felt towards her brother would put her in an intolerable position.

So, as running away wasn't really an option, and keeping the truth from Niccolo was virtually an impossibility, Dani had decided she had no choice but to come to Venice and tell Niccolo herself of his impending fatherhood.

So far there had been no response to her news except the shocked widening of his eyes and his continued silence. But knowing Niccolo as she did, that didn't mean there wasn't plenty going on behind those unfathomable brown eyes. Once Niccolo recovered from the shock of her announcement he was definitely going to have several things to say on the subject.

She moistened dry lips. 'Could you just say something, Niccolo?' she asked. 'Anything.' She grimaced. 'Just don't keep looking at me in that stunned way.'

But stunned was exactly how Niccolo felt!

Stunned. Shocked. Numbed.

Daniella had just told him— Had said—

He swallowed hard, realising as he did so that he had forgotten to breathe for the last minute. His normally astute brain had for once ground to a halt.

'Niccolo, please!' Daniella pleaded at his continued silence.

Niccolo knew he had to do something. Say something. He just had no idea what!

He finally drew in a ragged breath before speaking. 'Have you eaten lunch?'

Daniella blinked. 'I— What?' She stared at him in disbelief.

Niccolo breathed out. Then in again. That soft rising and falling of his chest was the only thing that seemed normal to him at this moment.

'You said you flew over from England this morning,' he pointed out evenly. 'I wondered if you had eaten since your arrival?'

Dani continued to stare at him. She had just told Niccolo that she was pregnant, with his child, and all he could do was ask her if she had eaten lunch?

She had expected disbelief—goodness knows she had expected that! But she had also expected that disbelief to be quickly followed by anger, and then Niccolo's arrogant demands for what he wanted.

If anyone had asked her what his first words would be after she told him of her pregnancy, her answer certainly wouldn't have been an invitation to lunch!

'Niccolo, did you hear what I just said?'

'Of course I heard you!' he snapped as he stood up abruptly to move around to the front of the desk, a nerve pulsing in his tightly clenched jaw as he looked down at her with glittering dark eyes. 'Daniella, you have had time to come to terms with your pregnancy; you must have known for several days at least—'

'Twenty-four hours,' she corrected softly, infinitely more comfortable with his explosion than with his silence, her chin rising challengingly as she added, 'I only found out myself yesterday, Niccolo.'

His eyes narrowed. 'That is something, I suppose,' he allowed. 'Have you seen a doctor? Are you well? You look to me as if you have lost weight, not gained it!' he accused.

This was more like the Niccolo D'Alessandro Dani knew!

Some of the tension left her shoulders and she relaxed back in the chair. 'I saw my doctor yesterday.' She nodded. 'And I'm very well.' She gave a tremulous smile. 'Weight loss can be perfectly natural in the early stages of—of pregnancy.'

She couldn't believe she was sitting here discussing her condition so calmly with Niccolo—still had trouble believing that she was pregnant at all.

Niccolo was right. She had lost weight these last few weeks. She had put her loss of appetite and extreme tiredness, the fact that food didn't even appeal to her, down to her stress over Niccolo's imminent return and her near obsession with keeping herself too busy to think about what she was going to say to him when he did.

It was natural to find food unappetising during the first few months of pregnancy, her doctor had assured her yesterday. And it was equally natural to feel tired and nauseous. She hadn't felt the latter yet, but there was still plenty of time for that!

'We will go out to lunch,' Niccolo stated. 'You need to eat, and we can discuss this further once you have done so.'

'Oh, but—'

'Do not argue with me on this, Daniella,' he warned tightly, his hands clenched into fists at his sides. 'You must eat, and I—I need a few minutes in which to process what you have told me,' he added harshly.

Yes, Dani could see that he did. She even understood why he did. She would just have preferred not to make a social occasion out of it by the two of them actually going out to lunch together.

She might have muddled things earlier, but she did

know how she wanted this to go. She had come here to tell Niccolo of her pregnancy, to assure him that he could have visiting access at any time he liked once the baby was born, and then she would return to London and get on with her life until the birth.

She should have known Niccolo would change the order of things—as he was doing so now, by insisting on taking her out to lunch!

Niccolo watched as first her understanding for his dilemma, followed by a look of stubborn resolve and then frowning determination flickered across Daniella's expressive face.

The first he understood. It had to be obvious to even the most casual observer—and Daniella was hardly that—that he was totally stunned by the news of Daniella's pregnancy.

The second he also understood—he already knew how stubbornly self-reliant Daniella could be when she chose, and he suddenly remembered her words earlier: 'I will continue to live in England, but you may visit whenever you are in London!'

Her look of determination was also easily understood—Daniella would not give in meekly to any demands he might choose to make concerning the child she carried.

But she would give in.

Oh, yes, Daniella would give in.

Eventually.

Because it was his child as well as hers, and Niccolo had no intention of giving in meekly to any demands she might choose to make concerning their child, either!

* * *

'This is nice,' Dani murmured as she looked around the quiet bistro Niccolo had brought her to, his hand having lightly but firmly gripped her arm as he guided her well away from the tourist-busy St Mark's Square to this small family-owned restaurant that overlooked one of the narrower canals. The owner had greeted Niccolo by name before showing them to one of the tables by the open windows.

'Eat, Daniella,' Niccolo instructed as the owner deposited breadsticks on the table, along with their menus.

Dani ignored his order and instead picked up the menu to use as a shield as she shot Niccolo frowning glances. He had barely spoken on the ten-minute walk here along the path-sided canals, but she knew from the slight pallor beneath his naturally swarthy complexion that this was only a temporary respite—that in actual fact Niccolo did have plenty to say, and was just choosing the moment when he would say it. Probably he would get started once she had eaten, as he seemed so determined to get some food down her!

'Stop thinking so much, Daniella, and instead choose what you would like for lunch.'

Dani looked up, not fooled for a moment by the pleasantness of his tone.

'Niccolo—'

'I believe there are certain foods that pregnant women have to avoid?' he prompted lightly.

'Smoked meat and fish, pâtés, soft cheeses, uncooked eggs,' she confirmed distractedly, having received a list of dos and don'ts from the doctor yesterday. 'But—'

'Then perhaps you would like the linguine with mushrooms and chicken?'

'Niccolo—'

'We will order our food before continuing this conversation, Daniella.' His tone was steely, uncompromising.

She drew in a breath to reply, but was prevented from further argument by the arrival of the proprietor to take their order, and waited until they were alone again before carefully placing her hands down on the red and white checked cloth that covered the small, square table to lean forward and look Niccolo directly in the eye. 'I do sincerely sympathise with the shock this has been to you—'

'Do you?' Niccolo drawled, perfectly relaxed as he leant back in his chair.

'Well, of course I do.' She groaned. 'It isn't every day you learn you're going to become a father.'

'No,' he conceded dryly. 'But it is not so much of a shock now as it originally was,' he admitted, that dark gaze lazily assessing. 'In fact, now that I have…adjusted to the idea, I find that the prospect of having a son or daughter is rather a pleasant one.'

Yes, Niccolo had certainly recovered from his earlier speechlessness, Dani acknowledged uneasily. And as she knew only too well, a totally self-possessed Niccolo was a force to be reckoned with.

What on earth had made her imagine that telling Niccolo herself about her pregnancy was the easiest option? What had possessed her to think that she could come here and tell Niccolo about the baby and that he would then just calmly allow her to return to England to continue her pregnancy without any interference from him?

Because the almost complacent way in which he had said

that he found the idea of having a child a pleasant one certainly implied he didn't intend letting her escape that easily!

'Niccolo, I don't think you've quite understood what's going to happen here,' she told him. 'You are biologically going to become a father in around eight months' time, yes, but not—not a hands-on father. Not a permanent, day-to-day fixture in this child's life!' she added slightly desperately.

Niccolo shook his head and smiled, seeming totally unconcerned by the vehemence in Daniella's announcement. 'I think that it is *you* who does not understand, Daniella,' he contradicted her. 'The child you are carrying is a D'Alessandro. More than that, as my son or daughter, he or she will be the D'Alessandro heir.'

She nodded. 'I do understand that, Niccolo—'

'No, you obviously do not.' He sat forward to lean across the table, his face only inches from hers now. 'As soon as the arrangements can be made, Daniella, you and I will be married,' he stated.

And watched with a wicked pleasure as she recoiled in horror!

CHAPTER SIX

'MARRIED?' Dani repeated incredulously when she finally managed to recover enough from the shock of Niccolo's announcement to find her voice again. 'I have no intention of marrying you or anyone else, Niccolo!'

He straightened abruptly, dark eyes suddenly glacial above his hard cheekbones and rigidly set jaw. 'Believe me, Daniella, there is no question of your marrying anyone else *but* me,' he bit out tautly.

She shook her head. 'You or anyone else, Niccolo,' she repeated determinedly. 'I told you weeks ago that I will never marry again.'

'The circumstances were different then,' he said with quiet violence.

'I wasn't pregnant, you mean?' Dani nodded. 'But that changes nothing—'

'It changes *everything*!' Niccolo glared at her. 'I have told you. The child you carry is the D'Alessandro heir, and as such—'

'It's also the Bell heir,' she reminded him, with no small measure of disgust, already able to imagine how thrilled her grandfather was going to be by the news. He was so filled with his own self-importance he would probably imagine she had become pregnant just to satisfy his demand for a great-grandchild—

Oh, God.

She shot Niccolo an apprehensive glance even as the colour drained from her face. If Niccolo learnt of the contents of her grandfather's will, would he think she had deliberately arranged this pregnancy in order to safeguard her parents' future?

Remembering Eleni's fleeting suspicions of that possibility four weeks ago, after Dani and Niccolo had spent the evening together, Dani had the dreadful feeling that he just might….

But there was no reason why Niccolo should ever know about that clause in her grandfather's will. And even if he did learn of it, it wasn't as if she was asking him for anything, was it?

Except the Bell heir…

No!

One thing at a time, she reminded herself. One problem at a time. And she had enough of those already without thinking of ones that hadn't even arisen yet!

'Daniella, what is it?' Niccolo queried urgently as he watched her cheeks pale. 'Daniella, you will tell me what is wrong!' he demanded forcefully, totally frustrated with her complete intractability concerning the idea of a marriage between them.

Could she not see that it was the only solution? That he would settle for nothing less?

And what of Daniella's wants and needs? came the unbidden thought….

He thrust it aside. Daniella was pregnant—a time during which a woman's hormones and emotions reputedly made logical thought and decisions virtually impossible. The fact that she was pregnant with his child, that he wanted to marry her, surely made her decision never to marry again totally illogical?

Dani firmly closed her mind to thoughts of what Niccolo might or might not come to think of her pregnancy if he learnt of that clause in her grandfather's will. At the moment her main difficulty was getting it through to Niccolo that she was not, under any circumstances, going to marry him. Although she would be lying if she said that she hadn't felt a slight thrill, a frisson of excitement, when Niccolo had announced his intention of marrying her.

It hadn't been her immediate reaction, of course. Initially she had been absolutely horrified just at the mention of a marriage between the two of them—had never even considered that Niccolo would make such an offer.

Although perhaps she should have done…

Niccolo was Italian, and more than that he was a D'Alessandro—a member of a Venetian family steeped in honour and tradition; the idea that the D'Alessandro heir might be born out of wedlock, so to speak, was probably enough to send Niccolo's ancestors spinning in their graves!

She gave a rueful shake of her head. 'What is wrong, Niccolo, is that I don't want to marry you,' she stated baldly, grimacing as she saw the angry glitter of his eyes and the way his mouth tightened inflexibly. 'Be totally honest—it isn't what you really want, either, now, is it?' she added reasonably.

This was all too new to Niccolo for him to know *what* he wanted. Admittedly, for the last three and a half weeks he had been quietly contemplating—relishing!—the idea of the two of them beginning a relationship, but he could not in all honesty say that marriage had ever entered into any of those fantasies.

But now that it had…

The prospect of having Daniella as his wife was not an unpleasant one. And the thought of having her permanently in his bed, of the two of them making love whenever and wherever they pleased, was extremely exciting.

Besides, there was no question as to whether or not it was what either of them really wanted—their child needed two parents, and parents who lived together, so that the child did not become some sort of human ping-pong ball.

'It *is* what I want, Daniella,' he insisted.

'But it can't be!' Dani protested fiercely. 'Until a few weeks ago the two of us couldn't even be in the same room without arguing—so nothing new there, then.' She sighed ruefully as she realised that was exactly what they were doing now. 'Niccolo.' She reached out and placed her hand on his, instantly regretting the action as she felt an electrical charge of physical awareness tingle up her hand and along her arm. She snatched her hand away. 'I promise you I will not make it difficult for you to see your son or daughter whenever you wish—'

'That would be every day, then,' he cut in harshly. 'A promise you could not possibly keep if you reside in England and my own home is here in Venice.'

Impasse.

Coming here and telling Niccolo about the baby

couldn't solve that particular problem. But Dani would not allow herself to be browbeaten into marrying him.

Oh, she knew he was nothing like Philip—that Niccolo possessed none of the insecurity or mental imbalance that had become manifest in Philip so soon after their wedding. But the thought of being any man's wife again, of placing herself in that position of vulnerability, was complete anathema to her.

She doubted she would be able to make Niccolo understand any of that without totally explaining the nightmare of her first marriage to him. Unfortunately, that was something she did not intend doing.

'I'm sorry, Niccolo, but the whole idea of the two of us marrying is unthinkable to me.'

Why? Niccolo was puzzled, completely aware that only minutes ago, when Daniella had touched his arm so impulsively, she had been as physically aware of him as he had been of her since the night of Eleni's masquerade party.

Probably before that night, he allowed ruefully, having had plenty of time to think in the three and a half weeks since he had last seen her. One thing he had come to understand was that he had already been aware of Daniella Bell and how she had grown into a beautiful young woman since he had helped Eleni move to England six years ago.

It had been the fact that Daniella had been only eighteen, while Niccolo was already thirty-one, and that she was also Eleni's best friend, that had put up a barrier so that Niccolo had felt he could never pursue that attraction.

And so had begun the verbal battles between them that

had punctuated every one of their meetings during the last six years.

Until the night of Eleni's masquerade party….

That night of anonymity had wiped away all those barriers, had allowed him to appreciate her even if he hadn't recognised her as Daniella. He had simply seen her as a beautiful and mature woman.

Damn it, she was *his* woman.

Carrying *his* child.

He would not allow her to walk away from him!

His mouth firmed with resolution. 'I too am sorry, Daniella—because the idea of the two of us *not* marrying is unthinkable to *me*.'

Dani sighed, but was saved from making any immediate answer by the arrival of their food. Not that she had any appetite for it, but the interruption was welcome.

What were they going to do?

She lived and worked in London. Niccolo lived and worked here in Venice. Niccolo was insisting that they get married. And she was insisting that they wouldn't.

Maybe she should have just followed her first instinct and started running—and kept on going….

'Does Eleni know about the baby?' Niccolo asked as soon as the two of them were alone again.

Daniella froze in the action of sprinkling parmesan over her pasta.

'No, of course she doesn't,' she denied. 'No one else knows but the two of us. I— It didn't seem…right that I should tell anyone else before I had talked to you.'

He gave an abrupt inclination of his head. 'That is something, I suppose.'

She looked pained. 'Niccolo, I am trying to be fair.'

'Fair, perhaps,' he grated. 'I would prefer reasonable.'

'I'm trying to be reasonable, too—'

'You call refusing to marry your baby's father *reasonable*?' Niccolo accused harshly.

Tears swam in her beautiful green eyes. 'I'm sorry.' She hastily wiped away the tears before they could fall onto the paleness of her cheeks. 'I believe pregnant woman tend to be a little—over-emotional,' she whispered.

Niccolo felt like a complete heel now. He hadn't intended to make Daniella cry—hadn't intended to upset her at all—but she was just being so damned stubborn by continuing to refuse to marry him!

He closed his eyes briefly, but could still inwardly see her woebegone face and tear-wet lashes.

He appreciated that this couldn't have been easy for Daniella. That it had taken great courage for her to come here like this today and tell him of the baby. She could have had no idea how he would react to the news.

He was just so frustrated with her refusal to marry him!

It was pretty obvious she wasn't going to change her mind without a fight, either. A fight Niccolo didn't believe she was emotionally or physically equipped to deal with right now.

He raised his lids, his eyes widening as he saw that her face had a slightly green tinge to it. 'What is it?' he asked with immediate concern.

Dani swallowed hard. 'I don't think I should have put this much parmesan on my pasta….' The pungent odour of the cheese on the hot food was making her feel extremely nauseous.

Niccolo reached across the table to remove her plate and replace it with his own ungarnished pasta.

'Oh, but—'

'Just eat, Daniella,' he told her wearily. 'Eat, and then we will continue our conversation.'

Dani wasn't sure that the delay was going to make any difference to the situation, but once her stomach had stopped churning from the smell of the melting cheese she realised that she was actually quite hungry. Not surprising, really, when she had been too nervous earlier this morning at the thought of seeing Niccolo again—at what she had to tell him—to even think about eating any breakfast.

She did feel slightly better once she had eaten Niccolo's pasta, and a rather delicious dessert something like an English trifle. But if their conversation was going to continue along the same impossible lines Dani knew she was just as likely to lose it all again!

She ran her tongue nervously over her bottom lip. 'Niccolo—'

'Not here, Daniella,' he said, before turning to ask for the bill. 'We will continue our conversation at my home.'

Considering that home to Niccolo was the D'Alessandro palace, Dani didn't think she was going to find talking there any more comfortable than she had here.

Eleni had once shown Dani photographs of her family home: a tall, five-storeyed building with a boathouse below, slightly Arabian in style, with an extensive garden on the roof. A home fit for the princes the D'Alessandro men had once been.

Her child—her son or daughter—was descended from princes!

From priests and pirates too, of course, she remembered wryly, but she doubted if members of either of those professions had actually lived in the D'Alessandro palace.

'Will you be comfortable travelling by boat, or would you rather walk?' Niccolo asked once they were outside.

Eleni had once gone into raptures about the thrill of approaching the D'Alessandro palace by boat, waxing lyrical about how beautiful it was viewed from the water.

'Boat will be fine,' Dani accepted huskily.

This really was a completely different way of life, she thought as she sat in the back of the small motorboat Niccolo piloted out into the busy Grand Canal, where dozens of boats similar to this one, as well as water-taxis and the much more romantic gondolas, glided smoothly through the water.

But it was Niccolo himself who held her attention as he sat behind the wheel, the slight breeze ruffling the darkness of his overlong hair, those beautiful brown eyes narrowed in concentration as he easily manoeuvred the boat through the slightly choppy water created by the passing of other crafts.

It was the first time Dani had had a chance to really look at him without the nerve-racking barrier of telling him of her pregnancy between them. She felt her heart actually skipping a beat as she gazed hungrily at the rugged handsomeness of his face.

She had been infatuated with him at the age of fourteen. Had remained fascinated by him and then, after her marriage, had shied away from his raw sexuality. Well, her fascination had been ecstatically satisfied just a few weeks ago!

She couldn't help wondering what her answer would have been if she hadn't been pregnant. If Niccolo had come to London on the weekend, as promised, to ask if she had changed her mind about entering into a relationship with him.

Would she have continued to say no?

Or would she have said yes, and happily grabbed the days, weeks, possibly months of having Niccolo as her lover?

Sadly, she would never know the answer to that now.

'Why the sigh?'

Dani shook off her mood of despondency and looked up to find Niccolo glancing back at her. 'I was just thinking how lucky you are to live somewhere so beautiful,' she said mendaciously.

It took great effort for Niccolo not to point out that Venice could become her home too, if she would only say yes to his marriage proposal; however, a motorboat in the middle of a Venetian canal was not the ideal place in which to begin yet another argument between them.

'Yes, it is,' he agreed casually. 'And here is the D'Alessandro palace.' He kept one hand on the wheel as he pointed with the other to the pale terracotta-coloured building that had been his family home for generations. He couldn't help but be inwardly pleased by the look of pleasure that instantly lit Daniella's features as she turned to look at it, her eyes glowing, an excited flush to her cheeks, her beautiful, kissable mouth curved into a rapt smile.

'Oh, Niccolo, it's *wonderful*!' she breathed.

Niccolo slowed the boat to manoeuvre it into its mooring beneath the house, before turning to help Daniella step onto the paved walkway that led to a staircase up into the main part of the palace.

'Could you bring tea up to the drawing-room, Edoardo?' he asked his manservant as the other man came into the spacious hallway to greet them. Niccolo kept his amusement contained as the elderly man showed none of the surprise he was probably feeling at the return of his employer in the middle of the afternoon, with a beautiful redhead secured firmly at his side, and he kept a light hold on Daniella's arm.

Dani, accompanying Niccolo up the wide staircase to the first floor, had never seen such a beautiful house. The decorations were ornately gold, the lavish furniture obviously genuinely antique. Huge paintings hung on the walls, and a crystal chandelier was suspended from the high ceiling above them.

She followed Niccolo as he threw open tall doors that led into what was obviously the drawing room. The domed ceiling of this room held Dani's attention, painted with cherubs and maidens, with more ornate gold filigree work and yet another crystal chandelier also suspended above them.

Having grown up in Wiverley Hall she was, of course, used to big houses, but the D'Alessandro palace was in a class completely on its own; it was unbelievably magnificent in its opulence.

She gave a choked laugh. 'Eleni told me it was beautiful, but I had no idea…'

'Come and look at the view,' Niccolo encouraged huskily as he opened the doors out onto the balcony before turning to hold out his hand to her in invitation.

Dani stared at that hand, feeling suddenly shy with him, never having quite appreciated before how in other circumstances Niccolo might have been Prince D'Alessandro. But it was all too easy, in these grand surroundings, to imagine him as such—to recognise his innate air of command, to acknowledge him as the powerful and much-respected head of the D'Alessandro family.

Niccolo was offering to share all of this with her, to make her his wife, the mother of his child—children…? For she didn't doubt that Niccolo would want more than one child to continue the D'Alessandro line. Any other woman would have grabbed the offer with both hands, Dani knew. Was she being rash in refusing to marry Niccolo? Was she being fair to their son or daughter by denying its birthright?

She was no longer as sure about that as she had been…

But maybe that had been Niccolo's intent in bringing her here?

Perhaps it was, but being here with him like this, with the magic of Venice and the D'Alessandro palace surrounding them, Dani was finding it more and more difficult to resist the allure…

'Daniella…?' Niccolo prompted again, his expression gently enquiring as he continued to hold his hand out to her.

She gave him a brief smile before stepping forward to take his hand and letting him guide her out onto the balcony. She released herself to step forward and rest both her hands on the railing as she gazed out across the water.

All of Venice lay before her, it seemed. The beautiful

Grand Canal was hazily lovely in the still-warm autumn sunlight as the boats moved continuously along its length, boatmen cheerily greeting each other as they passed. There was an elderly couple in one gondola floating majestically by, their rapt faces telling of their complete enthrallment with their surroundings. Another gondola accommodated a young couple, their arms wrapped about each other and with eyes only for each other.

Dani could see a small child sitting on the balcony of one of the buildings farther down the wide canal. A little girl with dark hair curling silkily onto her shoulders. Her whole attention was on the piece of fruit she was eating with relish, and the sound of her giggle sounded clearly across the water as a young woman, probably her mother, came laughingly out to join her.

And there were so many aromas to assault the senses too. The smell of fresh bread baking. The garlic that was added to most Italian dishes. The juices of many fruits mixed together, adding a freshness to the air that was intoxicating.

Niccolo stood slightly to one side, watching Daniella indulgently as she fell in love with the magic that was Venice.

He had been born here, had lived here all his life, but to him Venice was still a city like no other. A city that twined its tentacles into your heart and never let go. It was easy to see from the glowing fascination on Daniella's face that Venice had already started to take its hold on her heart too; her eyes were glowing mistily, her cheeks were tinged a delicate rose, and her lips slightly parted in wonder.

She shook her head slightly. 'How could Eleni possibly have chosen to leave all this?' she breathed.

'I do not know,' Niccolo murmured as he moved to stand behind her. 'Stay here with me tonight, Daniella,' he said, his hands sliding about her waist as he pulled her gently back to lean against him. 'Please spend the night here with me.' He groaned, lowering his head as he placed lingering kisses against the exposed column of her throat. 'Our child permitting,' he added achingly, 'I would very much like to make love with you in the Venetian moonlight.'

Dani leant weakly against him, her senses having soared the moment his arms moved about her. His lips travelled tantalisingly down the length of her throat, and her hands moved to cover his as they rested against the flatness of her stomach where their child nestled so safely.

'Your child permits,' she assured him throatily. 'As do I...' She turned in his arms to offer her mouth up to the feel, the taste of him as his lips claimed hers.

It was a searching kiss, a seeking, an affirmation that they wanted each other, that their bodies were as perfectly in tune today as they had been on that night four and a half weeks ago, when they had first made love and created a child together.

Dani moaned low in her throat as she felt the heat of her desire for Niccolo in the tingling awareness of her breasts, the nipples having tightened. That heat spread down her stomach, sparking fiercely out of control as it reached between her thighs. She felt Niccolo's own response as his own thighs hardened and his breath caught and became ragged.

Yes, they most definitely still wanted each other!

But...

Niccolo muttered in protest as Daniella gently but firmly moved her mouth away from his to tilt her head back. She looked up at him, the slight pallor to her cheeks telling him that she still had something to say.

Her throat moved convulsively before she spoke. 'Yes, I'll stay here with you tonight, Niccolo.' She nodded, her voice still husky. 'But only if you will promise not to talk of marriage again this evening.' She looked up at him uncertainly.

Niccolo frowned as he gave her a searching look. He could easily read the signs of strain in her expression, the look of almost apprehension—of fear?—in those slightly shadowed green eyes.

But what had she to be frightened of?

He reached up to cradle each side of her face and looked deeply into those troubled green eyes until Daniella deliberately dropped her gaze from his. 'You do know that I would never hurt you, do you not, Daniella?'

'Yes, of course,' she answered quickly.

Too quickly?

She had said she didn't want him to talk of marriage again this evening—would not even contemplate staying here with him until he made such a promise. So could it possibly be marriage itself that she feared? And if it was, what could possibly have happened to Daniella to make her look so fearful at the prospect of marriage? Had her husband hurt her in some way? Perhaps been unfaithful? Was that the reason for the short duration of the marriage?

Niccolo felt a wave of anger deep inside him as he contemplated anyone—most of all Daniella's ex-husband, a man pledged to love and protect her—having hurt her in any way.

But it was an anger he would control until he could return to England and possibly seek out the man Daniella had been married to so briefly; he certainly did not intend to shake their fragile relationship by questioning Daniella about it, either now or in the future.

His thumbs moved caressingly across the paleness of her cheeks as he smiled gently down at her. 'I promise I will not mention marriage again this evening, Daniella,' he repeated teasingly.

Dani looked at him intently, slightly suspicious of the ease with which Niccolo had agreed to her one condition for staying here at the D'Alessandro palace with him tonight.

Not that she doubted he would keep that promise. Niccolo was of all things a man of honour; having made her a promise he would most certainly keep it.

Maybe he was just hoping that their night together, their making love together, would convince her to change her mind?

But it wouldn't.

Would it…?

CHAPTER SEVEN

DANI lay back in the free-standing bath, totally relaxed by the deep warmth of the scented water, its bubbles tickling her chin as she smiled in dreamy contentment.

The luxurious gold fittings and porcelain bathroom suite were unlike anything she had ever seen before, and even this room, she noticed, had a painted ceiling of smiling cherubs. Three of its walls were mirrored, with intricately sculptured surrounds. A bathroom fit for a princess, in fact....

Once they had drunk their tea earlier, Niccolo had suggested that Dani take a nap, and as she was tired from the travelling, as well as the strain of her conversation with him, she had been only too happy to comply. Although she had been shocked by the bedroom Niccolo had told her was for her use—its proportions were immense. In fact, the whole of her apartment in London would probably fit into that one room!

But the beautiful silk-draped four-poster bed had proved to be so comfortable that Dani had fallen asleep in minutes, awaking completely refreshed a couple of hours later.

She hadn't been in the least surprised to find that Niccolo had sent one of his staff to collect her things from her hotel while she was resting. Although it was a little disconcerting to find that someone—probably a maid—had quietly entered the bedroom while Dani was asleep and unpacked the few things she had brought with her.

She had travelled over in tailored black trousers and a green lambswool sweater, but had deliberately brought the formal suit to change into for her interview with Niccolo. However, the delivery of her small overnight case meant that she could now change back into the tailored black trousers and a soft rose-coloured sweater she had intended wearing to travel home tomorrow.

She very much doubted there was going to be any need for formality between herself and Niccolo tonight!

Her heart skipped a beat and her stomach muscles clenched in anticipation as she thought of the night ahead. A night she had told Niccolo she would spend with him.

She felt a quiver of pleasure just at the thought of spending the night in Niccolo's arms. Of making love with him with each of them knowing the identity of the other.

Niccolo had been so wonderful earlier—so warm and caring as he'd solicitously poured a cup of tea for her and then tempted her into eating some of the delicious biscuits that had been on the tea tray. He'd personally showed her into the bedroom, which he'd explained adjoined his, and had made sure that Dani had everything she needed before he'd left her there to sleep.

How easy it was to be lulled into a sense of contentment by such attentions, Dani acknowledged ruefully. How much easier everything would be if she were to just accept Niccolo's marriage proposal and allow him to take charge, relieving her of all the worries of an uncertain future—

She was in love with him, Dani realised with sudden shock as she sat up in the bath.

Not just infatuated by him, as she had been at fourteen. And not just fascinated by him as she had been throughout her teen years. She no longer just suspected that she had loved Niccolo for years; Dani now knew without a doubt that she was totally, utterly in love with Niccolo D'Alessandro.

Dear God…

Her hands shook slightly and she tightly clasped the edges of the bath. She loved Niccolo!

But she had thought she'd loved Philip, too, once, she reminded herself sternly—and quickly followed that with the knowledge that there was absolutely no comparison between what she had felt for the insecure Philip and what she now felt for the self-assured Niccolo.

Maybe not, but she would be a fool—

Dani turned sharply as a knock sounded on the bathroom door. 'Yes…?' she asked tentatively.

The door opened softly and Niccolo stood in the doorway. 'You slept so long I was concerned you might be ill.'

Dani had sunk back beneath the bubbles in the bath as soon as she'd realised someone was actually about to enter the bathroom. Her cheeks burned hotly now that the 'someone' had turned out to be Niccolo. It was more than a little disconcerting to have him come in here like this when she had just discovered she was in love with him.

A discovery she must never, ever allow Niccolo to find out about!

'As you can see, I am perfectly well,' she told him with forced coolness.

He hadn't just been concerned for her physical welfare, Niccolo acknowledged privately to himself. When he had found Daniella's bedroom empty he had briefly thought that she had gone altogether—that she had reconsidered her decision to stay with him tonight and had instead fled the palace.

But then he had seen signs of her presence in the bedroom—a pair of shoes beneath the dressing table, a deep rose-coloured sweater draped on the bedroom chair—and realised that she must be in the adjoining bathroom.

He had spent the hours while Daniella slept in quiet contemplation, knowing that her decision to stay here with him tonight, although positive, did not mean that she would change her mind about marrying him. In fact, the promise she had insisted he make not to pressure her again tonight on the subject implied the opposite.

It went completely against his decisive nature to acquiesce to such a promise, but at the time Niccolo had known he had no choice—that if he didn't make the promise Daniella would not stay.

And he very much wanted her here beside him tonight—wanted to worship and adore her body long into the night, to show her that, although she didn't love him, the physical love between them was beautiful.

As *she* was beautiful, Niccolo thought as he looked hungrily across the room at her. The fire of her hair was secured loosely on top of her head, wispy tendrils curling damply against the slender curve of her neck, and her face was slightly flushed from the heat of the bath water.

A froth of bubbles was hiding her complete nakedness

from him. But that didn't mean that Niccolo couldn't easily envisage the gentle curves of her body: the fullness of her rose-tipped breasts, her slender waist and lithe hips and legs, the dark triangle of auburn hair at the apex of her thighs…

Dani was finding Niccolo's prolonged silence disturbing—especially as she was lying here naked in the bath, while he was fully dressed in a cream silk shirt and tailored brown trousers. And looking disturbingly gorgeous. She groaned inwardly. His overlong dark hair was slightly damp, as if from a shower, and the almost severe handsomeness of his face was dominated by glittering dark eyes as he continued to look at her so intently.

She drew in a ragged breath. 'Was that all, Niccolo?' she prompted pointedly. 'Because my bath water is getting a little cold.'

Instead of leaving, Niccolo stepped farther into the room to collect one of the huge, fluffy cream bath towels from the warming rail before moving to stand beside the bath. 'You must get out before you catch a chill,' he suggested as he shook the towel out invitingly.

Having Niccolo witness her standing up and stepping from the bath was not exactly what Dani'd had in mind when she'd made her pointed comment, intending him to leave.

But it was a little late to feel self-conscious, considering she had already been completely naked in Niccolo's presence the night they made love and that she had agreed to spend tonight with him too. Nevertheless, she did feel shy, and glad of the scented bubbles that still clung to her body as she stood up in the bath, her gaze no longer meeting his as she straightened.

But instead of handing her the towel, as she had expected, Niccolo reached out to wrap the towel around her, draping it over her body beneath her arms before securing the ends between her breasts. His hand briefly lingered there, warm and caressing, his dark gaze steadily holding hers as he stepped back to hold out his hand to her.

'Come,' he said softly. 'It is a very deep bath and I would not like you to trip and fall as you step out.'

Dani didn't want to risk falling either, but the air of intimacy in the room, the sudden awareness she could feel between herself and Niccolo, made her fingers tremble slightly as she placed her hand in his before stepping out onto the deep blue Persian rug.

Niccolo was standing very close, so close he could feel the warmth of Daniella's damp body as his arm lightly brushed against her breast, and he maintained his hold on her hand to look down at her searchingly.

'You're making yourself all wet,' she murmured huskily after a frowning glance at the sleeve of his shirt.

Niccolo would have been happy to make all of his clothing wet just for the chance to hold Daniella in his arms, to kiss her as he had been longing to kiss her again since holding her on the balcony earlier.

But the uneasiness with the situation that he could read in her expressive green eyes warned him to practise caution. Despite the fact that the two of them had made love, that they had created a baby together from that love-making, he knew that Daniella was still shy with him. And he wanted her to feel less, not more self-conscious with him, to give her time to feel at ease with their intimacy.

It took all of his considerable will-power, but somehow

he managed to release her hand and step away. 'I have arranged for us to dine upstairs in the roof garden as it is such a warm evening; I trust that meets with your approval?'

'Oh, yes!' Dani could imagine nothing more magical, her eyes glowing with anticipation as she looked up at him smilingly. No doubt the venue for their evening would make it a very romantic evening too. Which was probably his intention, she thought.

Whoever would have dreamt that the thought of a romantic evening with Niccolo—her adversary for the last ten years—would fill her with such pleasure, such excitement?

Who would ever have predicted she would be about to spend a romantic evening with Niccolo at all?

But she mustn't get carried away here, Dani reminded herself sternly, her smile slowly fading. Niccolo had his own reasons for making this evening as enjoyable for her as possible. And those reasons had nothing to do with romance. Yes, he might have made it more than clear that he wanted to make love with her again. But he had also left her in no doubt that his ultimate objective was to persuade her into marrying him, so that the two of them might share equally in the upbringing of their child.

It didn't matter that Dani had discovered only minutes ago that she was deeply in love with Niccolo; she had to remain on her guard this evening, so as not to be seduced into a false sense of security that might easily persuade her into accepting his proposal. Once tonight was over, Niccolo had to be made to see that she meant it when she said she would never marry again.

'If you wouldn't mind leaving now? I need to go and dress.' She deliberately moved away from him to cross the room and enter the adjoining bedroom, standing in front of the dressing table to study her reflection as she removed the pin from her hair and allowed it to fall down onto her bare shoulders, before picking up her brush and running it through the soft tangles.

She was totally aware of Niccolo following her from the bathroom seconds later. She could see his reflection in the mirror, but she also felt a frisson of physical awareness down the length of her spine that told her of his presence in the room behind her.

Niccolo's gaze was hooded as he studied the slender lines of Daniella's bare shoulders and upper spine, with her hair a tumble of red flame against the silky softness of her skin. He wanted her with a need that was bordering on obsession!

Each time he touched her, spent time with her, Niccolo's need to make love to her again intensified. Getting through the polite ritual of actually eating dinner with her was going to test his control to breaking point.

But it wouldn't break, he decided with determination; too much rested on his not alarming Daniella with the intensity of his need. So instead he forced a teasing smile. 'Can you find your way upstairs to the garden, or would you like me to come back in a short while and escort you?'

'Oh, I think I can find my own way, thank you, Niccolo,' Daniella turned to say lightly.

He gave a curt nod. 'Then I will see you later.'

Dani waited only long enough for Niccolo to leave the bedroom and close the door softly behind him before sinking weakly down onto the chair in front of the dressing table. One glance at her reflection in the mirror showed her that her cheeks were flushed and her eyes glowed deeply green.

It had all seemed so simple earlier, as the two of them stood on the balcony, Niccolo's arms around her and his lips travelling the length of her throat. He had told her that he wanted her to stay with him tonight—had asked her to stay with him, pleaded with her to do so. And as it was what Dani wanted too, she had agreed.

But now, with the prospect of a romantic dinner together followed by a night in Niccolo's bed, Dani was much less sure of the wisdom of accepting such an invitation…

She knew she had been right to have such misgivings when she joined Niccolo in the roof garden half an hour later, to find him sitting at a table beautifully laid with crystal and fine white linen. It was illuminated by several candles floating in a wide water bowl of gold, the only other lighting being several soft amber-coloured lamps that ran the length of the balustrade overlooking the Grand Canal.

Instead of joining Niccolo at the table, Dani moved to stand at that balustrade to gaze out over the breathtaking view that was Venice at night—majestically stunning with the moonlight and softly glowing streetlamps reflected in the water below, several gondolas gliding silently along its length.

Dani was once more so mesmerised, so enchanted, so moved by the beauty spread out before her, that she was incapable of verbally acknowledging Niccolo's presence as he came to stand beside her.

'It is magnificent, is it not?' he murmured.

Magnificent barely described it! No wonder so many couples chose to come here for their honeymoon.

Just the thought of a honeymoon, a natural progression

from the wedding that would have taken place before it, was enough to break Dani out of the spell that Venice— and Niccolo—had been so easily casting over her.

'It's very nice,' she conceded dryly, before deliberately turning her back on the view that was seducing her senses. 'Can we start dinner now? I'm absolutely starving!' She didn't even glance at Niccolo as she moved to the candlelit table and sat down.

Niccolo took his time joining her, his thoughts distracted. Daniella's slightly distant manner told him that she was regretting her agreement to spend the night here with him. That doubt came as no surprise to him, because he had felt those doubts earlier too. But he had no intention, by word or deed, of increasing that uncertainty. He wanted her to enjoy this evening—was even willing to accept that she wouldn't share his bed tonight after all, if that was what she ultimately decided. This was just too important—Daniella herself was too important—to his future happiness for him to ruin it all in one selfish night of need, of desire.

And so he deliberately set out to once more put Daniella at her ease, keeping his conversation light and well away from anything of a remotely emotional nature. Instead, as they ate, he drew her out to talk of her work as an interior designer. The enthusiasm with which she spoke of it, the pleasure in her face, told him of her deep satisfaction in her chosen career—which was one more thing standing in the way of Niccolo's wish that she would eventually agree to marry him and come to live here with him in Venice.

'I am not sure that I believe a woman could ever be that calculating!' he teased, after Daniella broke off telling him a rather amusing story of a woman who had lain on her bed to make sure that she could reach out and adjust her newly installed lighting so that it reflected in the mirrors above and would increase the pleasure for herself and her lover.

'Oh, I can assure you that some of them are,' Dani confirmed, her cheeks colouring bright red as she realised that the single glass of champagne she had allowed herself with her meal seemed to have loosened her tongue. Discussing another couple making love was definitely not something she should be doing with Niccolo, of all people. But despite her earlier nervousness, she had found the evening so relaxing, and Niccolo such easy company, that she had temporarily let her guard down.

Not a good idea when the meal was almost over and the night was rapidly approaching!

'I— This has been a wonderful evening, Niccolo. Thank you,' she told him with stiff politeness.

Niccolo was instantly aware of the return of Daniella's earlier doubts concerning the wisdom of the two of them spending the night together. While he had been totally captivated all evening by how beautiful Daniella looked, by how much he wanted to make love with her again, he'd already vowed to himself that he wouldn't until she was absolutely sure that it was what she wanted, too…

'I assure you, the pleasure has been all mine, Daniella,' he told her honestly.

She gave him a quizzical look. 'I'm curious to know why, when no one else does, you have always insisted on using my full name?'

Yes, he had—and deliberately so. Years ago, when Eleni had been so determined to remain at school in England with her new friend, and Niccolo had been just as determined that she would not, it had been his way of maintaining a disapproving formality between himself and Daniella. In latter years, he recognised ruefully, it had been for another reason entirely…

Niccolo easily held her gaze. 'But I'm *not* the only one who does so, am I?'

Her frown deepened. 'I don't— Oh!' She came to an abrupt halt, no longer relaxed. Her body stiffened. 'You're referring to my grandfather?'

Niccolo had indeed noticed the way in which Daniel Bell always referred to his granddaughter as Daniella when they'd met. He had also been very aware of the way in which the older man almost made it into an insult.

Niccolo reached across the table to cover her clenched hands with one of his own. 'But not for the same reason, Daniella, I do assure you.'

'I'm sorry?' Dani looked across at him uncertainly. The last person she wanted to talk about this evening was her machinating grandfather—although it had certainly brought her back down to earth with a bump!

Niccolo smiled gently at her. 'Unless I am very much mistaken, your grandfather uses your full name as a reminder that, despite being named for him, you are not the grandson he wanted.'

That was very astute of him after just a few hours' acquaintance with her grandfather, Dani thought heavily. It had taken her until she was in her teens to understand that her grandfather was taunting not just herself but her mother, who hadn't produced a male Bell heir. She grimaced. 'And you, Niccolo? Why do *you* insist on calling me Daniella?'

Niccolo could feel the tension in her hands beneath his, and he curled his fingers about them to move his thumb lightly, caressingly, across her tightly clenched knuckles. Her tension was evidence, if Niccolo had needed it, that her grandfather's disappointment that his only grandchild was a girl had been a constant source of hurt to her over the years.

'Because, Daniella, unlike your grandfather,' he said, 'I take total delight in the fact that you are feminine.'

'Oh!' Daniella blinked her surprise at his compliment.

Niccolo felt his inner fury towards Daniel Bell grow in intensity. How dared he cause this beautiful woman—*his* woman, even though she hadn't yet acknowledged it—a moment's pain simply because her gender was not what he had wanted?

'Don't blame my grandfather too much, Niccolo,' Daniella said. 'I'm sure you'll be disappointed, too, if the child I carry should turn out to be a girl and not the male heir you want—need—to carry on the D'Alessandro legacy.'

But Niccolo was an Italian, and to Italian men all children were loved and valued. His own parents, he knew, would have dearly liked more sons to carry on the D'Alessandro name, but after several miscarriages his mother had produced Eleni, thirteen years after Niccolo was born—a child who had been adored by all of them because to them she was a gift from God.

As the child Daniella carried was a treasured gift, regardless of whether it turn out to be a boy or a girl...

'You do not know me well yet, Daniella,' he told her quietly, and he stood up to move around the table to her side, gently pulling her to her feet so that she stood only inches away from him. 'But never doubt that this child—' he reached out and placed a hand possessively on the flatness of her stomach '—*our* child,' he emphasised, 'will be loved and wanted no matter what its gender.'

Dani's breath caught in her throat, her vision misting with sudden tears. She knew he meant what he said, and that he would indeed love their child—perhaps even already loved their child—whether it was a boy or a girl. She was grateful for that—knew that it could have turned out very differently.

Though Niccolo didn't just stop at declaring his love for their child, she reminded herself heavily. He was insisting on marrying the mother of his child too. But he didn't love *her*, did he?

She stepped away from the warm possessiveness of his hand on her stomach, able to breathe again once Niccolo was no longer touching her. 'That's reassuring to know, Niccolo. Thank you,' she said. 'And I want you to know that this has been the most romantic evening of my life.'

He regarded her with dark, unfathomable eyes. 'But…?' he finally prompted.

She quirked her lips. 'How clever of you to know there's a "but"!'

He gave a humourless smile. 'You have changed your mind about the two of us sharing a bed tonight, have you not?'

Dani looked at him warily. That was exactly what she had decided, and she wasn't sure, despite the mildness of his tone, how he was going to react to being told.

She swallowed hard. 'Are you going to be very angry if that turns out to be the case?'

Niccolo looked at her searchingly. Daniella expected his

primary emotion to be *anger* that she had doubts about their spending the night together after all?

She turned away to walk over to the balustrade, her back towards him as she spoke. 'Maybe if we had just made love this afternoon instead of waiting…' She stopped and made an attempt to control her ragged breathing. Once she was sure she would be coherent she tried again. 'I've had too much time to think, Niccolo. To realise… It really has been a wonderfully romantic evening.' She turned to face him, her back firmly against the balustrade. 'But now, if you don't mind, I think I would like to go to my own bedroom and sleep alone.' The last was added defensively.

Niccolo studied her beneath hooded lids. 'You say that as if you think I might try to force the issue.'

'Don't be silly, Niccolo!'

But her laugh sounded false to his ears. He was becoming more and more convinced by the second that he was being far from *silly*, as she put it.

He very much doubted that there had been any other man in Daniella's life in the two and a half years since the failure of her marriage… A marriage she had absolutely refused, on several occasions, to discuss with him. If he tried to talk to her about that marriage again now, would he succeed only in alienating her completely? Niccolo had a feeling that he might.

The relationship between the two of them was so very fragile. Too fragile for him to risk even attempting to discuss Daniella's previous marriage with her now. But he made a promise to himself that he would learn the truth about that marriage at the earliest opportunity. Not from

Eleni—because that would not be fair to either his sister or to Daniella. But he would find out the truth somehow.

He moved to Daniella's side, his gaze gently holding hers as he reached out to clasp one of her hands in his before raising it to brush his lips lightly across the softness of her skin. 'Of course I do not mind, Daniella, if that is your wish,' he reassured her gruffly.

Contrarily, a shiver of awareness quivered down Dani's spine as Niccolo's lips touched the back of her hand, and she instantly felt disappointed at Niccolo's easy acquiescence to her request to sleep alone tonight.

Her feelings made no sense whatsoever. Were completely illogical, considering *she* had been the one to say she would prefer not to sleep with him tonight.

But nevertheless, that feeling of disappointment persisted.

'It is,' she told him tersely as she snatched her hand from his grasp and moved sharply away from him. 'I—I'll wish you goodnight, then, Niccolo.' She hesitated at the top of the stairs to look back at him.

'Goodnight, Daniella.' He hadn't moved from where she had left him standing beside the balustrade, the expression in his gaze shadowed in darkness as the candles on the table flickered and died. 'Sleep well,' he murmured.

Dani gave him one last frowning glance before hurrying down the stairs to her bedroom on the next floor.

The bedroom that adjoined Niccolo's.

A fact she became very aware of when, only minutes later, she heard him let himself into the adjoining room.

Dani sat down shakily on her brocade-covered bed, not sure that she was going to be able to sleep at all knowing Niccolo was only on the other side of that connecting door…

CHAPTER EIGHT

'I HAVE brought you morning tea, Daniella.'

Dani roused herself sleepily at the sound of Niccolo's voice, extremely comfortable and warm beneath the bedcovers as she gazed up at him in the semi-darkness of her bedroom.

'I remembered your aversion to coffee yesterday,' he said as he stood beside the bed looking down at her.

'That's very kind of you.' Dani smiled her gratitude.

If she wanted tea or coffee in bed in the morning in London then she had to get up herself and prepare it. And asking any of the staff at the house in Gloucestershire for morning tea or coffee was frowned upon by her grandfather, when they were all perfectly fit and well enough to go down to the breakfast room for it.

She moved to sit up against the downy pillows. The gold brocade curtains were drawn across the huge French doors that led out onto the balcony, shutting out the view, making it impossible for her to tell what time of day it was.

Dani had tossed and turned in the bed for at least an hour the previous evening before falling asleep, and—unusually—she'd had to get up a couple of hours ago in order to be violently ill. She was feeling much better now, even more so after washing her face and brushing her teeth. Obviously this was the start of the dreaded morning sickness!

Still, she felt much better after a couple of hours' more sleep, and the tea sounded very inviting.

'Er—would you care to join me?' she offered as she turned, her eyesight having become accustomed to the semi-darkness, and found that there were two cups on the tray.

'Thank you,' Niccolo accepted, before moving to pick up the chair from in front of the dressing table and setting it down next to the bed. He lowered his long length into it, dressed casually this morning, in faded denims and a black cashmere sweater, his thick hair brushed back from his face.

'What time is it?' Dani asked lightly, in an effort not to feel self-conscious as her cream lace camisole top became visible above the bedclothes as she turned to pour the tea. Pregnant with Niccolo's baby, she would look slightly ridiculous pulling the covers up to her chin like some shy virgin!

'Almost ten o'clock,' Niccolo told her with satisfaction.

'In that case, shouldn't you be at work by now?' Dani frowned as she handed him a cup of tea before picking up her own cup and sipping gratefully. It tasted wonderful!

Niccolo shrugged broad shoulders as he added milk and a spoonful of sugar to his cup. 'I thought the two of us could spend the day together.'

'Oh, but…' Dani shook her head. 'I'm supposed to be flying back to England today,' she said doubtfully.

Niccolo nodded. 'And when you are ready to return to England the D'Alessandro jet will be at your disposal.'

Dani knew all about the family-owned D'Alessandro jet, and remembered teasing Eleni about the sheer luxury of it during their university years, when her friend had made frequent visits home to Venice in it. But Dani had never imagined flying in it herself...

Daniella even looked beautiful first thing in the morning, Niccolo thought distractedly, with her hair fluffed about her face in delicate disarray, her eyes like huge green pools in a face bare of make-up, and the creamy curve of her breasts visible above the low neckline of the lacy camisole she wore. If anything, he wanted her more this morning than he had the previous evening—as the hardening of his body was alerting him all too forcibly!

He shifted restlessly in the narrow confines of the bedroom chair. 'You have a problem with that arrangement?' he asked as he saw her frown.

'Not at all,' she assured him with a husky laugh. 'I was just musing on the luxury of owning your own jet and being able to fly wherever you want, whenever you want.'

'It is the D'Alessandro family that owns its own jet,' he corrected her, with his own frown as he sensed disapproval in her remark.

'Niccolo, as we both know only too well, you *are* the D'Alessandro family!' she teased.

Yes, he was. But he was also Niccolo. And as Niccolo he was becoming increasingly uncomfortable with the physical arousal he felt just looking at Daniella's flushed semi-nakedness.

He was thirty-seven years old, for heaven's sake, and had known many women in his adult life. Yet none of them had ever affected him in the way that Daniella did now just looking at her.

He stood up abruptly—at once realising his mistake as his body instantly betrayed his arousal. He would have to excuse himself. He did not dare risk alarming Daniella with this physical evidence of his desire—

'Niccolo?'

As Dani's eyes became more accustomed to the semi-darkness, the more she was able to discern. And at this moment, as she looked at Niccolo from beneath lowered lashes, she was completely aware of the hard arousal of his body. Her own body answered that arousal and her breasts seemed to swell, the nipples tingling into sudden awareness against the softness of her camisole.

Niccolo didn't reply, but he made no effort to disguise the heat that darkened his eyes or the flush against those hard cheekbones as he tightly clenched his jaw.

Dani swallowed hard, knowing that whatever happened next—or didn't happen—it was completely her choice. She knew from Niccolo's gentlemanly behaviour last night that he would not try to initiate anything between them that she didn't absolutely want.

At this moment she knew she wanted him.

Badly!

The reason for her initial sleeplessness last night had been a half-hope, half-dread, that there would be a knock on the communicating door announcing that Niccolo had changed his mind about leaving her to spend the night alone. When the knock hadn't come, Dani hadn't known whether she was relieved or disappointed!

But looking at him now, recognising his arousal, at least

she knew that Niccolo's decision not to come to her last night hadn't been because of any lack of desire on his part.

She turned to carefully place her cup back on the tray beside her. 'Niccolo...?' She held out a hand to him even as she threw back the bedclothes invitingly with the other one. 'Don't question, Niccolo,' she urged as she saw he was about to do exactly that. 'Just come to bed. Please,' she encouraged throatily.

The thrown-back duvet had revealed to Niccolo that Daniella wore French knickers of cream silk and lace to match the camisole top. Her breasts were pert and the nipples hard beneath the silky material, the knickers loose about her slender thighs, and her legs long and silky-soft.

His gaze returned to her face. Her eyes were warm and sultry, her lips—those pouting, full lips that he so longed to kiss—parted in soft invitation.

'Daniella!' He needed no second invitation he moved to join her.

She laughed as she sat up in the bed to swing her feet to the carpeted floor. 'Let's remove some of these clothes first, hmm?' she teased, and she reached out to pull the sweater up his chest and over his head before moving her hands to the fastening on his jeans.

Niccolo stood perfectly still only inches away from her as she unfastened the steel button there, and then the next, and the next, releasing his arousal.

His breath caught in his throat as her delicate fingers moved to touch him there. He groaned low, his eyes closing, as her hand slid beneath his boxers and she began to slowly caress him, fingers curving around him as she moved her thumb along the hard length of his shaft.

Niccolo had lain awake long into the night, unable to stop himself from imagining Daniella touching him like this, caressing him like this, kissing him like this…

Oh, God!

He vividly remembered her heat. Such warm, wet heat. Surrounding him. Drawing him in. Deeper and deeper into that molten fire until it threatened to send him spiralling out of control.

'Let me kiss you, Daniella,' he rasped urgently, and he moved his hands to cup either side of her face, drawing her up into a kneeling position on the bed so that he could claim her parted lips with his own. Their kiss was feverish as Niccolo's tongue plunged deep inside her, licking, tasting, thrusting, claiming that mouth for his own, and his hands ran restlessly down the length of her body to pull her close into his hardness.

As desire and need spun wildly out of control it was almost as if those hours since Niccolo had last kissed her had never happened—although Dani knew that they had, because she had spent most of them fervently wishing he would kiss her again.

Her arms were up about the broadness of Niccolo's shoulders, her fingers threaded into the wild darkness of his hair as she returned the fever of his kiss, and her moan was almost feral as one of his hands moved to cup beneath her breast and he rubbed the pad of his thumb over the already sensitised tip.

Dani's back arched as she moved against that caressing hand, her head dropping back as Niccolo's mouth left hers to travel the length of her throat and down, to capture the other throbbing tip through the thin material of her camisole top with the moist heat of his mouth. He drew it in, suckling fiercely in contrast to the gentle lap of his tongue against the roused hardness of her already engorged nipple.

Dani's fingers clung on to Niccolo's shoulders and her thighs parted as his hand moved the silk material aside to cup her centre, the pad of his palm pressing against her hardened nub as first one finger and then two sought and found her entrance.

Maybe it was because her body already knew the pleasure of Niccolo's, or maybe pregnancy had increased her sensitivity to his caresses, but as Niccolo's fingers continued to stroke inside her, and his lips, mouth and tongue suckled her, Dani felt her body arch anew with the rising force of her imminent release.

'Niccolo...?' Her cry was almost one of bewilderment, and her fingernails dug into the soft flesh of his muscled shoulders.

His hand shifted slightly. The palm was no longer against that hardened nub, but replaced by the caressing pad of his thumb as it moved rhythmically against her, again and again, until Dani could feel the increase in heat, in fire, and she shuddered against his hand in a fierce, pulsating pleasure that seemed as though it would last for ever.

'Oh, God—oh, God!' Her head dropped down weakly onto his shoulder and her mouth moved moistly against him, biting, nibbling in the ecstasies of release.

One of Niccolo's arms supported her back even as he continued to suckle her breast through the now damp material of her camisole. His fingers were stroking, possessing, extorting the last degree of pleasure out of her, and even the briefest caress of his fingers as they left her caused her to quiver in response.

He might not have known the woman he made love with all those weeks ago, but he certainly knew her now! Daniella was a goddess. A goddess of pleasure. Of love. An Aphrodite. And she was his. Every silken, glorious inch of her was *his*.

Niccolo raised his head to look down at her. At the wild tumble of hair about her face and shoulders. At her eyes, dark and slumberous from her recent release.

'You are beautiful, Daniella,' he told her throatily. 'So, so beautiful!' He reached down to swing her up into his arms before laying her down in the centre of the bed, his gaze never leaving hers as he gently slid the damp camisole and French knickers from her body before straightening to remove the last of his own clothing.

Dani gazed her fill of him as she hadn't been able to do the last time they were together, marvelling at the powerful width of his shoulders, his muscled chest, narrow waist and strong, powerful thighs and legs, before her hungry gaze returned to the hardness of his thrusting arousal, long and thick, like tempered steel encased in velvet.

Her gaze returned to his tensely waiting face. 'So are you, Niccolo,' she breathed. 'So are you!' She reached out her arms to him, drawing him warmly against her as he moved to lie down on the bed beside her, and she parted her lips to receive the fierce possession of his.

She could feel the muscles rippling in his back as he half lay across her, his mouth tasting the column of her throat, and she ran her hands down the length of his spine to cup the muscled contours of his buttocks.

Niccolo truly was beautifully male—like the statue of David. Although she thought, from her memory of that particular statue, that Niccolo was better endowed down below than—

My God, what was she *thinking*?

It was impossible to stop the burst of laughter from escaping, although her smile quickly faded as Niccolo raised his head to look down at her with enquiry; it really wasn't the time or place for her to have laughed.

'No, do not stop smiling, Daniella,' Niccolo encouraged as he saw the fading of that smile, the expression in her eyes almost wary now. 'I love to see you smile,' he assured her. 'And lovemaking is not always a serious business, you know,' he added.

She voiced her uncertainty. 'It isn't?'

'Not at all,' he reassured her gently, knowing that once again he had touched upon that area of physical intimacy that Daniella found so—so what?

From the sudden wariness in her eyes just now Niccolo would have said she was almost *afraid* of his reaction to her show of humour—as if she dreaded it might have angered him and feared his response.

He leant on his elbow as he smiled down at her. 'I am reminded of Eleni's reaction after our mother sat her down one day and gave her the "facts of life" talk. I am sure you know the one that I mean…?' He raised mocking brows.

'Oh, yes.' Dani grimaced as she easily recalled the embarrassment she had suffered at having that particular conversation with her own mother. She wondered where he was going with this—he seemed surprisingly relaxed about her laughter just now.

'Exactly.' He nodded. 'Eleni came to me afterwards and assured me that our mother could not possibly be serious about a man wanting to put that part of his body inside her. And that even if he did want to do such a totally gross thing, the woman could not possibly allow him to do it!'

Dani did try to hold back her laughter this time. She really did. But the thought of Eleni saying something like that to her much older and already sexually active brother was just too much for her, and she found herself once again convulsed with laughter.

'I can't believe Eleni really said that to you!' Dani choked once she got her breath back enough to talk at all.

'Oh, yes.' Niccolo lay down on the pillows beside her, one of his arms back behind his head. 'Like you, I found great difficulty in not laughing.'

'What did you say to her?' Dani asked wonderingly.

He shrugged. 'That when the time came she would not find the process quite so gross.' He shook his head. 'I wonder what my little sister would say now if I were to remind her of that talk?' he mused devilishly.

'I wouldn't remind her of it, if I were you.' Dani still grinned as she sat up beside him. 'Although *I* might,' she added mischievously.

Niccolo turned his head to look at Daniella as she sat up on the bed beside him, now totally unselfconscious in her nakedness—as he'd wanted and intended her to be.

He had no doubt now that there was some hidden pain inside Daniella connected with physical intimacy. He was also pretty sure that pain was somehow connected to her ex-husband. Philip Maddox was someone, Niccolo promised himself, with whom he would deal at a later date; it was Daniella who interested him now. And only Daniella.

'May I share your joke now?' he queried gently.

Embarrassed colour darkened her cheeks. 'It wasn't really a joke. I—I was—I was thinking of the statue of David,' she explained uncomfortably. 'About the fact that you—that you're—er…'

'That I am what?' Niccolo encouraged indulgently as Daniella's cheeks flushed anew.

'That you're much better endowed than he is,' she told him awkwardly, before turning her gaze away because she could no longer quite meet his.

'I will take that as a compliment, Daniella.' Niccolo surged up on his elbow beside her, his eyes glowing darkly. 'And that I am so aroused is due entirely to you.'

'It is?'

'Perhaps you would like to discover for yourself just how much I cannot resist you?' he murmured.

'Perhaps I might,' she said teasingly.

Dani hadn't ever imagined that lovemaking could be this much fun—least of all with Niccolo, a man she had only ever seen as either the serious head of the D'Alessandro family or her sarcastic protagonist of the last few years.

But Niccolo's teasing, their mutual laughter, had dispelled any awkwardness she might once have felt at being this intimate with him, and she slid down his body, placing featherlight kisses against his sensitised flesh until she reached her true goal.

'Let's see, shall we?' she whispered as she moved to take him in her mouth, instantly feeling his response as her tongue stroked and her lips caressed.

He felt so good, tasted so good. Her hand gently cupped him as he strained against her, as he groaned low in his throat, and his hands became entangled in the fiery tangle of her hair where it cascaded wildly on the flatness of his stomach.

'Daniella…' he muttered urgently seconds, minutes later, his whole body tensed, his hands clenched into the sheet beneath him.

She made one last stroke with her tongue before relinquishing him reluctantly and looking up at him in the half-light. 'I believe you desire me very much,' she teased, as another light caress of her hand visibly made him arch in a need for release.

'I believe you are right!' he told her fiercely, and he surged up beside her to gently push her back down onto the pillows. He laid claim to her pouting breasts, his hand caressing her before he trailed kisses down her still-flat abdomen to part the silky hair between her thighs and claim her with his lips and tongue.

Within seconds Dani knew that she was on the verge of another climax as Niccolo's tongue flickered against her hardened nub, lapping greedily.

'I want you inside me, Niccolo!' Dani cried achingly. 'I want— Oh…!' Her groan was one of pure pleasure as his tongue suddenly plunged inside her, thrusting rhythmically, taking her to a higher level of pleasure.

Higher.

And then higher still.

Until Dani thought she would disintegrate into a thousand, a million pieces!

'Niccolo, please…!' she whimpered urgently, and her hands moved restlessly against his shoulders. She wanted him inside her, deep, deep inside her, when the explosion came.

Niccolo gentled his stroking tongue before moving slowly, caressingly, back up the lithe length of Daniella's beautiful body, his hardness throbbing wildly for the possession she had just cried out for. 'It will not harm you or the baby if I—?'

'No,' Daniella assured him breathlessly, her eyes feverish, her lips red and swollen. 'The doctor told me it's perfectly safe for me to continue normal sexual relations. But as my "normal sexual relations" at the time were non-existent I—Oh…!' She moaned weakly as Niccolo moved between her thighs to position himself gently against her entrance.

Slowly, oh so slowly, inch by inch, Niccolo entered her, watching the deepening pleasure on Daniella's face even as he kept a tight rein on his control so that he wouldn't just surge deep within her in hard, thrusting possession, stroking rapidly until they both climaxed in wild, mindless ecstasy. His!

Daniella was his—all his, Niccolo cried silently as he buried himself inside her to the hilt, halting all movement as he gave her time to adjust to his hard length, his jaw clenched in his effort to slow down.

Dani, sensing the sheer effort of will Niccolo was exerting, and knowing his caution was unnecessary, began to move her hips against him, and his own groans of pleasure matched hers as seconds later he rolled over onto his back and took her with him, Dani above him now as he allowed her to take control.

Their gazes were locked as Dani rode him hard and fast, her back arching as Niccolo's hands moved to cup her breasts, as he caressed those fiery tips in that same instinctive rhythm. Then his hands left her breasts to grasp her hips, his expression fierce as he controlled her movements to take Dani with him into a breathtaking, bone-melting climax that raged fierily through every single part of them both.

Dani collapsed weakly down onto him minutes, hours later, to rest the dampness of her forehead against Niccolo's chest, her breathing as raggedly uneven as his own, their bodies still joined.

Niccolo reached up a languid hand to gently caress the fiery length of Daniella's hair as it lay like flame against the darkness of his chest, totally satiated, sure that he had died and gone to heaven in this siren's arms.

He didn't speak—wasn't certain that he could have done so if he had tried!—just held her, sure that a single word would break the spell. And he didn't want this to be over yet. He wanted to just lie here in Daniella's arms, to savour being with her like this. Without any arguments. Without any doubts whatsoever that she belonged to him and always would.

Because she truly was magnificent.

So beautiful. So responsive. So unselfish in her desire to give him as much pleasure as she was feeling herself.

Such lovers, Niccolo knew, were rare—unique.

As Daniella herself was unique.

Niccolo tightened his arms about her, instinctively holding to him what he knew to be his.

What *would* be his!

All he had to do was persuade Daniella into comprehending that too.

All...!

Daniella, as if sensing his fierce feelings of possession, began to stir above him, shifting slightly so that their bodies were no longer joined, before moving to lie down on the bed beside him.

Niccolo instantly turned on his side to face her, knowing by the sudden guarded look in her eyes as she looked at him that she had indeed sensed those feelings inside him and shied away from them.

'Daniella—'

'This changes nothing, Niccolo. You do know that?' Dani cut firmly across his reasonable tone, shaking her head determinedly. 'Physical pleasure is no basis on which to begin a ma—any sort of a relationship,' she amended quickly.

'It is a start,' Niccolo insisted darkly.

'No,' Dani denied.

'Yes, Daniella.'

'No, it isn't, Niccolo,' she repeated quietly, wishing things could be different, but knowing that too much stood between them to ever be overcome just by physical compatibility.

Her brief, disastrous marriage.

The contents of her grandfather's will.

The fact that Niccolo's only reason for wanting to marry her was because she carried his child.

That Niccolo didn't love her as she loved him!

The other things they could maybe have dealt with, given time and understanding, but the thought of loving Niccolo, being in love with him, and knowing that he had only married her out of a sense of Venetian duty and honour would surely destroy any chance of them finding happiness together.

It would certainly destroy *her*.

She could imagine nothing worse than loving Niccolo and being unable to ever tell him how she felt about him— knew that over a period of time, in the close intimacy of a marriage, it would destroy her more utterly than Philip's treatment of her had ever done.

She deliberately averted her gaze from Niccolo's as she moved away from him to sit on the side of the bed. 'I have to shower and dress if I'm to fly back to England today—'

'If *we* are to fly to England today,' Niccolo contradicted harshly, the mattress moving slightly behind Dani as he moved to sit on his side of the bed.

Dani turned sharply to look at him. *'We?'*

He raised dark brows challengingly. 'You did not seriously believe that I would simply let you return to England to face this alone?'

She frowned. 'Face what alone?'

'I believe you said that you have not yet told anyone else about your pregnancy?'

'Yes, that's right. What of it?'

Niccolo shrugged. 'It is my child too.'

'I know whose child it is, Niccolo,' Dani snapped, impatient with the turn this conversation was taking. 'I just don't see—'

'You do not see what, Daniella?' Niccolo's own patience finally snapped and he reached out to grasp her shoulders and shake her slightly. 'Did you really think that I would just remain here in Venice and leave you to face your family alone when you tell them of the child we have made together?' He scowled at her.

In all honesty, Dani hadn't really given much thought to telling anyone else but Niccolo about the baby—had told herself she had to deal with one confrontation at a time.

But Niccolo was right; telling her parents especially was not going to be a pleasant experience. As for her grandfather… The less she thought of her grandfather's self-satisfied reaction, the better!

Niccolo shook her gently again. 'If that really is the sort of man you believe me to be then perhaps you are right, and we do not have a basis on which to build any sort of relationship!' He released her to stand up and collect his clothes from the carpeted floor before crossing the room in measured strides and opening the door that connected to his bedroom. He closed it behind him with barely controlled violence seconds later.

Dani gazed after him in utter misery.

Who would have believed that only minutes ago the two of them had been making love together so beautifully?

CHAPTER NINE

'THERE really is no need for you to come with me to Gloucestershire,' Daniella insisted, for what had to be the tenth time, as Niccolo accompanied her inside her apartment after driving from the private airport where his twelve-seater jet had landed an hour or so ago.

And for the tenth time Niccolo made an effort to control the angry reply he wanted to make!

With nothing left to say between the two of them—as far as Daniella was concerned, that was—Niccolo still had plenty to say on the subject of their marriage—but he had arranged for his pilot to fly them back to England earlier that evening.

His suggestion that they drive down to her parents' home the following day had been quite sensible, it seemed to Niccolo, as Daniella was tired from the hours of travelling and he had some business to attend to in London this evening. But it was a suggestion Daniella was still protesting against most vehemently.

'There is no question of whether or not I will accompany you to Gloucestershire, Daniella,' he bit out forcefully. 'There is only the timing of the visit to decide.'

'I have already decided—'

'You are behaving ridiculously by even considering making that three-hour drive tonight,' Niccolo growled.

Her mouth twisted. 'In *your* opinion.'

Dani knew she was being awkward by insisting on driving to Gloucestershire tonight. Knew it, but couldn't control it.

She was tired and upset, completely over-emotional after hours of travelling with a silently disapproving Niccolo. Not even the luxury of flying in the private jet, with an attentive steward to see to her every need, had helped to alleviate the uncomfortable silence that had existed between herself and Niccolo for all of those hours.

And the same awkward discomfort still existed between them!

It was why she was feeling so contrarily determined not to do what Niccolo wanted her to do and wait until tomorrow to go and visit her parents. Even when she knew he was right. Especially *because* she knew he was right.

'In my considered opinion, yes,' Niccolo said tersely.

'Oh, your *considered* opinion?' she echoed sarcastically. 'Well, that makes all the difference, of course!'

Niccolo drew in an angry breath, knowing that Daniella was spoiling for an argument and that he was determined not to give her one.

She had to know how reckless it would be to make a three-hour drive this evening. It was already growing dark, and she was too tired—as was he—to make the drive safely tonight.

Besides, he really did have some business in London that he simply had to take care of this evening....

'Daniella, please.' He forced a calming tone to his voice. 'Do this for the baby's sake if not for mine, hmm?'

She flinched. 'That was pretty low!'

Niccolo almost ground his teeth with frustration. 'I will use whatever methods I deem necessary in order to make you see sense.'

'Obviously,' she scorned, dropping down into one of the armchairs in her tiny but comfortable sitting room. 'Very well, Niccolo. I will visit my parents tomorrow—'

'No, *we* will visit your parents tomorrow,' he contradicted her harshly. 'Do you have to fight me on everything, Daniella?'

She hadn't fought him this morning. In fact she distinctly remembered being the one to invite Niccolo into her bed!

Which was her main problem, Dani recognised heavily.

Being with Niccolo this morning—making love with him, laughing with him, teasing him during that lovemaking—had only made her fall in love with him even more. And she knew now just how wonderful it could have been between them if things had been different.

If Niccolo had loved her as she loved him.

Something that was never going to happen.

The duty and honour Niccolo offered, his taking responsibility for the child they had created together, had become a bitter taste in her mouth that simply wouldn't go away.

'Yes. I. Do,' she answered him quietly, firmly, knowing that to do anything else but fight the way Niccolo seemed so determined to take over her life was totally unacceptable to her. She could not become some sort of adjunct to Niccolo's life, just the mother of his child, simply because she was too tired or emotional to fight him anymore.

Niccolo sighed. 'I think it's best if I leave you now,' he said wearily. 'I have a meeting later this evening, but I will be staying at Eleni's tonight if you should need me.'

'I won't.'

His mouth tightened at the flat finality of her tone. 'I will be at Eleni's if you should need me,' he repeated, his tone of voice bordering on the savage. 'Tomorrow morning I will drive back here, and then we will go to see your parents together.' He knew he was being overly forceful, knew from the angry glitter in Daniella's eyes that she resented what she saw as his high-handedness, but Niccolo also knew it was either that or he would take hold of her and shake some sense into her.

He had no guarantee of what his next move would be once he touched her again. He had deliberately not touched her since leaving her bedroom this morning. Not even so much as a casual hold on her arm to help her in and out of the jet.

Because he dared not.

He could not be responsible for his own actions once he felt her warm softness beneath his hands. He had never wanted any woman as he wanted Daniella. In every way. Not just physically either. He wanted her laughter, too—and that easy teasing they had found together during their lovemaking. He wanted it all.

But her emotions were so fragile at this moment—*she* was so fragile—that he didn't want to risk saying or doing anything that might shatter their already shaky relationship.

This forced inaction was not an easy thing for a man used to dealing with hundreds of employees on a daily basis, as well as being head of the D'Alessandro family and managing all their finances. It was not an easy thing when dealing with the mother of his unborn child, the woman he—

The woman he *what*…?

Niccolo became very still, his gaze guarded as he looked across at the seated Daniella.

What *was* it he felt for this woman?

Whatever it was he had never felt it before. He was definite about that. He had never wanted to protect a woman as well as cherish her. To make love with her as well as laugh with her. To tell her all of his hopes and dreams as well as his fears.

All of those things he wanted with her.

Yet he knew he could never share his main fear with her—that she would never, ever allow him to have any of the things he wanted with her.

'I will leave you now, Daniella,' he repeated stiffly.

'Fine,' she accepted dully, her head resting back on the chair.

'Daniella, are you all right?'

'What do you want from me, Niccolo?' Her weariness faded as she turned to glare at him with fiercely angry green eyes. 'You've accompanied me to England against my wishes. You're coming to see my parents with me tomorrow, also against my wishes. What else do you want?' she challenged furiously, her hands clenched on the arms of the chair.

Niccolo bit back his reply, instead shaking his head before turning and striding quickly to the door of her apartment before all his good intentions fled and he said or did something he would definitely regret!

Dani watched him leave, angry with Niccolo, but most of all knowing she was angry with herself.

For needing him.

For loving him.

She was less angry the following morning, when Niccolo returned to her apartment to begin the drive to Gloucestershire. Less angry, but more determined.

She had made a mistake yesterday morning by making love with Niccolo. A mistake that would not be repeated. Not that Niccolo looked as if he would care for a repeat of that lapse either. His manner was curt in the extreme as he opened the car door for her to get into the passenger seat, his expression decidedly grim as he settled himself behind the wheel.

She shot him a sideways glance as he manoeuvred the car out into the busy London traffic. Apart from a terse greeting when Dani had answered the door earlier to his knock, Niccolo hadn't even spoken to her this morning.

Had these hours apart given him time to reflect too? To realise that his suggestion that the two of them marry had only been a knee-jerk reaction to knowing that she was pregnant with his child? After careful consideration, had he decided he didn't really want to marry her?

Perhaps it would be better for both of them if Niccolo had decided that.

'You seem a little—preoccupied this morning. Didn't your business meeting last night go as planned?' she ventured lightly.

Niccolo wasn't preoccupied—he was feeling murderous!

But not with Daniella. Never with Daniella.

No, his anger—this almost uncontrollable fury—was directed at another person entirely. But until he had his emotions under tighter control he would have to choose his words carefully.

'I don't remember saying that it was a business meeting, Daniella,' he countered with the same lightness.

'Oh…' Daniella finally murmured, after thinking over his remark for several tense seconds.

It instantly alerted Niccolo to his mistake—so much for choosing his words carefully!

'Neither was it a social occasion,' he assured her. 'It was more in the nature of a—' What the hell could he call his visit last night to Philip Maddox's apartment? A duty call? A need to know the truth about his marriage to Daniella?

Whatever it had started out as, Niccolo had ended up wanting to physically injure the other man. But that would have made Niccolo less of a man in his own eyes, his father having taught him long ago that a man's real strength lay in not resorting to physical violence. So, instead, Niccolo had chosen to rip Philip Maddox apart with words. Hard, cutting words of disgust for a man who had no right to call himself such.

Certainly Philip Maddox would not forget Niccolo's visit in a hurry.

He knew he couldn't talk to Daniella about any of that just yet—that she needed all of her emotional energy at the moment to deal with telling her parents about the baby they were expecting. But later they would talk…

Later Niccolo intended telling Daniella of his visit to her louse of an ex-husband. And he fully intended talking to her again about their own future together.

'It was a meeting that could not be put off any longer,' he concluded.

Which told Dani precisely nothing as to who the meeting had been with or what it had been about!

Perhaps he had no intention of telling her.

Very likely, she acknowledged heavily. Niccolo was a very private person, and had never felt the need to explain himself to anyone, so why on earth should she expect him to be any different with her? She shouldn't, was the answer.

'Sounds a bit boring,' she commented. 'I trust Eleni and Brad are both well?'

Eleni had rung her apartment that morning, but Dani had anticipated such a call from her friend and switched on the answer-machine; her parents first and then Eleni—that was how Dani had decided to deal with this situation. Besides, she had reasoned, if Niccolo wanted to tell his sister about the baby then no doubt he would do so.

'Eleni is intrigued,' Niccolo drawled. 'To quote my little sister exactly, she said, "First Dani disappears for a couple of days and then you turn up—what's going on, Niccolo?"' He gave a rueful grimace.

Dani felt some of her own tension leave her as she easily imagined Eleni's forthright curiosity. 'So what did you decide to tell her?'

He shrugged. 'Nothing. I thought we could join her and Brad for dinner later this evening and tell them our news together.'

Tell them exactly what? That was the question!

Just about the baby? Or did Niccolo also intend confiding in his sister and brother-in-law that he had offered Dani marriage and she had refused?

Eleni would never forgive Dani if Niccolo told her that!

Nothing would please Eleni more, Dani knew, for her

two most favourite people in the world besides Brad to actually marry each other.

Great—now Dani was going to have two lethally determined D'Alessandros to oppose!

Niccolo glanced at Daniella, knowing from her silence that she wasn't altogether happy with his reply. 'I will leave it up to you exactly what we tell them,' he said. 'I realise I am only allowed to be here at all on sufferance!' His voice had hardened with the frustration he still felt at Daniella's stubborn refusal to marry him.

Not that Niccolo intended letting the matter rest there—because, quite simply, he could not do that.

Three and a half weeks ago he had decided he had to give Daniella time to know whether or not she wanted to continue a relationship with him. But now that he had seen her again, spent time with her in his Venetian home, made love with her again, he could no longer bear to be apart from her.

That longing had absolutely nothing to do with the fact that she carried his child. Last night, as he'd lain awake long into the night in one of the guest bedrooms of Eleni's home, his thoughts—all of Daniella—had been enough to convince him of that.

'Perhaps you should tell me exactly how you wish to deal with this when we get to Wiverley Hall?' he asked.

Dani didn't want to 'deal with this' at all! But she appreciated she had no real choice—especially as there had never been any doubt in her own mind that she'd go through with the pregnancy. Not that Niccolo would have given her any choice in the matter; if she had so much as even suggested the possibility of a termination she knew he would have locked her up for the required eight months until she had given birth!

She grimaced. 'I don't intend stopping any longer than it will take to tell my parents about the baby.'

'And your grandfather?'

No, not her grandfather!

Dani had already decided that she simply couldn't bear the look of smug satisfaction that was sure to be on her grandfather's face when he learnt that she was pregnant and hopefully going to give him the great-grandson that he so wanted to continue the Bell name.

'No,' she stated flatly.

Niccolo gave her a brief glance. The look of almost stubborn anger on Daniella's face told him more than any words ever could have done that she had absolutely no interest in how her grandfather reacted to the news of her pregnancy.

'Do you fear that he will once again be disappointed in you?' Niccolo queried gently.

'Disappointed?' Daniella echoed. 'I imagine disappointment is the last emotion my grandfather will feel when he hears he is to be a great-grandfather at last! Or rather that there is to be a Bell heir at last,' she added, with a bitterness that was unmistakable.

That statement, as far as Niccolo was concerned, required clarification! 'Our child will be the *D'Alessandro* heir,' Niccolo reminded her pointedly.

'Not if my grandfather has anything to do with it!' Daniella retorted.

'Which he does not,' Niccolo snapped.

She shrugged, not wanting to carry on this thread of

conversation any longer. 'Then I suggest you take that up with him.'

'Daniella—'

'Look, Niccolo,' she interrupted him. 'You're going to find out later anyway, so I may as well be the one to tell you now…'

'Tell me what?' he prompted guardedly, already knowing from her tone that he was not going to like what he heard.

Dani drew in a ragged breath. She hated having to do this, but knew that if she didn't, then her totally insensitive grandfather was sure to. It was one of the reasons she hadn't wanted Niccolo to accompany her today, if she was honest. Only one of them, of course. But at the moment it was the most urgent.

Niccolo had already questioned the reason for her uncharacteristic behaviour the night of Eleni's party, and once he learnt of that clause in her grandfather's will, he was sure to draw only one conclusion.

An incorrect one, as it happened. But if Eleni, who knew and loved Dani, had felt compelled the day following the party to voice her doubts concerning Dani's motives for making love with Niccolo, how much easier would it be for Niccolo—who didn't know *or* love her!—to have those same doubts?

But it was no good believing—no, hoping—that Niccolo would never learn of that damning threat. As Dani knew only too well, her grandfather had absolutely no conception of the words 'sensitivity' or 'diplomacy', and was only ever interested in his own wants and needs.

It was far better that Dani tell Niccolo the truth now.

Better, but certainly not easier!

CHAPTER TEN

NICCOLO listened in stony silence as Daniella told him of the clause in Daniel Bell's will that could potentially disinherit Beatrice and Jeffrey Bell of not only the Bell money, but Wiverley Hall and the Wiverley Stables, if his granddaughter had not produced an heir before the time of his death.

His hands tightly gripped the steering wheel as he fought to control his inner fury. It was all too easy to guess why Daniella hadn't told him any of this yesterday.

Because she had feared his reaction.

His contempt.

His accusations!

And she was right to do so. His anger and contempt were so strong, so deep, that it was taking every effort of will he possessed not to voice those emotions.

Because he dared not.

Could not.

Not when he was all too aware of the fragility of Daniella's condition.

But that didn't mean there weren't plenty of things he would have liked to say!

'For goodness' sake, say something, Niccolo!' Dani all but shrieked as he remained icily silent.

She knew how bad it sounded—knew how damning it made her actions the night of Eleni's party look. Especially as those actions had resulted in her pregnancy. And she would much rather Niccolo vented his feelings here and now than just sat there in icy silence beside her.

That he was furious there was no doubt. His mouth was a thin line in his tautly set face, his knuckles showing white where his hands were gripping the steering wheel so tightly. He looked as if he would like to hit something or someone—although she knew absolutely that that someone would never be her. Niccolo had far too much honour to ever strike a woman in anger.

At least now she could be assured that Niccolo would never repeat his marriage proposal. Dani had to blink back the sudden hot rush of tears at that realisation. Not that she had believed for one moment that a marriage between the two of them would ever have worked—how could it when she was in love with Niccolo and he felt nothing but a sense of responsibility towards her? But knowing that choice had been firmly taken away from her was enough to make her want to curl up in a ball of misery and cry until there were no more tears left. About forty or fifty years should do it!

Niccolo drew in a harsh breath. 'I am not speaking because—' He broke off abruptly. 'Daniella, I think it is better if I say nothing at all on this subject until we can be alone somewhere more—suitable for such a conversation.'

The fact that Niccolo couldn't even talk about it right now was enough to tell Dani just how deeply angry he felt.

But what else had she expected? That Niccolo would agree her grandfather's demands were totally unreasonable as well as selfish? That Niccolo wouldn't view Dani's own actions on the night of Eleni's party as a deliberate ploy on her part to provide her grandfather with the heir he demanded?

Fat chance!

'Yes. Of course,' she agreed quietly, her throat actually aching from the effort of trying to suppress her tears. 'I'm sorry, Niccolo,' she added gruffly.

'You—' He broke off his explosion, his knuckles having turned even whiter. 'We will talk later, Daniella,' he said instead.

What was left for the two of them to talk about Dani had no idea. Although she was pretty sure the question of with which one of them the baby's future lay would come into that discussion somewhere….

'I'm very tired, Niccolo, so I think I'll take a nap, if you don't mind,' she told him wearily, and she rested her head back against the car seat and closed her eyes.

Niccolo glanced at her briefly, his mouth tightening as he noted her pallor and the dark circles beneath her closed lids, before determinedly turning his attention back to the road ahead. To allow his tumultuous thoughts full rein would only distract him from driving and so put both their lives in danger. Something he had no intention of doing.

There would be plenty of occasions for acting upon his thoughts once they reached Wiverley Hall!

Dani, as an only child, had always been very close to her parents, and telling them of her pregnancy when she wasn't married to the baby's father—or even intending to be—was probably the hardest thing she would ever have to do in her life.

Thankfully, she and Niccolo arrived an hour before lunch. Her parents would be in the sitting room together, talking over their respective morning activities before it was time to eat. Her grandfather, Dani knew, would have gone out for his late-morning constitutional, but he would be back in time for lunch, so this respite alone with her parents was limited.

'What a lovely surprise, darling!' Her mother stood up to hug her warmly, an older version of Dani herself, with her rich red hair and warm hazel eyes.

'Why didn't you let us know you were coming?' Her father gave her a brief, quizzical look as he received his own hug before turning his attention to their guest. 'Mr D'Alessandro—it's good to see you again.' He shook the younger man warmly by the hand.

'Daniella wanted to surprise you both,' Niccolo answered smoothly when it became obvious Daniella was at a loss as to how to begin telling her parents of the reason for their visit.

'Well, she succeeded.' Jeffrey Bell, a tall, thin, slightly weathered-looking man, after hours of working outdoors with his horses, with blond hair liberally streaked with grey and eyes of twinkling green, gave his daughter an indulgent smile before indicating they should all sit down in the comfortably worn chairs in the family's informal sitting room.

Niccolo waited until Daniella had seated herself on the edge of the faded gold-coloured sofa before deliberately sitting down next to her, and taking one of her hands firmly into his.

Daniella gave him a nervous glance, but left her hand where it was, her fingers curling slightly about his, as if drawing strength from this physical contact.

As she was meant to do. Niccolo's own parents were no longer alive, but he could still imagine the ordeal it must be for Daniella to come here today and tell her parents of her pregnancy. But whatever other circumstances had prevailed, Daniella had not become pregnant on her own, and the responsibility for this announcement was as much his as it was hers.

He knew by the way Daniella's throat moved convulsively that she was having serious trouble finding the right words with which to begin. He turned to the older couple. 'Daniella and I have something we wish to tell you both—'

'Well, isn't this cosy?' The loud voice of Daniel Bell interrupted suspiciously.

Niccolo stood up slowly to turn and stare coldly at the elderly man where he stood in the doorway, looking at them all with shrewd green eyes. The same green eyes that in his granddaughter were warm and gently loving.

'Major Bell,' he bit out in icy recognition, before turning back to Daniella as she still sat frozen into immobility on the sofa, her guarded gaze fixed on her grandfather. 'Will you forgive me, *cara*—' Niccolo spoke to her gruffly '—if I take your grandfather away for a few minutes?'

Dani raised startled eyes to look at Niccolo. Why on earth—?

'I will not be long, I promise.' Niccolo gave her a gently encouraging smile.

'I— Of course.' She nodded, at the same time blinking her eyes in confusion at this development.

Was Niccolo—aware from their earlier discussion that she did not want her grandfather present during this conversation—just giving her some privacy in which to talk to her parents? Or did he have some other reason for spiriting her grandfather away? Whatever Niccolo's reasoning, Dani could only feel relief at his giving her these few minutes alone with her parents.

'Thank you.' She gave Niccolo's hand a grateful squeeze.

'You are more than welcome, *cara*,' he assured her, and he raised her hand, his gaze intent on hers as he placed the lightest kiss against the back of that hand before releasing her and turning back to her grandfather. 'Major Bell, I wish a few minutes' private conversation with you, if you would be so kind?' It was voiced as a question, but the hard determination of Niccolo's tone brooked no argument against the request.

Dani had been slightly thrown by Niccolo's endearment, and that kiss on the back of her hand, but nevertheless she saw the surprise that widened her grandfather's eyes at the younger man's tone before he brought the emotion under control.

He looked at Niccolo with mocking enquiry. 'Well, of course, D'Alessandro,' he drawled confidently. 'We can go to my study.' He stepped back to allow Niccolo to precede him out of the room, a move Niccolo deftly avoided as he stood aside deferentially to allow the older man to lead the way.

Dani's breath left her in a whoosh of relief once the two men had left the room—an emotion echoed by her parents, if their weary sighs were anything to go by. Although the fact that Niccolo and her grandfather had gone now meant

that Dani had to tell her parents about the baby by herself
before the two men returned—something that was proving
a lot harder than she had imagined.

After all, she was twenty-four years old, and ran her
own successful business in London; it wasn't as if even
without Niccolo's emotional support she couldn't keep
herself and her unborn baby. But it wasn't really about that.
Her parents, as Dani knew only too well, had been deeply
distressed for her when her first marriage had ended in the
way that it had. In fact, it had taken all of her persuasion
at the time to talk her father out of going to London to
confront Philip and tell him exactly what he thought of
him!

And now Dani was about to tell them that their only
daughter was going to be an unmarried mother in around
eight months' time!

It was—

All three of them turned towards the door in alarm as the
sound of Daniel Bell's shouting could clearly be heard all
the way down the length of the hallway that led to his study!

Dani rose unsteadily to her feet. 'What…?'

Her parents seemed frozen in their chairs. Her father
was the first to recover enough to speak ruefully. 'Exactly
what did Mr D'Alessandro want to talk to your grandfather about?' he murmured.

There were a few seconds' silence, as Niccolo obviously
replied softly to the older man, followed by yet more
shouting from Dani's grandfather.

'I have no idea!' she replied.

If Niccolo had told her grandfather about the baby then
anger was the last reaction Dani would have expected. But

if Niccolo was discussing anything else with her grandfather then she really didn't have a clue what it could be.

She certainly intended finding out!

'I don't think that's a good idea, Dani.' Her father reached out to grasp her arm as she would have hurried from the room to go to her grandfather's study. 'Mr D'Alessandro strikes me as the sort of man who can take care of himself,' he told her. 'And anyone else who comes along, hmm?' he added softly.

Dani turned back to her father, and the gentle questioning in his eyes was almost her undoing. It *would* have been her undoing if at that moment she hadn't heard the door to her grandfather's study being opened and then closed again with studied force, followed by the sound of someone walking down the carpeted hallway.

Who—?

A grimly satisfied Niccolo entered the room. 'Major Bell has decided not to join us, after all,' he announced.

There was complete silence in the room, and then Jeffrey burst into appreciative laughter. 'I have no idea what you said to my father, Niccolo, but anyone who can best him in an argument—I take it you *did* best him?' He waited for Niccolo's nod before continuing. 'Then you deserve a medal!' he exclaimed, and he crossed the room to slap the younger man on the back.

Jeffrey Bell's lack of rancour on his father's behalf came as no surprise to Niccolo now that he understood the overbearing way in which Daniel Bell had ruled this household for the last twenty-five years. It was the total look of bewilderment on Daniella's face that concerned him at this moment.

He crossed swiftly to her side. 'I assure you that your grandfather is perfectly well. He is merely sulking in his study,' he said dryly.

Sulking?

Her grandfather was *sulking*?

Surely only young children who couldn't have their own way did that?

Then Dani realised that was exactly how her grandfather behaved like: a spoilt and petulant child who always wanted his own way. The only tried and tested way to deal with a spoilt and petulant child was to deny them what they wanted—and Dani knew only too well what her grandfather wanted most!

'Exactly what did you say to him, Niccolo?' Dani wanted to know.

He shrugged. 'The truth.'

She frowned. 'About…?'

'Perhaps I should have said that I told your grandfather a few home truths,' Niccolo amended.

Dani swallowed hard. 'Such as?'

Niccolo looked at her searchingly, easily able to see the strain in her face as she looked up at him anxiously.

He turned to look at her parents. 'I wonder, Beatrice and Jeffrey, if you would mind allowing me a few minutes alone with Daniella? We have some very exciting news to share with you both, but I believe I first need to—to talk to your daughter.'

'Niccolo—'

He reached out and once again took her hand in his. 'We could have this conversation in front of your parents, if that is your wish. But I believe they may find it a little embarrassing to witness me going down on one knee while I propose to you!'

She shook her head. 'I've already told you that I won't—'

'*Cara,*' Niccolo silenced her gently, lifting her hand to brush his lips against her softly scented skin, his gaze intent upon hers. 'It occurred to me, while you were asleep on the drive down here, that when we talked yesterday I somehow failed to propose properly to you. With your permission, it is an omission I intend correcting before we talk to your parents.'

Dani was still rather dazed. Niccolo didn't need her 'permission' to do anything. Neither could she see what difference his *asking* her to marry him rather than telling her was going to make.

'I think it's best if we do leave you two alone for a while,' her mother told her gently as she came over to squeeze her arm understandingly. 'Daddy and I will just go through to the kitchen and tell Cook there will be two more for lunch.'

'But I believe we'll leave Father to sulk for a while longer,' Dani's father added.

'That arrangement sounds perfect.' Niccolo was the one to agree.

'I thought it might.' Jeffrey laughed. 'Don't keep us waiting too long for this news of yours, hmm?' he added warmly.

Dani waited until her parents had left the sitting room before turning back to Niccolo. 'I'm sorry, Niccolo, but don't think you getting down on one knee and proposing is going to make the slightest difference to what my answer has to be.'

'*Has* to be?' he echoed softly, his head tilted slightly as he looked down at her.

Dani removed her hand from Niccolo's clasp before moving away, totally unnerved by his close proximity. 'I simply can't marry you, Niccolo—'

'Why not?'

'Because I *can't!*' she groaned.

So much for her earlier certainty that Niccolo would never repeat his offer of marriage!

But to be married to Niccolo, loving him, *in* love with him, when he didn't return those feelings, had to be her idea of hell on earth....

'It wouldn't work, Niccolo—'

'Everything works between us, Daniella,' he cut in softly.

She gave a weak smile. 'You're talking about sex, Niccolo—'

'I'm talking about making love,' he corrected. 'And we do make love, Daniella.' His voice lowered to a sensuous murmur that made Dani shiver. 'Even that first time we made beautiful love together. Deny it if you can.'

Dani couldn't. She already knew that what she and Niccolo shared physically was exceptional. Perfect.

She shook her head. 'I'm not going to deny it, Niccolo.' She sighed. 'But what happens when I'm huge with our child and no longer sexually attractive? If we were married would I be expected to just sit by while you went out and found yourself a mistress—?'

'No!' Niccolo exclaimed, frowning darkly at the mere

thought of ever making love to any other woman but Daniella. 'No,' he repeated gently as he crossed the room to her side. 'Daniella, perhaps our…courtship has been a little brief. Certainly the nature of it has been reversed, in as much as we made love first and then afterwards got to know each other—and are still learning about each other,' he acknowledged ruefully. 'But I do not just want you in a sexual way, Daniella. I want all of you.'

She looked up at him, heartbreakingly earnest. 'What does that mean?'

He smiled. 'It means that I know you are not in love with me yet, but that I hope, given time, to persuade you into loving me as much as I love you. And I *do* love you— a great deal, Daniella,' he added throatily. 'I love you as I never thought I would love anyone,' he told her intently. 'I love you more than life itself!'

Dani stared at him, completely dumbstruck, completely overwhelmed! 'I— But— You can't love me!' she finally managed to gasp.

Niccolo's smile deepened. 'The fact that you are the only person I know who would dare to tell me who I can or cannot love is one of the reasons that I do love you.'

'But—but you never even approved of me as a friend for Eleni.'

'I was guilty of that arrogance, yes.'

'And even less so after my marriage and divorce,' she continued, frowning now.

He drew in a sharp breath. 'You are in no way responsible for the brevity of your marriage to Philip Maddox!' he told her harshly.

Dani looked up at him cautiously, seeing the fierce

anger in his gaze. And yet it was an anger she was some-how sure was not directed at her....

What did Niccolo know of her marriage to Philip? How did he know? Surely Eleni couldn't have told him?

'The meeting I told you I had in London yesterday evening was with Philip Maddox,' Niccolo continued, his eyes narrowed intently as he recalled that meeting.

'You went to see Philip?' Daniella gaped.

'I certainly did. And I cannot believe that any man could have treated you in that way. He was your husband, and had only just promised before God to love and protect you!'

He shook his head in disgust as he thought of his con-versation the evening before with Daniella's ex-husband. The sorry excuse for a man had admitted that, in a fit of uncontrollable jealous rage, he had all but raped his own wife on their wedding night.

Niccolo had already guessed that it had to be something as awful as that after sensing Daniella's aversion to even the idea of marriage. A few minutes' conversation with Philip Maddox had confirmed his own worst fears.

He looked at Daniella with concern now as she moved to one of the chairs to sit down heavily, her face very pale. 'I don't understand. What made you go and see Philip in the first place?'

'You did, *cara mia*,' Niccolo confirmed as he went down on his haunches beside her chair, his gaze intent on hers. 'These last two days in Venice, you several times looked at me warily, almost with fear, when you thought you might have angered or displeased me, as if you were frightened of what my reaction might be. But please believe me when I tell you I would never force you to do anything you did not want to do, Daniella.'

She already knew that!

Just as she knew—had always known—that Niccolo was nothing like Philip. Niccolo was strong where Philip was weak. Niccolo was honourable where Philip was selfish. Niccolo would never use physical force on any woman. Because Niccolo was—well, *Niccolo*!

The man she loved.

Enough to marry him? Enough to forget the aversion to the commitment of marriage that Philip had so forcefully instilled in her? Enough to entrust her love, the rest of her life, into Niccolo's hands?

God, yes!

Loving Niccolo and knowing that he loved her in return, wiped away any doubts she might have had about marrying again. Because, she realised wonderingly, loving Niccolo, knowing that he loved her, made her strong, not vulnerable.

Niccolo clasped one of her hands tightly in his. 'I will never allow anyone to harm you ever again, Daniella,' he vowed passionately. 'Not Philip Maddox. And certainly not your grandfather,' he added grimly.

Dani felt some of the tension of the last few minutes leave her as she looked ruefully at Niccolo. 'What *did* you say to him just now?' she asked.

Niccolo shrugged. 'I merely explained that I was thinking of setting up my own stables and going into the horse-training business, and that Jeffrey would be the perfect partner for that business. A move that would, of course, necessitate Beatrice and Jeffrey moving from Wiverley Hall to the more modern facilities I intend purchasing. I explained how sorry I was that this would mean he would lose his unpaid housekeeper as well as a source of income, but that I believed the move to be necessary for the happiness of my future wife.'

'It is,' Dani assured him happily.

'I also informed him, without telling him that you are already pregnant, that it is our intention for any children you may or may not have in the future to be D'Alessandros and not Bells. It *is* our intention, is it not…?' Niccolo prompted, suddenly touchingly uncertain.

'It most definitely is,' she breathed shakily, her fingers tightening about his. 'But—Niccolo, earlier in the car, when I told you about my grandfather's will, I thought you were angry with me because you believed I had deliberately set out to become pregnant by you.'

'The anger I felt at that time was directed solely towards your grandfather, for threatening you and your parents in this despotic manner,' he corrected with an impatient shake of his head. 'No man has the right—and especially not a father and a grandfather—to use emotional and financial blackmail in that way.' He raised one dark eyebrow. 'If it is any consolation, I do not believe, once your grandfather has thought the situation through, that he will carry out any of his threats.'

Dani had a feeling that Niccolo would turn out to be right—that her grandfather really had no wish to end up alone and lonely at Wiverley Hall.

Just as she appreciated that it was Niccolo, in his desire to protect her and all she loved, who had made all this possible…

Because he loved her.

Niccolo *loved* her!

She swallowed hard. 'You can go down on one knee and propose now, Niccolo,' she encouraged throatily.

Niccolo looked at her intently and saw the slight flush on her cheeks, the smiling curve to her lips, the warm glow in her eyes.

He moved down onto one knee, her hand held tightly in his. 'Daniella, I love you. I will always love you, and only you, with all of my heart. You are the woman I adore, the body I worship—that I will desire even when you are big with our child,' he added teasingly. 'Will you please marry me and so make me the happiest of men?'

Dani heard every wonderful word of his proposal, cherished every syllable. 'Niccolo,' she began shakily, 'I love you. I will always love you, and only you, with all of my heart. You are the man I adore…' her voice strengthened as she echoed his words '…the body I worship—that I will desire even when I am big with our child,' she added ruefully. 'Yes, I will marry you—and gladly make you the happiest of men, as it will make me the happiest of women to be your wife!'

'Daniella…' Niccolo groaned even as he reached up to take her in his arms and claim the warm invitation of her lips with his own.

She was finally his!

And she would remain his for all time, to be loved and adored as she so deserved to be loved and adored. And he knew Daniella would love and adore him in return.

Niccolo asked for no greater happiness….

EPILOGUE

THEY were married only three weeks later, in a wedding—despite the speed with which it had been organised—that was every bit as beautiful as Eleni's had been the previous year.

All of the D'Alessandro family was present, with Eleni herself beaming proudly at Dani and Niccolo throughout the service as she watched her beloved older brother marry her beloved best friend.

All the Bell family were there too. Dani's happily proud parents. Her grandfather too. Even if he was a little more subdued these days than he'd used to be.

But Dani had no doubt that he would soon bounce back to his normal obnoxious self. Once he got over the fact that his new grandson-in-law could buy him out a hundred times over, and was a man who wouldn't allow anyone to bully or threaten the people he loved—namely Dani and her parents.

And during the months following the wedding, after Dani moved to Venice to live with Niccolo and the two of them eagerly anticipated the birth of their child, Dani knew herself to be very much loved and adored. Their love for each other became deeper and stronger as the two of them came to know each other more intimately.

Seven months later Niccolo cried unashamed tears of pride and happiness, with Dani's hand tightly clenched in his, when their daughter, Sofia Beatrice D'Alessandro, entered the world and claimed their hearts.

A child created by their love.

A cherished and beloved daughter who would one day be joined by two younger brothers: Daniele Niccolo D'Alessandro and Pietro Cesare D'Alessandro.

The D'Alessandro heirs....

Although born in England, **Sandra Field** has lived most of her life in Canada. She says the silence and emptiness of the North in particular speaks to her. While she enjoys traveling and passing on her sense of a new place, she often chooses to write about the city that is now her home. She's been very fortunate for years to be able to combine a love of travel (particularly to the North—she doesn't do heat well) with her writing, by describing settings that most people will probably never visit.

Kayaking and canoeing, hiking and gardening, listening to music and reading are all sources of great pleasure. But best of all are good friends, some going back to her high-school days, and her family. She has a beautiful daughter-in-law and the two most delightful, handsome and intelligent grandchildren in the world (of course!).

Sandra has always loved to read, fascinated by the lure of being drawn into the other world of the story. Her first book was published as *To Trust My Love*. Sandra says, "I write out of my experience. I have learned that love, with its joys and its pains, is all important. I hope this knowledge enriches my writing, and touches a chord in you, the reader."

CHAPTER ONE

As the Malagash Island ferry eased into the dock, Cade Lorimer turned on the ignition of his beloved Maserati and prepared himself for what would undoubtedly be an unpleasant interview.

Saluting the ferry attendant, he drove up the metal ramp onto the narrow highway. He knew exactly where he was going. He owned most of the island, after all. An island now awash in early September sunlight, its thickets of evergreens hugging the cliffs, the sea sparkling as it dashed itself against the rocks.

He was here at the request of Del, his adoptive father. Here on a fool's errand, one that could lead to nothing but trouble—because the woman he was to track down was, in theory, Del's granddaughter.

Del's granddaughter? That had to be the joke of the century. She was a fake. Of course she was.

According to Del she'd been born in Madrid, and had spent most of her life in Europe. Yet for the last eleven months she'd been living a mere forty miles from Del's summer mansion on the coast of Maine.

Cade didn't believe in coincidence. Tess Ritchie was an imposter who'd heard of Del's considerable fortune and was biding her time to lay claim to it.

So it was up to him to stop her. And stop her he would.

On the meadows above the road, three deer were peacefully grazing; Cade's eyes flicked over them, barely registering their presence. Del—so he'd said—had known about Tess ever since she was born, had supported her financially for her entire life, but had never been in touch with her directly or breathed a word about her existence to anyone.

Through local gossip, Cade had long ago found out about Del's biological son, Cory, the black sheep of the family who was, supposedly, Tess Ritchie's father. Del had never breathed a word about Cory's existence, either.

The two best kept secrets on the eastern seaboard, Cade thought, his fingers drumming the soft leather on the steering wheel. If by any chance Tess Ritchie wasn't a fake, then she was related to Del by blood. As he, Cade, was not.

This simple fact rankled; he resented even the possibility of Del having a granddaughter. Stupid of him, no doubt. But wasn't his reaction one more indication of how he'd always felt cheated of any true connection to Del?

Cade rolled down the window, the breeze tugging at his hair. Another minute or two and he'd be there. The investigator's report had stated that Tess Ritchie was renting a converted fish shack just past the village.

The investigator was one Cade himself had used; his reputation was impeccable. But this time, he was out to lunch.

As for strategy, Cade figured he'd wing it once he was face-to-face with Tess Ritchie. For sure, he'd have to fight her off. The woman wasn't born who could resist Del's money, let alone Cade's far more substantial wealth. Billionaire had a certain ring, he had to admit.

So there were two rich men in the family. Yeah, he'd have to fight her off.

He rounded a corner, and there, on the shore of the cove,

was a fish shack that had been turned into a small winterized cabin. An image of Moorings, Del's summer place, flashed across Cade's mind; Del wanted him to bring Tess Ritchie to Moorings on the return trip. The contrast with the fish shack was so laughable that Cade's anger jumped another notch.

He turned down the dirt track to the cabin. No car parked outside and no sign of life. Tess Ritchie worked full-time, Tuesday to Saturday, at the local library, that much Cade knew; it was why he'd arrived well before nine on a Saturday morning.

He drew up outside the cabin and climbed out of his car. Waves murmured on the shingled beach; a pair of gulls soared overhead, their wings limned in light. Filling his lungs with cool salt air, Cade briefly forgot his errand in a moment of sheer pleasure. His own love of the sea was a rare bond between him and Del.

With an impatient sigh, he strode over to the door—painted an ebullient shade of yellow—knocked hard and knew instinctively that the silence on the other side of the door was the silence of emptiness. Fool's errand, indeed. She wasn't even home.

On ponderous gray wings a heron flew past; and to Cade's ears came the rattle of footsteps on the pebbles. Swiftly he circled the cabin. A woman wearing brief shorts and a tank top was jogging toward him along the crest of the beach. She was agile, tanned and lithe, her hair jammed under a vivid orange baseball cap.

Then she caught sight of him. She stopped dead in her tracks, her breast heaving from exertion, and for the space of ten full seconds they stared at each other across the expanse of pebbled beach.

At a much slower pace, which was imbued with reluctance— or was it fear? Cade wondered—she started toward him.

On his way to the cabin, he'd pictured a bleached blonde with a slash of red lipstick and a lush, in-your-face body.

He'd been wrong. About as wrong as he could be. His mouth dry, his eyes intent, he watched her come to a halt twenty feet away from him, her back to the sun.

No lipstick. A sheen of sweat on her face, most of which was shadowed by the oversize brim of her cap. Workmanlike sneakers on her feet, and legs to die for. He stepped closer and saw her, almost imperceptibly, shrink away from him. She said sharply, "Are you lost? The village is back that way."

"Are you Tess Ritchie?"

"Yes."

"My name's Cade Lorimer. I need to talk to you."

He could easily have missed the tiny flicker of response that crossed her features as he said his name, so swift was it, and as swiftly subdued. Oh, yes, he thought, you're good. Just not quite good enough.

"I'm sorry," she said, not sounding at all sorry, "I don't know you and I don't have the time to talk to you—I need to get ready for work."

"I think, when you know why I'm here, you'll make the time," he said softly.

"Then you think wrong. If you really want to see me, come to the public library. Half a mile down the road, across from the post office. I'll be there until five this afternoon. And now if you'll excuse me—"

"Lorimer," Cade said. "The name doesn't ring a bell?"

"Why should it?"

"Del Lorimer is my father—he's the one who sent me here. His other son—Cory—was your father."

Her body went rigid. In a staccato voice, she said, "How do you know my father's name?"

"Let's go inside. As I said, we have things to talk about."

But she was backing away, step by step, her gaze glued to

his face. "I'm not going anywhere with you," she said, her fists clenched by her side so tightly that the knuckles were white.

Terror, Cade thought, puzzled. Why the hell would she be terrified of him? She should be jumping up and down for joy that Del Lorimer had finally sent someone to seek her out. "If you don't want to go inside," he said, "we can talk out here. There's lots of time—the library doesn't open for an hour and a half."

"Talk about what?"

"Your grandfather. Wendel—better know as Del—Lorimer. Who just happens to spend his summers forty miles down the coast. Don't tell me you don't know about him because I won't believe you."

"You're out of your mind," she whispered. "I don't have a grandfather. My grandparents died years ago—not that that's any of your business. Whatever your game is, Mr. Lorimer, I don't like it. Please leave. And don't come back, or I'll set the police on you."

The sheriff on Malagash Island was a longtime friend of Cade's. He should have come up with a strategy, Cade thought irritably, because this wasn't going the way he'd imagined it would. "Who told you your grandparents died?"

A tiny shiver rippled through her body; she hugged her arms to her chest. "Go away—just leave me alone."

"We have several options here, but that's not one of them." Cade's jaw tightened. Above her thin tank top, he could see the enticing shadow of her cleavage. Her arms were smoothly muscled, her fingers long and narrow. Ringless, he noticed, and in a sudden spurt of rage recalled the Lorimer family diamonds.

He'd had enough of this ridiculous fencing. In a blur of movement, he closed the distance between them, gripped her by the arms and said forcefully, "Your grandfather sent me. Cory Lorimer's father."

Ducking her head, she kicked out at him, as vicious and unexpected as a snake. As Cade automatically evaded the slash of her foot, she tore free and took off at a run up the slope.

In five fast strides, Cade caught up with her, grabbed her by the shoulder and tugged her around to face him. But before he could say anything, her body went limp in his hold. Oh, yeah, he thought cynically, oldest trick in the book. Digging his fingers into her shoulder because she was a dead weight, he wrapped the other arm around her waist.

Then, to his dismay, he realized it wasn't a trick. She'd fainted, a genuine, no-fooling faint. Face paper-white, eyes shut, body boneless. With a muttered curse, he lowered her to the ground and thrust her head between her knees.

So the terror had been real. What in God's name was going on? Impulsively he pulled the ball cap off her head, loosing a tumble of dark chestnut curls from which the sun teased streaks of gold. It was soft between his fingers, silky smooth. She was too thin, he thought. But her skin was like silk, too.

Then she stirred, muttering something under her breath. He said with a calmness he was far from feeling, "I'm sorry—I shouldn't have frightened you like that."

He could hear her trying to steady her breath; the small sounds smote him with compunction. He added, "I've never in my life terrified a woman into fainting—not my style. Which is something you'll have to take on trust. Look, let's start again. I have a very important message for you, one I've promised to deliver. But we can do this outside, so you'll feel safe."

Slowly Tess raised her head, her hair falling around her face. She needed a haircut, she thought distantly. Time to get out the scissors and hack the ends off.

The man was still there. Through her tumbled curls she saw hair black as the ravens that flocked the beaches, eyes the harsh gray of the cliffs that ringed the island. His face was carved like the cliffs—hard, unyielding, craggy. And undeniably, terrifyingly male.

A stranger. But worse than a stranger, she thought with a superstitious shiver. Her fate. Dark, dangerous and full of secrets.

Pushing her hair back, terror rising in her throat again so that she could scarcely breathe, she said raggedly, "I've nothing here worth stealing. No money, and I don't do drugs, I swear I don't."

Cade Lorimer said blankly, "Your eyes. They're green."

Panic-stricken, she gaped at him. Con artist, or certifiably mad? What did green eyes have to do with anything? She pushed hard against him and said frantically, "There's nothing here for you. Cory's dead—he's been dead for years. Can't you just leave me in peace?"

Cade's heart was thudding in his chest; her words scarcely registered. In all his life, he'd only known one other person with eyes that true, deep green, the green of wet leaves in springtime. That person was Del Lorimer.

She must be Del's granddaughter. She had to be. "Do you wear contact lenses?" he rapped.

Temper streaked with a flash of humor came to her rescue, briefly subduing fear. "Which mental ward have you escaped from? You're here to rob me and you want to know if I wear contacts?"

"Just answer me," Cade said brusquely. "Your eyes—are they really green?"

"Of course they are—what sort of stupid question is that?"

"The only question that matters," he said heavily. So she wasn't a fake; he'd been way off base. That wasn't his style, either.

As for her, her whole body was taut with tension; she was looking at him as warily as if he really was an escapee from a mental institution. Or a thief, the other accusation she'd thrown at him.

Logically he should explain the significance of her eye color. But he wasn't quite ready to do that. "I'm no thief—I have all the money I need," Cade said, "and I'm entirely sane. As for drugs, I've never touched them—more than enough excitement in day-to-day living without dosing myself with chemical additives." He hesitated, then added with huge reluctance, "I'm here to give you something, not to take anything away."

"There's nothing you can give me that I would want," she said stonily. "Nothing."

"How can you say that, when you haven't heard me out?" His smile didn't reach his eyes. "The first step is for both of us to stand up, how about it?"

He took her by the elbow. The coolness of her skin seeped into his pores; her nearness sent heat licking along his veins, liquid heat, primitive and lethal. Oh, no, he thought, appalled. He wasn't going to lust after Del's granddaughter. That really wasn't in the cards.

But as he eased her upright, his senses were assaulted by her body's fragility, and by the scent of lavender, delicate and uncomplicated, that drifted from her skin. Again desire ravaged him, unasked for, totally unwelcome. With all the willpower at his command, a willpower honed over the years, Cade kept his face an unrevealing mask and forced himself to relax.

Shrugging off his fleece vest, he wrapped it around her shoulders. "You're cold," he said. "Go inside and get something warm on. You could call the police, too—Dan Pollard's the sheriff's name, I've known him for years. Give him a description, and he'll vet me. Then we'll talk."

Tess swallowed. Cade Lorimer was standing too close to her, much too close. But while there was concern in his voice, and remorse overlying the gray depths of his gaze, she had the strong sense that both these emotions were, at best, superficial. Lorimer, she thought, and shuddered. How could she trust anyone with the same last name as Cory, her father? "I'll call the police right away," she said flatly. "Don't follow me into the house."

A gull screamed overhead as she walked steadily toward the cabin. The door shut decisively behind her, and Cade heard the snap of the lock. Restlessly he began prowling up and down. If she really was Del's granddaughter, why had she never contacted Del? She'd been here for nearly a year, and not once had she put the touch on him. So what kind of game was she playing? Lying to him, telling him both her grandparents were dead, acting as though he, Cade, was a combination of Attila the Hun and Hannibal Lector.

What was taking her so long?

Swiftly he walked around the back of the cabin, wondering if he'd fallen for the second oldest trick in the book—escape via the back door. But through the plate glass windows that overlooked a small deck and the ocean, he could see Tess Ritchie inside the cabin, her back to him as she did something at the stove. Declining to spy on her, Cade turned and stared out to sea.

No answers there.

The back door scraped open. Tess said, "I've made coffee. I'll give you sixteen minutes of my time and not a minute more."

"Did you phone the sheriff?"

As she gave a choppy nod, Cade pulled up one of the cheap plastic chairs and sat down. She set a tray on the low table. Her movements swift, she poured two mugs of steaming coffee and pushed a plate of muffins toward him. "Home-made?" he asked casually.

"Blueberry. I picked the berries two weeks ago. I've lived here nearly a year—why did you pick today to turn up?"

He knew exactly how long she'd lived here. "A month ago

my grandfather had a minor heart attack. It scared the pants off him—his first intimation that he, like everyone else, is mortal. That's when he hired an investigator to—"

"An investigator?"

The terror was back, full force, nor was she making any effort to mask it. "That's right," Cade said, all his suspicions resurfacing. "Del wanted to discover your whereabouts. Eventually the investigator came up with this location. You must have known of Del's existence, or why else would you be living so close?"

Tess buried her nose in her mug, inhaling the pungency of the dark Colombian blend. "I'm living on the island because I was offered a job here and I love the sea." And because, she thought, it was a very long way from Amsterdam. "Why would Cory lie, telling me both my grandparents were dead?" she flashed. "My grandfather died years ago, in New York City. Not long after, my grandmother succumbed to pneumonia."

"Was Cory a truthful man?"

Her fingers tightened around the handle of her mug. "He had no reason to lie."

"He did lie. Del's very much alive and wants to meet you. That's why I'm here—to bring that about."

Coffee sloshed over the rim of her mug. "No."

"You haven't even heard me out."

"I don't want to meet him! Ever. Go home and tell him that, and don't either of you bother me again."

"That's not good enough."

"Maybe you should try looking at it from my point of view," she snapped, color flagging her cheeks.

Cade looked at her in silence. Her cheekbones flared like wings; her lips were a soft and voluptuous curve, infinitely enticing, while her eyes, so exotically shaped, so vivid in hue, drew him like a magnet. She was—he knew this without a shadow of doubt—the most beautiful woman he'd ever seen.

He'd seen—and bedded—more than a few beautiful women.

"So what is your point of view?" he said in a hard voice.

Fractionally she hesitated. "I disliked my father," she said evenly. "Disliked and distrusted him. I therefore have no wish to meet his father—a man who, let's be frank, has ignored my existence for twenty-two years."

Cade leaned forward, clipping off his words. "He's supported you financially for twenty-two years. Or are you forgetting that?"

She gave an incredulous laugh. "Supported me? Are you kidding?"

"Every month of your life, money's been deposited in a Swiss account for your use."

She banged her mug on the table; more coffee spilled over the rim. "You're lying—I've never seen a penny of that money."

"Or are you lying?" Cade said with dangerous softness. "There's a lot more money where that came from."

She surged to her feet. "Don't insult me—I wouldn't touch Lorimer money! It's the last thing I need."

Cade stood up, too, and deliberately let his gaze wander over the plastic furniture and the roughly shingled walls of the little cabin. "Doesn't look that way to me."

"Money," she spat, "you think it can buy everything? Look around you, Cade Lorimer. I go to sleep at night to the sound of the waves. I watch the tides come and go, the shorebirds feed, the deer wander over the hill. I'm free here, I'm in control of my own life and I'm finally learning to be happy—and no one's going to take that from me. No one! Including Del Lorimer."

Abruptly Tess ran out of words. Dammit, she thought, why did I spout off like that? I never talk about myself to anyone. And then to bare my soul to Cade Lorimer, of all people. A man who screams danger from every pore.

He was watching her, those storm-gray eyes focused on her, intent as a hunter who sees movement in the underbrush. "One of us is lying," he said, "and it isn't me."

"Then why are you so anxious to introduce me to my grandfather?" she said sweetly, "if I'm nothing but a money-grubbing liar?"

"Because he asked me to."

"Oh, so you dance to his tune? But of course, I'm forgetting, he's a very rich man."

Cade's breath hissed between his teeth. Had he ever known a woman to get so easily under his skin? "Del gave me a secure and happy childhood," he grated, "and taught me a great deal over the years. Now he's old and he's sick, and it's payback time."

Tess said, going on intuition, "You didn't mean to tell me that, did you? Any more that I meant to sound off about freedom and happiness."

Infuriated by her accuracy, Cade picked up his mug and drained it. "You make a mean cup of coffee, Tess Ritchie," he said with a wolfish grin. "In your lunch hour, go on the Internet and look up Lorimer Inc.—check me and Del out, get a few facts. I'm taking you out for dinner after work. I'll pick you up here, sharp at six-thirty, and we'll continue this conversation."

She raised brows as elegant as wings. "Are you giving me orders?"

"You catch on fast."

"I have my faults, but stupidity isn't among them."

"I didn't think it was," he said dryly.

"Good. Then you'll understand why I'm not going out for dinner with you. Goodbye, Mr. Lorimer. It's been…interesting."

"So interesting that I'm not about to say goodbye. Come off it, Tess—you're certainly smart enough to know I won't vanish just because it suits you. Six-thirty. If nothing else, you'll get a free meal at the hotel, prepared by one of the finest chefs along the coast." His smile bared his teeth. "Besides, I've been told I'm a passable dinner date. Now hadn't you better get ready for work instead of standing there staring at me with your mouth open? I wouldn't want you to be late."

"I'm not—"

He took the two steps off the deck in a single stride, loped around the corner of the cabin, got in his car and roared up the slope.

He'd gotten away from her without touching her again. For which he deserved a medal. And he knew exactly what he was going to do next. A self-imposed task, the potential results rather more important than he liked.

CHAPTER TWO

CAREFULLY Cade steered the Maserati between the potholes in Tess's driveway. He was twenty-five minutes early. Only, he assured himself, because he'd completed his task, and the paperback novel he'd brought with him had failed to hold his attention.

Nothing to do with Tess, and the itch under his skin to see her again.

He climbed out of his car and knocked on her door. No answer. He knocked again, feeling his nerves tighten. Had he been a fool to take her for granted, and assume she'd be meekly waiting for him? She was no pushover. If she didn't want to see him again, she'd take measures to put that into effect.

He tried the door, which, to his surprise, opened smoothly. Stepping inside, he closed it behind him. Ella Fitzgerald was crooning on the stereo; the shower was running full-blast.

Tess was home. She hadn't run away.

It shouldn't matter to him as much as it did.

Cade looked around, taking his time. Clothes were flung over the chair: a black dress, hose and sleek black underwear that raised his blood pressure a full notch. Dragging his eyes away, he took in the cheerful hooked rugs dotting the worn pineboard floor, and an array of cushions that brightened the sagging chesterfield. Books overflowed the homemade shelves. The room was spotlessly clean.

Absolutely no evidence that she'd ever had any access to Del's allowance, or to any other substantial source of money, Cade thought. Basically it was the room of someone who lived off a minimal paycheck.

Someone who'd be far from immune to the Lorimers' wealth.

The CD came to an end. He flipped through a stack of discs, discovering old favorites of his own, intrigued by how eclectic a collection it was. He selected a CD and snapped open the cover.

The shower shut off. As he leaned down to push the play button, a door opened behind him and he heard the soft pad of bare feet on the wooden floor. He turned around.

Tess shrieked with alarm, clutching the towel to her breasts. Her hair was wrapped in another towel, turban-fashion, emphasizing her slender throat and those astonishing cheekbones; her shoulders were pearled with water and her legs went on forever. He wanted her, Cade thought. Wanted her here and now. Fiercely and without any thought for the consequences.

He wasn't going to do a damn thing about it. For starters, she was Del's granddaughter and strictly off-limits. Plus— more importantly—he was far from convinced she was as innocent as she looked. Too much money was at stake.

She said shakily, "You're early."

"I did knock. The door wasn't locked."

"I usually don't bother locking it. Although I guess I should when you're around."

He said hoarsely, "Tess—"

"Don't come near me!"

The terror was back full force. "Sometime—soon—you're going to tell me why I frighten you so badly," he said. "I made a dinner reservation for seven—charming though you look right now, a towel won't cut it."

Her heart was still racketing in her chest. Sure, he'd startled her. But it was more than that. In his light gray suit, blue shirt and silk tie, Cade looked formidably sophisticated and wholly, disturbingly male. Not to mention sexy, a word she avoided like the plague.

She was the nearest thing to naked.

Power, she thought slowly, that's what he breathed; although he was quite possibly unaware of it. Power. Money. Sexual charisma. All three put his danger quotient off the chart.

She didn't do sex.

To her horror, she heard herself blurt, "If Del Lorimer's my grandfather, that makes you my uncle." This all-too-obvious fact hadn't struck her until five minutes after Cade had driven away from her cabin this morning.

"I'm Del's adopted son," Cade said curtly. "No blood relation to your grandfather at all. Or to you." Just as well, he thought savagely, given the way his hormones were acting up.

Adopted. Not a blood relative. But not her fate, either, Tess thought in a sudden snap of fury. Merely a man who was a total stranger to her, and who would remain just that—a stranger.

Unfortunately her thoughts didn't stop there. Because she'd grown up in an environment where she could trust nothing, she'd always endeavored to remain honest with herself. If she were to be honest now, relief had been her predominant emotion that Cade Lorimer wasn't related to her by blood; close on its heels had been utter dismay at all the implications of that relief.

It didn't matter who Cade was. She just didn't do sex.

Deeply grateful he couldn't read her mind, she said tartly, "So you're an adopted son. If I'm the newly discovered grand-daughter, aren't you afraid I'll supplant you?"

"No," Cade said coldly, and watched her lower her lashes, her face unreadable.

Then she looked up, meeting his gaze in unspoken challenge. "My clothes are on the chair," she said. "Turn your back."

Unwillingly admiring her spirit, he tore his eyes from the silken slopes of her bare shoulders and did as she asked. "You okay with this music?"

"Meatloaf, Verdi, Diana Krall," she said wildly, "play what you like. And I'm not wearing a towel for dinner, I'm wearing a dress. The only one I own, so if it's not up to your standards, too bad."

"You'd look gorgeous wearing burlap."

"Mr. Cade Flattery Lorimer," she retorted, picking up her clothes and holding them like a shield in front of her.

Suddenly angry, Cade turned to face her. "I mean it. Look in the mirror, for God's sake—you're an extraordinarily beautiful woman."

Her jaw dropped. "I'm too skinny and my hair's a mess."

He grinned at her, a mocking grin sparked with so much energy that it took her breath away. "Slender, not skinny," he drawled. "Although you're right about the hair—a good cut would do wonders."

"What *is* your angle? If money doesn't work, try sex?"

"What a wildcat you are. Hissing and spitting if anyone gets near you."

"Whereas you're like a panther! Sleek and dangerous."

She hadn't meant to say that. Only to think it.

"Now who's pouring on the flattery?" Cade said. "Get dressed and dry that mop of hair, or we'll be late for dinner."

Oddly enough, beneath a storm of emotions she couldn't possibly have labeled, Tess was very hungry. Scowling, she marched out of the room with as much dignity as she could muster when swathed in an old blue bath towel, and shut her bedroom door with more than necessary force. For the first time in her life, she wished she owned a real dress. Something out of *Vogue*, stunningly simple, reeking of money and sophistication.

With a vicious snap she switched on her hair dryer. She didn't have time to cut her hair, but she was going to slather on eye shadow and mascara. For courage, she thought, picking up her brush.

Because wasn't one of the several reasons she'd decided to keep this dinner date the simple fact that running away was the coward's way out?

In the last few years, she'd done too much running.

Cade had put on Mozart by the time Tess walked back into the living room. Taking his time, he looked her up and down, noticing instantly that her fingernails were digging into her palms, and her jaw was tight. Her dress was a plain black sheath, teamed with sheer black hose and stiletto heels. She'd swept her tangle of hair into a knot high on her head; clustered black beads dangled from her earlobes. Her mouth—his own went dry—was a luscious raspberry-red. He said, "Beautiful's such an overused word—you take my breath away."

Her heart lurched in her breast. She said coolly, "I made my dress from a remnant that was on sale. The shoes come from Second Time Around—I only hope the original owner won't be eating dinner at the hotel."

"I bet she never looked that good in them."

"You're too kind."

Part of her liked this verbal banter, Tess thought uneasily. Quelling a stab of fear, she took a white mohair sweater from the cupboard, flung it around her shoulders and stalked out the door.

Cade's car smelled of leather; he drove with smooth competence, making small talk about the scenery. Ten minutes later they were seated in the hotel dining room by a window overlooking the ocean, the applewood in the fireplace crackling cheerfully. Trying not to panic at the alarming array of silverware, Tess took a deep breath and went on the offensive. "Your company—Lorimer Inc.—owns this hotel. And many others, worldwide, all part of the DelMer chain of fine hotels."

"Del has rather a large ego—he liked the idea of combining his two names. So you checked him out."

"Him and his adopted son. I'd be a fool not to meet him, wouldn't I? A rich old man—every woman's dream."

"No more shoes from Second Time Around," Cade said.

"No more hose from the dollar store." The waiter put a menu in front of her, a thick leather binder embossed with gold. She wasn't going to be intimidated by a menu, Tess thought resolutely, and opened it to the first page. "Once I've hooked up with Del, I could buy the dollar store. A whole string of them."

"You could," Cade said. "Do you like martinis?"

She'd never had one. "Of course."

"Straight up or on the rocks?"

"On the rocks. I could buy a car like yours."

"Several, I should think."

Her eyes narrowed. She was doing her best to act like the crassest of fortune-hunters, and Cade wasn't even reacting. If anything, he was laughing at her. Chewing on her lip, she added, "I'd inherit a ton of money when my grandfather dies. Enough to buy diamond earrings and go on a world cruise."

"Lorimer Inc. owns a fleet of cruise ships—you could take your pick. Stateroom, the works. I'm sure by then you'd have found some diamonds to your taste."

She'd never liked the look of diamonds. Too cold, too flashy. "Emeralds, to go with my eyes," she said dreamily.

"Excellent choice…have you decided on an appetizer?"

The menu was in Italian with the English in script below.

When she was eleven, she'd spent a year in Rome with Cory and Opal, her wayward mother; Tess said in impeccable Italian, "I'll have *fegato grasso al mango*." She flipped the page. "With *stufato di pesce* for a main course."

Each was the most expensive item on the page. Blanking out the actual dollar amount, she said with as much innuendo as her conscience would allow, "How is your grandfather's health? You mentioned a heart attack."

"Oh, I suspect he's got a good many years in him yet. You might have to wait for that inheritance."

"Or is the inheritance like the support—nonexistent?" she retorted. "If, as you claim, I really am related to him, I could always go to the press. Illegitimate Granddaughter Cheated Of Her Rights—I can see the headlines now, can't you?"

With a flourish, the waiter put the martinis on the table, and took their orders. Tess loathed olives. She picked up the frosted glass and took a hefty swallow. Her face convulsed. "That's straight antifreeze!"

"Your first martini?" Cade said innocently.

"They don't serve them at the chicken takeout." She grimaced. "I see why—who'd want to eat olives pickled in ethylene glycol?"

Cade signaled the waiter, asked for a brandy Alexander, and said smoothly, "Del hates martinis, too. And loves the ocean."

"Does he? How nice. You know, if allegedly he's been supporting me since I was born, he owes me quite a backlog." She smiled at Cade, batting her mascaraed lashes. "I'd better hire a good lawyer."

"It would have to be a very good one to take on Lorimer Inc."

"Then there's you," she said in a voice like cream, brushing his fingers with her own, letting them linger until every nerve in his body tightened. "You make Del's fortune look like small change."

It was the first time she'd touched him voluntarily; and how he loathed her motive for doing it. Holding tight to his temper, Cade watched her pout her raspberry-red lips, heard her purr, "I'd be a fool to turn my back on you or Del, Cade. But especially you."

His voice taut, because there was a limit to what a man had to put up with, Cade said, "Do you want to know what I did today? I wandered around the village talking to people about you. People who've known you for the better part of eleven months." The pout was gone, he noticed with mean pleasure, replaced by blank shock. Calmly he kept going. "I'm sure you'd agree with me that the islanders to a man—or woman— are sober New Englanders who don't go in for flattery. They described you as reliable, honest, frugal, hardworking. Likes to walk the beaches by herself. Hardly ever goes off-island. No friends. No wild parties. No men."

Tess gripped the edge of the table. "You spent the day *gossiping* about me? How dare you! And why would they talk to *you*? The islanders aren't just sober, they're closemouthed to a fault."

"Several years ago, I paid top dollar to buy up ninety percent of the island. Made it into a nature conservancy to protect it from development—the only concession being that I build this place." Cade waved his martini at his surroundings. "So I'm in like a dirty sock—the islanders love me. You might as well drop the gold-digger act, it's wasted on me. You can't fool an islander—if they say you're honest as the tide turns, I'll go along with that."

For now, he added silently.

With exquisite timing, the waiter deposited a creamy drink sprinkled with nutmeg in front of her. She glared at it, trying to gather her wits. She'd just made a total fool of herself. Good job, Tess. What's the follow-up?

"Try your drink," Cade said, giving her the full benefit of his smile. One of his women had called it lethal; another, dynamite. It was a weapon he wasn't above using when it suited him.

But instead of blushing in confusion or smiling back, Tess said furiously, "I've never laid eyes on one red cent of your grandfather's money."

His smile faded. "That was the next item on my agenda." He waited while her antipasto was put in front of her. "I talked to Del today. He's a stubborn, cantankerous old man, who likes control and claims he's mislaid the investigator's report—"

"You haven't seen it?"

The emotion in her face was unquestionably relief. Cade picked up his fork. "No. But I did get out of Del—by sheer bloody-mindedness—the investigator's discovery that ever since your father died six years ago, your allowance has been siphoned off the account by your mother. Opal Ritchie. I can only presume Cory took it prior to that."

Briefly Tess shut her eyes. Opal and Cory. Her parents. Cory with his unpredictable rages, his drug-induced highs. Opal, wild, willful, never to be trusted. The rooms, she thought. Oh God, those awful rooms...

"What's wrong?" Cade demanded.

When she opened her eyes, she was back in the elegant dining room, with its high-arched windows and vaulted ceiling, its polite murmur of conversation; and a pair of stormy-gray eyes boring into her soul. "I'm fine," she said flatly, and with superhuman effort pulled herself together. The brandy Alexander, which was delicious, slid down her throat. The array of silver looked a little less intimidating. Carefully she selected the mate of the fork Cade had used and took a bite of mango, chewing thoroughly, tasting nothing. "You called me a liar back at the cabin."

"I shouldn't have doubted you," Cade said curtly. At least with regard to Del's monthly support, he shouldn't have. But he still had plenty of other questions about the all-too desirable and highly enigmatic Tess Ritchie.

The tight knot in her chest easing somewhat—for hadn't he more or less apologized?—Tess said shrewdly, "You still wish I was a thousand miles away from Del, don't you? So you and I are on the same wavelength. The distance'll be forty miles, not a thousand—but forty miles is plenty. Because I don't care about the Lorimer money. His or yours. I like my life here on the island, it's all I want and I'm not leaving here. You can tell my grandfather I'm grateful he did his best to support me—it wasn't his fault that I never saw the money. But it's too late now. I don't need his support anymore."

Her green eyes blazed with honesty. Disconcerted, Cade discovered in himself a contrary and ridiculous urge to take her words at face value. To trust her.

He'd never trusted a woman in his life other than Selena, his mother, whose every motive had been on the surface for all to see. Tess wasn't Selena. Tess was mysterious, fiery and unpredictable.

Trust her? He'd be a fool to be betrayed by a pair of emerald-green eyes.

He'd been holding a weapon in abeyance. Deciding now was the time to use it, Cade said coolly, "Del told me something else today—that the investigator drew a complete blank for the year you turned sixteen. The year your father died. What happened that year?"

Her skin went cold. A roaring filled her ears. She couldn't faint again, she thought desperately. Not twice in one day. She shoved the fork in her mouth, and concentrated on chewing. She might as well have been eating cardboard.

She'd slept wrapped in cardboard for over two months.

Forcing herself to swallow, desperate to change the subject, she said jaggedly, "Where does my grandfather spend his winters?"

Cade sat back in his chair, gazing at her, his brain in overdrive. Mysterious was a euphemism where Tess was concerned. She was secretive and closemouthed, a woman for whom terror was a constant companion. What had she done at sixteen—or what had happened to her—to induce that blank-eyed stare, those trembling fingers?

He shoved down an unwelcome pang of compassion, allowing all his latent distrust to rise to the surface instead. She'd been a model of good behavior ever since she'd arrived on Malagash Island. But preceding that? What then?

"Are you in trouble with the law?" he demanded.

"No," she said. But her gaze was downcast, and her voice lacked conviction.

Fine, he thought. I might just do some investigating on my own behalf. Del likes to think he holds the reins, but I'm the one in control here.

With equal certainty Cade knew that if he didn't bring Tess Ritchie back to Moorings, Del would order the chauffeur to drive him to the island and find her for himself.

He said casually, "You speak very good Italian."

"When I was twelve, I lived for a year in Rome." She glanced up, her eyes shuttered. "I also speak German, Dutch, French and a smattering of Spanish. A European upbringing has its advantages." Which, she thought bitterly, really was lying.

"Favorite artist?"

"Van Gogh. I don't see how anyone could live in Amsterdam and not love his work. Rembrandt and Vermeer close seconds."

"Your tastes in music are eclectic and you like espionage novels."

"You should be the investigator," she said nastily. "I also like medieval art, lavender soap and pizza with anchovies."

Lavender, he thought, remembering the fragrant, misty rows of blue in the fields of Provence. It was an unsophisticated scent, earthy and real, that somehow suited her. Trying to focus, he said at random, "Which university did you attend?"

Her lashes flickered. She said edgily, "There are other ways of getting an education."

"Where's your mother living now?"

She dropped her fork with a small clatter. "I have no idea."

Her main course was put in front of her. Tess grabbed the nearest knife and fork and started to eat. Red wine had been poured in her glass, the firelight dancing like rubies in its depths. In sudden despair, exhausted by memories she only rarely allowed to surface, she craved to be home in her little cabin, the woodstove burning, a mug of hot chocolate on the table beside her.

And the clock turned back, so that she'd never met Cade Lorimer; never heard of a putative grandfather who lived only forty miles away.

Cade said, "I've upset you."

"You're good at that."

"I'd noticed. I'll book myself into the hotel and get in touch with Del tonight—we'll go see him tomorrow morning. The library's closed Sunday and Monday—I checked."

"I'm sure you did. I'm not going."

No point in arguing now, Cade thought. But at least there was some color back in her cheeks.

What *had* she done at sixteen? Quelling a question he couldn't possibly answer, he began talking about the Vermeers he'd seen at the Metropolitan Museum, segueing to the political scene in Manhattan; and discovered she was well-informed, her judgments acute, occasionally slanted in a way that fascinated him. Then, of course, there was the play of fire-light in the thick mass of her hair, the shadows shifting over her delicate collarbone and ivory throat.

Wanting her hadn't gone away; it had, if anything, inten-sified. Good thing he was known for his willpower; he was going to need all of it. Because to seduce Tess Ritchie would be a very bad move.

They were sipping espressos when his cell phone rang. "Excuse me a minute," he said, and took it from his pocket. "Lorimer," he barked.

Tess straightened her shoulders, trying to work the tension from them unobtrusively. In half an hour she'd be home, her door locked, her life resuming its normal, peaceful pattern.

Peace was all she wanted. Peace, order and control.

Then, abruptly, her attention switched to Cade's side of the conversation. "He's *what*?" Cade was saying. "How bad? So you're at the hospital now. Okay, I'll be on my way in five minutes. I'll see you tomorrow, Doc. Thanks."

He pushed the end button and thrust the phone back in his pocket. The color had drained from his face, his jaw a tight line. He said flatly, "Del's had another heart attack. A minor one, according to his family doctor." He waved to the waiter. "We'll leave as soon as I've paid the bill."

So Cade loves his adoptive father, Tess thought, and felt emotion clog her throat. Cory hadn't loved her. Ever.

She never cried. Couldn't afford to. So why did she feel like crying now? She forced the tears down, watching Cade pass over his credit card.

What if Del Lorimer had another heart attack in the night, and died? She'd never meet him. Never find out if he really was her grandfather, or if this whole farrago was the product of an overeager investigator. But if Del was, by any chance, truly her grandfather, blood of her blood, shouldn't she see him, find out if he was a replica of Cory or someone entirely different?

We...Cade had said a few moments ago. *We'll leave*...she thoroughly disliked the way he'd taken it for granted that she'd go with him.

It was her choice, and only hers.

Stay or go.

CHAPTER THREE

TRYING to decide what she should do, Tess gazed at Cade in silence; he was frowning at the bill, his mind obviously elsewhere. What if he drove off the road because he was thinking about Del rather than his driving?

Somehow the decision had made itself. Tess said evenly, "If I come with you, I'll need some clothes."

"No time," Cade said. "We can get anything you need tomorrow. Let's go."

As obediently as a well-trained hound, she followed him out of the dining room to his car; and felt her heart contract when it took him two attempts to get the key in the ignition. "Are you all right to drive?" she asked.

"Don't worry—I won't put you in the ditch."

It's you I'm worried about, not me. As she fastened her seat belt, the soft leather seat enveloping her, Tess knew her words for the truth. How long since she'd allowed anyone else to matter to her?

Forever and a day.

Or, more accurately, not since that hot summer's night when she was five, and she and her parents had fled Madrid on the midnight train. Just the three of them: they'd left behind Tess's beloved nanny, Ysabel, without Tess even having the chance to say goodbye to her.

That long-ago heartbreak, so laced with betrayal, had cured Tess, once and for all, of letting anyone close to her.

The last person she should allow to bend that rule was Cade Lorimer. Yet for some reason Tess found herself gazing at his hands, wrapped around the leather-coated steering wheel. Strong hands with a dusting of dark hair, and long, lean fingers that made her ache somewhere deep inside.

She dragged her eyes away, staring out the window. The brief ferry trip was soon over, the forty-mile drive passing in a blur of black spruce, dark rocks and the glitter of the moon on the sea. Although Cade showed no inclination to talk and she had nothing to say, the silence was far from restful. It was a relief when he pulled into the parking lot of an imposing brick building, and she could get out of the car and stretch her legs. "Hospital's state of the art," he said without a trace of emotion, striding toward the entrance. "Del endowed it after my mother died two years ago."

"Oh…I'm sorry she's dead."

"Del's lost without her," Cade said tersely, pushing open the door.

And you, she wondered, did you love your mother just as you so obviously love Del?

Then, to her dismay, Cade took her by the hand. His palm was warm, his fingers clasping hers with automatic strength. With shocking speed, heat raced through her body, fiery and inescapable. Her steps faltered, every nerve on high alert. The ache in her belly intensified, and she could no more deny it than she could shut out the long corridor with its antiseptic smell and polished tile floor. Desire, she thought helplessly. I've never felt it in my life, yet recognize it as though I've always known it. How can that be?

It was more than she could do to pull her hand away. Because Cade needed her, or because she was a total fool?

Desire wasn't on the list, any more than sex.

They'd arrived at the elevator. As they rose to the second floor, Tess stared at the controls, her body a tumult of longing that both terrified and bewildered her. She forced her features to immobility. She couldn't bear for Cade to guess her feelings, for then she would truly be naked in front of him.

As they left the elevator, the nurse on duty smiled at Cade. "Room 204," she said. "He's resting well."

"Thanks," Cade said briefly. Outside the room, he hesitated, inwardly steeling himself for whatever he might find.

Tess tried to tug her hand free. But his fingers tightened, and—short of causing a scene—she had no choice but to follow him into the room. Standing at his side, tension singing along her nerves, Tess looked down at the man in the bed.

Del Lorimer was asleep, his mane of silver hair spread on the pillow, his strongly corded arms bare to the elbow. Automatically she recorded a beak of a nose, an obstinate chin and the facial wrinkles of a man who's lived his life at full tilt.

She felt not the slightest flicker of recognition. Not even remotely did he remind her of Cory.

Swiftly Tess switched her gaze to Cade; and with dismay saw a man closed against any emotion. His features were tight, his jaw clenched, while his eyes were like dark pits, unreadable and unreachable.

In unconscious antipathy she moved away from him so that their shoulders were no longer touching. She'd been wrong: Cade didn't love his adoptive father. By the look of him, love wasn't a word he'd even recognize.

In a way, she was glad to see his true colors so clearly; it made it easier to dismiss him as a ruthless interloper who was interfering in her life with results she could neither anticipate nor desire.

Desire. That word again.

Desire someone incapable of loving the father who—on Cade's own admission—had given him security and love as a boy? She'd have to be crazy to do that.

To her relief, a white-jacketed doctor came to the door. Cade joined him there, holding a low-voiced conversation, then came back into the room. "We might as well go," he said impersonally. "Del will sleep the night through, there's no point in staying."

For a split second Tess looked down at the man lying so still in the bed, a man who, other than common human concern, meant nothing to her. Then she preceded Cade out of the room, walking fast down the hushed, immaculate corridor.

Sixteen minutes after they left the hospital, Cade slowed at two impressive stone pillars and turned down a driveway that wound between stiff Scotch pines and a forest of rhododendrons. Del's stone mansion boasted grandiose white pillars, a formal array of windows and huge chimneys, and equally formal gardens, raked, clipped and weeded to a neatness nature never intended.

Tess disliked it on sight.

For the first time, she broke the silence since they'd left the hospital. "You'll take me home tomorrow," she said.

Cade rubbed his neck, trying to get the tension out. "You can sleep in the west wing," he said. "You'll hear the sea through the windows."

"Tomorrow," she repeated inflexibly.

He shifted in his seat so that he was gazing into her vivid green eyes. Against his will, an image of Del flashed across his mind: a shrunken old man lying too still in a hospital bed, the bars raised on either side. "Give it a rest, Tess," he said sharply. "Haven't we argued enough for one day?"

"Then perhaps you should try listening to me."

Whatever her background, she'd learned to fight for herself, he thought, watching the night shadows slant across her face. Her skin gleamed pale, infinitely desirable, the pulse throbbing gently at the base of her throat. Flooding him as irresistibly as a storm surge, he longed to rest his face there, close his eyes and let the warmth of her skin seep through his pores.

Not since he'd started dating had he ever been pulled so strongly to a woman. It wasn't the way he operated. Easy come, easy go, everything pleasant and on the surface, that was him. He sure as hell wasn't going to break that pattern with Tess Ritchie. Might as well step into a minefield.

Anyway, judging by the look on her face, she'd rather clobber him than hold him close.

"Let's go in," he said, and climbed out of the car.

When he unlocked the massive oak door, four large dogs came scrabbling across the marble floor, barking in excitement, white teeth gleaming. With a gasp of pure horror, Tess grabbed Cade, thrusting him between her and the dogs. *The alley, the dog snarling...crack of a gunshot.*

"Down!" Cade said, and all four subsided, jaws agape, tongues lolling. Swiftly he turned. "You're afraid of dogs, Tess?"

Wrong word, he thought. For terror, once again, was etched into every line of her body, her eyes saturated with emotions he couldn't begin to name, let alone understand.

"I—yes, I'm afraid of them," she faltered. Flushing, she dropped her hold on his suit jacket.

"They thought I was Del."

"I don't care what they thought—just keep them away from me."

"You get bitten as a kid?" he said casually, signaling for the dogs to stay as he led her up the magnificent curve of the stairwell.

"Yes. Yes, I was."

Accusing her of lying would start another argument, Cade decided. But she was definitely lying. Again. He opened the fourth door along the hallway. "The Rose Room," he said ironically. "My mother was, in many ways, very conservative."

An ornate brass bed, too much ruffled chintz, an acre of rose-pink carpet, and a bouquet of real roses on the mantel. "My whole house would fit in here," Tess said.

Cade opened a drawer in the Chippendale dresser and pulled out a nightgown. "Towels and toothbrush in the bathroom," he said brusquely. "Come down for breakfast in the morning any time you're ready."

The gown was a slither of green silk that had probably cost more than her entire wardrobe. As Tess gingerly took it from him, a spark of electricity leaped between them. She jumped back, giving a nervous laugh, tossing the gown on the bed. As though he couldn't help himself, Cade took her by the shoulders. "All too appropriate," he said tightly.

His fingers scorched through her dress; his eyes skewered her to the wall. She tried to twist free. "Don't!"

"You're so goddamn beautiful—I can't keep my hands off you."

Deep within, feelings she'd never experienced before uncoiled in her belly, slowly, lazily, unarguably. Her knees felt weak. Her heart was juddering in her breast. With all her strength, she pushed against the hard planes of Cade's chest. "If you brought me here to seduce me, you've got the wrong woman. Let go, Cade! *Please...* "

She wasn't a woman who would beg easily. She wasn't playing hard to get, either—he was almost sure of that. Plain and simple, she hated being touched. By him? Or by anyone?

His usual women were willing. All too willing, tediously and predictably so; which was probably why it had been a considerable while since he'd shared his bed.

Cade released her, rubbing his palms down his trousers, and stated the obvious. "You feel the attraction, too. But for some reason you're fighting it."

"I don't feel anything! Or is your ego so inflated you can't stand rejection?"

The wildcat was back, eyes glittering. "You do feel it, Tess. I can read the signals." He gave her a mock salute. "We'll pick this up in the morning. Good night."

The door closed softly behind him. Tess locked it with a decisive snap, then sank down on the bed. She'd never in her life met anyone like Cade Lorimer.

A few moments ago, desire had almost overwhelmed her. Desire was a phenomenon she'd read about, always with faint derision; it wasn't something she'd ever expected to attack her like an enemy from within.

When Tess woke the next morning, the sound of the sea was drowned by the hard pelt of rain driven against the windowpanes.

Trying to shake off a strange sense of oppression, she sat up, and saw with a jolt of unease that an envelope had been pushed under her door.

Opening it as warily as if it contained a deadly virus, Tess unfolded the sheet of heavy vellum. *I'll stay at the hospital all day*, it said. *The housekeeper will find something for you to wear and the dogs will be kept in the kennels. Cade.*

His handwriting was angular, decisive and very masculine. Cautiously Tess unlocked the door, peeked down the empty hallway and grabbed the small heap of clothes on the floor. Tights, a scoop-necked T-shirt and a pair of sandals that looked brand-new: the housekeeper had come through.

Quickly she dressed and went downstairs for breakfast. She spent the rest of the day curled up in the library, reading and listening to the rain, birch logs snapping in the fireplace. But to her intense annoyance, from midafternoon onward, she found herself straining for the sound of Cade's car.

She wanted him to drive her home. That was the only reason she was interested in his return.

She got up, pacing back and forth, wishing the rain would let up so she could go outdoors. Then, from the corner of her eye, she noticed a collection of framed diplomas on the wall of the alcove beyond the fireplace. Walking closer, she saw degrees from Harvard, awards from the London School of Economics, the letters dancing in front of her eyes.

All the diplomas were Cade's.

Humiliation wasn't an emotion new to Tess; but she'd never before felt it so keenly or so painfully. She hadn't even graduated from high school.

Worse, she was the daughter of a small-time crook and his unscrupulous mistress.

Cade Lorimer was way out of her league. One thing was certain—she'd never be *his* mistress. Not that she wanted to be, of course.

Viciously Tess dug the poker into the glowing coals, tossed another log on the fire and went back to her book.

Dinner was a welcome break, even though her appetite had deserted her. But when Cade still wasn't back by nine o'clock that evening, Tess clumped downstairs to the kitchen. She was trapped in this horrible house for another night, she thought irritably, making herself a mug of hot chocolate, stirring in too many marshmallows, then taking an experimental sip.

Behind her, the swing door swished open. Cade said, "You've got marshmallow on your chin."

She glowered at him. "Nice to see you, too."

"I need a drink—something stronger than hot chocolate."

"How's Del?" she countered; and realized to her surprise that she really wanted to know.

"Cranky as a bear in a cage. Coming home late tomorrow afternoon. Whose clothes are you wearing?"

"The butler's granddaughter's," she said.

The tights were too short and the T-shirt too small. Trying very hard to keep his gaze above the level of her breasts—which were exquisitely shaped—Cade opened the door of the refrigerator, took out a beer and uncapped it. Taking a long draught, he said, "Hospital food has to be the worst in the nation and their tap water tastes like pure chlorine."

He'd dropped onto a stool by the counter and was loosening the collar of his shirt. He looked tired, she thought reluctantly, watching the muscles in his throat move as he swallowed.

His body hair was a dark tangle at the neckline of his shirt; the thin cotton clung to the breadth of his shoulders. As he rolled up his sleeves, corded muscles moved smoothly under his skin. Moved erotically, Tess thought, and buried her nose in her mug. What was wrong with her? She never noticed the way a man moved.

The silence had stretched on too long. She said politely, "Is it still raining?"

"Supposed to stop tomorrow morning." He took another gulp of beer. "What did you do all day?"

"Read in the library."

"Right up your alley," he said with a faint smile.

One smile. That was all. No reason for her to feel as though he'd given her the sun, the moon and the stars. The man had charm to burn, she thought crossly; but she'd always considered charm a slippery attribute at best. Picking up her mug to drain the last of the hot chocolate from it, she said tautly, "If you're not able to drive me home tomorrow morning, I'm sure there's a chauffeur hidden away in this barn of a house. I'll get him to drive me…good night."

"Wait a minute!"

Furious, she glanced down. His fingers—those elegant fingers—were clamped around her left wrist. "Let go," she flared. "I'm not in the mood for macho."

"Del won't be home until the afternoon, and he wants to meet you—so you can't go back before that. And when you meet him, don't say or do anything to upset him. He's to be kept quiet for the next while, and he's not supposed to worry about anything."

"You told him I was here? That I'd meet him?" she said, her voice rising.

"Of course I did. Why else are you here?"

"How was I supposed to leave? I don't have a car, there's no bus to Malagash Island and I don't like hitchhiking in a downpour."

Cade stood up, still clasping her wrist. "You'll meet him, Tess. You don't have to throw your arms around him. But, by God, you'll be polite."

"Is this your CEO act?" she snapped. "Well, whoop-de-doo."

Her eyes were like green fire. Not stopping to think, Cade dropped his head and kissed her, hard and fast and with all the pent-up emotion of the last two days. Then he stepped back, his heart juddering in his chest. "I've been wanting to do that ever since I saw you jogging on the beach," he snarled. "You be around when Del comes home, and watch what you say. If you're half the person the islanders say you are, you wouldn't want an old man's death on your conscience."

His kiss, so unexpected, so forceful, had seared through her like a bolt of lightning. Her adrenaline sky-high, any caution lost in rage, Tess wrenched her wrist free and blazed, "You're the one who brought me here—what about *your* conscience?"

"My conscience is my concern. Just behave yourself tomorrow."

"Don't tell me how to behave—I'm twenty-two, not ten,"

Tess retorted, itching to throw her empty mug in his face. Banging it on the counter instead, she pivoted to leave the room.

Like a steel clamp, Cade's hand closed around her shoulder. "I'm not only telling you how to behave, I expect to be obeyed. Have you got that straight?"

"I'm not an employee you can fire when the whim takes you!"

"No," he said in a voice like ice, "you're Del's grand-daughter." Then, with a deliberation that was subtly insulting, he released her and stepped back.

Was she really related to the old man she'd seen in the hospital? Or was this whole setup as unreliable as a bad dream? Unable to think of a thing to say, as furious with herself as she was with Cade, Tess marched out of the room with as much dignity as she could muster. As she raced up the back stairs, she realized she was scrubbing at her mouth, doing her best to erase a kiss that had been shattering in its heat, its anger and its imperious demands.

No wonder words had deserted her. No wonder she was on the run.

Once again, she locked her bedroom door.

CHAPTER FOUR

BY THE time the rain stopped the next day, an hour after lunch, Tess was in a foul mood. She'd go mad if she didn't get some exercise.

She'd always hated being confined.

While Moorings must be worth a mint, she wouldn't trade it for her cabin for all the money in the world. But would Cade believe her if she told him that? Somehow, she doubted it.

She slipped out the front door. The air was filled with the heady scent of wet pine needles mingled with salt from the sea. Breathing deep, she set off down a narrow path that, she hoped, would lead her to the ocean.

The path ended at a secluded cove ringed by rocks, where the water sparkled and danced, riffling onto a pale sand beach. Quickly she shucked off her borrowed sandals, and dipped her toe in. Cold, yes, but not unbearably so. She looked around. No one in sight, and Cade wouldn't be back until late afternoon.

Like the mischievous little girl she'd never been allowed to be, Tess stripped to her underwear and, giggling breathlessly, ran into the water. In a mighty splash she flopped forward and thrashed toward the rocks.

She'd learned to swim at a local pool the year she'd spent in Boston as a housekeeper; her strokes were strong, if not particularly stylish. The exercise warmed her, and all the kinks—physical and emotional—of the last forty-eight hours washed away.

Heaven, she thought, turning on her back and floating so she could gaze into the guileless blue sky.

Cade settled Del in the master suite at Moorings, promising to bring Tess to meet him in an hour or so. He then went in search of her.

He drew a blank in the library, the dining room, the solarium and her bedroom. Her black dress was still hanging in the closet; so she couldn't have left.

The beach, he thought. That's where she'd go. Unless she'd left Moorings altogether: she hadn't liked his ultimatum or his CEO act, and he wouldn't put it past her to start walking the highway toward Malagash Island. He hoped to God she wouldn't hitchhike; even on the back roads of Maine, that wasn't a good idea.

If she wasn't at the shore, where would he look next?

He hurried to his room, changed into running gear, and took off down the path. Wet leaves brushed his bare arms, and it was unseasonably warm. He was sweating by the time he emerged onto the beach.

A little heap of clothes lay on the sand and the beach was deserted. Cade jolted to a stop and scanned the surf, his pulse pounding in his ears.

Where the hell was she?

Then he caught sight of a wet head, sleek as a seal's, out by the rocks. Tess. She was cavorting in the waves, diving, splashing and kicking. His relief was instantly engulfed in anger.

He yelled her name. Her head swiveled. She waved at him, and even from that distance he could see she was laughing. Anger notched up to sheer fury.

He ran the length of the beach, his sneakers sinking into the sand. Then, with ferocious speed, he leaped from rock to rock along the long outcrop of granite. When he was level with her, he shouted, "Come closer—I'll lift you out."

Treading water, she gazed dubiously at the chunks of rock. "I'll swim back to the beach and meet you there."

"Do as you're told. Or so help me, I'll jump in and haul you out."

A wave sloshed over her bare shoulders. Laughing with delight, she said pertly, "It's a gorgeous day! Why are you so angry?"

"Because you could have easily drowned in the undertow—why do you think I'm angry?"

Tess's mouth dropped open. What a ridiculous time to realize that while she'd always been petrified of Cory's rages, Cade's anger didn't frighten her at all. It challenged her instead, invigorating her. And what did that mean?

As another wave slopped up her chin, she swallowed a mouthful of saltwater. Choking and sputtering, her brain grappling with this latest twist, she edged toward the rock and waited for a gap in the surf. Then she reached up for Cade's outstretched hands.

With insulting ease, he lifted her from the water. She found her footing on the rough granite and shook her head like a dog. "You should have come in," she said wickedly, "the water's great."

She was wearing nothing but a skimpy black bra and black bikini underwear. Her image burned into Cade's brain: the thrust of her breasts; her waist's delicate concavity; the flare of hip. Like a peregrine plummeting to its prey, he took her in his arms and found her mouth. Her lips were cold and wet, tasting of salt; as he drank deep, he wasn't so angry that he didn't sense the sudden rigidity of her body and her total lack of response.

From somewhere deep within, he dredged up the willpower to restrain his kiss, seeking rather than demanding, giving rather than taking; and was rewarded when he felt her hands creep up his chest and her body grow pliant. Her first shy response rocketed his heartbeat. He fought for control, nibbling on her lower lip, his tongue seeking out the heated warmth of her mouth.

With the same trust, the same hesitancy, she opened to him. God, how he wanted her!

He pulled her slender frame the length of his, the fit perfect, the cold nubs of her breasts through her bra further inflaming him. Her hands crept around his neck, her fingers digging into his scalp; the tentative touch of her tongue ripped through him. Fiercely he traced the long curve of her spine, then circled her naked hips, drawing her into the hardness of his arousal.

Tess shuddered, fear ripping through her, banishing an exploration that had totally beguiled her. She pulled her mouth free, and had neither the will nor the strength to mask the turmoil of emotion that was tearing her apart.

Cade said urgently, "Don't be frightened—yes, I want you, no disguising that. But I won't hurt you, I swear I won't."

She was shivering, for the lovely liquid heat of Cade's embrace had vanished. He'd taken her somewhere she'd never been, she thought numbly, and in so doing, had changed her unalterably.

She whispered, "I'm cold. I need to go back to the house."

"Tess, you wanted me as much I wanted you."

She could scarcely deny it. Fighting for control, she said, "If I'm to meet Del this afternoon, there's a condition attached—you mustn't touch me again. Or kiss me. Do you promise?"

"No."

Her lashes flickered. They were wet, he noticed, stuck together in little clumps. He said, "The only promise I'm prepared to make is that I'll never do anything against your will."

"That's downright manipulative!"

"Is it? Think about it."

She was chewing on her bottom lip. The slope of her shoulders, the delicate flare of her collarbone, juddered through him. "We'd better go back," he said curtly. "Didn't anyone ever tell you not to swim alone? This is the ocean, not some suburban swimming pool."

"I couldn't stand being caged up in that house for one minute longer!"

"You were a fool to take such a risk," he said in a clipped voice. Bending, he gathered her in his arms.

Tess gave a gasp of dismay. One moment she'd been standing on her own two feet; and now she was cheek to chest with the man who was undermining her whole sense of identity. She said in a smothered voice, "Put me down."

But Cade had started back toward the beach, treading carefully over the heaped boulders. "The granite's rough and your feet are bare."

Not up for discussion: that's what he meant. His arm beneath her bare thigh was hard as rock; against her rib cage she could feel the strong, steady beat of his heart, an astonishing intimacy that streaked through her veins like wildfire. How could she feel so threatened by him, yet, paradoxically, so safe?

She closed her eyes, biting her lip to keep the question unspoken. When they reached the beach, Cade dumped her unceremoniously on the sand beside her clothes. "Put them on—I'll find you something dry when we get to the house."

Yanking the tights up her wet legs, she said peevishly, "You weren't supposed to get home until later."

He gave a mirthless smile. "The hospital couldn't wait to get rid of Del. He's home resting. We'll visit him once you're cleaned up."

"I'm not going to meet him wearing a T-shirt that's two sizes too small!"

"Guess it'll have to be the little black dress then." Cade grinned with an aggressive flash of white teeth. "Or one of my T-shirts, which will be four sizes too big."

She tugged her borrowed shirt over her head, noticing with dismay how her nipples were faithfully outlined under the thin fabric. With a sigh of exasperation, she shoved her toes into her sandals. Meeting her alleged grandfather couldn't be nearly as challenging as keeping one step ahead of Cade Lorimer.

An hour later, Tess was ready. She was overdressed, she thought, and decided to do without earrings and to leave her hair loose around her face. Her sweater draped over her black dress, she went in search of Cade; and found him waiting for her in the solarium. It was the only room in the house in which she felt even slightly at home, with its massed ferns and semi-tropical plants.

Cade swept her from head to toe in a single comprehensive glance. She was nervous, he thought, and doing her best to hide it. "Let's get this over with," he said.

She tossed her head. "I'm not scared of Del Lorimer."

"Good," Cade said blandly. He tucked her arm in his; her fingers were as cold as when he'd pulled her from the ocean. His jaw tight, unable to think of anything to say, he led her out of the room.

Upstairs, he tapped on Del's door. "Come in," Del growled.

His hand at the small of her back, Cade pushed Tess ahead of him.

Del Lorimer was sitting up in a vast iron bed, the sunlight full on his face. Tess stopped dead in her tracks, making a tiny, shocked sound.

His eyes were the same true, deep green as hers.

He really was her grandfather. He had to be. Only now did she realize that, deep down, she'd never fully believed Cade's story.

Del, she noticed, looked every bit as shocked as she felt. He said gruffly, "So you inherited the Lorimer eyes. They skipped Cory. As did so much else." He patted the white bed-spread. "Come closer, girl. Let me look at you."

Like a robot, she walked nearer to the bed, and watched him devour every detail of her appearance with those vivid green eyes. He said brusquely, "Let's get the apology out of the way first. I'm sorry the money I sent never reached you. I should have known Cory would take it. But Opal—guess I expected better of her."

Tess blinked. "Apology accepted."

"I owe you, girl. I'm—"

"My name's Tess," she said.

"So you've got claws. Good. Never did like females to be doormats for a feller to wipe his feet on." Del cleared his throat. "Like I said, I owe you. You'll live here in the summers, and in Manhattan in my penthouse the rest of the year. I'll arrange for a monthly allowance starting tomorrow. You can travel, go to college, do what you like. And when I pop off, which at this rate could be any day, you'll inherit a big whack of money."

Battling a mixture of outrage and amusement, Tess said, "I don't think you're going to pop off—you wouldn't be able to call the shots if you did."

He gave a surprised bark of laughter. "Can't call 'em with Cade. Learned that a long time ago. Might as well try my hand with you."

"What if I'm as contrary as Cade?"

"All that money? Don't make me laugh."

"Surely I'm the one who should be laughing—all the way to the bank."

"I owe you," he repeated stubbornly.

"You don't owe me anything!"

From behind, Cade kicked her ankle with the toe of his shoe. *Behave yourself...* Tess said coolly, "I'll think about everything you've said, Mr. Lorimer—it's a very generous offer. By the way, your beach is beautiful."

"Not bad. Get whales offshore all summer. You can go back to Malagash later today, quit your job, pack your stuff and move up here. I usually head for the city mid-October."

Stubborn, Del most certainly was. But underneath the bluster the old man was exhausted, Tess realized with a pang of compassion. Not that he'd ever admit it. Hadn't she inherited the same will to survive, the same stiff-necked pride? Without them, she might have gone under, years ago.

Impulsively she leaned forward and kissed him on the cheek. "I'm glad we've met...I'll talk to you later." Then, without looking at Cade, she walked out of the room.

Moments later, Cade joined her, closing the door quietly behind him. "We'll go back to the solarium," he said.

It was as good a place as any. When they reached it, Tess stationed herself against a magnificent hibiscus in full bloom, and said with a calmness she was far from feeling, "I understand now why you reacted to the color of my eyes."

"No DNA tests required," he said dryly.

"None are needed anyway—I'm turning down Del's offer." As Cade's breath escaped in an angry hiss, she said passionately, "Hear me out, Cade. And do your best to see where I'm coming from."

He jammed his hands in his pockets. "Okay, give—I'm listening."

She paused, trying to marshal her thoughts. "First, I don't need a grandfather who would serve as a constant reminder of my father. I told you I disliked Cory. The truth is, I loathed him—he never loved me, never saw me as anything but an impediment, an inconvenience."

Cade said intuitively, "You were afraid of him."

"Maybe I was," she said in a brittle voice. "But that's not your concern."

"Why were you afraid of him?"

Ignoring a question she had no intention of answering, she said evenly, "As for Del's money, it would stifle me. I'm financially independent, in debt to no one, with a job I like and my own place to live. I'm not giving that up to move to this house—it's too formal, and I hate tripping over servants all the time. It'd be like living in a velvet-upholstered cage!"

"You want control over your own life."

"Why wouldn't I?"

"Why not try compromise instead of control? You're not giving Del a chance."

"It's my life. He might feel he owes me—but I don't owe him anything. Can't you understand? He's nothing to me. Nothing!"

"Who are you trying to convince—yourself?"

"You! But you aren't listening."

Cade's eyes narrowed. "My problem is, I'm listening to both of you—you and Del. Let me tell you something. I own a house a couple of miles down the road, and you can stay there in the summers, use the place as if it's your own—I'm often away. You'd be close enough to Del, yet preserve your independence."

"What's the point? I'd only be substituting one cage for another."

"My house is very different from Moorings. Modern, full of light and open to the ocean—you'd like it, I know you would. It's my favorite, I have to admit."

"Favorite? You own other houses?"

"Sure—a brownstone in Manhattan. A château on the Loire, a lodge at the vineyard in South Australia."

The question was out before she could censor it. "Just how rich are you, Cade?"

He named a number and watched her jaw drop. "I was a computer whiz kid," he said. "Made a bundle early, invested it, and haven't stopped since. I took over Lorimer Inc. from Del seven years ago, when he turned sixty-five, and I've expanded it considerably." His smile was sardonic. "Your inheritance from Del won't come near my net worth, but it'll be sizable just the same."

Tess gave a sudden shiver. "I hate it when you talk that way."

"Do you? Do you really?"

She walked over to the window without answering him, staring out at the formal gardens, her fingers pleating and re-pleating the black fabric of her skirt. Cade followed her, his gaze fastened on her face. She was thinking, he decided, and thinking hard. Which was, of course, an all too natural reaction. Money—the amount he'd mentioned—would give a saint cause to think; and Tess, being a woman, was by definition no saint. Besides, she was dirt poor.

So what if he was a cynic? He'd had plenty of cause to become one in the last several years.

Tess said so quietly Cade had to strain to hear her, "Why did you tell me how rich you are?"

"You did ask. And isn't it better to get it out in the open?"

"So much money…" she breathed, resting her forehead on the glass pane and closing her eyes.

So she'd succumbed, Cade thought. And why not? Money was an extraordinarily potent weapon. Money, in the circles in which he moved, was the equivalent to power.

He should know.

He raked his fingers through his hair. Disconcertingly a big part of him wished Tess had held out. That she was different from all the other women he'd met.

How silly was that?

CHAPTER FIVE

SLOWLY Tess straightened, turning around to face Cade, the leaves of the hibiscus brushing her arm. End this whole charade now, she thought, before it's too late. She opened her mouth to speak, with no idea how she was going to end anything.

The late sun was firing her hair with gold. Cade said, moving smoothly into the next phase of his strategy, "As the Lorimer heiress, there are things you'll need to know—we have a lot of ground to cover. We'll start by touring the headquarters of Lorimer Inc. in Manhattan, then move to its international holdings. It'd be best to visit them one by one. Nothing like seeing a setup in person, and talking with the employees, to get a grasp on the way things operate."

Her face pale, Tess pushed away from the window ledge. "Are you crazy?" she croaked. "I'm not—"

"No wealth without social responsibility and intelligent understanding—that's Del's credo, and it's one I endorse," he said. "The château on the Loire that I mentioned, we'll go there after New York. Then we'll stay in the DelMer hotel in Venice—that'll show you another part of the operation. After that, there's the thoroughbred farm in Kentucky, our oil holdings in Venezuela, and the vineyards near Adelaide."

She was gaping at him, temporarily speechless. Good thing

she couldn't read his mind, Cade thought. The prospect of traveling around the world with her—necessary though it was—appalled him. How was he going to keep his hands off her? Or get a decent night's sleep, knowing she was on the other side of the wall?

Seducing Tess Ritchie wasn't part of his strategy; it would be neither responsible nor intelligent.

"You have to be educated to your new position," he went on. "It's important you take your rightful place in Del's world, and be comfortable in it. Afterward, you can be as proactive in Lorimer Inc. as you wish. This plan, by the way, has Del's blessing."

"You talked it over with him?" Tess said with the calm of extreme rage.

"Of course. At the hospital today while we were waiting for him to be discharged."

Cade stepped closer, tweaking a strand of her hair. "I guess the first step—rather than Manhattan—should be a proper haircut and some decent clothes." Of its own volition, his hand strayed to her cheek, stroking the silken sweep of her skin, lingering there. His loins tightened.

She struck his hand away. "I'm not going to Manhattan. Or Venice. I'm not going anywhere with you."

"The haircut and the clothes—enough clothes to start with, anyway—we can deal with those in Camberley."

Camberley was a nearby shopping area patronized by the very rich. "If I'm not going with you, I don't need to go to Camberley," Tess seethed. "I have a job waiting for me— they're expecting me to show up tomorrow morning at nine. If you won't drive me back to Malagash, I'll call a cab and go on my own."

"Your job isn't waiting for you—I phoned yesterday and arranged for an extended leave of absence."

"You *phoned* them? Behind my back, without even telling me?"

"There was no point in telling you—you'd have raised the roof."

Cade was standing between her and the door. Tess put a hand to his chest, pushing him as hard as she could; and was further infuriated when he didn't move an inch. "Where's the nearest telephone?" she demanded. "It'll be the shortest leave of absence on record."

He dropped his hands to her shoulders, his nails digging into her skin. "Stop being so childish."

Her eyes like green pools of fire, she spat, "You think you can *buy* me? Wave a million dollars in front of me and I'll meekly fall into line? Some things can't be bought, Cade Lorimer, and my freedom is one of them. Now get out of my way!"

"I never thought you were a coward," he said.

"Coward?" she repeated incredulously. "Because I'm not genuflecting to you and your precious money?"

"Because you're turning your back on the chance to make something of yourself," he retorted, his voice like a whiplash. "You've got a two-bit job on an insignificant island and you live in a fish shack. Is that what you want for the rest of your life?"

"I'm twenty-two, Cade. Not sixty."

"You're turning your back on world travel. On gaining insider information about one of the largest international corporations in existence. On the opportunity to further your education anywhere and in any field you want. Yeah, you're a coward. A coward and a fool."

White-faced with rage, she seethed, "I'm neither one. I'm a survivor who's lived in places you've never dreamed of. I don't need you, your money or your fancy international connections. Or your ivory tower existence—what do *you* know about the real world? You're totally insulated from it!"

He knew a great deal about the real world, knowledge that had been hard earned. Not that he was going to tell her that. Some things he'd learned long ago to keep to himself.

Cutting to the chase with the speed of a predator, he said, "You never went to university—am I right?"

Her shoulders slumped. "You have a genius for finding my weak points," she said with the honesty of despair. "I've never even finished high school—the only reason I got the job at the Malagash library was that they were desperate."

"You'd like more education, wouldn't you?"

"Of course. But I have my living to earn."

"No, you don't—Del's giving you an allowance. That's the whole point."

"A kept woman," she said bitterly.

"Stop wallowing in clichés, you're far too intelligent for that. Fact number one—you're Del's granddaughter. Fact number two—he's a very rich man who wants to make amends for the past. Fact number three—his health's not great and he mustn't be stressed. It wouldn't hurt you to go along with him for now and it sure as hell could benefit you."

He made it sound so easy, so logical. Yet panic was engulfing Tess at the mere thought of leaving the life she'd carefully and painstakingly fashioned for herself. "I don't want to leave the island," she cried. "I'm afraid to."

There. She'd said it.

"I know you are—that's where the courage comes in," Cade said straightforwardly; and somehow, in the midst of it all, she noticed with a twinge of respect that he wasn't offering her empty sympathy. "We'll start small," he added. "The haircut and the clothes first, then we'll go from there. One step at a time."

She said slowly, "What's in this for you?"

An opportunity to test my willpower, he thought crazily.

To practice celibacy in the company of a woman who drives me—and my hormones—up the wall. "I'm doing it for Del," he said, and knew he was skirting the borders of truth.

Tess wrapped her arms around her chest. "Why does everything have to be so complicated?"

"Because simplicity's boring?"

"You're not boring."

"Neither are you," Cade said with such vehemence that Tess's mouth twitched in an involuntary smile.

She said, "By the time you've finished shepherding me around the world, you'll be bored out of your skull."

"I wouldn't count on it," he said grimly, brought her hand to his lips and kissed her palm with a sensual pleasure that melted every bone in her body.

Hot color flooded her cheeks. She snatched her hand back. "When you act like that, I want to run in the opposite direction!"

"You can't—it's too late to run away."

He was right, although she couldn't have said at what point it had become too late. "So I'm cornered," she retorted, biting off her words. "Del mustn't be upset or worried— guess I can't march into his room and tell him I'm heading back to Malagash on the first ferry, can I? You've manipulated me from the very beginning, Cade. Congratulations."

"We'll go shopping tomorrow," he said evenly, "then head for Manhattan the day after. In the meantime, I have work to do in my office here. See you later."

The door to the solarium closed behind him. Tess sat down hard in the nearest chair and kicked off her shoes. Camberley, Manhattan, France and Venice. With Cade.

The die was cast. And her predominant emotion was— heaven help her—excitement.

* * *

Swathed in a purple cape, Tess gazed at herself in the mirror. Pierre, the stylist, lifted one long strand of her hair and scrutinized the ends. With a theatrical shudder he demanded, "Who cut your hair?"

"I did," she said. "With the kitchen scissors."

He struck his forehead with the back of his hand. "What brand of conditioner?"

Her budget hadn't included such luxuries. "None."

"*Madame*," he said, "you have come to the right place and only just in time. We will get to work." He bundled her hair back from her face, pulling it this way and that. "Yes. I see the way to go." Imperiously he waved to one of his acolytes. "Shampoo and a treatment first."

An hour and a half later, Tess was again gazing at her reflection. "That's me?" she croaked.

"It is my creation," Pierre said grandly. "You will come back in six weeks, not one day longer."

But Tess wasn't listening. Pierre had cut off great chunks of her hair so that it now framed her face in soft curls. Experimentally she tossed her head, feeling light and somehow free, all the weight gone.

Without any false vanity, she knew she also looked astoundingly beautiful, as though her features had come into their own. Perhaps, she thought slowly, she'd been hiding behind her mass of curls for years, using them as camouflage, as protection; and now she was standing in the open. Exposed.

Cade had accused her of cowardice. She tilted her chin, daring her own reflection. "I—thank you, Pierre," she said inadequately.

Pierre gave a satisfied smile. "You were a challenge—*mon plaisir, madame*."

Cade was waiting for her outside, Tess remembered. Cade,

who from the beginning had found her beautiful. Feeling absurdly shy, Tess walked out into the autumn sunshine.

Cade had browsed the local bookstore, and was leaning against the Maserati, trying to keep his attention on the book he had bought. He couldn't. His mind persisted in wandering, and everywhere it went it came up against a chestnut-haired woman with a mind of her own.

Either Tess Ritchie was a brilliant actor, or she really didn't want Del's money. Del's or his.

Considering the amount of time he and Tess had spent together, he knew very little about her. Acting could well be one of her major talents.

Could he trust her? Hadn't he be burned too many times by women who'd wanted him solely for himself—so they'd claimed—only to demand financial recompense when he'd ended the affair? Not one of them had been able to separate him from his money, or to value him for himself.

Poor little rich guy, he thought ironically. Self-pity had never, in his opinion, been an admirable trait. But—just once— he'd like to be seen as a man, not as a walking bank account.

Then something caused him to look up.

Tess was coming down the salon steps toward him. His heartbeat stuttered in his chest. He pushed away from the car, watching her until she was standing only five feet from him. Bravado masking shyness, he thought, and shoved down a totally unwanted flick of respect. "I've already told you you're beautiful," he said flatly. "So now what do I say?"

She blushed. "If I ever cut my hair again with the kitchen scissors, Pierre will hunt me down. Mercilessly. I was a chal- lenge, or so he said."

"He and I are in total agreement. You are, very definitely, a challenge."

"The head of Lorimer Inc. challenged by a woman who lives in a fish shack?" she said incredulously. "It's the other way around, Cade."

"Is it? Why?"

She scowled at him. "Clothes are the next step in your plan," she said, "not interrogation."

She was right, of course. He wasn't interested in the way her mind worked. It was her body that was obsessing him, not her mind.

"The boutique's one block down the street," he said, and mockingly crooked his elbow. "Shall we go?"

With the sense she was doing something of enormous consequence, Tess rested her hand on his arm. She said provocatively, adjusting her stride to his, "If you pay for my clothes, it'll be all over town that I'm your mistress—or don't you care?"

"I've let it be known that Del's granddaughter, who's been living in Europe, is here for a visit—I prefer gossip to be at least minimally accurate." He glanced down at her. "Would you like to be my mistress?"

"No!"

"Probably just as well, seeing as I haven't asked you."

She dropped his arm as if it was scalding her, the rose-bushes that lined the entrance to the boutique brushing against her legs. "How will I know what to buy here?" she demanded.

"I've spoken to Susan, the owner—she'll see that you have everything you need."

"You're not coming in with me!"

Cade had learned a long time ago that on occasion it was strategic to be seen to retreat; he owed the boardrooms of Europe a debt of gratitude, he thought wryly. "I'll be waiting near the car," he said.

Tess watched him walk away, letting out her breath in a small hiss. She'd been primed for a fight, and he'd denied her the satisfaction. He moved, she thought unwillingly, with the grace and economy of an athlete; he had the shoulders of an athlete, too.

Furious with herself, she pushed open the door of the boutique. A bell chimed; an attractive, middle-aged woman said, "Can I help you?" Her eyes widened. "You must be Tess Ritchie," she said with genuine warmth, "I've been looking forward to meeting you. Selena—Cade's mother—was a good friend of mine, such a lovely woman."

With a swift glance Tess ascertained they were alone in the boutique. She said, "My hose are from the dollar store, my shoes are secondhand and my dress is homemade. Tomorrow Cade and I are going to New York, then on to France, Venice and heaven knows where. I need help. Major help."

Susan laughed. "You've come to the right place." She marched over to the door, switched the Open sign to Closed and drew the gauze curtain. "Let's have some fun."

Linen, leather, fine wool, silk. Slacks, bras, shoes, earrings. Casual, semiformal, elegant. And always, in the mirror, a woman who was a stranger to Tess: a woman who bore little resemblance to a small-town librarian on a coastal island.

At the end, when Susan was adding up the bill, Tess said, "I'll be paying the first $900." She knew to a penny the amount in her savings account; she was leaving enough money to fly back from Adelaide should she need to.

Susan's fingers paused on the till. "Cade didn't mention you paying for anything," she said dubiously.

"Cade Lorimer is much too used to getting his own way." Tess held out her credit card. "The first $900."

"He's in for a shock with you."

"It'll be good for him."

Tess signed the receipt and gave Susan a quick hug. "Thank you so much. You've been a lifesaver."

"My pleasure," Susan said, uncannily echoing Pierre. "I'll see that everything's delivered to Moorings later today. Have fun on your travels, Tess—I mean that."

"I'll do my best," Tess said, smiling, and walked outside into the sunshine.

Her pumps were Italian leather, her hose silk. Her underwear was also silk, edged with the finest of lace. Her suit, with its cheeky little flared skirt and neat-fitting jacket, was cerise linen, teamed with a cream silk blouse; her earrings were simple gold hoops. With a new confidence in her step, Tess crossed the road and saw Cade walking down a side street toward her.

She met him partway, flipped her new Chanel dark glasses up into her hair, and passed him the bill. "I cost you plenty," she said. "I really liked Susan, by the way."

He flicked down the bill. "Not as much as I'd expected."

"I paid the first $900," Tess said calmly. "That way I'm only partially a kept woman."

"You can't afford to do that!"

"You let me decide what I can and can't afford," she said softly, and knew she was talking about far more than clothes.

"Sometimes I will," he replied with the same dangerous softness, "and sometimes I won't."

"Then you'll keep me on my toes, won't you?" she said, glancing down at her exquisite new shoes.

"While I was waiting, I arranged our flights to Manhattan and Paris."

"You said one step at a time! That's two steps. Don't push your luck, Cade."

A muscle twitched in his jaw. "You're the most contentious woman I've ever met."

"Flexibility in the face of opposition is a sign of maturity," she remarked airily.

The seawind was gently flipping her skirt, exposing even more of those glorious long-stemmed legs. For wasn't she like a flower, Cade thought, colorful, graceful, burnished with sunlight? *Flowers are for picking,* a voice said in his head.

Not this flower.

So now you're the coward, Cade?

With an incoherent exclamation compounded of frustration, lust and fury, Cade put his arms around Tess, pulled her to his body and plunged for her mouth. In sheer shock, she opened to him. He thrust with his tongue in an assault as unsubtle as it was steeped in raw hunger. More hunger slammed through him, his heart like a piston in his chest, his loins hard with primitive need.

Her scent, her softness shafted his body with lethal speed. He was lost…

He wasn't lost. He was on the main street of Camberley ravishing Del's granddaughter in full daylight. As though someone had thrown cold water in his face, Cade wrenched his head free.

And met a pair of wide-held green eyes, turbulent with emotions he couldn't begin to guess. Patches of color rode high in Tess's cheeks. Her shoulders were rigid in his grip. Cade said choppily, "If I was smart, I'd head for Manhattan on my own on the first plane."

"Go right ahead," she gasped.

"No way—I never back down from a challenge." He gave his wolfish grin. "It would ruin my reputation."

His answer wasn't in any way reassuring. Tess gazed up at him blankly, her breath lodged somewhere in her throat, and her knees on the point of collapse; she was also, she realized distantly, trembling. The desire that had streaked through her veins from Cade's kiss was indeed her enemy, its sole aim to drive her into intimacy with a man who screamed danger from every pore. For if his kiss had been passionate, it had also been passionately angry.

Intimacy? The word was as much a stranger to her as the man. Yet she'd agreed to traipse around four continents with him in the next few weeks.

She was out of her mind.

Her voice thin in her ears, she said, "I can always run away, Cade. And I will, if you push me too far."

"I can always bring you back."

"I'm good at vanishing," she said, "I've had lots of practice. You might want to remember that."

Even now, knowing he'd just made a major mistake in judgment—lust blinding him to any remnant of reason—Cade had to fight the urge to seize her in his arms and kiss her again. He'd never felt so out of control, so at the mercy of a woman's body. Although that's all it was, a body. Dammit, the only thing he was feeling was the basic attraction between male and female. Lust. Chemistry. Testosterone.

Nothing else.

And that's the way it was going to stay.

CHAPTER SIX

SIXTEEN minutes later, Cade pulled the Maserati to a halt outside Moorings. He reached for a leather briefcase in the back seat, opened it and said, "I might as well give you this stuff now, Tess."

He passed her some papers, a checkbook and a credit card. "Everything's been set up in your name. This is the balance in the account, and this amount will be added on the first of every month. Oh, and here's the limit on the credit card."

Tess sat still, gazing at numbers that scarcely seemed real; once again, the ground had shifted under her feet. "That's far too much," she said.

"You'll get used to it," he replied cynically.

"Gee, thanks for the vote of confidence. Who's money is it?"

"Del's—I'm just the messenger."

Just wasn't a word that applied to Cade Lorimer, she thought, drumming her fingers on her knee. "Do you know how I feel?" she said tightly. "As though you're robbing me of everything I cherish—my solitude and independence, my job, my little house, my freedom." She riffled through the blank checks. "And you've got the gall to substitute money in their place…all to prevent an arrogant old man from getting upset."

Are you for real about the money?

Cade looked at her in silence. She gave every impression of speaking from the heart, he thought, and along with the distrust that was his constant companion, felt a flicker of remorse. How long since anyone had caused him to question his motives, or to see firsthand the results of his own actions?

It's for your own good... while this was true enough, maybe she deserved better of him. But his mind remained stubbornly blank of alternatives, the silence stretching in front of him like a sun-baked desert.

In sudden impatience, Tess ran her fingers through her hair. "I don't know why I thought you'd understand—silly of me. When all's said and done, I agreed to this charade, didn't I? Let's go and see Del and get it over with."

"Not until you've calmed down."

She said bitterly, "Don't worry, I'll behave myself. In my fancy clothes and my expensive new shoes."

He pounced. "Why *are* you embarking on this charade, as you call it—what's the real reason?"

Tess bit her lip; he couldn't have asked a more difficult question. "I haven't figured it out yet," she said evasively.

"When you do," he said nastily, "let me know, won't you?"

"Maybe. Maybe not." She tilted her chin. "My reasons might be private."

"I'm sure they are—and with good reason."

"You persist in suspecting me of the worst!"

She was right. He did. With impersonal briskness Cade said, "We'd better go visit Del—he needs to settle down early, and we're leaving first thing in the morning. So this is your only chance to say goodbye to him."

If only she had a weapon—any weapon—that would force Cade to see her as she really was. That would make even a minimal impression on him. But the prospect was laughable;

the mighty Cade Lorimer had a hide as tough as his leather briefcase. Tess preceded him into the house and up the stairs, carrying the sheaf of papers under her arm.

Del's bedroom door was open. The old man was sitting in an armchair that overlooked the blue waters of the cove; although his face was turned away, there was both sadness and frustration in his bearing. Pity sliced through her. He was a widower who'd lost a beloved wife; and during the last few weeks, he'd been exiled from health and vigor.

Tapping on the door to give him a moment to recover, she said lightly, "This is the new me. Do you need an introduction?"

Stiffly Del turned his head; his eyes widened. "You remind me of Selena," he said unevenly. "My second wife. Cade's mother. She was a beauty—stole the breath from my body until the day she died."

More moved than she cared to admit, Tess said softly, "Thank you, Mr. Lorimer. That's a lovely thing to say."

"What do you plan to call me, girl? Because you can drop the Mr. Lorimer crap."

"I'll call you Del if you'll quit calling me girl."

He gave a bark of laughter. "Done deal. So you're off to Manhattan tomorrow."

"Yes," she said. "Although I reserve the right at any time to go home to Malagash Island."

"Cade better make damn sure you don't."

"It may not be up to Cade—I have a mind of my own."

"So does Cade," Del said with a fierce grin.

"Then may the better man—or woman—win," Tess said, tossing her head.

"If you two have finished squaring off like a couple of roosters," Cade said, "I've got work to do."

But Tess wasn't finished. Indicating the sheaf of papers under her arm, she said awkwardly, "Thank you for this, Del.

You've been extremely generous and I promise I won't waste your money."

"Have fun with it," Del said gruffly. "Reckon there hasn't been much fun in your life up to now."

"I will." Quickly Tess stepped closer, kissed his wrinkled cheek and whispered in his ear, "Thanks, Gramps."

His snort of delighted laughter followed her out of the room. Cade was close on her heels. When they were out of earshot of the bedroom, he grated, "You've got him eating out of your hand already—well done, Tess."

She whirled in a flare of skirts. "You don't want him upset—but when I'm nice to him, you don't like that, either. What's your problem?"

For my whole life I've wanted something Del wouldn't give me...yet already he's giving it to you. Cade sure wasn't going to say that. But his brain—his much-vaunted brain—wouldn't come up with anything else. Action. That's what he needed. He grabbed her around the waist, pulled her toward him and kissed her hard on her lips. She kicked out at him. Ignoring the sharp pain in his shin, he deepened the kiss, demanding from her a different response, calling on all his considerable skills to evoke it.

Tess surrendered, suddenly, generously and completely, for what other choice did she have? Her body was melting in his embrace, and of their own accord her arms wound themselves around his neck, her fingers digging into his scalp. It was a kiss she wanted never to end...

Her mouth, that exquisite mouth, melded with Cade's in a way that drove him to the brink. He was steeped in her. Scorched by her. If he didn't have her, he'd explode.

His tongue laced with hers. His hands pushed aside the lapels of her jacket, finding, under the silken fabric, the warm swell of her breast. Her shudder of response rocketed through him; her nipple had hardened, her body arching into his until there was nothing in the world but this woman, so willing, so achingly desirable.

He was ravishing her not thirty feet from Del's bedroom door.

With a muffled sound of self-disgust, Cade thrust her away. "I don't know what happens to me when I'm around you," he snarled. "My brains go into reverse."

She was trembling, he saw with renewed fury. Her lips were swollen from his kiss, her eyes dazed. "You can't do that to me!" she cried. "Kiss me as though I'm the only woman in the world, then shove me away as if I revolt you."

Nothing could be further from the truth, that much Cade knew. But how much easier it would be if Tess believed he was only toying with her. "I'll do what I want," he said, and watched her quiver as if he'd struck her.

Recoiling, she whispered, "You hate me."

"I hate what you do to me!"

"Yet we're supposed to travel together?"

His own question, precisely: one that had haunted him the last two nights. "You know what the problem is?" he said with deliberate brutality. "I need to find myself a woman. One who knows the score."

Pain tore through her defences. "So you're not really kissing *me*—anyone would do."

"Not just anyone. She has to be beautiful, sophisticated and temporary. Too many stars in your eyes for my liking."

Her nostrils flared; even her hair seemed to spark with electricity. "I'm not afraid of my feelings, if that's what you mean."

"Wearing your heart on your sleeve is plain stupidity."

"Not having one is worse."

"That's—"

"Right now, I wouldn't kiss you if you were the last man in Manhattan. Your whole life's a lie, Cade. Going behind my back with my job, tricking me into protecting Del, manipulating me to suit your own ends. I don't hate you—I despise you!"

So he'd succeeded, Cade thought. She'd avoid him as much as was possible in the next few days; and he, heaven help him, wouldn't lay as much as a finger on her.

To his fury, there was an icy lump lodged in his gut. He said curtly, "Be ready to leave at eight in the morning. I'll have Thomas bring some suitcases to your room."

Then he turned on his heel and marched down the hallway. Lust, that's all it was. Straightforward lust.

Of an intensity and degree beyond his experience.

The next afternoon, Tess was waiting for Cade in the atrium of Lorimer Inc.'s Mahattan headquarters. Steel, glass and light, she thought, gazing upward at the soaring ceiling. Meant to impress, and succeeding brilliantly.

Just as, against her better judgment, Cade had impressed her throughout the day. The empire over which he exercised control was vaster and more complex than she could possibly have imagined; yet every detail was at his fingertips. Furthermore, his employees, from the cleaner on the fourth floor to the vice president on the eighteenth, clearly respected him, responding to him with a warmth he must have earned.

He couldn't have fooled everyone on eighteen floors... could he? Okay, so at work he wasn't just frighteningly intelligent and enormously efficient, he was also a charmer. He'd remembered that the cleaner had a new grandson. He'd inquired with real concern about the vice president's sick wife. He'd listened to a secretary's problem with her medical insurance, and acted on the spot to fix it.

Cory had had charm. He'd turned it on—and off—like the kitchen tap.

So was Cade a classic case of Jekyll and Hyde? After all,

she had yet to meet any of his mistresses, the women who consorted with him after working hours. They might have a very different tale to tell than the cleaning lady.

She, Tess, wouldn't be joining their ranks. She was too starry-eyed, too unsophisticated. He was going to hook up with a woman who knew the score.

That would be just fine, Tess thought fiercely. She herself didn't do sex, and she avoided intimacy like the plague. Another woman would get Cade—dangerous Cade—off her back and let her settle into her new role as the Lorimer protégée.

She had no idea what this role would entail. A further loss of freedom? Or an opening to vistas she'd never dared imagine? Either way, the sooner Cade found himself a new mistress, the better.

Then, with a lurch of her heart, she saw him striding across the expanse of marble floor toward her. Dark navy business suit, silk tie, black hair impeccably groomed: if only that were all. Add his height, his breadth of shoulder, the way he moved. Add muscles toned to an animal grace. Add light and shadow falling across the hard planes of his face, across unfathomable gray eyes and features that were infused with strength and character.

The grand total was a magnetism so powerful that every woman from the basement to the penthouse would flock to him.

Including her? Was she fooling herself, big-time?

Gritting her teeth, Tess stood her ground. Cade said with chilling formality, "My chauffeur's outside in the limo, he'll drive you home. We have tickets to the opera tonight—we'll eat before we go, because we have another early start tomorrow and you look tired."

She was. But he didn't have to say so. He didn't look tired, she thought petulantly. He looked like he could work a forty-eight-hour day and go to six operas.

"Oh," he added, "wear a long gown, won't you?"

"Yes, Mr. Lorimer."

His eyes narrowed. "I hoped the tour would have taught you that I value initiative more than compliance."

"Will there be a quiz?" she said naughtily.

"Stow it."

"Do your mistresses turn into paper dolls when you use that tone of voice?" she asked with genuine interest.

"You'll have to ask them. I'll be back before six."

Turning on his heel, he strode toward the elevators. Tess dragged her eyes away, and hurried outside. The chauffeur drove her back to Cade's elegant brownstone near Central Park. She let herself in, ran upstairs to her bedroom, where they'd dropped off her suitcases this morning, and tore off her classy pantsuit. Then she showered in the ultramodern bathroom with its granite counters and heated towel rails, dressed casually in jeans, and laid out on her bed one of the three evening gowns Susan had helped her choose. This one was a deep moss-green, and very becoming. She needed all the help she could get, for wasn't she dreading an outing that would bring her face-to-face with Cade's peers? Or, worse, with the women in his past?

What would it be like to make love to Cade? To surrender herself to him, to be naked in his arms?

With a tiny sound of distress, she tossed the dress on the bed and started prowling the brownstone. Cade liked bold colors, furniture with clean lines and modern art whose impact was visceral. She lingered in front of an array of photographs on the mantel in the living room, in particular one of a much younger Del with his arm around his beautiful, raven-haired Selena. Cade—perhaps nine or ten—was standing on the other side of Del. Del, Tess thought in puzzlement, was making no effort to draw the boy into the photo: all Del's attention and certainly all his feelings were directed toward his new wife.

Already Cade's eyes were full of secrets…

Unexpectedly behind her, with the slightest of sounds, a door swung on its hinges. Tess grabbed a soapstone sculpture from the mantel, whirled in a blur of movement and crouched, holding the statue like a weapon in front of her.

Cade was standing in the doorway.

Slowly Tess straightened, wishing the marble hearth would swallow her and the statue, wishing Cade to the eighteenth floor of Lorimer Inc. She said inadequately, "You startled me."

He walked into the room, took the sculpture from her nerveless fingers, replaced it on the mantel, then stepped back; her reaction, so swift, so practiced, had horrified him. "Don't lie to me!"

"I'm—"

"Your reaction when you heard the sound of the door— what kind of upbringing did you have?"

"That's got nothing—"

"Give it up—you were ready in an instant to defend yourself. To the death, by the look on your face. It's time to come clean…I need to know the facts. The places you've lived. Why you were so terrified the first time you met me."

"Give me one good reason why I should tell you anything! You don't like me. You don't even trust me—you think I'm after every cent you've ever made."

Cade gazed at the defiant flags of color in Tess's cheeks, scarcely hearing what she said, making no attempt to close the gap between them. Keep it that way, he told himself. Don't touch her no matter what you do. But damn well make sure you get some answers. "You were afraid of Cory—why? Did he abuse you?"

"I don't owe you an explanation." Tess backed up until the ledge was digging into her shoulders. Until she could retreat no further, she thought frantically, and like a cornered animal, went on the attack. "Why do you always call your father Del, and not Dad?" she demanded, and made a wild guess. "Because he didn't love you as a little boy?"

Cade's jaw tightened; she had a talent for striking where he was most vulnerable. "That's none of your business."

"Not a bad reply. I'll use the same one."

A worthy opponent...where had those words come from? "Maybe Del didn't welcome me into the family the way I would have liked," Cade said tautly. "But he gave me a secure childhood, happier than most kids get, and he did his best to send me out into the world prepared for what I'd find. I'd stake every dollar I ever made that you had none of that."

"If you're so interested in my childhood, why don't you hire your own investigator?" she flared. "You can afford to, we both know that."

The truth slapped Cade in the face. He said baldly, "I don't want to. I don't want to go behind your back, or have a complete stranger ferreting out the details of your life. I want you to tell me yourself."

"You want me to *trust* you?" she said with an incredulity that grated on his nerves.

"Anything you tell me will never go beyond this room, and I'll never use it against you."

"Even if that were true, why would I unload on you? I've never told anyone about my parents or my past."

"If you don't tell me, then I *will* hire my own investigator."

"You know what your problem is—you can't bear to lose."

"You got it. So which is it to be, Tess?" He jammed his hands in his pockets. "Confession's good for the soul, isn't that what they say?"

"Psychobabble."

"Wisdom. Either way, give it a try."

She let out her breath in a small sigh and wandered over to the window, with its view of a quiet, tree-lined street: an oasis of peace in a huge city. Keeping his hands in his pockets, Cade followed her, stationing himself where he could watch her face.

He had no idea what he was about to hear. But he did know it was essential he hear it.

Speaking more to herself than to Cade, Tess said, "Cory's casual acquaintances always liked him. He was astonishingly good-looking, with charm to burn. He was also a heroin addict who stole, cheated and lied. As for Opal, she was beautiful, rich, wild and willful, with the morals of an alley cat—they were well-matched. I, of course, was an accident. I put a big crimp in their style until I was old enough to be left alone."

"How old was that?"

"Five. Six. They used to lock me in my room and go out, and I never knew when they'd come home or what shape they'd be in...I used to fantasize about running away. But I had no money and nowhere to go. No relatives, Cory said, no grandparents—of course they never told me about Del and his money."

"Are you suggesting they were model parents until you were five?"

She winced, and with one finger began tracing the molding on the window, up and down, up and down. "We lived in Madrid until I was five," she said tonelessly. "I had a nanny called Ysabel. I adored her. She was a fiery-tempered Spaniard who stood up to my parents, made sure I got proper food and rest, and took me to the park to play with other children...I used to call her Bella because I couldn't get my tongue around Ysabel."

"What happened to her?"

"Two days after my fifth birthday, Cory, Opal and I got on a train late at night and traveled from Madrid to Vienna. I never saw Ysabel again. Even though I cried and cried, my parents wouldn't give me her phone number so I could call up and say goodbye…a couple of weeks later, they told me she'd died."

"It broke your heart."

For the first time, Tess looked full at him. Dry-eyed, he noticed, for all that those eyes were green pools of pain. "I've never loved another human soul since Ysabel," she said. "Love betrays you. Leaves you bereft, and lonelier than you thought possible."

"Not always," he said harshly. "Sure, I grieved when my mother died. But I was the richer because we loved each other."

Once again, Tess realized, Cade had given honesty instead of easy sympathy. She said stonily, "That hasn't been my experience."

"You never called your parents Mum and Dad?"

"They wouldn't answer if I did."

"Not roles they aspired to," Cade said, remembering Del. Del hadn't wanted to be his father. It had taken Cade years to admit that simple, devastating truth.

"*Did* Cory abuse you?" he asked.

"No. Oh, I got slapped around a few times, usually when they were desperate for a fix and out of money. But nothing major."

That last phrase, he thought, revealed a great deal about the little girl Tess had been: her daily life so frightening that to be slapped around was unimportant. Although he was almost sure he knew the answer, he said, "Why did you leave Madrid?"

"Creditors were after Cory. It set the pattern—stay in a city until it became too risky, then run away in the night and set up somewhere else. Sometimes the money flowed like water, sometimes there was none." She shivered. "No stability. No safety."

"Until you ended up on Malagash."

"You see why I'm a loner, and why I loved my little cabin? It was mine. I was in control. And I was safe."

"You're safe here," Cade said forcefully.

With equal force Tess said, "One thing I've learned over the years is to create my own safety."

"You can ask others for help."

"You, you mean?" she said with another incredulous laugh. "I don't think so."

Why was he so angry, when, basically, she was telling him what he wanted to hear? He'd never gone out of his way for any of his mistresses; to have done so would have been counter to the whole way he ran his life.

Yet Tess had trusted him with her narrative; and it had had the ring of truth. Or rather, he thought, she'd partially trusted him; for he was aware of the gaps in her story, gaps that left plenty for the imagination. The year she'd turned sixteen, for instance, was still a blank, as were all the years after that.

Later. Bide your time, Cade, choose when to push deeper. In the next few days, there'll be plenty of opportunities.

He would push. He knew he would. Even if he didn't fully understand why.

"We should eat, Tess," he said. "Then we have to get ready—the opera starts at eight."

She was twisting her hands together. "You still want to go with me?"

He raised his brow. "Why wouldn't I?"

"Cade, don't you get it? My father was a crook. My mother went from man to man as if she was changing her shoes. And you want to introduce me to New York society?"

"Do you think I'm a total fool? You're nothing like your parents."

"You don't have a clue what I'm like!"

"I know quite a lot about you," Cade said, the words playing and replaying in his head. Although he had no idea where they'd come from, they had the unmistakable ring of truth.

"I'm so ashamed of my parents," Tess said in a low voice.

"I thought if I ever told anyone about them, I'd be dropped quicker than a rotten apple."

"You've got the wrong man."

"You're angry," she whispered.

"Not at you. At them. For the horrendous way they treated a little girl who was too young to defend herself."

"Oh." In genuine perplexity, she added, "Will I ever figure you out?"

"I'd hate to be too predictable."

Tess looked at him in silence. He crackled with suppressed energy, pullling her into his orbit by sheer force of personality. Predictable? What a joke. He'd listened to her sordid story without judging her, an act so unexpected that she was filled with gratitude. Not once in the last few minutes had he offered cheap pity; nor had he touched her. If he had, she might well have broken her self-imposed rule and wept all over him. Which wouldn't have been predictable, either.

Oddly the thought of going out this evening, of being surrounded by strangers and distractions, pleased her; right now she felt as though she'd been flayed, the memories crowding her mind too close and much too painful. "You're right, we'd better eat," she said, and managed a smile. "You'll like my dress—Susan picked it out because it's the same color as my eyes."

He should have bought her emeralds to go with it, Cade thought. But there'd be plenty of opportunities for that, too.

CHAPTER SEVEN

To say he liked Tess's dress was the understatement of the year, Cade thought, as he stood in the foyer and watched her descend the staircase. She was wearing a slender sheath of green, the taffeta skirt rustling as she walked, the tiny cap sleeves and abbreviated bodice heavy with gold embroidery. Her shoulders rose from it like polished ivory, topped by her flare of chestnut curls.

Desire slammed into him, rocking him to his foundations. Forcing his features to impassivity, he said, "Very nice."

"I'm not sure nice was the effect I was striving for."

He let his gaze wander from the toes of her gold spike-heeled sandals past her enticing cleavage to her exotic eyes, artfully shaped with eye shadow, her lashes impossibly long. "What were you striving for?"

"*Vogue. Elle. Flare.*" She grinned at him. "Aim high."

"Too much character in your face for a model—vapid, you're not. Before you wear that dress again, I'll buy you some emeralds."

"You will not!"

"You argue too much," he said, and held out his arm. "Shall we go?"

Tess hesitated on the bottom step. Cade looked disturbingly

handsome in a black tux teamed with an immaculate pleated white shirt. Handsome, sexy and magnetic, she thought, with that undercurrent of animal grace that his highly civilized clothes only emphasized.

He knew more about her than anyone else in the world; and he hadn't run away.

He terrified her.

With a poise of which she was inwardly proud, she rested her hand on his sleeve. "My shawl is on the table by the door."

As he draped the swath of gold fabric around her shoulders, his fingers brushed her collarbone. A shiver of desire rippled through her. So that hadn't changed. If anything, it had intensified.

She glanced up and blurted, "When you look at me, what do you see?" Then she clapped her hand over her mouth. "Oh God, forget I asked that."

Cade let the weight of his hands fall on her shoulders and, for once, left his tongue unguarded. "I see a beautiful woman who isn't yet convinced she's beautiful. Who has no idea of the power she wields, and who might not wish to wield it even if she did know. A woman on the brink of the future…"

Startled, Tess stored the words away so she could think about them later. "You tell it as you see it."

"Is there any other way?"

"For you, no." Going on impulse, she reached up and kissed him, the softest of touches to his lips before she hurriedly stepped back. "You make me feel beautiful," she whispered huskily. "Thank you."

It wouldn't do to throw her over his shoulder and carry her off to bed—that went out of fashion years ago. With a huge effort, Cade managed to speak more or less normally. "Let's go slay 'em at the Met."

"You haven't even told me what opera we're to see."

"*La Traviata*. Star-crossed lovers."

Tess could have said, *I've never had a lover, star-crossed or otherwise*. But she'd done more than enough talking for one night; and wasn't her virginal state yet another of the secrets she'd guarded for years?

The chauffeur drove them to the opera house, where they were ushered into Cade's private box. The orchestra tuned up and the overture began.

When the curtain descended at the end of Act I, Tess wasn't ready for the break. Cade said, under cover of a storm of applause, "You like it."

"Oh, yes," she breathed. "So much emotion, and those delicious voices."

He'd never seen her face so open, so vulnerable. All her defences were down, he thought grimly. But he'd be the lowest of the low to take advantage of it. He'd damn well better find himself another woman, and soon; it was called self-preservation. "Would you like some wine?"

"I'd just like to sit here," she said. "But you go."

Good idea, Cade decided, and headed for the bar. However, at the end of the second act, Tess said, "I need to stretch. It's not going to end happily, I know…I wish it would."

"A glass of wine'll fix the blues," Cade said heartlessly.

He led her through the crowds in the lobby, introducing her to several people whose names she immediately forgot. Then a tall, slender blonde in a patrician white gown approached them. Ignoring Tess, she laid her hand confidingly on Cade's sleeve and reached up to kiss him. A kiss she'd intended for his lips, Tess thought; but Cade, at the last minute, moved his head so that the kiss landed on his cheek. "It's been so long since I've seen you, Cade," the blonde said. "Too long. We must get together."

"Hello, Sharon…may I introduce Tess Ritchie? Sharon Heyward, Tess."

Sharon assessed her with insulting brevity. "Hello," she said. "Are you enjoying the opera? The production's by no means as good as Zeffirelli's."

"As I've never seen it before, I can't compare."

"Your first visit to town?" Sharon smiled, her eyes ice-blue. "I thought you looked a little out of place."

"I grew up in Europe," Tess said, smiling back. "Amsterdam, Vienna, Paris. So it's pleasant to visit Manhattan with Cade."

Sharon's lashes flickered. "Cade, I'm in town until Tuesday. Surely you're not tied up all weekend."

Tied up, Tess thought with an inner quiver of amusement. The woman wasn't born who could do that to Cade Lorimer.

"Tess and I are leaving for France first thing tomorrow," Cade said easily.

Sharon's mouth tightened. Turning to Tess, she said, "Don't expect it to last, will you? Sooner or later, Cade always moves on."

"Leaving a trail of broken hearts behind him?" Tess said. "Somehow, Sharon, I don't think mine will be among them. But thanks for the warning…Cade, should we go back to our box?"

With an undeniable flounce, Sharon turned her back. "Nice to have met you," Tess added wickedly. Then, as she and Cade walked up the stairs, she hissed, "How often am I going to meet your ex-mistresses?"

"I wouldn't worry about it—you're more than capable of holding your own."

She was also, Tess realized, extremely angry for no real reason. "Or perhaps I shouldn't assume she's an ex? She didn't seem to think she was."

"Money, Tess, money. If I was down and out, Sharon would trample me under her Ferragamos."

"So why did you sleep with her?"

"You find me a woman who doesn't give a damn about the Lorimer millions!"

Tess gaped at him; it hadn't occurred to her that money could be, in certain situations, a liability. With painful truth, she said, "I'm no better than Sharon—I'm dressed from head to toe in stuff you paid for. And if you had your way, I'd be draped in emeralds as well."

He closed the curtains of their box with a decisive snap. "You'd be enjoying the opera just as much in the back row of the family circle," he said curtly.

"Huh…at least you didn't give Sharon the down-and-dirty about my life in Europe."

"Let's get something straight, Tess. We both come with a past. Yes, I've had affairs, of course I have. As for you, you're twenty-two years old, you've been on your own since you were sixteen—there've been men in your life and maybe we'll bump into one of them at the Paris airport."

She really should tell Cade the truth, Tess thought uncomfortably. She'd never get a better time than now. But as she opened her mouth, the conductor mounted his podium and bowed to the applause; and the moment passed.

As did the moment to ask Cade who would be his next mistress. He was on the lookout—he'd told her so.

She'd hate her. Whoever she was.

As the curtain rose on Violetta's bedroom, Tess's thoughts marched on. How could she hate someone she'd never met? It wasn't as though she wanted to be Cade's mistress herself. Dog in the manger, she thought, that's you.

Besides, Cade's a free man, who's doing Del a favor by traveling four continents with you in his wake. You're nothing to him. Just one more beautiful woman in a string of beautiful women.

From the bed, Violetta began to sing, and Tess tried her

best to sublimate her own feelings in those of the doomed courtesan. Gradually she lost herself to everything but the music. The tragic ending touched her to the heart, and she was very quiet as they walked out into the cool of evening, where water cascaded in shades of pink and gold in the huge fountain.

Violetta, so young and beautiful, had longed for her handsome lover with a depth of emotion that had been a revelation to Tess. But Violetta had died.

She, Tess, was very much alive. And hadn't Cade's kisses, passionate and passionately irresistible, also been a revelation, evoking cravings she hadn't known she was capable of?

She'd been fooling herself: she didn't want Cade to make love to another woman, or to find someone else to be his mistress. She wanted him to make love to her.

Her steps faltered. Revelation number three, she thought dazedly. Not that she had any idea how to seduce Cade.

"Tess, are you all right?"

"Oh—oh yes," she stammered, flushing as she realized that Cade's quizzical gaze was fastened on her face. Heaven knows what he'd been able to read there.

Nothing, she prayed. Her certainty that she wanted Cade for herself was too new, too raw, to bring it into the open. Let alone act on it.

She took a deep breath, calling on all her poise. "I loved the opera, Cade. Thank you so much for taking me."

"My pleasure," he said tritely, guiding her toward the waiting limo.

What would it be like to be Cade's lover? As she traveled round the world with him, would she find the opportunity—and the courage—to invite him to her bed?

She didn't do sex.

But would it be just sex with Cade? *Just* sex? What did that mean? Or would it be something else altogether, something operatic in intensity, unquenchable and all-absorbing?

There was no way Tess could tell, for she was operating from a basis of total ignorance. Although she'd read a lot of novels over the past few years, many containing sex, not one of them had prepared her for Cade Lorimer.

A few minutes later, when she walked into the foyer of Cade's brownstone, she was achingly aware of the silence. They were alone together. Cade's bedroom was upstairs. She'd checked it out this afternoon before he came home, had even sat on the bed on the dark blue spread and wondered— heaven help her—if he slept naked. She said raggedly, "I'm going to bed, it's been a long day."

He was tugging at his tie. "Whoever invented these damn things didn't have comfort in mind," he muttered. "Good night. Set your alarm so that we can leave by six-thirty tomorrow."

His mind wasn't on her, she thought, scurrying up the stairs. Or on sex. Which was, of course, a very good thing.

Tess dreamed that night about Opal singing a pizza ad at the top of her voice as she lay dying of an overdose, while Cory, in the next room, was fighting a duel with knuckle- busters...she woke with a start, sitting bolt upright in bed. Her heart was hammering in her chest and she knew from long ex- perience that she wouldn't easily get back to sleep.

So much for opera.

She pulled on a silk robe over her nightgown, and on bare feet padded down the stairs. Surely she'd find hot chocolate, or at least tea, in Cade's highly impressive kitchen.

Rooting in the cupboards, she found an expensive brand of Amaretto-flavored cocoa. Trying to read the dates on the milk cartons, she propped the refrigerator door against her hip and stuck her head in the whole way.

"What's up?"

With a shriek of alarm, Tess backed up, bumped into Cade and turned in his arms. "I—I thought you were a burglar," she stuttered.

"I thought *you* were," he said dryly.

He was wearing a low-slung pair of sweatpants and nothing else. Dark hair tunneled from breastbone to navel; he was so close she could smell, elusively, a tantalizing combination of herb-scented soap and warm, male skin. Her palms were pressed to his chest; she could feel its muscled hardness through every pore, a sensation that made her melt like a candle to the flame.

The robe she'd flung on to come downstairs had fallen off her shoulders, and her nightgown was one of Susan's more minimal choices. Say something, Tess, she thought frantically. Anything. "I c-couldn't sleep."

"I thought I heard someone call out—that's what woke me." Oh God. "I had a bad dream."

His arms tightened their hold. "I said you were safe here."

Safe, she thought. Was this his idea of safe? And was safety what she really wanted?

Violetta hadn't opted for safety.

Her heart was racing as though a wild bird was trapped in her rib cage; beneath her fingertips, his muscles were iron-hard. He was so beautiful, she thought helplessly. Why had she never realized that a man's body could emphasize so seductively her own femininity?

"Dammit, Tess, don't look at me like that."

"Is that the power you were talking about?" she faltered. "I feel so different with you, as though somehow you free me to be myself—and yet that woman is someone I don't even know."

Like a man driven to the brink, Cade sought out her mouth. She met him more than halfway, her lips parted, willing and eager. He nipped at her lower lip, then slid his tongue along its sweet curve, his hands skimming the length of her body under the slippery silk. Heat throbbed through her, swirled and shuddered. She moaned deep in her throat, arching against him. Then he plunged with his tongue and the world dissolved into nothing but desire.

It didn't take courage at all, she thought dimly, to be in Cade's arms; for it was the most natural place in the world for her to be.

She buried her hands in his hair, pulling his head down, aching for more, more, always more…and felt, with a thrill of possessiveness, the hard jut of his own needs.

He wanted her.

With a recklessness new to her, she rubbed herself against him and heard him gasp her name. He clamped one arm tight around her, pulling her into his body, the thin silk no barrier at all to an intimacy that drenched her in liquid fire. Drenched and destroyed her.

Clinging to him with the last of her strength, she dug her nails into the taut muscles of his shoulders. *Take me, take me,* she thought dazedly, and knew she was ready to travel to an unknown country. With Cade. Only with Cade.

Each tiny jab of her fingernails lanced straight to Cade's loins. With a muffled groan, he let his teeth graze the long line of her throat, thrown back, bared for him, before he dragged the thin strap of her gown down her shoulder. Her breasts' pale glimmer nearly drove him out of his mind. He dropped his head, tracing the soft rise of her flesh, then flicking her nipple with his tongue until it was rock hard. Until she was whimpering, incoherently begging him for more.

Muscle, blood, bone and sinew, he wanted her. Had to have her, had to satiate a need beyond any he'd ever known. He was drowning in her. Losing himself. He'd die if he didn't take her. Here. Now.

Somewhere, deep within, a red warning light flashed on. Drown? Lose himself? Die?

What the hell was going on? He'd never felt like this in his life. Never needed a woman as, right now, he so desperately needed Tess.

He didn't want to need her.

From the same deep place, he found the strength to drag his mouth from the sweetness and heat of her body, to fill his lungs with air and say in a voice that didn't sound remotely like his own, "I'm ending this. Right now."

She shuddered in his hold, opening green eyes that were drowned—that word again, Cade thought savagely—in desire. "I don't understand," she whispered. "What's wrong?"

How could he possibly explain something he scarcely understood himself? If Tess, at the age of five, had decided against love, hadn't he, equally young, decided against need? For as far back as he could remember, his real father had derided a small boy's need for love and approval; and Del had always kept him at a careful distance.

Surface relationships, Cade thought caustically, those were his specialty; and over the years they'd served him well.

He wasn't going to change, dammit. If Tess's body drove him too close to the edge, then he'd deny himself that body.

Simple.

"It's all wrong," he said implacably. "If we go to bed together, we'll both regret it in the morning."

Tess straightened, bracing herself with her palms to his bare chest, and said with ragged honesty, "I don't want you to stop—I won't regret it, I swear I won't."

The terror that had so puzzled him on the pebble beach of Malagash was gone; in its place was surrender, pure and simple. Cade said brutally, "But I will."

She flinched visibly. "So it was all an act?" she quavered.

"No!"

"You're lying—you've got to be!"

"I'm not—some things you can't fake."

"Then what's going on? I don't understand…"

"I'd be taking advantage of you," he said stonily. When all else fails, fall back on clichés, he thought with savage self-derision.

"How could you take advantage of me when I've just told you I'm willing?"

Cade moved back so that Tess's hands fell to her sides. He should have pushed her away the first moment she backed out of the refrigerator into his arms, he thought furiously.

His willpower was impressive. But not that impressive.

Pride stiffened Tess's spine; like a cornered animal, she went on the attack. "Do you enjoy making women beg for your attention? For sexual favors? If so, I was right to despise you."

Then her eyes widened with comprehension. She gasped, "There's someone else. You've already found another woman. Of course—how stupid of me not to guess."

"Don't be—"

"I'll go through with this trip to France tomorrow because I don't want Del to be disappointed," she said raggedly. "But keep your distance, Cade—do you hear me? Or I'll damn well go back to Malagash on the first plane and leave you to explain why."

In a swirl of silk she marched out of the kitchen. The swing door swooshed shut behind her.

Cade let out his breath in a long sigh. Well done, he thought. He hadn't wanted to admit to himself, let alone to her, even the possibility that he might need her. So now he'd driven her away and—he wasn't completely blind—hurt her feelings into the bargain.

He was a brilliant CEO, yeah. But he was bottom of the class when it came to Tess Ritchie.

He might want to check his morning coffee for arsenic. On which less than comforting thought, Cade went to bed.

Alone.

CHAPTER EIGHT

AT CHARLES-DE-GAULLE Airport, Cade's rented Maserati was waiting for them; it was scarlet. The color of passion, he thought. The color of blood.

Ever since they'd left Manhattan for the airport where his personal jet had been parked, Tess had maintained an icy silence, sleeping her way across the Atlantic, now ignoring him as if he didn't exist. As the valet loaded their suitcases into the trunk, he climbed in and turned on the ignition. Two could play that game, he thought vengefully. Besides, driving in Paris always took his full attention.

As a couple of taxi drivers intent on mayhem swerved in front of him, she didn't even flinch. Her defenses were firmly in place and he thoroughly disliked being ignored.

You're not used to it, Cade. Your other women spent their time falling all over you.

Unlike Tess.

He covered the seventy or so kilometers to the château in record time. As he turned into the long driveway through imposing wrought-iron gates, their pale stone pillars topped with heraldic knights in armor, he said, "Welcome to Château de Chevalier."

"Thank you," Tess said coolly. She was determined not to

be impressed. But after the car had wound through a dense forest, which opened into formal gardens of clipped shrubbery and autumn flowers, she saw the château and gave an involuntary gasp of pleasure. It was riding the banks of the river in creamy splendor, its Renaissance turrets and windows shining in the early evening sun.

A palace out of a fairy tale, she thought, where all the endings were happy.

There'd be no happy endings for her.

"The tufa cliffs are to our left," Cade said. "Caves were dug into them generations ago, for aging and storing the wine. The vineyards are behind the château. It's a good time to be here. Some of the early-ripening grapes are nearly ready to be harvested, others are waiting for the first frost...we'll get rid of our stuff, you can change into something less formal, then I'll take you around. I haven't been here for two months, so I have a lot to do."

As he spoke of the harvest, his voice had warmed. So he cared, she thought, and blurted, "Learning the complexities of winemaking will be a breeze compared to understanding you."

"Then you'd better stick to the wine," Cade said.

Stifling both pain and anger, she did just that, until her brain was stuffed with a wealth of information about pruning, tannin content, Sancerre, rare vintages and wooden vats.

Somehow, the day had fled and it was evening. Wriggling her shoulders to rid them of fatigue, Tess followed Cade out into the courtyard. A full moon had risen through the trees, the walls of the château a ghostly white, poised over the still waters of the Loire. She said, "We haven't even touched on the marketing aspect of the vineyard."

"We'll do that tomorrow morning. It's a science in itself."

"Just don't let me do so much tasting tomorrow," she

remarked, picking her way over the cobblestones with exaggerated care. "I've never had much head for drink."

"You're cut off." Moonlight gleaming in his hair, he said abruptly, "I'd like us to walk some of the rows before we have dinner. Because, in the end, it's the grapes that count."

She was beginning to like him, Tess thought blankly. The depth and acuity of his knowledge, the respect and affection that the workers held for him: they were as real as the *parterres* with their well-tended blossoms, and the bronze statues reflected in stone-edged pools.

She was a long way from home.

Impulsively she said, "I'd rather be here than in the library on Malagash Island. I guess I'd outgrown safety and didn't even know it."

Cade stopped in his tracks. "You have this continual capacity for taking me by surprise."

"I bet Sharon never took you by surprise."

"Not once…you didn't like her any more than she liked you."

Without finesse, knowing the question was too important for her to hedge, Tess asked, "Is she going to be your mistress again?"

They'd climbed the slope behind the château. Rows of vines ranged the hillside, the canes heavy with grapes. Cade said, "These rows are Sancerre. Over there are Bourgueil."

"Is that a polite way of telling me to mind my own business?"

"I won't get involved with Sharon again."

Involved, Tess thought, what a horrible word. And used it herself. "Are you involved with anyone else yet?"

"What is this, an inquisition?"

"It's a straightforward question," she said, hoping he couldn't hear the sick pounding of her heart.

"No. Not yet."

So she had her answers. Glancing around at a world bathed

in the moon's pale radiance, Tess realized with a tightening of her nerves how isolated they were up here, out of sight of the château and the outbuildings of the vineyard. She stooped to admire the carefully spaced bunches of grapes on the vines, taking a moment to gather her courage. Then, standing tall, she looped her arms around Cade's neck and kissed him full on the mouth.

Stepping back, she said, "I did that because I wanted to. Not because you're rich."

A breeze stirred her hair. An owl hooted from the forest, hauntingly sad; her heartbeat was like thunder in her ears, so loud she was sure the owl could hear it. Cade was standing dead-still, and as the seconds ticked by, the gamble she'd just taken seemed more and more foolhardy.

Anyway, it had failed.

Then Cade brought his hands up and cupped her face, his fingers digging into her skin. His gray eyes hard, he said, "In the long run, I'll hurt you, Tess. You're not the type for a casual fling and I'm not into commitment. Never have been."

"So do we do nothing because we're afraid of being hurt?" she cried. "That's what my life was like for the sixteen years I lived with Cory and Opal. Smooth the troubled waters. Keep a low profile. Don't rock the boat. I lived every cliché in the book, over and over again—until I was sick of them. But now I'm ready to take a few risks. After all, I'm here in France with you, aren't I?"

Her skin was cool to his fingertips, smooth as the finest silk. And wasn't he being offered, freely, the woman he'd ached to bed ever since his first sighting of her on a rocky beach in Maine?

He'd be a fool not to take her.

He said harshly, "So this isn't related to the fact that I'm a billionaire?"

"No!"

The words forcing themselves out, their raw truth rough-ening his voice, Cade said, "You can't be bought, Tess. You know it, and so do I."

Her eyes jerked to meet his own. "Do you mean that?"

"Yes," he said shortly. "Can't you tell? Or do you disbe-lieve everything I say?" Then, to his horror, he saw that her eyes were brimming with unshed tears. "For God's sake, don't cry—I meant it as a compliment."

She blinked furiously. "You trust me," she gulped, "that's what you're saying. And I never cry."

"You're giving a damn good approximation."

"It's so stupid—way back, when we were eating dinner at the hotel on Malagash, I was doing my level best to convince you I was after every cent you and Del ever earned. But now I'm nearly in tears because you understand that what's at stake here has nothing to do with money. Absolutely nothing."

So had he finally, Cade wondered, found a woman who didn't see him as a walking bank account? He said tersely, "This doesn't change the way I feel about anything long-term. Falling in love isn't an option. Marriage certainly isn't."

She raised her chin defiantly. "Mistress is an okay word."

"As long as you're sure of that."

"I'm sure." Her lips, those delectable lips, curved in a slow, provocative smile. "I'm beginning to think you're the one who's afraid of risk, Cade."

"Are you calling me a coward?" He whipped his arms around her waist and pulled her toward him. Her eyes widened and her smile vanished; her body was suddenly rigid.

"I take it back," she said, keeping her voice level with a huge effort. She was the one who was afraid; and was desper-ate to keep that fear to herself.

Take the initiative, she thought. Before you run like a rabbit.

She let her palms slide up his chest, feeling through his shirt the heat of his skin, the hardness of bone and muscle. Feeling, distantly, the first stirrings of desire. She lifted her face, her lips parted, and with mingled excitement and terror watched his eyes narrow with purpose, points of fire in their dark centers.

He said with ferocious intent, "I've waited too long for this." Then his mouth plummeted to hers, his tongue lacing itself with hers, plundering her, robbing her of everything but a fierce, shocking need.

Somehow, from depths she hadn't known she possessed, Tess answered him with a hunger that matched his own; for if he had plunged to her mouth like a peregrine to its prey, then she was his mate, his equal. So she met him, fire with fire; and felt his arms tighten around her waist, hauling her into him, hip to hip.

She was burning all her bridges, she thought dimly. Which was another cliché. She was abandoning any notions of safety to embrace a man who would lead her into an unknown country...

Her response had rocketed through every cell in Cade's body. Holding to a vestige of control—for had he ever lost it so fast?— he slid his lips down the pale column of her throat to the little hollow at the base of her throat, and felt her pulse skitter under his tongue. "So you like that," he muttered hoarsely, and without waiting for a reply, pushed her jacket aside to find her breast, his breath catching in his throat as she shuddered with desire.

"I like it," she said weakly.

"I wouldn't want you to be in any doubt." With lightning speed he lifted her off her feet, pulling her into his body, and kissed her again, kissed her as though he'd been waiting all his life to be with this one woman in the moonlight beside an ancient river.

Her little gasp of shock was smothered by his mouth. He demanded and took, he sought and coaxed, and only when he felt her surrender in every bone of her body did he lower her to the ground.

Tess lay back, the long rows of grapes enclosing her, the darkly luminous sky over her head. Cade's big body was hovering over her, covering her; never had she felt so purely feminine, yet so certain of her own power. She opened her arms to him, welcoming his weight, his warmth. His face closed off the sky and his lips, once again, drank deep of her mouth.

Far away, the owl hooted. Cade barely heard it. He was steeped in the woman embracing him, his control shattered, and still he took and still she answered him, kiss for kiss, caress for caress. He tore her jacket from her shoulders, letting it fall back on the clipped grass, and to his huge gratification, felt her fingers fumble with the buttons on his shirt. As her fingers tangled themselves in his body hair, then swept over his nipples, he juddered in response.

His own jacket joined hers on the ground. Ripping at the buttons, Cade tore her blouse away from her body; her breasts, cupped in white lace, made his breath hitch. Swiftly he undid the clasp on her bra, gazing at her in a passion of pleasure and hunger before dropping his head to seek out her breasts' rosy tips with tongue and fingers.

She bucked in his hold, her sharp cry of delight inflaming him. Distantly he felt her yank his shirt down his back and take his bare shoulders in her hands, clasping them as though she never wanted to let him go. "You're so beautiful," he muttered, "so goddamned beautiful…I want to see you naked."

He raised his head, kissing her again, laving her tongue with his and plundering all the sweetness of her mouth. Then he pulled off his shirt, tossing it toward the vines.

Cade's shoulders gleamed in the moonlight, broad, tautly

muscled; had she ever seen anything so beautiful, so infinitely desirable? And if he wanted her naked, then naked she would be. Her fingers trembling, passion conquering shyness, Tess unbuttoned her slacks and lifted her hips in a single graceful movement to ease them from her body.

Her legs, so long, so slender, flooded Cade with primitive possessiveness. She was his. Only his. With brutal strength, he ripped her bikini panties down her hips. She kicked them off, her hands instinctively covering herself.

"Don't be shy…there's no need."

"But I've—"

Stopping her words with his mouth, Cade drank deep. Then, lifting her hands one by one, he kissed her palms; from there, with mouth and hands, he began exploring the silken smooth curves and hollows of her body, from throat to collarbone to breast to navel. She was trembling all over, whimpering his name, and all he wanted to do was bring her pleasure. He slid down her body, parting the damp pink petals of her flesh, then stroking them rhythmically, erotically.

Swamped with sensation, Tess gasped in shock and delight, her body arching, her nails digging into his bare shoulders. "Cade, don't stop," she muttered, "please don't stop…"

Then Cade felt the climax seize her, feral, lethal, her broken cries echoing in his ears as she tumbled over the edge. Swiftly he gathered her in his arms, her body boneless, her heartbeat like a trip-hammer against his rib cage.

"Cade," she whispered again, "oh, Cade…"

He traced the long curve of her belly, clasped her by the hips and lifted her into his erection, flame shuddering through his limbs, primal and unstoppable. "There's more," he said hoarsely. "God, how I want you!" And kissed her again, ravaging her mouth.

She wrenched free, her breathing ragged. "I want you so

much, beyond anything I've ever known…but be gentle with me, won't you? I've never done this before…it's all new to me."

His heart stopped in his chest. Riveted to the ground, he lashed, "What do you mean?"

"I'm a virgin," she said, a flush rising in her cheeks. "I should have told you before, but somehow the time never seemed right to—"

"A virgin?" he repeated blankly, a chill rippling down his spine.

"I've never even kissed anyone the way I kiss you. Let alone the rest…why are you looking at me like that?"

"Why didn't you tell me after the opera? We were talking about our pasts, I told you about the women I'd been with."

"I should have, I know. But you had so much experience and I had none. Absolutely zero. It's no big deal, Cade, it's not as though I've done anything shameful. Just the opposite, in fact."

He reached over and grabbed a fistful of their clothes. Then he surged to his feet. Roughly he hauled her up to join him. "Here, get dressed."

"What are you talking about? I don't want to."

"This isn't going any further—it went too far as it was."

"Don't treat me like a child!"

"I don't do virgins," he said coldly. "The women I bed know the score."

She said incoherently, "You're behaving like those job applications where you have to have experience to get the job—yet the job's the only way to get the experience. Don't you understand? I'm trusting you. With my body. With myself. Surely I don't have to spell it out?"

"The other thing I don't do—as you know—is commitment," he grated, buttoning up his shirt. His reasons were deep-rooted, powerful and profoundly private; the last person he'd share them with was Tess. "I'm not into long-term.

Hell, Tess, do *I* have to spell it out? How can I have a temporary affair with you? Apart from being a virgin, you're part of the family. *Oh, by the way, Del, I initiated your granddaughter into sex while we were away. Not going to marry her, of course, but it was fun while it lasted*—is that what you're suggesting?"

"Del's got nothing to do with this," she seethed. "It's *my* body. I do with it what I choose."

"Not with me, you don't."

She stamped her foot. "How dare you treat me this way, as though I'm not capable of making up my own mind?"

The moonlight fell softly over her bare breasts, for she'd disdained to put on her blouse. His whole body was one big ache of frustration and lust. Fighting to subdue an anger that he knew was out of all proportion, Cade said flatly, "Quite apart from any other considerations, I'd be taking advantage of your inexperience. When you get married, you'll want—"

"Married?" she interjected furiously. "After living for sixteen years with Cory and Opal, you think *marriage* is on my list?"

"If it isn't, it should be. You can't let them run the show."

"I will if I want to," she retorted. "So why don't you want to get married, Cade? Del and your mother loved each other—you had the best of examples."

"Too constricting," he said evasively. "Too predictable, too dull. I like variety. Playing the field."

She winced. "With me as just one more player."

He pulled on his trousers and shoved his shirt into his waistband. Tess was different. That was the whole problem. Just by being herself, she overturned all his rules, made nonsense of them.

She was also a virgin.

"Get dressed," he repeated, his voice unyielding.

Tess's shoulders sagged. "I've run out of arguments," she

said helplessly. "It's like battering my fists against the walls of the château."

He glanced around at the silent rows of canes with their precious burden of grapes. "We should never have come up here."

So briefly she could have imagined it, he looked as though he was being torn in two; but then that illusory flash of pain was gone. She hardened her heart. She wasn't going to feel sorry for Cade Lorimer.

She wasn't going to feel sorry for herself, either, she thought forcibly, fumbling to do up her blouse. No, sir. She was going to dump all the rules she'd come up with over the years to keep herself safe, and live life on her own terms.

Starting tomorrow, she'd learn everything she possibly could about running a vineyard, and when she got back to Maine she'd ask her grandfather if she could have a job here.

Ask? No way. She'd demand he give her the job.

On the sole condition that Cade Lorimer never be allowed near the place.

It was a condition she'd insist on, Tess thought three days later, as the plane touched down on the runway in Venice. In the last seventy-two hours, she'd concentrated to the best of her ability and absorbed information through her pores. But the whole time, Cade had avoided her assiduously, delegating her education at the vineyard to his underlings whenever possible; on the rare occasions when he'd been forced to speak to her, his frosty politeness had been far worse than outright rudeness.

She should have been happy to have seen so little of him, she thought, unlatching her seat belt. Among the grapevines in the moonlight, hadn't he treated her like a teenager who didn't know her own mind? She hated him for that callous dismissal, of course she did.

Or did she?

She wasn't happy. She was unrelentingly and acutely miserable instead. If *La Traviata* had shown her the power of emotion, the aborted lovemaking in the vineyard had taught her all too much about desire, and its dark companion, frustration.

She still wanted to make love with Cade, lose her virginity with him, take that enormous leap into physical intimacy with him. He was indeed, as she'd recognized instinctively on the pebble beach at Malagash, her fate.

None of this made any sense, logically. Why would she still want to make love with a man who'd turned her down as casually, as cruelly as if she were one of the château's marble statues?

But then, *La Traviata* hadn't made much sense, either.

What made even less sense was the way she missed Cade's companionship and laughter, the warmth of his rare smiles, his touch. At the château she'd dreamed about him every night in her big four-poster bed, embarrassingly erotic dreams charged with emotions that each morning left her heavy-eyed and heavy-hearted. Day by day, her unhappiness had intensified; now, as she stood up and stretched her legs, she knew she was dreading their stay in Venice.

She soon discovered that she and Cade were staying in a luxurious DelMer hotel on one of the small islands in the lagoon; from her window Tess could see the nearby island of Burano with its brightly painted houses and wooden fishing boats. Obediently she toured the hotel with Cade, learning what went on behind the scenes to produce a seemingly effortless level of comfort and service for the guests.

It was interesting, and often an eye-opener; but it didn't captivate her as the vineyard had. Once again, though, Cade treated his employees with respect and genuine warmth: an attitude that emphasized, all too cruelly, the way he was treating her. Again, the anger she'd been aware of ever since

Cade had ordered her to put on her clothes—ordered her as if she was a child—flicked along her nerves.

Anger felt better than misery.

At the age of sixteen, she'd taken control of her destiny. Wasn't it time she did the same again? Be damned if she'd be his victim, helpless, suffering in silence.

Fine words. But how was she going to put them into effect?

Midafternoon, when they took a break, she said to Cade with a casualness that, even to her ears, didn't ring true, "My brain's in overdrive, I can't do any more today…will you arrange for me to have a gondola ride on the Grand Canal?"

"I can take you by water ferry to far more interesting places."

"Tomorrow, perhaps. For now, I'd like to be an ordinary tourist. You don't have to come," she finished, risking a dart of sarcasm, "I wouldn't want to bore you." If he didn't come, she'd take it as an omen; and cancel—or at least delay—her ill-formed plan.

He could hardly deny her, Cade thought, for he wasn't blind to how hard she'd worked the last four days. Nor had she made any effort to reopen that disastrous moonlit conversation between the silent rows of vines: for that alone she deserved to ride a dozen gondolas. "I'll come," he said brusquely. "We'll have dinner in a little restaurant I know near the Rialto Bridge—you can sample Italian wine for a change."

So the die was cast, Tess thought with an inward shiver. Hadn't she known all along that Cade would accompany her? To keep her safe. Choking back a giggle that might have bordered on hysteria, she wondered if she'd have the nerve to go through with her plan.

The risk was astronomical, the chance of success…she had no idea if she'd succeed, or what would be the cost if she did.

But she couldn't go on as she was.

CHAPTER NINE

IN THE hotel bedroom, Tess took one of her dresses off the hanger. It was long, flowing and ultrafeminine, in a soft shade of tangerine: sexy without being too obvious about it. Her pretty sandals were encrusted with crystals, and she inserted delicate crystal earrings in her lobes. Then she added makeup to enhance her eyes; her hair was a knot of curls with tendrils that sculpted her cheeks, and a warm tangerine lipstick flecked with gold coloured her lips. War paint, she thought; and in a surge of cold terror wondered—when the time came—if she'd dare embark on this particular battle. Let alone win it.

I'm not one of Cade's typical women, and I know he wants me…keep that in mind, she told herself fiercely. After taking several deep, steadying breaths, she left her room and floated down the winding staircase to the lobby.

As always, her beauty struck Cade like a physical blow. More than one male head turned to watch her progress, he noticed with a possessiveness that was scarcely appropriate. He walked forward to meet her. "I found this shawl in the boutique," he said, "it can be cool on the canal."

The shawl was woven of the finest wool, a creamy-white that reminded her of the stone walls of his château. "It's lovely—thank you," she said with unaffected pleasure.

Sharon would have turned up her well-bred nose at so simple a gift. But Tess was wrapping herself in the shawl, stroking its soft folds. She's not for you, Cade thought viciously. She's a virgin. Out of bounds.

They traveled to Venice, *La Serenissima,* by water ferry, then boarded the gondola Cade had reserved; the gondolier was dressed in a striped shirt and straw hat. Tess sat on a fat cushion, facing the six-pronged, iron *ferro* on the stern. She was also facing Cade, impossibly handsome, impossibly sexy Cade.

The long wooden oar splashed peacefully in the water. Cade interjected the occasional explanation: of the colorfully striped mooring poles outside the *palazzi;* of the Gothic splendor of Ca'D'Oro; of the origin of the Church of the Salute, bathed in a fiery sunset. He was more relaxed than she'd seen him in days, she thought; and was glad she'd suggested this simple outing, even though her motives were suspect. Besides, he was speaking to her without that deadly politeness that had so crushed her spirits.

As the gondolier serenaded her in Italian, the glorious architecture further distracted her from her nervousness. The plan, after all, didn't have to be implemented until after dinner.

"I'm having a wonderful time, Cade," she said impetuously. "The canal's so evocative of the past. So romantic."

"It smells," Cade said pithily.

"You've got the soul of a businessman."

"I am a businessman." He gave her one of his rare smiles, producing an armload of yellow roses from behind his seat. "So I should toss these? They were intended as an antidote to the smell."

"You arranged for them to be here?" she said, charmed, burying her nose in the silky petals. "That was sweet of you."

In front of his eyes, she'd changed from the strictly businesslike partner of the last few days to the desirable and all too approachable woman he'd so nearly seduced at the vineyard. Cade's loins tightened. Furious with himself, he pointed out a *fondaco*, a twelfth century warehouse, and told her a little of its history. But she was still cradling the roses, her cheek brushing the delicate blooms seductively, her lips gently curved.

To his infinite relief, he realized they'd reached their destination. The gondola bumped against the mooring, then they walked along a crowded street past faded old buildings to the restaurant. Cade had chosen small and intimate, rather than imposing. Bad mistake, he thought, watching candlelight flicker over Tess's features at their secluded table. He said at random, once they'd chosen their meals, "The gondolier was pleased to be given the roses."

"After he told me his wife was pregnant, I wanted to do something for him—you didn't mind?"

He shook his head. Her lovemaking, inexperienced though it had been, had had that same generosity: a thought Cade squashed as soon as it surfaced. One more day at the Venetian hotel, a quick side trip on the way home, then they'd be back on his own turf. Maybe there it would be easier to keep his hands off her.

If the worst came to the worst, he'd call Cecilia. Or Jasmine. Or Marylee.

Tess's dress clung softly to her breasts; desperate to bury his face in her cleavage, so shadowed and enticing, Cade averted his gaze. The breeze on the canal had tousled her curls, and as she smiled at the waiter, her green eyes shone like jewels.

Desperate? When had he ever been desperate for a woman before?

Maybe abstinence was affecting his brain. Up until now, hadn't he always taken what he wanted?

Up until now, he'd always been in control.

"You look very fierce," Tess said edgily.

With a jerk, Cade came back to the present. "Sorry," he said with unaccustomed awkwardness. "How's the *insalata*?"

"Delicious," she said, spearing a sliver of sun-ripened tomato. "The dressing's to die for."

It's you who's to die for, Cade thought; and for a horrible moment thought he'd said the words out loud. Trying to pull himelf together, he began to talk about some of his early experiences in Venice, when he was wheeling and dealing to procure the renovation permits for the hotel.

To his relief, she declined dessert. He paid the bill and in no time was ushering her onboard the hotel's private water ferry. Half an hour, he thought. You can keep a lid on lust for thirty more minutes.

The soft putt-putt of the motor discouraged conversation. But the moon—the same full moon that had shone in the vineyard on Tess's naked breasts—was shimmering on the waters of the lagoon. At least he was sitting across from her; to have felt her thigh pressed to his would have been more than he could bear.

He'd never in his life been so glad to reach one of his own hotels. His jaw tight, he escorted her to the top floor, where her suite—next door to his—overlooked the spires and domes of the city. "I'll see you in the morning," he said.

"I'll look forward to it," she replied, gave him an enigmatic smile and closed the gilt-scrolled panels in his face.

In his own suite, Cade ripped off his tie, took a shower, which he tapered to cold, threw on sweatpants and turned on the TV. He wasn't going to get any sleep—he might as well brush up on his Italian.

Five minutes later, after he'd just poured himself a glass of Tuscan wine, a soft tap came at his door.

He hadn't ordered room service; and he had his own fax machine and laptop, so it couldn't be someone from the front desk. Puzzled, he peered through the peephole.

Tess was standing in the hallway.

Swiftly he unlocked the door. "Is anything wrong?"

"Aren't you going to invite me in?"

Her cheeks were pale, her eyes enormous. He took her by the elbow, drew her into the room and snapped the door shut. "Are you ill, Tess?"

Her robe was full-length, a virginal white. Beneath it, her nightgown reached to midthigh. It was diaphanous and not remotely virginal, he thought, his mouth dry. The plunging neckline alone was calculated to drive a man to drink. He said with impersonal crispness, "If you're not feeling well, I can call the hotel doctor."

In a staccato voice she announced, "I'm sick of being a virgin—that's all that's wrong with me, and that's the first thing I have to say."

Her chin was set at an obstinate angle, her face was still paper-white, and once again she'd taken him totally by surprise. Along with lust, admiration for her sheer effrontery entangled itself in Cade's chest. Doing his best to bank both down, he said, "You get first prize for initiative, I'll give you that. What's next on the list?"

"Don't you dare laugh at me—I'm scared out of my wits."

He was still holding her by the elbow, Cade realized, and dropped it as though it had scalded him. "How about a glass of Fontarollo?"

"I plan to stay stone-cold sober. I'm here to seduce you."

"You chose the right nightgown," he said nastily. "I turned you down—remember?"

"I sure do. But I've had three days to think about all your reasons, starting with Del. I'll never tell him I lost my virginity with you, and I don't see why you would—so he's out of the picture. That's the second thing on my list."

"Just how long is this list?"

Her eyes narrowed militantly. "I want to seduce you. And you want to go to bed with me, I know you do. That's the third thing—seducer and seducee."

"Maybe I'll be the one doing the seducing," he said with dangerous softness.

A hectic flush stained her cheekbones. "I didn't think this would be so difficult," she said wildly. "You can pour me a glass of that wine after all."

Turning his back, Cade filled a crystal, long-stemmed glass with ruby-red wine. Passing it to her, he said, "You're playing with fire, Tess—you know that?"

"I sure don't feel the slightest bit romantic." She took a big gulp of wine, plunked the glass down on the priceless antique desk and said, ticking off her fingers, "Del's no longer an issue. You're not involved with anyone else. And at twenty-two, isn't it time I played with fire?"

"I won't marry you," he said with no diplomacy whatsoever.

She tilted her chin even higher. "Affair versus commitment," she said, hoping she sounded more confident than she felt. "That's number four on the list. This will be a Venetian affair. Short and sweet. I don't want marriage, or anything approaching marriage, I told you that already. Freedom, independence and lots of space are what I need. You don't want marriage or long-term commitment—high potential for boredom and too predictable. So we're in total agreement."

It was ridiculous to be irked because her dislike of marriage equaled his own. Although, Cade had to admit, he was as far from bored as he could be, and once again she'd proven herself utterly unpredictable. She'd also had control of this discussion for too long. He said curtly, "If freedom means you can seduce six other guys along with me, the deal's off."

Her jaw dropped. "Are you nuts?"

"No. For as long as we're lovers—assuming that's what's going to happen—I'll be faithful to you. And I'll expect the same of you."

"Well, of course." Her eyes narrowed. "Although you're talking as though this affair's going to last a whole lot longer than two days."

"Who knows?" he said. "We might have to prolong our stay in Venice."

"Not indefinitely, we can't."

He raised one brow. "On the other hand, we might decide to leave tomorrow morning."

Her frown deepened. "Are you playing games with me?"

"It's a fine concept—A Venetian Affair. Should I choose to extend into An Adelaide Affair—which I admit doesn't have quite the same ring—I'll no doubt like that, too."

"You don't want commitment!"

"I want fidelity," he said in a hard voice. "And when either one of us decides to end this affair, we say so. Up-front. Whether that happens in Venice, Adelaide or Tierra del Fuego."

By now Tess was scowling. "You're doing your CEO act again."

"I'm the one calling the shots—that's the way I operate. So now it's my turn to ask a question. You're a virgin. There must have been men in your life, but for your own reasons, you didn't let them close enough to get to first base—"

"I'm not a baseball game—I'm a woman!"

"I'm very aware that you're a woman. Why me? Why now?"

"That's two questions," she said fractiously.

"So it is," Cade said, and waited for her to answer.

She took another gulp of wine. Folding her arms over her

chest, she said rapidly, "I've been into control for as long as I can remember, probably because I had none as a child. But you and I—when we get within ten feet of each other, control goes into a tailspin. I'd never even felt desire for a man until I met you." She grimaced. "How naïve is that—and if you ever tell anyone, I'll kill you. But, Cade, whether I call it desire or lust or chemistry or hormones—or even romance," she added with a weak grin, "it's still the most powerful feeling I've ever experienced. And I want to act on it. Now. With you."

"Even though you're scared out of your wits."

Again she swallowed, the muscles moving in her throat. "Guess so."

"So you agree to all my terms? Fidelity, no commitment, and when the time comes, a good, clean ending?"

"Are you always this cold-blooded?"

"Yes," he said, "I am. Saves trouble in the long run."

"All right, I agree," she said in a smothered voice.

"Then what are we waiting for?"

He moved closer, watching her eyes dilate. The fear was all too real, he thought; if bedding her was to mean anything to either of them, it was up to him to lay it to rest. In one swift movement, he picked her up, holding her against his bare chest. "Come with me," he said.

She made an indecipherable sound in her throat; her body was a bundle of rigid muscles, and he could almost feel her nerves vibrating. From nowhere came a flash of admiration for her courage. It was up to him to relax her, too. More strongly than he'd wanted anything for a very long time, he suddenly realized he wanted Tess to enjoy being in bed with him.

It was her first time.

So this lovemaking was more about her than about him, he thought, kicking open the bedroom door. Not totally altruistic—that would be pushing it too far, and he was no saint; but definitely focused on the woman in his arms rather than on his own needs. Wasn't that new for him?

He'd never gone to bed with her, and already she was changing him in ways he didn't understand.

He walked across the spacious, elegant living room into his bedroom, where through the open blinds moonlight splashed across the dark waters of the lagoon. Putting her down beside his bed, he stripped back the covers. "Lie down, Tess. I'll be right with you."

She sat down on the very edge of the bed, looking as though the slightest provocation would send her into full flight. Quickly he went to his toilet kit in the bathroom, found the foil envelopes and brought a couple back into the bedroom, laying them on the bedside table. "Oh God," Tess gasped, "I never even thought of that."

"Then it's a good thing I did," Cade said. Taking his time, he lit every candle in the room and pushed the door shut, so that the only light came from the moon and from the clustered blue and yellow flames.

Then he walked over to the bed and sat down beside her. She was clutching her robe to her chest, her hands white-knuckled. "I'm the one who instigated this," she blurted. "I don't know why I'm so scared."

He chafed her cold fingers. "You've never been with a man before—why wouldn't you be scared?"

In the dark depths of his irises, Tess could see tiny pinpoints of fire. To her nostrils, unmistakable, drifted the scent of his skin. She'd know him anywhere, she thought; and how could she possibly lose her virginity with anyone other than him?

She was behaving like a wishy-washy Victorian heroine who was terrified of her fate. Sitting up straight, she said, her voice scarcely quavering at all, "If you kissed me, I bet I'd feel better."

"You have the courage of ten lions," Cade said, lowering his head. His lips brushed hers with a sensuality that shivered along her nerves. She closed her eyes, the better to savor it, and felt his hands, warm and very sure of themselves, drop to her shoulders. With a small whisper of surrender, she brought her own hands to rest on his chest. The roughness of his body hair, the heat of his skin, licked along her nerves with delicate flickers of fire.

As though he was so closely attuned to her that he knew her every mood, Cade deepened his kiss, his tongue dancing with hers, his teeth grazing her lower lip. She let her palms glide over his chest, searching out the hard curve of rib bone, then the bumps of his spine: learning his body. Within her, heat leaped to flame. Against his mouth, she whispered, "I'm where I want to be. Here. With you."

"Right now, I wouldn't want you to be anywhere else in the world," he muttered and was suddenly devouring all the sweetness of her mouth in a kiss that ripped through her.

In a flood of gratitude and desire, she twisted in his arms. He pulled her onto his lap, her robe slipping from her shoulders. She shrugged out of it, longing to feel skin on skin, her breasts aching for his touch. As if he'd read her mind, he cupped their weight in his palms, teasing their tips until she threw her head back, whimpering his name.

"So beautiful," he said hoarsely.

Emboldened, she wrapped her arms around his neck, her legs around his body; and felt his hardness thrust between her thighs. He wanted her. But had she ever doubted that? Shuddering, her breath caught in her throat, she whispered, "We've got too many clothes on."

"Look down," he said.

He was stroking her breast through her diaphanous gown, her flesh like the ivory petals of a rose, the aureole a darker bud. Again she shuddered, wondering if she could die from sheer pleasure.

Gracefully she lifted her arms over her head; and watched him draw her gown up her body, then slide it over her head. His eyes drank her in, such an intensity of passion in them that, suddenly, Tess wanted to weep.

He slicked her nipples with his tongue. Sensitized, scorched, so aroused she scarcely knew where she ended and he began, she molded herself to him, clasping him by the hips, glorying in the jut of bone and tautness of muscle. With a gentleness that was laced with both daring and shyness, she edged the waistband of his sweatpants downward, and wrapped her fingers around his silken, heated center.

His face convulsed. He said roughly, "You destroy me."

"I—"

His eyes speared into her. Into her soul, she thought helplessly. "Tess, with me you're free—free to do whatever you want to."

"So making love can be another kind of freedom?"

He'd never thought so. "For you, right now, it can be," he temporized.

The words tumbled from her lips. "I've never touched a man like this. Never been naked with a man before."

It was an odd time for Cade to feel a sudden flick of fear. Pushing it away, he brought her palm to his mouth, smoothing it with his lips, feeling her fingers curl confidingly in his. Then he found the pulse in her wrist, feeling it flutter beneath his lips. "Do you like what we're doing?"

Her chuckle was spontaneous. "Like it? Understatement of the year! Oh, Cade, I didn't realize lovemaking was like this. So overwhelming, so powerful, yet there's a place for laughter."

"We've only just begun," he said. Swiftly he rolled over, carrying her with him. Stripping his sweats from his body, he kicked them aside. Then he drew her to lie beside him, length to length.

He was magnificent, Tess thought. Aroused. Male to her female. So focused on her that it made her tremble.

He was kissing her again, long, drugged kisses that throbbed through her until her whole body was liquid with longing. Lifting himself on his elbows, he hovered over her, his mouth lingering on her throat, on the delicate hollows beneath her collarbone, on the twin peaks of her breasts, swollen and agonizingly sensitive.

She arched, running her nails down his spine, feeling his thighs push hers apart and sink between them. His fingers, infinitely skillful, found her warmth and wetness, teasing, skimming, until it was unbearable; until she bucked under his touch; until the rhythms mounted to a climax that plunged her into that place where she was most intensely herself yet suffused with him in every cell of her body.

Very slowly she came back to herself. "You did it again," she whispered, sliding her fingers down his body, burying them in the tangled dark hair on his torso. "But I want more. I want to be filled with you, Cade. To know what that's like...won't you show me?"

No barriers, he thought. Only trust. And felt again that fugitive nibble of fear.

Holding tight to restraint, wanting her to be more than ready when he entered her, he traced all her curves again with lips and hands. Her heartbeat was like a hammer in his ear, her quickened breathing and her roaming hands assaults to his control. But not until she was frantic with need did he deal with the foil envelope, then gently ease himself between her legs.

She was lying beneath him, her hair a chestnut swirl on the pillow, her eyes like dark pools in which he could drown. She grasped him by the waist, opening to him. Inexperienced, generous and heart-stoppingly passionate—she was all of those things, he thought. And, right now, she was his.

He thrust deeper. A flash of pain crossed her features, and was as quickly subdued. Braced, he held himself still with a huge effort. "I don't want to hurt you," he gasped.

She arched upward, gathering him in. "You won't. You aren't. Cade, take me, oh please…"

Deeper and deeper he thrust, until she closed around him like a silken glove, her inexpert movements inflaming him beyond bearing. But even then, he waited until he saw the same storm gather in her face, heard her broken cries and felt her inner throbbing. Pushed to the edge, to the very brink, Cade could hold back no longer. His own rhythms seized him, powerful and implacable. Watching her face, he fell with her; and spiraled to release.

Trying not to let his whole weight rest on her, he dropped his forehead to her shoulder, his chest heaving. Her skin smelled sweetly of lavender; he could feel her blood racing in her veins. Fighting for breath, he muttered, "Are you okay?" And raised his head for her response.

She took his face in her hands, her smile radiant. "I feel—oh, Cade, what words do I use? Joined to you. Fulfilled. Light as air, joyous as a rainbow." She laughed, a deep belly laugh that, involuntarily, curved his own mouth in response. "I feel wonderful, fantastic, splendiferous. If you want to add okay to that, go ahead."

"You're very good for my ego," he said dryly.

Sobering, she murmured, "You took care of me. Waited for me, made sure I was ready. Thank you for that—because it cost you, I could tell."

"You weren't supposed to see that," he said uncomfortably.

"Next time, I don't want you to hold back."

"I figure we could manage that in about five minutes—how about it?"

"Oh." She blushed entrancingly. "Really? That soon?"

"That soon."

"You still want me? I mean, I wasn't exactly—"

"You were perfect," he said briefly. "And in a few minutes, I'll show you how much I still want you."

She gave another ripple of laughter. "I like being in bed with you!"

"Good. Because I plan on spending a fair bit of time here in the next few hours. I don't have any meetings until noon tomorrow, and I'm sure the hotel can manage without me all morning." He eased out of her embrace. "I'll be back in a minute."

In the bathroom, Cade regarded himself in the mirror. Same face, he thought. Same body. But something was different. In the big bed in the next room, with a chestnut-haired woman, he'd shifted to a new place.

Tess's generosity, untutored and shy though it had been, was the essence of Tess: nothing to do with the fact that he was filthy rich. Tess hadn't been responding to the Lorimer billions; she'd been responding to him, Cade. So for him, also, this lovemaking had been a first time, he thought—the first time he'd ever been able to fully trust his bed-partner's passion.

Wasn't that, deep down, what he'd always wanted? Yet for some unknown reason, every nerve he possessed was on edge.

He took a couple of deep breaths, making himself relax. One thing he knew: the Venetian Affair was going to travel to Venezuela and Australia, and even back to Maine. It could take quite a while to get Tess Ritchie out of his system.

He wasn't done with her.

Not anywhere near.

CHAPTER TEN

CADE and Tess stayed for two more days on the little island in the Venetian lagoon. As she folded her clothes into her suitcase on the morning of their departure, Tess knew she wasn't ready to leave. Cade was shaving in her bathroom; she could see him through the open door. Naked to the waist. Lean, muscular and sexy.

She had sex on the brain, she thought irritably.

When they left here, was the affair over?

She'd told Cade it would be a Venetian Affair, finished when they left the hotel. Which just went to show how ignorant, how totally out of touch with reality a twenty-two-year-old woman could be.

While he hadn't exactly agreed to her conditions, not for a million dollars would she ask him if it really was over. Too humiliating.

Cade leaned forward over the sink and splashed water on his face. Catching sight of her in the mirror, he smiled at her, a smile that tugged at her heartstrings. She should end the affair now, she thought frantically, before she got in any deeper. Although wasn't she way over her head already?

Clutching the scrap of white nightgown she'd worn that first night, Tess said, "We've spent a lot of time in bed the last couple of days."

He grinned, a piratical grin that caused—once more, she thought in horror—desire to uncurl lazily in her belly. "Be accurate," he said. "We've spent a lot of time making love. Occasionally we managed to do it in bed."

In a strangled voice she said, "In the bathtub up to our necks in bubbles. On the Aubusson carpet halfway under the table. Up against the wall right here in this room—we nearly knocked the picture down."

"I never liked that picture."

"Where haven't we made love?"

"The lobby?" Cade said with another of those devil-may-care grins.

"A girl has to draw the line somewhere," she said primly.

He laughed, striding back into the room, catching her by the waist and waltzing her around the very same carpet. In embarrassing detail, she remembered how she'd straddled him, ridden him, her naked breasts cupped in his hands…

Cade stopped by the chaise longue and looked her up and down. She was wearing a business suit tailored in dark green linen, her cream silk blouse very feminine, her exquisite legs in silken hose. "You look good enough to eat," he said, bent his head and kissed her.

So much for makeup, she thought distantly, wrenched her head free and heard herself say, "Is that our last kiss?"

His eyes narrowed. "What are you talking about?"

"We're leaving Venice."

"Are you telling me you want the affair to end?"

She couldn't bear it if it did. She tilted her chin. "Do you?"

"Where the hell have you been the last two days?" he said, exasperated.

"Men turn sex on and off. I've read about it in books."

If it hadn't been for the desperation in her voice, Cade might have laughed. Schooling his features to impassivity, he said, "You're stereotyping me—you're guilty of sexism. Oh, Tess, I'm disillusioned."

She glared at him. "Stop making fun of me!"

"Do *you* think I want our affair to end?"

"I—I guess not."

"Brilliant deduction," he said dryly. "If anything, I want you more now than I did two days ago."

The blush started at her throat and crept up her cheeks all the way to her hairline. "Me, too," she said in a small voice. "But we're going back home, we can't—"

"We can do what we like—we're consenting adults."

"A Venetian Affair, the sequel?" she said, engulfed in a flood of emotion that she hastily labeled relief.

"You catch on fast." He hesitated. "We've got to stop at another DelMer hotel before we head back to the States. But it won't take long. Then we'll fly directly to Kentucky."

"Kentucky?" she said, puzzled. "I thought we were going back to Manhattan first. Or Maine."

"Del deeded me his Kentucky thoroughbred farm a few years ago. I just found out that the nearest neighbors are throwing a big party on the weekend—a good chance to introduce you to society."

"Thanks for consulting me first!"

"There wasn't time," he said impatiently. "Are you finished packing? We should leave soon."

Relief was swallowed in temper. "A Venetian Affair II—sequels can always be canceled."

"Yeah?" he said, plummeted to her mouth, laced his tongue with hers, and with one hand found the silken curve of her breast. And judged the precise moment when temper flared into passion.

He'd jammed her against an antique table bearing a priceless fourteenth century gold vase. Tess gripped him by the buttocks, thrust against his erection and wondered how she could have contemplated ending an affair that had wound itself around her, body and soul.

Soul? This was about her body, she thought wildly. And only her body. Then she stopped thinking altogether.

With an abruptness that shocked her, Cade pushed her away. He was breathing hard, his steel-gray eyes fired with emotions she couldn't have begun to guess. "The water ferry will be at the dock in ten minutes," he said. "I'll meet you in the lobby."

The door shut decisively behind him. Tess said a very rude word and shoved the nightgown into her suitcase. This affair was about sex, nothing but sex; it wasn't even remotely about her soul. She'd do well to remember that.

She marched into the bathroom and repaired her lipstick. Her cheeks were still bright pink, and her blouse was halfway out of her waistband.

What was happening to her?

It wasn't until Cade's jet landed at Barajas Airport that Tess realized their destination. She said uncertainly, breaking the silence between them for the first time since the jet had taken off, "Madrid? Why here?"

"The hotel's having staff problems—I'd rather deal with it face-to-face than by fax."

Madrid: the place where she'd been born, and where she'd lived for the first five years of her life. Not sure how she felt about being back, Tess sat quietly during the drive into the city. The baroque-style hotel was in old Madrid, near the Plaza Mayor; the lobby, with its silk wall hangings, gold-leaf columns and sumptuous paintings, took her breath away.

As always, Cade was greeted with respect and warmth. He held a low-voiced conversation with the manager, then turned to Tess. "There's a private room off the lobby, we'll have a snack there before we start work," he said.

She followed him past a huge vase filled with a bouquet of orange and purple birds of paradise and admitted to herself that she wasn't up for dealing with staff problems. Maybe she could suggest that she test the mattress in one of the rooms, she thought wryly. Alone. To catch up on her sleep.

Cade pushed open a door marked *Privado* and ushered her ahead of him. She walked in, then stopped dead.

A woman in an austere charcoal suit was standing on the Persian carpet. She was middle-aged, her sleek black hair wrapped in a chignon, her profile as imperious as an eagle's. All the color drained from Tess's face. Grabbing the door handle for support, she gasped, "*Bella!* But—they told me you were dead."

"They were wicked, selfish and cruel," the woman announced. "May they languish in limbo. May they burn in hell." A fierce smile lit up her face. "I am very much alive—as you see."

"It's really you? It can't be!" Then the older woman smiled again, a smile so full of love that Tess was wrenched backward through the years to a little girl in a playground whose nanny was smiling at her as she pushed her higher, higher and ever higher on the red wooden swing.

"You've grown up, *chica*," Ysabel said.

"Oh, Bella…" Swiftly Tess crossed the room and flung her arms around the other woman.

"I would have known you anywhere," Ysabel said raggedly, tears trickling down her cheeks. "I always knew you would be beautiful—I worried for you because of that beauty."

"You use the same perfume," Tess said in a choked voice.

Ysabel held her tight. "*Querida*," she murmured. "When I came to your lodgings that day and found you were gone, all three of you, in the night—no address, no word of where you'd disappeared—I was heartbroken. I tried to find you, but with no success. I missed you, *chica*, I missed you so much."

Tess straightened, gazing into Ysabel's dark brown eyes, the color of the chocolate treats she'd adored as a child. "I cried for days…until Cory finally told me you'd died. I believed him—why wouldn't I? But I shouldn't have."

"Cory Lorimer could say the sky was green and the whole world would believe him," Ysabel snapped, wiping the tears from her face. "It was his only talent."

"But—" Tess's brain finally began to work. "How did you get here? How did you know I'd be here today?"

"Signor Lorimer," Ysabel said, glancing over her shoulder at Cade. "He contacted me three days ago, told me he'd bring you to Madrid if I wished to see you again." She raised elegantly plucked brows. "See you? Of course I wanted to see you! His news made me so happy, Tess, so very happy."

Cade shifted his feet; he'd positioned himself near the door. When Tess turned to face him, her delicate features were glowing with a happiness that matched Ysabel's. But, he noticed, not even being brought face-to-face with a woman she'd loved, and whom she'd thought dead for years—not even that had made her cry. Why was she so afraid of tears?

Was he complaining? Hadn't he dreaded the prospect of two weeping females in the same room, he who never involved himself in the private lives of his women?

He said rapidly, "It was nothing. A matter of hiring a couple of investigators."

"You couldn't have given me a better gift," Tess said huskily. "Anyone with a credit card can buy emeralds. Or diamonds. Or even yellow sweetheart roses. But to find Ysabel for me…thank you, Cade. Thank you from the bottom of my heart."

She'd never looked more beautiful. With uncomfortable

truth, his thoughts marched on. Over the years, he'd bought various women diamond earrings, bracelets and watches, forking over his credit card as casually as if he was ordering a martini. It was the way he operated, and it had served him well.

If pushed to the wall, could he remember the names of all those women?

No. He couldn't. What was it about Tess that made her so different from the rest? That made him behave so atypically?

He said abruptly, "We're booked into the suite on the top floor, Tess. Why don't you spend the day with Ysabel—there's a limo available for you near the front entrance. Then we could all have dinner together, and you and I will leave for the States tomorrow morning."

A martial glint in her eye, Tess said, "The appropriate response when someone thanks you is to say, *you're welcome, no hay de qué, no problem*…I could go on."

"You're welcome," he said dryly, and heard the commonplace phrase echo in his ears. *You're welcome…you're welcome in my life.*

He was losing it. And Ysabel was glancing from him to Tess with a speculative glint in her remarkable dark eyes. With a brief salute Cade left the room, heading for the front desk and the far more manageable problems of a cashier who might have been dipping into the till and a chef who wanted a forty percent raise.

Yes, he was running away. So what?

At nine-thirty that evening, Tess and Ysabel were standing near the front door of the hotel, where the limo was waiting to drive Ysabel home to her charming little apartment with its flower-bedecked balcony; she and Tess had had lunch there. Throwing her arms around the older woman, Tess said, "*Buenas noches*…it was a wonderful day, Ysabel. And you'll come for a visit in October, won't you?"

"*Si Dios quiere…buenas noches, querida.*" Swiftly Ysabel tapped over the sidewalk to the limo, waved once and was driven away. Again, there had been tears on her cheeks.

Tess hurried back into the lobby. She knew exactly what she was going to do; and knew, too, that Cade would be busy in the kitchen observing the chef and his underlings at the height of dinner preparation for at least another half hour.

Upstairs in the suite, she lugged the chaise longue around so it faced the door. Next she showered, smoothing body lotion over her skin and painting her toenails a vibrant scarlet. Finally she took out the bag she'd carefully packed away in Venice, donned its contents and arranged herself on the chaise longue.

Nothing left to do but wait.

Outside the suite, Cade yanked off his tie. If he ever saw another temperamental chef in his life, it would be too soon. Trouble is, the man could cook like a dream—and didn't he know it.

He'd gotten a twenty-nine percent raise and had promised never to hold a deboning knife to the pastry chef's throat again.

All in a day's work. Cade turned the key in the lock and pushed open the door.

His heart gave a great thud in his chest. As he pulled the door shut and clicked the latch, the flames of perhaps a hundred candles wavered in the air. "Well," he said, "should I call security? Tell them there's a strange woman in my suite? Although, come to think of it, the body looks familiar."

The woman on the chaise longue gave a smothered snort of laughter. She was wearing a Venetian carnival mask painted gold with black-rimmed eyes, high cheekbones and brilliant red lips; it was surrounded by a froth of scarlet net.

A net ruff circled her throat; a scarlet and gold fan had been strategically placed at the juncture of her thighs. Otherwise, she was as naked as the day she was born.

"Jazzy toenails," Cade added, leering at her. "Not bad breasts, either."

She raised the fan and waved it languidly over her mask. Again the candles flickered. "Or should I be the one to phone security?" she said, her voice muffled by the mask. "Would it be premature to warn them that I'm in grave danger? Of being seduced, that is."

He tossed his tie on the heavy mahogany table, following it with his shirt. Then he loosened his leather belt. "I'd say you have about five seconds to make that phone call."

"I could wait. A little danger adds spice to life," she whispered, her green irises gleaming through the eyeholes in the mask.

By now his heart was hammering against his rib cage. He kicked off his shoes and socks, let his trousers drop to the floor and yanked down his underwear. Fully aroused, he walked over to the chaise longue, knelt beside it and buried his mouth in the curve of her instep.

Her skin smelled delicious. Taking his time, he moved to her ankle, slid his lips up the inside of her calf and heard her gasp his name. Raising himself higher, he eased her thighs apart and eased his finger into all the wetness and heat he knew would be waiting for him. Her body arched, slender, smooth as silk, utterly familiar and unbelievably erotic.

She was moaning, her hips undulating, her rapid breathing all the encouragement he needed. Swiftly he rose to hover over her and plunged. As she cried out, rising to meet him, the fan dropped with a small clatter to the floor. Writhing, her movements driving him mad, she took him in, deeper, deeper, until he was lost. His hoarse cry of release mingled with her scream of ecstasy, their blood beating as one.

He let his head drop, feeling sweat bead his forehead. "You've wrecked me," he said.

She'd fallen back on the brocade pillows, her breasts rising and falling as she tried to catch her breath. "I have to take the mask off," she muttered.

"Can't take the heat?" He let himself rest on top of her, fumbling with the ruff and tugging it free of her throat. Then he reached for the elastic at the back of her head and eased the mask from her face.

She smiled at him with sudden, endearing shyness. "I wanted to surprise you," she said.

He gave a bark of laughter. "You more than succeeded—I forgot all about my homicidal chef."

"I aim to please," she said demurely.

She did please him, he thought, staring at her without really seeing her. She pleased him beyond measure. And what the hell did that mean?

A delicate flush wafted over Tess's cheeks; she had no idea what he was thinking. "I can't thank you enough for today," she said. "For the gift of Ysabel."

He flicked her nipple with his tongue, watching her eyes widen. "So is this about gratitude?"

"I don't know what it's about," she said with raw honesty, reaching up to stroke his raven hair back from his forehead. "But I wanted to give you something in return for what you did today. Not something from one of the boutiques…that's too easy—and you have everything you need, anyway."

Did he? If that were true, why was he desperate to ravish the women he'd just ravished only moments ago? He said, "We could move to the bed. I'm the one in danger now—of falling off this goddamned chaise longue."

"It wasn't designed for two. Why do I have the feeling you don't like gratitude?"

He grinned at her. "Because I don't. Hell, Tess, of course

I did my best to locate Ysabel. I'd have to have a heart of stone not to—she's the only person you ever loved."

"It was the most wonderful gift you could have given me." Then her own grin flashed across her face. "Glad you liked my mask."

"It was the fan that did me in." He stood up and lifted her into his arms. "Bed," he said. "Are any of these candles about to set the place on fire?"

"You and I are going to do that," she murmured, tracing his lip with her fingertip.

Sensation, raw and primitive, surged straight to his loins. His last thought, before he carried her into the bedroom, was that tomorrow he was going to buy her emeralds—because he wanted to make love to her when she was wearing nothing but an emerald necklace.

Would he ever have enough of her?

The day—or night—he thought with a touch of grimness, would arrive when he would have had enough of her. Or, for that matter, she of him. That was the way it worked.

Inevitable.

CHAPTER ELEVEN

THE next day, under a moody gray sky, Tess fell in love.

Cypress Acres was a sprawling expanse of rolling green fields, freshly painted white rail fences and groves of tall trees whose leaves rustled in the wind. And horses, she thought, getting out of the car to stretch the day's travel from her limbs. Like a woman hypnotized, she crossed neatly cropped grass and leaned on the top rail of the fence.

Mares were grazing in the field, lazily swishing their tails against the flies, their coats glossy with good health. Foals slept on the grass, frolicked on the hillside and nudged for their mothers' milk. When Cade came up behind her, she said dreamily, "I'd made up my mind I wanted to work at the château. But now I want to be a stablehand, and learn all about the horses."

"You can do both," he said, watching her rapt face.

"They're so beautiful."

He'd always loved Cypress Acres, ever since he'd taken it over on his twenty-fifth birthday seven years ago. "Have you ever ridden one?"

"Never."

"I'll give you a lesson before dinner—want to check out the barn?"

"Oh, yes."

"Let me go ahead and make sure the dogs aren't around."

Her face changed. "How many dogs?"

"Three. Purebred German shepherds. Very well trained."

Something he couldn't decipher flickered across her features and was gone. She rolled her shoulders, as if trying to rid them of tension. "I'll wait here for you," she said.

Once Cade signaled to her from the door, she entered the dim, spacious barn, which smelled sweetly of hay and was immaculately clean. Taking her time, Tess went from stall to stall, rubbing aristocratic noses and doling out carrots. She met Zeke, the head groomsman, and won him over by her frank avowal of total ignorance and her wish to learn all she could in the next few days.

Ten minutes later, dressed in a pair of old jeans and a sweatshirt, she had her first lesson with a currycomb and a mild-mannered gelding named BillyJ. Then she was put to work with a can of saddle soap and an old leather harness. Cade left her to her own devices and went inside the house to phone Tiffany's.

When he came back out, wearing jodphurs and well-worn riding boots, Tess was in the ring with the same gelding, as Zeke supervised her first lesson with the lunging line. While BillyJ wasn't about to break any of the rules, Cade could tell right away that Tess had an instinctive feel for the animal at the other end of the line, the kind of feel that couldn't be taught.

Bow-legged and grizzled, Zeke strolled over to the fence. "She's got the touch," he said briefly. "Thought I'd put her up on Arabesque."

"Good choice. Believe it or not, she's never been near a horse before today."

Zeke pushed back his greasy ball cap. "She listens," he said. "Doesn't forget what you tell her."

"High praise."

"We'll see if she's got lasting power."

Cade's conscience gave him a nasty nudge. It wasn't Tess's lasting power that was the issue, it was his own. Love-em-and-leave-em-Lorimer…he'd been called that ever since he was old enough to date. "I'd suspect she has," he said, and knew he was talking about more than horses.

Zeke shrugged. "You'll take Galaxy later?"

Galaxy was Cade's bay stallion. "After Tess has a riding lesson. If you can keep the dogs away from her, I'd appreciate it—she's got a real phobia."

"I'll only leave them loose in the barn at night. But we should introduce her to them."

When BillyJ was back in his stall, placidly munching hay, Cade said, "Tess, you have to meet the dogs, just in case you come across them unexpectedly. They're trained guard dogs, and once they know you're a resident, they won't bother you. Zeke and I will be here—you don't have a worry in the world."

She bit her lip. Nothing came without a cost, she'd learned that a long time ago. If, in order to spend time with the horses, she had to face three dogs, she could handle it.

"Okay," she said in a small voice.

"Zeke, would you bring them in?" Cade asked.

Zeke ambled off. Although Tess braced herself, when Zeke came around the corner with three large German shepherds on leather leashes, she shrank backward.

"You're safe," Cade said. "I won't let anything happen to you."

You don't understand the first thing about me… Again Tess bit her lip, forcing the words back where they belonged. Zeke brought the dogs closer. "Just let them sniff you," he said. "Spirit, Tex, Ranger—friend. Friend. Got it?"

Three tails wagged. Then Zeke wheeled in a half circle and led the dogs away. "That's it?" Tess mumbled.

Cade rubbed the tension from her shoulders. "To think I once called you a coward," he said wryly. "I should have been shot on the spot."

Her body jerked as though he'd hit her; her eyes were barricaded against him. "You did say riding lesson?"

"Anytime you're ready."

The riding lesson was a revelation to Tess. She sat quietly on the white mare named Arabesque, her hands relaxed on the reins, and before the lesson ended had mastered the art of posting in the saddle. As she slid to the ground, her smile was brilliant. "Can we have another lesson tomorrow?"

"You're going to be sore tomorrow."

"You trying to get out of it?"

"Ten a.m.—after you've cleaned three stalls and polished a couple of saddles. In the afternoon, I'll give you a crash course on the finances of breeding thoroughbreds."

"Slave driver," she said amiably, and led Arabesque into the barn. She rubbed the mare down, told Zeke she'd see him in the morning and trailed behind Cade to the house. It was an antebellum mansion, painted white like the fences, with a host of brick chimneys and mullioned windows shot with the golden rays of the setting sun.

As Cade opened the side door, she said, "You have such good rapport with Zeke—with all your employees for that matter—it doesn't fit your CEO act."

He gave a short laugh. "I worked on a cattle ranch in Argentina and a dude ranch in Montana—I know what it's like to look after other people's animals."

"You did?" Her frown deepened. "When? And why?"

What was the harm in telling her? "When I was twenty, I traveled around the world for two years on a shoestring—no money other than what I earned with my own two hands. I loaded pulpwood in Alaska, sorted scrap iron in China, portered in the Himalayas—you name it." He shrugged. "You could say it was the making of me. It certainly shaped the way I run Lorimer Inc., and how I relate to my employees."

Tess said with painful truth, "Back in Maine, I accused you of living in an ivory tower...I'm sorry."

"Ivory towers, I'd be willing to bet, are dead boring places to live." He ushered her indoors. "You must be ready for a shower and dinner?"

Her mind still occupied with the image of Cade sorting scrap iron, she said absently, "More than ready—in Madrid it's eleven at night."

"Shower, dinner and bed," he said. "Maybe you should sleep alone tonight. Sleep being the operative word."

Tess stumbled on the staircase, forgetting about that younger Cade. Perhaps, she thought sickly, their affair had been a European Affair: fine in Venice and Madrid, but finished now that they were back on home territory. Scrabbling for a vestige of self-control, she said coolly, "I am quite tired."

"It's been a long day."

Cade was marching her along a dimly lit hallway lined with depressing portraits of family ancestors. Scurrying to keep up with him, Tess blurted, "Are you trying to break it to me gently?"

He stopped so suddenly that she cannoned into him. "Break what?"

"That the affair's over."

"All I want is for you to have a decent night's sleep!"

Her shoulders sagged. "So it wasn't just a European Affair—it's transatlantic?"

"Multinational, if we head out for Venezuela and Australia next week. This is the second time you've brought this up. Are you sure you don't want to end it yourself?"

"Yes! Or do I mean no?"

"What do you mean?"

"I don't want it to end!" Then she blushed, furious that she'd sounded so vehement. Pulling away from him, she muttered, "Well—that was a dead giveaway."

Unease now added itself to the stirrings of Cade's conscience. He said carefully, "I'm the first man you've ever made love with, Tess. Don't mistake it for more than it is, will you?"

He couldn't have given her a clearer warning, she thought, gazing up at him. "Don't fall in love with you—that's what you're saying."

"Precisely."

"I don't love you," she said sharply. "But when we're together in bed…we both call it *making love*."

Choosing his words, aware even as he spoke how bland they sounded, Cade said, "We care for each other."

"I like you," she said.

He should have expected her to speak her mind. "Liking's fine," he said. "Just don't carry it to the next step, that's all."

"I promise I won't," she snapped. "Where's the nearest shower? I stink of horses."

Cade opened the door to his left. "These are your rooms. Mine are next door. Bedroom, bathroom, balcony overlooking the rose garden—you'll find all you need. Dinner's in half an hour."

His smile was impersonal. From somewhere Tess dredged up one that was equally cool and shut the door in his face, jamming the lock with vicious strength.

She'd gotten the worst of that discussion. So Cade cared for her. He cared for his Maserati.

Probably more. It didn't argue with him.

Why did she want to fling herself facedown on the bed and indulge in a storm of weeping? She never cried.

She went through every swear word she could think of in every language she knew. Then she had a shower and put on a slinky black dress that, unlike her homemade one, screamed haute couture. It also screamed sex.

After dinner, a meal where she ate sparingly because her appetite seemed to have deserted her, she pushed back her chair and said, her eyes glittering, "I think I'll take you up on that offer to sleep alone. Good night, Cade."

Cade surged to his feet. Candlelight, from the ornate silver candelabra placed at intervals down the mahogany table, burnished her hair and glowed on the soft swell of her breasts. He said, "If you're interested in sleeping alone, you chose the wrong dress."

Her nostrils flared. "I'll wear what I want."

He stepped closer, watching her fight the desire to retreat. "You want me," he said roughly.

"I want you to go straight to hell."

"Then let's go together," he said, and swept her up into his arms.

She kicked out at him, pummeling him on the chest with her fists. "Put me down!"

He thrust the door open with one knee. "Quit struggling," he grunted. "You're not going to win."

White-faced with rage, she seethed, "Because you're bigger. Stronger. Tougher. Because you're a guy. Put me *down*, Cade."

So suddenly that she staggered, he dumped her, feetfirst, to the floor. Then he thrust her against the wall, took her chin in his fingers and planted a kiss on her mouth so searing, so torrid, that Tess locked her arms around his nape and kissed him back.

She was furious with him, she thought dimly. She wanted him. Oh God, how she wanted him…

He pulled his mouth free, then reached up and jerked her arms apart. "Now you can go to bed," he snarled. "Alone."

Rage scorched her cheeks. "What was that all about? Punishment because I dared to oppose the mighty Cade Lorimer?"

"I wish it was that simple."

"So what *was* it about?"

"None of your goddamned business!"

Hands on her hips, Tess glared at him. "I'm not the slightest bit in love with you—get that fact through your thick skull. In fact, at this precise moment, I don't even like you." His jaw dropped. "Oh," she said blankly. "So that's what's wrong—you're in love with *me*."

"I am not!"

In dulcet tones, Tess misquoted, "The man doth protest too much, methinks. Shakespeare. I'm a librarian, remember?"

Determined not to be outdone, Cade dredged his memory. *"I understand your kisses and you mine."*

"Love goes toward love... Romeo and Juliet."

A thing of beauty is a joy forever. He wasn't going to say that. Anyway, it was Keats. "Tess," Cade said, "in plain English, I am not in love with you. Got that?"

She staggered artistically, drawing the back of her hand across her forehead. *"A poor lone woman."*

Regrettably Cade laughed. "Oh sure. How about a compromise? We go to bed together and go straight to sleep."

"What are the odds of that?" she said, a gleam in her eye.

"Only one way to check it out."

"Your place or mine?" she said demurely.

He was still laughing as he ushered her into his bedroom. They didn't go straight to sleep; Cade had known they wouldn't. But eventually they did fall asleep, naked, tangled in each other's arms. And the next morning, at dawn, Tess woke to find Cade leisurely tracing the long curve of her spine with his lips, his erection pressed into her hip. She lay still, reluctant to let him know she was awake, her whole body in a trance of desire.

He was kissing her shoulders, pushing her hair aside to kiss her nape, his fingers seeking out the soft fullness of her breast. Slowly, sensuously, she turned over, opening her arms to him. In utter silence, he made love to every inch of her body. As though he was worshipping it, she thought. As though she was infinitely precious to him.

Or was her imagination working overtime?

The storm, inevitably, gathered them both, lifted them, then hurled them toward release. Still without saying a word, Cade enfolded her in his arms, dropped his cheek to her shoulder and drifted off to sleep again.

But Tess found herself wide-awake. Not moving a muscle, her body satiated, she gazed at his sleeping features. He had, truly, made love to her; there could be no other way to describe his generosity, or his attention to her every need.

She was the one who'd better phone security, she thought crazily, because she was in danger: in danger of falling in love with Cade. How could she make love with him, day after day, night after night, with such aching intimacy, and not fall in love with him?

She'd be a fool to do anything so risky. Sooner or later, the affair would end. Maybe not on this continent. Maybe not for weeks. But end it would.

Terror, her old enemy, seized her in its grip. She didn't want it to end. She couldn't even contemplate letting another man into her bed. It was Cade she wanted, and only Cade.

Now and—her mind quailed—forever.

That day Tess mucked out three stalls, watched Zeke apply strong-smelling linament to a swelling on the foreleg of a stallion called Hyperion and had a riding lesson at ten with

Cade. Knee grip, use of the bit, pressure on the turns and this time a thrilling, although too brief, canter around the ring. She then rubbed Arabesque down.

After that, she worked a yearling on the lunge, closely supervised by Zeke. A brief lunch, then Cade took her through the account books, and introduced her to the intricacies of tracking a thoroughbred's lineage.

A shower had never felt so good. After dinner, in preparation for the neighbor's ball, she and Cade had a dancing lesson in the empty, echoing ballroom. She loved music and he had an innate sense of rhythm; her brow knit with concentration, she added the foxtrot and waltz to her list of new skills. Then she followed him upstairs to his room, changed and fell into the bed. "You haven't seen this nightgown yet," she mumbled. "I've been saving it up."

It was midnight-blue, see-through, so seductive Cade forgot his half-formed plan to cool their affair for now. But as he leaned forward to brush her parted lips with his own, her lashes had already drifted to her cheeks; her breathing deepened.

There were faint blue shadows under her eyes. Very carefully, Cade eased down beside her on the bed. Tess had solved any question of him implementing his plan by falling asleep.

He didn't know whether to be glad or sorry.

Tess woke sometime in the middle of the night. She'd been dreaming. The images fled as soon as she opened her eyes; but the dream's mood, its sense of entrapment, of fear and foreboding, lingered.

Cade was deeply asleep beside her, his hair black on the pillow in the light of a waning moon. One of his arms was flung over her ribs; against her back, she could feel the strong, steady beat of his heart.

She should feel safe with him so close to her; all she had to do was wake him and he'd comfort her.

What if she got used to asking him for help? What then?

Managing not to wake him, she slipped out of bed, found her barn clothes in a heap on the floor where she'd dropped them before dinner and got dressed. Trying to avoid floor-boards that creaked, she crept to the door and slid into the hall. A bewigged ancestor with a pursed mouth stared at her dis-approvingly from the wall.

The stables, she thought, that's where I'll go. The horses will make me feel better.

Her dream must have been about Cory and Opal; no one else had the power to so drench her in dread. But she wasn't in her parents' power anymore, she thought stoutly, checking that she had her keys before letting herself out the side door. Because of Del, she had money; because of Cade, she was learning about corporations, hotels, vineyards and thorough-breds; and she'd reconnected with Ysabel.

She had choices now. As a child, she'd had none.

The night air was cool and damp, clouds smothering most of the stars. Soft-footed, she walked to the barn, unlocked the grooms' door with her key and closed it behind her. A horse whickered a welcome, poking its head out of the stall. "Hello, Galaxy," she said softly and started over the concrete floor toward him.

In a rattle of claws, three German shepherds lunged around the corner and ran right for her. Even in the dim light, she could see their teeth, white, sharp and deadly. With a tiny gasp of dismay, she held her ground.

There was nowhere to run.

"I'm your friend," she squeaked. "Zeke said so."

The dogs surrounded her, avidly sniffing her sneakers and jeans. Their tails were wagging, she realized. Then the largest of the three sat back on his haunches, mouth agape as though he was laughing at her.

Her dog in Amsterdam, her beloved Jake, had had a strong streak of German shepherd in his mixed ancestry; his eyes had been filled with the same golden, alert intelligence.

Tess dropped to her knees. Tentatively she put out her hand to the dog's collar, angling the tag so she could read the name inscribed on it. "Spirit," she whispered, and patted him on the shoulder.

He swished his tail on the concrete floor. The other two dogs were busily nosing her shirt, and suddenly it was too much. In a great upsurge of memory, she put her arms around Spirit and buried her face in his fur.

The first sob pushed its way from somewhere so deep that, instantly, she was undone.

CHAPTER TWELVE

CADE wasn't sure what woke him. A sound? The sense that he was alone in the big bed? "Tess?" he said, wondering if she'd gone to the bathroom.

He was answered by the silence of a sleeping house. Sitting up, switching on the bedside light, he saw that the bed was indeed empty and that the untidy heap of Tess's barn clothes was gone.

Every instinct he possessed warned him to find her, and find her fast. He got up, threw on jeans and a T-shirt and headed out the door. He'd be willing to bet she'd gone to the barn, although he had no idea why.

The dogs, he thought with a stifled curse. Zeke had been leaving them loose in the barn at night.

He took the stairs two at a time and hurried out the side door. No lights in the barn, and not a sound from the dogs. If she wasn't there, where was she?

He unlocked the outer office door, where stud books were neatly arranged on the shelves and the small green lights on the computer shone coldly. The inner door, to the barn, opened smoothly.

Horror jolted through his body. The dogs had dragged her to the floor.

He leaped forward. But then, belatedly, he realized that she had her arms around one of the dogs, and that she was weeping. Weeping as though her heart was broken, he thought, and stopped in his tracks. He'd never heard such desolation, such profound sorrow—the sorrow of a lifetime, surely.

Two of the dogs raised their heads, and one of them trotted over to him, burrowing a cold nose into his hand. But the third dog stayed where he was, unmoving, for Tess was sobbing into his fur, her shoulders heaving.

Cade said quietly, "Tess, don't be scared—it's me." Then he knelt beside her and put his arms around her, turning her into his chest. Unresisting, her body shuddering in spasms of weeping, she fell into his embrace. Spirit nuzzled closer. Cade held on to the woman and the dog, knowing there was nothing he could do until she'd emptied herself of tears.

She never cried. She was terrified of dogs. Yet he'd found her weeping her guts out in the middle of the night, surrounded by three very large dogs, one of whom she was wrapped around as though she never wanted to let go.

Thank God he'd woken up; and he had the rest of the night to find out what was going on.

Gradually her sobs became less frequent, her body sagging against him in utter exhaustion. Fumbling in his pocket, he found a handkerchief and pressed it into her hand. "Blow your nose," he said. "Then I'll take you back to the house."

Head lowered, she scrubbed at her nose and wet cheeks. "I had a dog," she quavered. "In Amsterdam, the year I was sixteen. His name was Jake. Spirit looks like him."

All his senses on high alert, Cade said, "What happened to him?"

Her breath heaved in her chest. Gazing at the buttons on Cade's shirt, she said jaggedly, "Soon after I turned sixteen, Cory's luck ran out. He was shot dead outside a drug dealer's only three blocks from where we lived. I heard about it and ran home to tell Opal. She was terrified. Told me to stay away from the flat for the next week, threw a couple of bills at me and said she'd meet me at the nearby hostel that night."

Tess drew another deep, shaky breath. "She didn't turn up that night, or the next two nights—she probably left on the first train the day Cory was shot."

Cade's breath hissed through his teeth. "When my money ran out," Tess said flatly, "I had nowhere to go. I was too frightened to go back to the flat. So I started roughing it on the streets. I found Jake the third day—he was a stray, hanging around a Dumpster. I panhandled at the station for the two of us, and for a couple of months it went okay. He was a big dog, wouldn't let anyone near me…so I felt safe."

"But you weren't."

"One of the local gang leaders had his eye on me. Ysabel was right—I was too pretty for my own good. I was saving for a train ticket to Den Haag, and I nearly had enough money. But one day when I went to the back door of a restaurant looking for a handout, Hans was waiting for me."

In the dim light, Cade could see her eyes were drowning in remembered terror. Tess at sixteen, he thought—the year the investigator hadn't found a trace of her.

"He grabbed me," she said in a rush. "When Jake went for his throat, Hans shot him. Full in the chest. But even then, Jake managed to knock Hans down." She stifled a sob. "I ran. Ran faster than I've ever run in my life, and by a miracle I managed to shake Hans off. I hopped a freight train that night and got out of town. The rest's history."

Cade said the obvious. "You had to leave Jake behind. You couldn't even bury him."

Her face convulsed. "Jake and Ysabel—they both loved me, and I lost them both."

"Jake saved your life," Cade said, throttling down emotions that threatened to choke him, for her bleak account had shaken him to the roots. "No wonder you didn't want anything to do with the dogs at Moorings. At the time, I misunderstood. You weren't scared of the dogs themselves—it was the memories that terrified you."

"When I reached Den Haag, I got a job washing dishes in a Chinese restaurant." She gave a watery smile. "From there, it was uphill all the way. Cleaning offices at night, ushering in a theater, making cold calls for a market agency...you name it, I've done it."

"How did you get to the States?"

"Housekeeper on a cruise ship." She hesitated, adding in a low voice, "I should have told you all this back in Manhattan. But I couldn't. I just couldn't."

He had to take that look off her face. Cade said calmly, "You could make a donation to an animal shelter in Amsterdam in Jake's memory—you can afford to do that now."

Her face brightened. "That's a wonderful idea—I'll do it."

Cade got to his feet, drawing her up with him. "You're exhausted," he said roughly. "Past time you were back in bed."

She looked right at him, her eyes like dark pools. "Thanks, Cade. For letting me cry. For listening."

He didn't want gratitude, that much he knew. His shoulders tight with tension, he said, "Do me a favor, will you?"

"Of course."

"Every day, write down some of the details of those weeks in Amsterdam. Describe where you slept every night, for instance. What markings Jake had."

She shivered. "He'd lost the tip of one ear. I'll never forget how he snarled when Hans grabbed me...."

"Tess, you got yourself out of Amsterdam and you made it all the way to Malagash Island, where you built a life for yourself. But in the process, you buried those nightmare sights and sounds." He gave a faint smile. "Time to resurrect them, that's all I'm saying."

He gazed down at her, wishing he could banish the same images: a raised gun, a bleeding dog, a terrified teenager running for her life through dark, garbage-strewn alleys. He had the feeling they'd be with him for the rest of his life. He was also, he realized, seething with anger. At a world that allowed such things to happen. At Del, for not making any effort to track Tess down when she was young and in desperate need. At himself, because six years ago he hadn't been there for her, hadn't even known she existed.

She could have gone under so easily, and been forever lost.

He couldn't let the anger out now: it was the worst of times. He put his arm around Tess's waist. "Right now, let's call it quits," he said. "You've done more than enough for one night."

It was a measure of her tiredness that she made no argument. Keeping his emotions under tight rein, Cade walked her back to the house; and chose her bedroom, rather than his, for her to spend the rest of the night. With impersonal briskness he undressed her, found a nightgown in her drawer and pulled the covers over her. But before she closed her eyes, she reached for his hand and pressed it to her lips. "Thank you," she whispered. Still clasping his fingers, she fell into a stunned sleep.

But Cade stayed awake, sitting beside the bed. Keeping vigil, he thought soberly, as darkness faded from the sky and the first birds began to sing in the tall trees.

He should never have started this affair. Tess had been damaged more than enough in her short life, without him adding to it. His affairs were always short-lived. Worse, this particular one was with the woman who was Del's granddaughter; he, Cade, would have an ongoing relationship with her for the rest of his life, whether he wanted to or not. Avoiding her totally would be impossible.

He'd been an idiot in Venice, thinking with his hormones, not his brain cells. He should have sent her straight back to her room in her virginal-white gown.

Damage control, he thought heavily. How was he going to accomplish that?

One thing he could do, tangential though it was. He could confront Del with Cory's chequered past, and ask why Cory's existence had been kept a secret. Ask, too, why Del had never tried to contact Tess. It was due time for those ghosts to be laid to rest.

As for him, he'd better start keeping Tess at arm's length. Arm's length? he thought with vicious irony. He should end the affair right now, before any more damage was done.

Which meant that never again would he hold her in his arms, naked, breathtakingly beautiful, so generous she made nonsense of any concept of distance...

When Tess woke up, she was alone in her bedroom. It was sixteen minutes past midday.

The events of last night crowded into her mind. In a barn in Kentucky, she'd broken one of her inviolable rules: never to tell anyone about the events of those terrible days after Cory died. But she'd told Cade. Nor, she thought, stretching the stiffness from her limbs, had the sky fallen.

She scrambled out of bed, showered and went downstairs for lunch, hoping to find Cade there. However, she had the vast dining room to herself. A note and a flat package were sitting beside her plate, the handwriting on the envelope Cade's. She slit it open and quickly read the scrawled words. He'd had to go to Manhattan but he'd be back tomorrow in time for the ball. Zeke would give her riding lessons the next two days. The package had been delivered this morning and he hoped she'd wear the contents with her green dress. His signature was a slash of black ink: Cade.

No reason to feel uneasy. What had she expected, that he'd sign it *Love, Cade*? Or that he'd mention what had happened last night?

Eating a deliciously light omelet, she looked at the flat box suspiciously. She might not be sophisticated, but she recognized the name Tiffany's.

Open it, Tess. It's not going to bite you.

In the end, she took the package up to her room to open it in privacy. Anchored to a bed of soft white velvet, emeralds flashed green fire: a pendant with a single stone on a delicate gold chain; earrings with more emeralds dangling from tiny gold chains; a gold bracelet set with emeralds. She'd never in her life seen jewellry so beautiful.

Cade should be here. Why hadn't he waited to give them to her himself, tomorrow night? To circle her throat with the pendant, to kiss her nape…

How could she be so ungrateful as to be critical of him?

The uneasy feeling hadn't gone away; if anything, it had magnified. She shoved the slim leather box into her top drawer; mucking out stalls and pitchforking hay would improve her mood.

Cade didn't phone, that day or the next.

She shouldn't have told him about Amsterdam, Tess thought sickly, as she twisted to do up the zipper on her green dress the second evening. Sure, he'd listened. But what choice had he had when she was blubbering all over him?

If only she could undo that scene in the barn.

Through the open window, she heard the sound of a car approaching. Gazing out, she watched a limo draw up in the circular driveway. Cade climbed out, carrying an overnight bag and a briefcase, and hurried to the front door.

Her hands were cold and her pulses racing. She was dreading the ball tonight, she realized, the speculative glances, the inevitable questions about her whereabouts for the last twenty-two years. She'd know only one person there—Cade—and she'd had exactly one dancing lesson in her entire life.

But she'd be adorned with a small fortune in emeralds, she thought with a spurt of anger.

Footsteps hurried along the hallway outside her room, passing her door. Cade's door shut with a crisp snap. Two minutes later she heard his shower start.

If she was half as brave as he claimed she was, she'd go to his room and offer to dry his back. He hadn't even taken the time to tap on her door, or to kiss her. It was as if she no longer existed.

By making love with him, she'd trusted him with her body. But by telling him about Jake and Hans, she'd trusted him with her soul.

Her thoughts marched on. The decision never to talk about Amsterdam wasn't just about repression; it was about self-preservation as well. She'd been smart to keep her past to herself. How many people wanted to associate with a woman who'd once been as homeless as a stray dog, on the run from drug dealers and gangs?

Obviously Cade didn't. He'd disappeared for two days and now he was ignoring her.

She'd told him once that anyone with a credit card could buy emeralds. The jewels lying in their velvet-lined case were indeed an empty gesture if he no longer respected her. If he no longer wanted her.

Or was there more going on than that?

Cold terror had uncoiled like a snake in her belly. Desperately she tried to smother it. She wasn't going to fall apart again, not twice in forty-eight hours. Once had been once too often.

You've done more than enough for one night…as clearly as if she was back in the barn, she heard Cade's words echo in her head. At the time, she'd taken them at face value. But now, they were more ambiguous.

He hadn't asked her to tell him the details about that past: he'd asked her to write them down for her own use. The difference was crucial.

He didn't want to know the details.

Her fingers ice-cold, Tess did up her thin-strapped gold sandals. Quickly she inserted the earrings into her lobes and fastened the bracelet around her wrist. But despite her best efforts she couldn't manage the clasp on the pendant. Then she sat down on her bed and waited.

The shower shut off. Five minutes later, she heard Cade's door close again, and a decisive tap came at her door. She stood up, drawing composure around her like a cloak.

"Come in," she said.

Cade strode into Tess's bedroom. She was standing very still, a slim, wary figure in a gold-embroidered dress that fit her like a glove. Tiny sparks of green shot from her earlobes and wrist. "Sorry I'm late," he said abruptly. "Are you ready?"

He looked formidably elegant in his tux, yet as untamed as the panther Tess had once compared him to. Neither had he, in her opinion, sounded overly sorry. She said with formal exactitude, "Thank you for the emeralds."

"*No hay de qué*," he said, his touch of sarcasm grating on her nerves. "You're not wearing the pendant."

"I can't do up the clasp."

Cade looked at her in silence. Damage control, he thought. Keep your distance.

She hadn't taken a single step toward him; so his strategy was working. Now all he had to do was maintain it. Easy enough when he was in Manhattan and she was in Kentucky. Not so easy face-to-face with her, when she looked delicious enough to eat and was stationed scarcely two feet away from a very wide bed.

Clumsily for him, Cade lifted the pendant from its velvet bed—he had beds on the brain, he thought savagely—and looped it around her neck. As she bent her nape, his fingers brushed her skin; a shiver rippled through her. His jaw tightened. Fumbling with the small gold clasp, he fastened it and stepped back.

"I'm ready," she said.

Her spine was ramrod straight. Knowing better than to touch her, for if he did he'd be lost, Cade said, "We should go. It's a ten-mile drive." Then he heard himself add, "You're not a horse going to the glue factory, Tess—you're a beautiful woman going to a high-society shindig that lots of people would give their eyeteeth to attend."

"I'm not lots of people," she said crisply, and draped her gold shawl around her shoulders.

Yet another Maserati—a black one this time, she noticed—was parked outside waiting for them. Cade turned on the radio, effectively drowning out conversation, and drove fast along the dark, winding highway: fast enough that she didn't want to distract him. Or was that just an excuse for her silence?

As the shadowed fields and black silhouettes of trees flashed by, the pride that had sustained Tess through years of unfulfilling jobs and mean lodgings came to her rescue. Be damned if she'd beg for Cade's attention, or fall all over him because he'd given her a few pretty green baubles. Let his other women do that. She wasn't going to.

But her nerves, she knew, were stretched to the breaking point; and as Cade drove along an *allée* of live oaks toward a mansion whose every window gleamed with light, they tightened another notch.

If she could sleep wrapped in cardboard, she could face a roomful of strangers. Cade pulled up by the wide arch of steps and turned off the ignition. "I'll stick with you," he said briefly. "And if they play a rhumba, I'll make sure no one else asks you to dance."

"Too bad I have such a limited repertoire," she said, her green eyes flashing; she was, she realized, spoiling for a fight. "I can always head for the powder room—I'm sure you'll find someone else to dance the rhumba with you."

"I'm sure I could," he grated, got out of the car and opened her door.

They climbed the steps side by side, between an array of antique pots full of scented camellias, and were ushered in the massive oak door by a uniformed butler. A middle-aged couple bustled toward them, the woman plump in yellow satin, her husband plumper in a tux with a bright yellow cummerbund. "Cade, darling," the woman exclaimed. "And this must be Del's granddaughter—you have his eyes, honey. Wasted on a man, I always said. I'm Bee Alden, and this is my husband, Chuck." She leaned forward and kissed Tess on the cheek. "Welcome to *Belle Maison*."

Chuck said, "Tess, you're a whole lot prettier than Del ever was. Now you be sure to save me a waltz or two. Bee's been at me for years, but seems like a waltz is the only dance where I don't tramp all over my partner's feet."

Tess chuckled. "I'd be delighted to. We could even risk a foxtrot—I'm good at dodging."

"Well now, aren't you a sweetheart?" Chuck said. "Cade, good to see you, boy. Why don't you take your pretty lady inside and get her a glass of bubbly? Soon as the guests stop arriving, honey, I'll be right along to claim you."

As they passed out of earshot, Cade said softly, "Bee wears a different color satin every year with her hair dyed to match, and she's got the kindest heart in the south. Ah...now this couple, they'll give you the third-degree."

A couple as disapproving as the ancestral portraits at Cypress Acres was walking toward them, the woman's thin lips coated with what was no doubt Dior lipstick. Tess tensed, then soon discovered she'd scarcely needed to. With a skill she had to admire, Cade fielded questions that were more than pointed and observations that verged on bitchy. Then he whisked her away to meet a white-maned senator who'd gone to college with Del.

One by one, the expensively dressed guests paraded past her, openly curious, overly tactful or—rather more than she'd expected—just plain friendly. She waltzed with Cade, with Chuck and with the senator; and gradually she relaxed. She couldn't fault Cade's behavior; he was taking every measure he could to ensure she enjoyed herself, and his physical closeness as they danced together set her heart to singing. As they filled their plates at a buffet so colorful, so enticing that she forgot everything in pure delight, she heard herself laughing and chatting as though she'd been attending society funtions all her life.

Amsterdam was another world.

Where had that thought come from? Tess shoved it away as she helped herself to tiny rolls of puff pastry stuffed with shrimp and avocado. Amsterdam was in the past. Over. Done with.

The contrast between this world and that was too cruel.

She took another gulp of champagne, bubbles tickling her nostrils. After they'd eaten, Cade led her onto the dance floor again; his steel-hard muscles under his formal jacket brought a flush to her cheeks, a liquid grace to her movements. Eyes shining, lips parted, she abandoned herself to the sheer pleasure of being in his arms.

But then the band struck up a Latin rhythm, catchy and sensual. She said, smiling up at him, "The powder room—I'll be back in a minute."

"I'll keep an eye out for you," he said.

It wasn't the moment to remember how, at dawn two mornings ago, those same eyes had roamed from the rosy tips of her breasts to her writhing hips, his big body hovering over her. Blushing, she mumbled, "Won't be long."

The powder room wouldn't have been out of place in a DelMer hotel, for it boasted gold-framed mirrors, fragrant bouquets of freesias, and a luxurious array of creams, soaps and linen hand towels. Trying not to gape, Tess discovered a small sitting room off the bathroom, wallpapered in the same heavy brocade, and tucked herself in one corner. Easing off her sandals, she decided to repair her lipstick and take some breathing space before she went back to the ballroom.

The outside door opened. A well-bred voice said languidly, "Del Lorimer's granddaughter is a pretty little thing."

Tess froze to her seat. "Marcia," a younger voice replied, "the gal's a raving beauty. Head over heels in love with Cade, of course."

"Naïve of her to be so obvious about it," the languid voice replied. "Someone should warn her. Won't be any wedding bells in that direction, Caro."

Caro sighed. "If I was twenty years younger and forty pounds lighter, I'd be in love with him, too."

"Wouldn't get you anywhere, darling," Marcia drawled. "Cade's not the marrying type. Pity. All those lovely green-backs."

"You remember Talia Banks?—she's here somewhere with

her latest man. She had an affair with him a year or so ago. Generous to a fault, she said, but he called the shots."

"Guess that's how you end up a billionaire...shall we go back? What *do* you think of Bee's hair?"

Caro sniggered. "I'm waiting for the year she chooses turquoise satin."

"Darling, really..."

The door closed behind them. Tess let out her pent-up breath, deeply thankful they hadn't checked out the sitting room. With some difficulty, because her fingers were trembling, she did up her gold shoes. *In love with Cade.*

Head over heels in love with Cade...

CHAPTER THIRTEEN

SHE was in love with Cade, Tess thought. Of course she was. The truth had been staring her in the face for days, but it had taken two gossipy socialites to make it sink in. Happiness rose like sunlight within her, brilliantly bright and warm. How astonishing, she thought. How amazing! She, Tess Ritchie, had fallen in love with a man so handsome, so sexy, that he turned her bones to water.

She had no idea when it had happened—so gradually she hadn't noticed, or very suddenly in the barn when she'd sobbed all over him. Did it matter?

Her reflection in one of the mirrors was staring back at her, a radiant smile on its face; her heart was racing as though she'd been waltzing for thirty minutes nonstop. Hastily she took her lipstick from her gold evening bag and slicked it over her mouth, trying to subdue the smile. She couldn't hide here forever. But how was she going to face Cade knowing that she loved him?

You've always had secrets, she told herself. This is a happy one, for a change. But it's still your secret. Just pray he's not in intimate conversation with a woman twenty years too old and forty pounds overweight whose name is Caro.

She ran a brush through her hair and walked back into the ballroom. The band was playing a tango, music so aggressively sexual that her steps slowed. She saw Cade immediately. He was dancing with a tall, leggy brunette in a backless black dress, a sultry smile on her lips.

Dancing? He wasn't dancing. He was publicly making love to her. Dipping her backward, whirling her in circles, pulling her toward him only to thrust her away.

An untamed mix of fury and knife-sharp pain ripped through Tess's body, red-hot, ice-cold. Cade, who had promised to watch out for her, had totally forgotten her.

The brunette didn't have a limited repertoire.

So this, Tess thought, was jealousy. The dark side of love, its ugly sister. Although she'd never felt it before, she knew what it was instantly. She wanted to tear the brunette from Cade's arms. She wanted to run for the door and keep running until she was—where? Where could she run? For Cade was everywhere, and wherever she ran, she'd carry him with her.

And that, too, was love.

The band ended on a triumphant chord. Cade had whipped the brunette into his chest and was holding her to his body. He was laughing.

Bee said briskly, "Now, honey, you mustn't wear your heart on those cute cap sleeves of yours for everyone to see. Here, have some more bubbly. I always say to Chuck that there isn't a trouble invented a glass of champagne can't fix."

Numbly Tess took the proffered crystal flute. "I'm in love with him," she blurted.

"Of course you are. Who wouldn't be? Just because I'm happily married doesn't mean I can't admire the finest set of pecs this side of California. But, honey, I should warn you, marriage is a dirty word as far as Cade's concerned. His mother's divorce—messy, very messy. And then the custody battle—well, who can blame him for being gun-shy?"

"Custody battle?" Tess faltered. She'd always assumed

that Selena, Cade's mother, had been a widow. Certainly Cade had never mentioned divorce.

Bee gave a sigh that was partly pleasurable. "What a spectacle it was—the country club dined off it for weeks. Cade's father didn't want Cade, never had—but he didn't want Selena having him, either. Well, the lawyers got rich, which is always the way, and in the end the judge voted for motherhood." She gave Tess a shrewd glance. "This is news to you? Cade's been closemouthed since he was a boy, with very good reason."

When had she, Tess, ever asked Cade about his real father, or what had happened to that father? She hadn't. She'd been too absorbed in her own troubles; and had, she thought guiltily, too easily jumped to the conclusion that Cade, so rich, so handsome, so accomplished, had no real troubles of his own other than a less-than-close relationship with Del.

So two fathers hadn't wanted Cade: his biological father and his adoptive father. The mystery that was Cade was suddenly clearer to Tess. No wonder commitment was a dirty word to him. A double-edged rejection had scarred him for life, marked him so deeply that he wouldn't allow himself to need her, or be needed by her.

To love or be loved.

"There now," Bee said, "Cade's looking for you. Off you go, honey, and take my advice—play your cards close to your emeralds."

Tess gave an involuntary gulp of laughter that was all too close to tears. "Thanks, Bee," she said, and started across the room toward Cade. The brunette had vanished. He was standing at the edge of the dance floor, watching her approach, waiting for her. Out of duty?

In spite of herself, anger was hot in her breast again. She'd told Cade the sordid story of her past; but had he confided in her? No, sir.

Anger was preferable to swooning at his feet because she'd been stupid enough to fall in love with him. Or bursting into tears because he'd never marry her.

Marriage, she thought blankly. She was the woman who'd said—fairly adamantly, as she recalled—that she never wanted to marry anyone.

She'd changed her mind. A total about-face. But would Cade ever change his?

He said curtly, "You were gone a long time."

"You managed to entertain yourself while I was gone."

"Talia asked me to dance."

Her heart clenched in her chest. "An old friend?" she said silkily.

"She and I were lovers a year or so ago," he said impatiently. "I'm only telling you before you hear it from someone else."

A devil had control of her tongue. "So we've had Sharon and now Talia. Are we working our way down the alphabet?"

"If I didn't know you better, I'd say you were jealous."

"You know me very well. In bed, at least."

"Tess," he said with treacherous gentleness, "if you want to have a knock-em-down fight, I'll be happy to oblige. But not here and not now."

A headache was brewing behind her eyes. "I wish I'd never left Malagash Island," she said with the truth of desperation. "Never met you!"

"You've done both," he said brusquely. "The senator wants you to meet his brother and sister-in-law—they have a summer place in Maine. Come along."

For a moment she contemplated marching straight out of the ballroom into the cool, star-spangled night: that would really set the tongues wagging, and not just in the powder room. The thought cheered her up somewhat; and the senator's family turned out to be as charming as the senator.

Dancing with Cade, though, in what was only a facade of intimacy, was more painful than Tess would have believed possible. She couldn't bear for him to guess that she was in love with him; when, briefly, she was introduced to a group that included Talia, she kept her poise by sheer force of will. But her headache worsened; a dull throbbing had settled behind her eyes, interspersed with sudden sharp flashes of pain.

As he took her onto the dance floor in yet another waltz, Cade said evenly, "What's wrong?"

"I have a headache."

"Why didn't you say so? I'll take you home."

To her own bed at Cypress Acres. Alone. Because she would use the headache, Tess thought with unhappy truth; the other thing she didn't dare do was make love with Cade, knowing that she loved him. In the intimacy of his big bed, how could she possibly disguise her feelings? "Sounds good," she said in careful understatement.

Ten minutes later, they were accelerating down the driveway under the dark canopy of trees. "Do you have any aspirin?" Cade said.

"No. I never get headaches."

"Why tonight? You were a great success."

The words escaped in spite of herself. "What have you got against marriage, Cade?"

He glanced over at her, his eyes hooded. "I already told you—a high potential for boredom."

"Nothing to do with your parents' custody battle?"

His fingers tensed on the wheel. "Who told you about that?"

"Not you."

"Why would I?"

Hurt slammed through her. So love was also vulnerability, she thought, and said carefully, "I told you about Jake and Hans."

He said flatly, "My father insisted on a cold, businesslike

marriage that would advance his medical career and give my mother plenty of time for volunteer work. Then she met Del and, I suppose, discovered what she'd been missing. She filed for divorce, my father hired the shark-lawyer-of-the-year, and the fight was on."

"You were a pawn in that fight."

"She impoverished herself in the courts," he said harshly. "But she stuck with it, and she won. End of story."

"Beginning of story, I'd say, if you've been running from marriage ever since…Cade, I'm so sorry I never asked. I always assumed Selena was a widow."

"She and Del were good together. But The Rose Room at Moorings says it all—at heart, my mother was a conventional woman. They were settled. Comfortable. Content." Unconsciously he was banging his fist on the wheel. "If that's all there is, I'd rather stay single."

"You and I aren't like that."

"Lust, Tess. It'll burn out. It always does."

"And what if it doesn't? Are you still going to run away?"

"Dammit," he exploded, "it's not that simple. You're Del's granddaughter, I'm responsible for you."

"I'm responsible for myself!"

"I don't care if this sounds arrogant," he said. "I'm worried if we continue our affair you'll get in too deep."

"You're afraid I'll fall in love with you," she said with deadly accuracy, and watched him nod. "What if I already have?"

"Don't play games."

"What if I asked you to marry me? What would you say?"

Abruptly he pulled over to the side of the road, and turned in his seat to face her, his eyes burning into hers. "Am I missing something here? What the hell's going on?"

"Answer my question."

"I'd say no."

In spite of herself, she flinched. "Just like that."

"Tess, you're not in love with me. In less than three weeks, you've been lifted out of a backwater island, presented with a new grandfather and thrust into high society. It's no surprise that—"

"You left something out," she said icily. "I also lost my virginity. Or had you forgotten?"

"I should never have started this affair! When you knocked on my door in Venice, I should have sent you back to your room. I was the one with experience—and I don't care what you say, I was the one responsible for you."

"But you didn't send me back," she said softly and knew at some deep level that she was fighting for her life. "I'm the woman who makes you break the rules. Who destroys your control, who drives you out of your mind—and now I'm the one who's sounding arrogant. Cade, do you seriously think you and I would have a boring marriage? Or that we'd ever use our children as pawns even if we did divorce?"

"For God's sake—one more reason I'm against marriage is so I'll never have to go anywhere near a divorce lawyer."

"Was your father a good man? A loving man?"

"Neither. He was cold-blooded, selfish and manipulative." The words forced from him, he added, "I've never ceased being grateful to my mother for not abandoning me to him all those years ago."

"You're a good man at heart," Tess said passionately. "You love Del, I know you do, in spite of the fact he's always held himself aloof from you. You're different from your father. As different as you could be."

"Since when did you get to be such an authority?"

"Since you first took me into your bed. I may be inexperienced, but some things can't be faked. Your care for me, your generosity, your passion—they're you. Your essence."

She was leaning forward, speaking with the intensity that was so characteristic of her. The sweet rise of her breasts above her embroidered bodice clawed Cade with desire; the single emerald was swinging gently in her cleavage, shooting green sparks. When he'd chosen the pendant, hadn't he pictured making love to her with it as her only adornment? Right now, he ached to take her in his arms, to end this ridiculous discussion the only way he knew how.

She *was* in danger of falling in love with him. Tonight had proved it. And there was another way to end the discussion. A brutal way, yes—but brutally effective. Not stopping to think, because if he did he might back off, Cade said, "When we started the affair, we made an agreement—when the time came to end it, we'd do it up-front. That time's come, Tess. I'm ending it. Now. My only regret is starting it in the first place."

She shrank back in her seat. "You regret making love with me?" she faltered.

"That's not what I meant."

"That's what it sounded like!"

"In Adelaide and Venezuela we'll act as business associates only," he said, biting off the words. "After that, you're on your own—I'll keep out of your way at Moorings, or wherever else you choose to go."

Clutching straws, she said, "What about Del?"

"If you're wise, you'll never tell Del we've been involved."

"As though I'm ashamed of the most beautiful thing that's ever happened to me?"

"Because it's none of his business!"

"Keep everything compartmentalized," she said bitterly. "That's how you've always lived, isn't it? Sex over here, business over there and no place for feelings."

"I'll live my life the way I choose. Right now I'm ending

our affair before I do more harm than I've already done. It's not open for negotiation—my mind's made up."

As suddenly as he'd stopped the car, Cade swung back on the highway. The Maserati surged forward into the darkness. Tess leaned back on the cool leather and closed her eyes, her hands clenched in her lap. Other than confessing she'd fallen in love with Cade, and begging him to marry her, what more could she say? She'd fought for her life—for her newly discovered love—and she'd lost. The Venetian Affair had just come to an end on a country road in Kentucky.

Into her mind dropped the image of her little cabin by the sea. She was going back there, she thought desperately. As soon as she could. Del could visit her there, if he chose to. But she was through dancing to Cade's tune.

Her headache was a vicious, throbbing reality, as though a dozen rock bands were tuning up inside her skull. All she wanted was to be alone—so that for the second time in as many nights she could cry her eyes out.

But not yet. She had too much pride to show Cade how deeply he'd hurt her.

The drive home seemed to last forever; as she followed Cade up the front steps at Cypress Acres, she was swaying with fatigue. He said tightly, "I've acted for the best tonight, Tess. You don't agree with me now, but in time you will."

"Don't try to control my feelings," she seethed. "You may be a billionaire, but if you won't risk falling in love with me, you might as well be poverty-stricken."

His fingers dug into her elbow. "That's ludicrous and you know it."

"Let go of me," she said with iciness of true rage. "You don't want to have an affair with me—so I'm off-limits. No touching allowed."

Her skin was cool, and silken-smooth. He was right to end the affair, he knew he was. Yet all he wanted to do was pull Tess into his arms and kiss her senseless. Cade dropped her elbow, matching her rage with his own. "You're assuming I want to touch you."

"Go back to Talia. Or Sharon. But leave me alone," she said and pushed open the door. To her infinite relief, Cade didn't follow her up the stairs. Alone in her own bedroom at last, she locked the door and leaned back on the panels. But her eyes were dry, burning in their sockets.

She kicked off her gold sandals, stepped out of her dress and flung the emerald earrings and bracelet on the dresser. However, once again, she couldn't manage the clasp on her pendant. Swearing under her breath, she left it dangling around her neck, and grabbed the least sexy of her nightgowns.

Then she stationed herself on the window seat overlooking the paddock and the gently rising hills, leaned against the cold glass and waited for night to be over.

At seven the next morning, Tess threw on a pair of jeans and started downstairs. Her plan was to go to the barn. For comfort, she thought, and as she turned the corner saw with a stab of pure agony that Cade was standing in the foyer. Cade and his overnight bag.

With all her willpower, she forced herself to continue her descent. Then he glanced up, caught sight of her and took a step toward her. She froze on the bottom step.

He said choppily, "I'm heading to Maine for a couple of days—I want to see Del. Best thing is for you to stay here."

Her decision was instant. "I'm coming with you."

"Tess, you're not—"

"You're through running my life," she said frigidly. "I have to see Del, too. He's my grandfather, and he's not well."

Cade said reluctantly, "So it's not a charade anymore—you and Del."

She let out her breath in a small sigh. "He meant nothing to me initially, I was being honest when I told you that…and he's not the rock to cling to that I needed so desperately when I was small. But he shares my blood, and in his obstinate way he's trying to do right by me." In spite of herself, her voice shook. "I can't turn my back on him—he's all I've got."

"He needs you as much as you need him," Cade said harshly. "He needs you, too."

"Don't kid yourself. He told me the day he married my mother that he didn't want me to call him Dad. Ever. I was only eight, but I knew there was a message there. Del doesn't need me. He never has."

Frowning, Tess said slowly, "Cory must have caused him so much grief…perhaps he couldn't let you close because he was afraid of being hurt all over again."

Cade's gut clenched. Of course. It was so blindingly obvious that he hadn't seen it. Cory would have broken Del's heart over and over again. Why wouldn't Del keep his adoptive son at a distance?

The look on Cade's face stabbed Tess to the core. "Maybe it's time to ask Del why he wouldn't let you near. If it really was self-protection."

Cade wasn't about to make any promises, to her or to himself. "If you're coming with me, Tess, you'd better hurry."

Once again Cade had retreated, his face a tight mask. Tess said briefly, "Give me five minutes to pack my bags."

She ran upstairs, past the disapproving ancestors, and dragged her suitcase out of the closet. Leaving the elegant green gown on its hanger because she never wanted to see it again, she flung in some of her more casual clothes and changed into an uncrushable silk pantsuit. Hastily she tucked the emerald pendant beneath her camisole and snapped the case shut.

In a few hours she'd be back in Maine. She'd go to Malagash Island; and this time she wouldn't leave.

She hurried downstairs. Cade was waiting for her in the car. After she'd slammed her door, he put his foot to the accelerator. In a voice devoid of feeling, he said, "The cook filled the thermos with coffee and there are a couple of freshly baked Danish in the box."

"The cook deserves a medal," Tess replied and put on her dark glasses, ostensibly against the early morning sun, in actuality to hide from Cade. She was hungry, she realized in faint surprise, and poured herself a mug of steaming coffee. In between chewing apricot croissants and taking naps to catch up on her sleep, she kept up a patter of light conversation during the journey: for which she herself deserved a medal, she thought derisively. But she was damned if she was going to let Cade know that he'd broken her heart.

What a trite phrase. Yet her rib cage felt sore, her muscles ached from tension and a cold knot had lodged itself in her belly. Unromantic symptoms, but all too real.

She'd tell Del her plans tonight, and tomorrow she'd go home to Malagash.

Once again, it would be the haven she'd always needed.

CHAPTER FOURTEEN

Several hours later, Cade pulled up in front of Moorings. He said tersely, "I'll go see Del first. When it's your turn, don't upset him."

It had been a long day. Tess said flippantly, "No, Mr. Lorimer."

He turned in his seat, his gray eyes turbulent. "Do you think it's easy, ending our affair when all I want to do is haul you off to the nearest bed? But I'm doing the right thing, I know I am. So quit making snide remarks!"

"If it's that difficult, why is it the right thing?"

He seized her by the shoulders, planted a furious kiss full on her mouth, then pushed her away. "The butler will bring your case in," he snarled. "I won't be with Del for very long."

Inside the house, Cade took the stairs two at a time. Hastily he scrubbed at his mouth before he tapped on the door; the last thing he needed was lipstick smeared on his face.

As he walked in Del's room, the old man's face changed. "Thought you were the doc. Got me on a new medication, seems to be doing wonders. But he insists I sit around like a broody hen half the day."

"Then maybe you should listen," Cade said. His voice tight, he added, "I need to talk to you."

"Talk all you like. I got time."

There was no point in subtlety. "Through spending time with Tess, I've come to understand what a huge grief to you Cory must have been, Del. Is that why you were so reluctant to take on a second son? And why you never wanted me calling you Dad?"

"He nearly destroyed me," Del said harshly. "From the time he was a little boy, he was dishonest, aggressive and casually cruel. I couldn't fathom him or tolerate him. Couldn't make him change his ways, either. When I divorced his mother—my first wife—for adultery, the two of them took off to Europe, and good riddance. After she died a few years later, Cory contacted me for money." Del shrugged. "I paid him off on the condition he stay in Europe. And once Tess was born, I sent a monthly allowance. Well, we know what happened to that."

"You didn't try to see her," Cade said stiffly.

Del passed his hand over his face; he looked, Cade thought in compunction, every year of his age. "I never told Selena just how bad Cory was. Thought she'd quit loving me if she knew I had a rotten egg for a son. So I couldn't tell her about Tess, either. I loved your mother, Cade, but I never really understood why she loved me."

"You didn't think you deserved her," Cade said in sudden enlightenment.

"That's about it. So I kept it all a secret—and Tess is the one who suffered, along with you. Because you're dead on— I kept you at a distance on purpose. I'm sorry, Cade. More sorry than I can say."

It was as though a great weight he'd scarcely been aware of carrying had lifted from his chest. Cade said slowly, "If you're willing, it's not too late to bridge the gap."

Del cleared his throat. "Yeah, I'm willing."

"Tess has done us a good turn," Cade said huskily.

"She's okay, is Tess." Del sat up straight. "So what do you think of the latest vote in congress?"

With alacrity, Cade dove into the murky field of politics, an area where he and Del had never seen eye to eye. Half an hour later, he went to his office to check his faxes from Los Angeles; he was planning to fly there tomorrow, put some space between him and Tess.

There'd be no Venezuelan Affair. Let alone Australian, Asian or Argentinian.

Early the next morning, Del's chauffeur left Tess at the top of her driveway on Malagash Island. Fog had rolled in during the night. Waves washed softly onto the beach, rattling the pebbles. A gull mewed eerily.

She started down the slope; and knew that with every step she took, Cade was flying further and further away from her, on his way to Los Angeles. *Pressing business,* he'd said. *A good time to put a little distance between us.*

Startling her, a crow cawed from its perch on a piece of ghost-white driftwood. She'd slept badly, and had spent the black hours of night trying to convince herself that she was confusing lust with romance, and sex with love. It hadn't worked. She loved Cade, irrevocably.

Unrequited love was another cliché, she thought miserably, digging in her purse for her house keys. How was she to live with it, day after day? Where would she find the resolve to get up in the morning?

The cabin smelled musty and unlived in. Her plants had died from lack of water, and a storm had crusted the windows with salt spray. Why had she never realized how small the cabin was?

She shivered, trailing into her bedroom, where she'd slept alone so happily, content to hear the tides rise and fall and the seabirds cry. It, too, felt claustrophobically small.

She should open a few windows, cycle to the store, get some food in. Instead she walked out onto the deck, the deck where she'd served Cade coffee and homemade muffins on a morning that now seemed a lifetime ago. The fog was cool on her cheeks, dampening her hair.

The other man she loved was, of course, Del. *Gramps,* she'd called him on their last couple of visits, not realizing the name was concealing true affection. But when she'd seen him yesterday, caged in his room like a ruffled old eagle, she'd understood how much he meant to her.

Love, in two very different guises, had trapped her. She couldn't run off to a château in France and make a new life for herself thousands of miles from Cade; she needed to be closer to Del.

Close to Del meant close to Cade.

Trapped, indeed. In the last three weeks, her world had expanded its boundaries immeasurably. From Manhattan to Madrid, from hotels and gondoliers to horse barns and vineyards, she'd discovered a whole new existence; and in Cade's arms, she'd found a fulfillment that had drenched her in intimacy.

She couldn't go back to the life she'd known on the island, she thought, gazing into the thick folds of fog. It was too late. She'd outgrown her little cabin.

Yet, at this precise moment, she had no idea what was to replace it.

As though the fog had shifted, clearing the view, she suddenly remembered herself as a little girl, the day she fell off the red swing at the playground. She'd scraped her knee; it had oozed a nasty mixture of blood and gravel. She'd run for her nanny, knowing that Bella would hold her and comfort her, and the pain would go away…

That's what I'll do, Tess thought. *I'll go to Madrid and see*

Ysabel. She'll understand. Maybe, just maybe, she can tell me what to do next.

Quickly she fumbled in her pocket for the chauffeur's cell phone number. If Cade could fly west, she could fly east.

Perhaps he was right, and distance was what she needed.

Cade got back to Moorings the next day. With immense reluctance, he stared up at Del's seaside mansion. Tess was inside. In a few moments, he'd have to face her.

He'd driven himself—and his employees—into the ground in Los Angeles. It hadn't helped. Day and night, he'd been saturated with Tess's absence: darkness, of course, far worse than daylight.

Withdrawal symptoms, Cade thought with vicious emphasis, as he mounted the front steps. He'd gone from a heavy dose of the most amazing sex in his life to none at all. No wonder he was sleeping badly.

Inside, the dogs greeted him with wild enthusiasm; then the butler handed him a note. "From Miss Ritchie," he said. "And Mr. Lorimer would like to see you before he settles for the night."

In the privacy of his room, Cade tore open the envelope and read the brief message.

By the time you get this, I'll be in Madrid with Ysabel. Then I may go to Amsterdam. You're right, Cade, we need to put distance between us. Tess.

He should be relieved that he didn't have to face her, that she'd gotten the message that his way was the right way. The only way.

He wasn't.

Madrid was bad enough, Cade thought furiously. But Tess, alone, in Amsterdam? What was she thinking?

He was going after her. Amsterdam was, for her, a city of nightmares, and be damned if she was going to face them on her own.

So much for distance, a little voice sneered in his ear.

Shut up, he snarled, went to the phone and made a couple of calls. Then he unpacked and repacked, showered and had a brief visit with Del: a visit during which he determinedly confined the conversation to matters of business.

Several hours later, Cade was standing in the lobby of Madrid's DelMer Hotel talking to the receptionist. "Tess Ritchie," he said, his voice gravelly from jet lag. "She hasn't checked out, has she?"

"No, sir. She's checking out tomorrow morning. Let me call her room."

Although Tess didn't answer, Cade at least knew she wasn't in Amsterdam. He ordered a cab, and went straight to Ysabel's apartment. Ysabel opened the door. Her accent more pronounced than usual, she said, "Cade—I wasn't expecting to see *you*."

Cade stepped inside, his eyes sweeping the small, cluttered room. "I'm looking for Tess."

Ysabel stepped back. "Why?"

Her voice was far from friendly, and she wasn't asking him to sit down. He said flatly, "To go to Amsterdam with her."

"She's not caught in your—how do you say?—apron ties. She's a grown woman, and your affair with her is over."

"So she told you that."

"It's not your business what she tells me."

"I couldn't risk her falling in love with me, Ysabel!"

Ysabel's magnificent dark eyes flashed. "Love isn't a disease. It's what makes us human."

He wasn't in the mood for a sermon. "Fine," he said "Where is she?"

"You've come a long way to see her."

"Where *is* she?" he repeated, holding tight to his temper "I have to talk to her."

"She left here two hours ago to go back to her hotel."

"On foot?"

"Of course. It wasn't then dark."

"She's not at the hotel," Cade rapped.

"Then she's gone into a bar to hear flamenco. Or into a res taurant for…" she fumbled for the word "—*la merienda*…the snack. I suggest you go back to the hotel and wait for her." Ysabel straightened to her full height. "If you hurt her again you will have me on your coattails—you understand?"

"I never intended to hurt her," he said roughly.

"Then you should have been more careful of her heart."

Cade stood still, the truth hitting like a blow. "So she ha fallen in love with me."

"That is for you to find out."

He said abruptly, "She was very fortunate that you were ir her life when she was so young—thank you, Ysabel, for al that you've done for her." He then wheeled on the faded carpe and let himself out, running down the stairs and emerging onto the street.

Under orange awnings, couples were seated on the sidewalk, drinking beer and *vino tinto*. Music rollicked from a nearby *taberna*. Taking out his cell phone, Cade called the hotel; but Tess still wasn't in her room. He began to walk trying to picture the route she'd take, his eyes darting back and forth across the heavy traffic; the whole time he was reining in an anxiety that would cripple him if he allowed it to.

Once he thought he saw her: a chestnut-haired woman with her back to him in a bar, eating *tapas* and laughing a something the man next to her had just said. His heart contracted with a hot pang of what was unquestionably jealousy; but when the woman turned her head, he saw she was older than Tess and nowhere near as beautiful.

Tess was entirely free to spend her time with whomever she wished. Or, he thought savagely, to take another man to her bed.

He crossed a busy square, taxis honking their horns, a policeman watching the chaos with a bored eye. Then, from two streets over, he heard sirens wailing; he turned down the street as though the sound was a magnet, his pulse racing. A truck was veered to one side with its hood badly dented, while a small sedan was crushed against a lamppost. Serious enough, but nothing to do with Tess.

What if it had been? What if that were her body being loaded into the back door of the ambulance?

What if, what if? What the devil was wrong with him?

She was a woman alone at night in a city that had the usual quota of crimes, large and small. He couldn't bear not knowing where she was or whether she was safe.

It was no longer anxiety cruising his nerves; it was fear.

An unruly gang of punks surged along the sidewalk toward him. Young males, high on testosterone and drugs, carelessly and loudly aggressive in their studded black leather and dangling chains. Cade knew from experience that in a flash they could change to something much more dangerous.

A straggler, obviously drunk, bumped into Cade; to his overwrought imagination, the man could easily have been Hans, the gang leader who'd threatened her life seven years ago. "Get away from me," Cade snarled, adrenaline racing through his veins, his fists bunched at his sides. He knew any number of nasty moves from his two years of roughing it; if he had to, he'd use them.

Something must have shown in his face; the punk staggered off, belching. Cade straightened, his muscles taut in a ferocious mixture of aggression and rage.

If anything happened to Tess tonight, he'd never forgive himself.

Because he loved her.

No, he didn't, he thought wildly. He wasn't in love with anyone. And knew the words for a lie as soon as they'd flashed across his brain.

He, Cade Lorimer, had fallen in love with the green-eyed, fiery-tempered woman who'd turned his life upside down.

For a moment, all his other emotions were submerged in pure amazement at the simplicity, the rightness of a truth that was dazzlingly obvious. He stepped to one side of the pavement, the crowds eddying in around him. His jealousy, his mounting fear, his increasingly desperate search for her on the busy streets of a Spanish city, were all clues he'd ignored.

He had to find her. Tell her. Take her in his arms and make love to her the night through.

Providing she'd have him.

He couldn't go there. Not now.

Cade took off down the pavement at a fast clip. It took him thirty minutes to reach the hotel. Its baroque facade and decorated columns mocked him with their solidity; until he found Tess, nothing in the world was solid.

He marched into the lobby and phoned her room, hearing a shrill, repetitive ringing until the voice mail clicked on. Then he checked the bar and the lounge. His last stop was the dining room, paneled in ornately carved mahogany, with tropical plants creating small oases of privacy among the scattered, gloriously hued Moroccan carpets.

At the far end, tucked into a corner table, Tess was having

dinner. A book was open in front of her. She was absorbed in it, absently sipping a glass of *vino rosado*.

She looked as if she didn't have a care in the world.

Suddenly enraged beyond any bounds of common sense, Cade strode the length of the room, bamboo brushing his shoulders, the occasional waiter skipping nimbly out of his path. He came to a halt beside her table. "You look very much at home," he said.

The book slipped from her fingers, knocking over a silver dish filled with elaborate curls of butter. "Cade!" she gasped, pushing back her chair and scrambling to her feet. "What are you doing here?" Then she paled. "Del—he's had another heart attack?"

"Del's fine."

"Then what—"

"Tell me you're happy to see me," he said hoarsely.

Her chin snapped up. "Why should I? You ended our affair as casually as if—as if you were tossing aside a book you'd read."

"I was wrong. I made a mistake."

She swept on as though he hadn't spoken. "I came here to put distance between us. Distance that you insisted on, not me. So why are you here when I'm doing my best to forget about you?"

Her eyes were ablaze with fury; but around her neck, he saw the glimmer of a gold chain. "You're wearing the pendant I gave you."

"I can't undo the clasp," she retorted. "If you want it back, it's all yours."

"I want you to marry me," he said.

Her jaw dropped; she gripped the edge of the table as though it was all that was holding her up. "Are you out of your mind?"

"No," he said with a sudden feral grin. "I'm jet-lagged, I've been half-crazy with worry ever since I found out you'd left Ysabel's apartment three hours ago, and I nearly started a brawl on the sidewalk. I don't have a ring and I haven't composed any fancy speeches—so if you want diamonds and poetry, you're out of luck. But I do want you to marry me."

"Why? Because instead of chasing after you, I headed in the opposite direction?"

"Because I love you," he said.

Tess gaped at him. "This isn't happening...I'm dreaming and any minute I'm going to wake up all by myself in bed."

Cade took her in his arms, running his hands up and down her spine, then kissing her, sinking into the kiss until there was nothing else in the world but this one woman. With all her strength, Tess pushed him away. "Stop it! One day the affair's over, the next day you're kissing me as though there's no tomorrow?"

He said forcefully, "I want you today and tomorrow. Only you, and for all my tomorrows."

She was pummeling him on the chest. "I'll bore you. I'll make demands on you. I won't let your nasty, cold-blooded father run your life. You don't want me."

He captured her hands in his, gazing down into her furious eyes as he put all the conviction of his newfound love into his voice. "My body wants you, that hasn't changed. Never will. But my heart wants you, too. My heart and my soul. And they're what really count."

"Oh," she said, and he watched as fury was replaced by an emotion he couldn't decipher. "That sounds sort of like poetry to me."

"I was a fool to end our affair. I was running scared, you were right. You were so different, you made nonsense of all my rules, and I didn't have a clue how to handle the way you made me feel."

"How do I make you feel?" Tess asked, knowing the question was all-important. In spite of herself, her hands crept up his chest, seeking the warmth and hardness of his body, so achingly familiar, so agonizingly missed.

"As though I was born to find you," he said hoarsely. "To need you and to love you. To marry you."

"You hated needing me," she said pithily. "It made you run in the opposite direction."

"I've stopped running," he said wryly. "About time, wouldn't you say?" He raked his fingers through his hair, searching for an argument that might persuade her, coming up with nothing but the strength of his own feelings. "Say you'll marry me. Or if you don't want marriage, that you'll at least live with me."

Her eyes narrowed. "There's something you're forgetting. Something crucial."

"Tell me what it is."

"You haven't asked how I feel about you."

"Hell, Tess, I'm scared to. I've done everything in my power the last few days to push you away—and now I'm supposed to ask if you love me?"

"You got the question right," Tess said with a sudden, radiant smile that caught at his heartstrings.

"So what's the answer?" he said roughly.

Finally she said the words she'd been longing to say for what felt like forever. "I do love you, Cade. I realized it at the ball, when I was skulking in the powder room—the very night you ended our affair." She bit her lip. "Terrible timing."

"I thought I was doing the right thing. For both of us. I've been wrong a few times in my life, but that night took the cake." He linked his arms around her waist. "Tell me again that you love me."

"I love you, love you, love you." Her smile broke out again. "And I'll do my best not to bore you."

"That's the least of our worries," Cade said, and kissed her again, a kiss fueled by a gratitude as deep and as passionate as his love; and this time he felt her yield. More than yield, he thought in a flood of joy, her response rocketing through him. "Marry me, Tess," he whispered against her lips. "I'll be as good to you as I know how, I swear I will. And I'll love you as long as there's breath in my body."

"I'll marry you, Cade."

"Even though you swore off marriage years ago?"

"If you can change your mind, I can change mine."

His own smile broke through. "I want you to wear white. Like the white you were wearing when you came to my room in Venice."

"We could honeymoon in Venice."

"A Venetian Marriage," he said huskily. "Sounds fine to me."

She gave a sudden ripple of laughter. "You won't be able to back out—we have a whole dining room full of witnesses."

"Then maybe I should order champagne all around, and ask everyone to charge their glasses to my future bride."

"Maybe you should."

So he did.

* * * * *

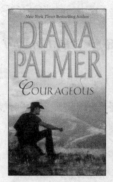

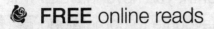